Pearl S. Buck

PEONY

Wakefield, Rhode Island & London

Published by Moyer Bell
This Edition 1996

Second Printing, 2000

**LIBRARY OF CONGRESS
CATALOGING IN PUBLICATION DATA**

Buck, Pearl S. (Pearl Sydenstriker), 1892-1973
Peony / Pearl S. Buck

p. cm.

1. Jews—China—History—19th century—
Fiction.
I. Title.

PS3503.U198P46 1996
813'.52—dc20 95-44446
ISBN 1-55921-168-7 CIP

Printed in the United States of America
Distributed in North America by Publishers Group West, 1700 Fourth Street, Berkeley, CA 94710, 800-788-3123 (in California 510-658-3453) and in Europe by Gazelle Book Services Ltd., Falcon House, Queen Square, Lancaster LA1 1RN England.

Ruth Stern

Pearl S. Buck

Pearl Sydenstricker Buck was born in West Virginia and taken to China as an infant before the turn of the century. The daughter of Presbyterian missionaries, she lived with her family in a town in the interior instead of the traditional missionary compound. Buck grew up speaking Chinese as well as English and received most of her education from her mother. She received an M.A. from Cornell and taught English literature in several Chinese universities before she was forced to leave the country in 1932 because of the revolution.

She wrote eighty-five books and is the most widely translated American author to this day. She has been awarded the Pulitzer Prize, the William Dean Howells Award, and the Nobel Prize for Literature. She died in 1973.

Good reading and a new field

—*Kirkus*

The conflicts inherent in the Chinese and Jewish temperament are delicately and intricately traced with profound wisdom and compassionate understanding in this tale . . . This is an enchanting story, the theme of which is tolerance. Highly recommended.

—*Library Journal*

[Ms. Buck's] zealous study has enabled her to give vivid impressions of a 4,000-year-old culture through carefully drawn minor characters and much colorful detail about such things as burial and marriage rites, and court etiquette.

—*The New York Times Book Review*

Other Novels by Pearl S. Buck

Dragon Seed
East Wind: West Wind
A House Divided
House of Earth
Imperial Woman
Kinfolk
Living Reed
Mandala
The Mother
The Pavilion of Women
Sons

AT VARIOUS times in history colonies of Jews have gone to China and lived there. The city of K'aifeng, in the province of Honan, was a center for them. In China they have never been persecuted, and if they have suffered hardships, these were only the hardships of life in the community where they were.

In its basis, therefore, this novel may be said to be historically true, although the characters, with unimportant exceptions, are the creatures of my imagination. The story takes place at the period, about a century ago, when the Chinese had accepted the Jews, and when, indeed, most Jews had come to think of themselves as Chinese. Today even the memory of their origin is gone. They are Chinese.

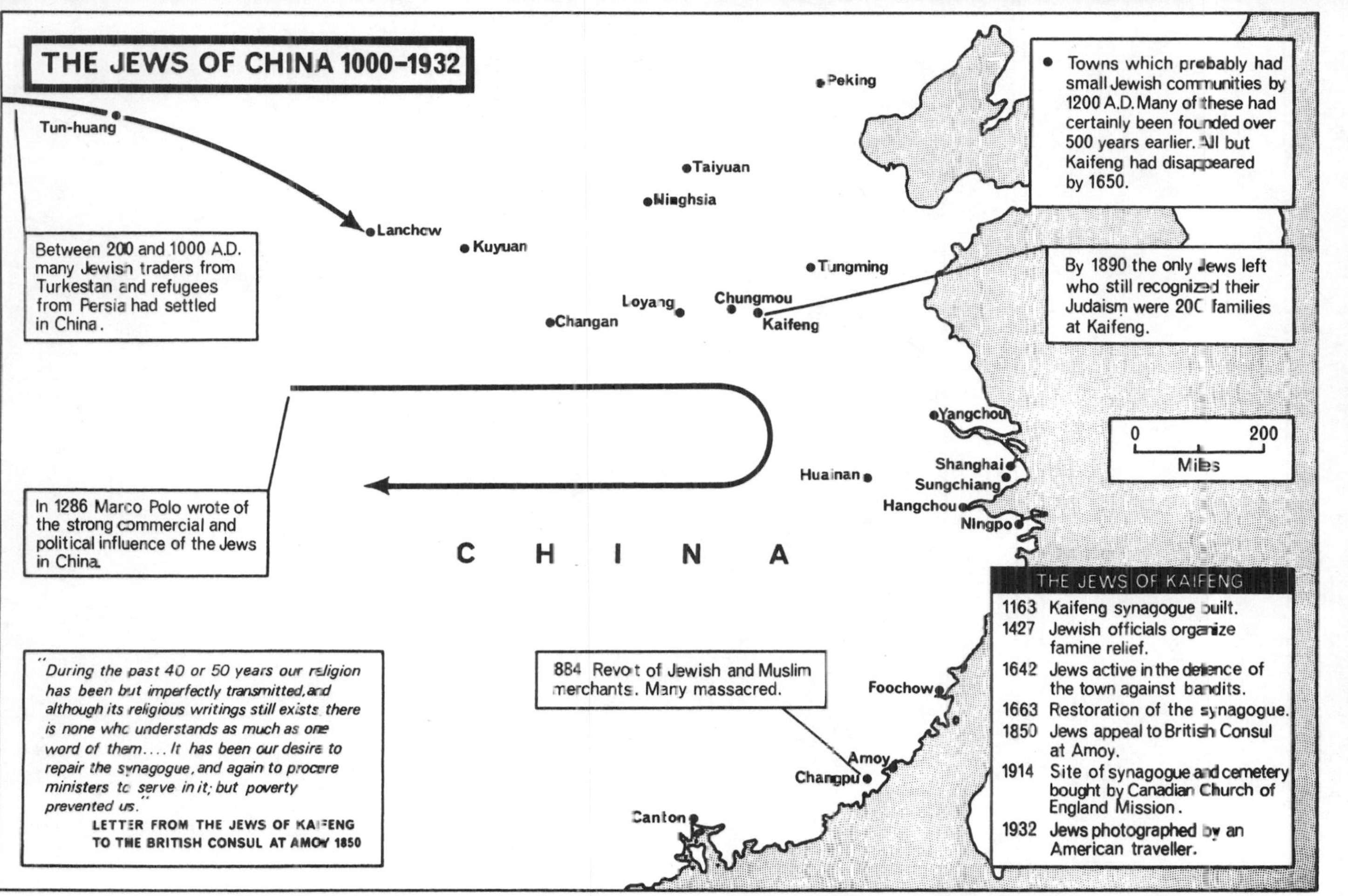
THE JEWS OF CHINA 1000–1932
Tun-huang
Lanchow
Kuyuan
Peking
Taiyuan
Ninghsia
Tungming
Loyang
Chungmou
Kaifeng
Changan
Yangchou
Shanghai
Sungchiang
Hangchou
Ningpo
Huainan
Foochow
Amoy
Changpu
Canton
CHINA
0 200 Miles
Towns which probably had small Jewish communities by 1200 A.D. Many of these had certainly been founded over 500 years earlier. All but Kaifeng had disappeared by 1650.
Between 200 and 1000 A.D. many Jewish traders from Turkestan and refugees from Persia had settled in China.
By 1890 the only Jews left who still recognized their Judaism were 200 families at Kaifeng.
In 1286 Marco Polo wrote of the strong commercial and political influence of the Jews in China.
884 Revolt of Jewish and Muslim merchants. Many massacred.
"During the past 40 or 50 years our religion has been but imperfectly transmitted, and although its religious writings still exists there is none who understands as much as one word of them.... It has been our desire to repair the synagogue, and again to procure ministers to serve in it; but poverty prevented us."
LETTER FROM THE JEWS OF KAIFENG TO THE BRITISH CONSUL AT AMOY 1850
THE JEWS OF KAIFENG
1163 Kaifeng synagogue built.
1427 Jewish officials organize famine relief.
1642 Jews active in the defence of the town against bandits.
1663 Restoration of the synagogue.
1850 Jews appeal to British Consul at Amoy.
1914 Site of synagogue and cemetery bought by Canadian Church of England Mission.
1932 Jews photographed by an American traveller.

PEONY

挑筋教

I

IT WAS spring in the city of K'aifeng, a late spring in the northern Chinese province of Honan. Behind the high city walls the peach trees, planted in courtyards, bloomed earlier than they did upon the farms spreading over the level plains around the moat. Yet even in such shelter the peach blossoms were still only rosy buds at Passover.

Within the courts of the house of Ezra ben Israel the peach blossoms had been cut several days early and had been forced to bloom in time for the feast. Each spring Peony, the Chinese bondmaid, made it her task to provide thus for the branches of flowers that stood against the walls of the great hall. Each year Ezra, her master, and Madame Ezra, her mistress, took notice of what she had done. Knowing how cold the spring had been this year and how long the dusty northwest winds had blown upon the city, they had given her special praise when they entered the great hall this night for the feast.

"See what magic our little Peony has wrought this Passover," Ezra had said, his plump hand gesturing toward the flowers.

Madame Ezra had paused to admire. Her impetuous look grew kind. "Very pretty, my child," she had said to Peony.

Peony had remained properly silent, her small hands folded above her flowing sleeves. David's eyes she met and avoided as he smiled, but Leah's warm smile she accepted, answering it with a small quiver of her lips. The old rabbi had given no sign. He was blind and so he saw nothing. As for Aaron, his son, Peony did not look at him.

They took their seats at the ample round table that had been placed in the middle of the hall, and Peony began to direct the serving of the food in her noiseless graceful fashion. Four menservants obeyed her, and Wang Ma, the elder woman servant, poured the tea.

As long as she could remember, Peony had watched this evening feast in early spring in the house of Ezra. She had directed the placing of every dish and utensil upon the table and the servants had obeyed her because she knew, as well as though she had been a daughter in the house, exactly where each dish was to be found and each placed. The dishes were kept the year round, unused except for this night before Passover. The silver spoons and chopsticks, the great seven-branched candlesticks, all were shining in the light of the lanterns hung from the high red beams. Upon a vast silver tray she herself had placed the symbols she did not understand, but which each year she prepared, a roasted egg, bitter herbs, apples, nuts, and wine. They were curiosities of a foreign religion.

But the whole day was a strange one in this unheeding Chinese city. Although Peony knew the rites well, each spring she wondered at them again. The search through the house for bits of leavened bread! Ezra, the master, had made the search this morning as he always did, laughing as he went carelessly from spot to spot, and asking her if that were all. Madame Ezra used always to hide the bits of leavened bread for him to find, but now for several years she had let Peony do it, and Ezra had commanded her to count the bits so that he would know when he was finished. He made a joke of it, as though he were somewhat ashamed before the servants. When Peony and David were children, they had laughed immoderately at the search and had joined in it with merriment, pointing out each crumb of the forbidden bread. But then she had not known that she was only a bondmaid.

Now she knew. She stood quietly watchful, as the feast proceeded. Each person at the table was known to her in some fashion. David she knew best. For David's sake she had been bought in a year of famine, when the Yellow River had burst its dikes and had swept over the low-lying land. She had been too young to remember that sale of herself. Try as she might, she could remember no face before

David's face. He was her first memory, a gay boy, two years older than she, always much taller, much stronger, so that instinctively she turned to him and depended upon him. In those days she had told him all her little thoughts and sorrows, and it had been a habit hard to break. Yet her own wisdom had taught her that it must be broken. It was not sensible to think that the bond between two children could continue beyond childhood, not when one was master and the other bondmaid.

She did not repine, knowing herself fortunate in this kindly Jewish household. Ezra ben Israel, the head of the house, was a cheerful, stout-bodied merchant. Did he cut his full beard, Peony often thought, he would have looked Chinese, for he had had a Chinese mother. This was a grief to Madame Ezra, and so none spoke of it. She took comfort in the knowledge that David, her son, looked like her rather than his father, and she was fond of declaring, indeed, that David was most like her own father, for whom she had named him. All the house feared Madame Ezra not a little, even while each depended upon her for some private good, for her great kindness was likely to be undone at any moment by a sudden temper. She was a woman nearing fifty years of age, tall and large, handsome if one did not dislike a high nose and bright color. With all her warmth, she had also certain rigidities of belief and habit that could not be shaken. Thus, as usual on the Passover feast, Madame Ezra had invited the Rabbi and his two children, Aaron and Leah. Aaron was a pale secretive youth of seventeen, whom Peony despised for his pale splotched face and his corruption. Whether his family or Ezra's house knew of his evil deeds she did not know, and it was beneath her to inquire. Perhaps none of the Seven Surnames and Eight Families, as the Jews were called in K'aifeng, knew all that the Rabbi's son did, and the Chinese were too kind to tell them.

Leah was different. Leah was good, one of those rare creatures born beautiful and good together. From her waiting place near the table Peony watched Leah with a sad pleasure that she would not allow to become envy. Tonight in her wine-red robe girdled at the waist with a gold band, Leah was wholly beautiful, except perhaps that she was too tall. The Chinese did not like tall women. Yet against this defect, Leah had a cream-pale skin and large dark eyes glowing between long curled lashes, and her lips were red and full. The nose, again, was too high for Chinese beauty, although it was not large as Madame Ezra's was.

Leah was more than beautiful. She was filled with some spirit, a high quality, which Peony admired and did not understand. The Chinese said of her, "She is heaven-good." They meant that her goodness was natural and that it flowed from a fountain within herself. As she sat beside her father, quick to help him when he moved his head, she illuminated the feast with joy, even though she seldom spoke.

Something of this, perhaps, came from her father, the Rabbi. A man of great height and spare frame, he was clothed with saintliness as with a robe of light. Years ago he had caught a disease of the eyes from which many Chinese suffered, and since no cure was known, he had become blind. Being foreign, he had no immunity, and upon him blindness fell quickly. He had not seen his dead wife's face after she was thirty years of age, and Leah and Aaron he had seen only as little children. Whether, not able to see these human faces, he was compelled to look only upon the face of God, or whether from his natural goodness, he appeared now to be all spirit and no more flesh. His hair, which had grown white soon after he became blind, framed his white and beautiful face. Above his long white beard his high nose and sunken eyes were proud and calm.

Thus they sat at the feast table and Peony saw every movement and smile. She saw David look at Leah across the table and look away again, and she repressed the pang this gave her. He was Leah's equal in height, and Peony thought him even more beautiful. At nineteen David ben Ezra was nearing the fullness of his young manhood. His Jewish garments became him; this Peony had to admit, although she did not like them because they made him strange to her. On usual days he wore Chinese robes because he said they were more comfortable. But tonight he wore a blue and gold robe, and on his head his blue silk Jewish cap pressed down his dark short curls. She could not keep from looking at him, and then he caught her eyes and smiled at her. Instantly she bowed her head, and turned away to bid Old Wang, the eldest manservant, to fetch the Passover wine jug.

"Take it to the Master," she directed.

"I know," he hissed. "You need not tell me after all these years. You are as bad as my old woman!"

As he spoke Wang Ma, his wife, came in with more servants, bearing basins and pitchers of water, and towels ready for the ceremony of hand washing. But Ezra, instead of blessing the wine, rose from the heaped cushions of his chair and filled the Rabbi's glass.

"Bless the wine for us, Father," he said.

The Rabbi rose and lifted his glass and blessed the wine, and they all rose and drank. When they were seated again Wang Ma led the servants and they poured water into the silver basins, and each person at the table washed and dried his hands. Then each took a bitter herb and dipped it in the salt and ate it.

It was all familiar to the Chinese servants and yet always strange. They stood about the room, silent, their dark eyes watching in fascination and wonder and respect. Under their gaze Ezra was not wholly at ease as he proceeded with the rites.

"David, my son, Leah is younger than you, and she will ask the four questions this time," he said.

And Leah, blushing a little, said the questions four times in her deep and sweet voice, which still was somehow childlike.

"Wherein is this night different from other nights?"

Four times she asked and four times the answers came from those about the table, the Rabbi's great solemn voice louder than any:

"On all other nights we may eat leavened bread but on this night only unleavened.

"On all other nights we may eat other kinds of herbs but on this night only bitter herbs.

"On all other nights we need not dip an herb even once, but on this night we do so twice.

"On all other nights we eat sitting upright, but on this night we may recline."

When the four questions had been asked and answered, Ezra said, "Tell us the story now from Haggadah, Father."

But here Madame Ezra spoke with reproach. "Oh, Ezra, it is you, the father of our family, who should tell the story! I do believe you have forgotten it, for every year you will not tell it. If only you read Hebrew you could read it to us."

"I would not dare, in the presence of the Rabbi," Ezra said, laughing.

So the old rabbi told the ancient story of how once their people were bondmen in a foreign land and how one of them named Moses rose up to set them free, and how he bade his people bake bread quickly without leaven and kill a lamb and mark their door-posts with its blood, and how after many plagues the last plague came upon their rulers so that the first-born son in every family died, and at last the king of that country bade them go. Thus forever each year this day was their festival of freedom.

"Until," the Rabbi said, lifting his head high, "until we return to the land that belongs to us, our own land!"

"May it be soon!" Madame Ezra cried and wiped her eyes.

"May it be soon," Leah said gravely.

But Ezra and David were silent.

Four times during the long story Peony had motioned to the servants to pour wine, and four times all drank in memory of what she did not know, but she knew the wine must be poured. The very meaning of the word "Jew" Peony did not know, nor did any Chinese know, beyond the fact that these foreigners, who prospered so well in the rich city, had come long ago from a far country, Judea, or as it was called, the Country of the Jews. Through Persia and India they had come by sea and land to China. At many times in history, in one generation after another, they had come as merchants and traders in a small steady human stream. But every now and again they came in a sudden crowd of some hundreds at a time, bringing their families and priests with them. So had Ezra's own ancestors come, scores of years ago, one of seventy families, through India, and bringing with them bolts of cotton goods, which was treasure to the Chinese, who only knew the making of silk. This gift, presented to the emperor of that early dynasty, had won them favor, and upon them he bestowed the Chinese family name of

Chao, by which surname Ezra was known to this day in the city of K'aifeng.

The Chinese in the city viewed these modest invasions with tolerant eyes. They were a clever people, these Jews, full of energy and wit, and often a Chinese, indolent with years of good living, employed a Jew to manage his business. Almost as often he gave a second or third daughter to the Jew for his wife, but the Jews never gave their daughters in return.

"Quick, you turnip!" Wang Ma now whispered to Old Wang as the Rabbi sat down. "Fetch the eggs!"

Wang Ma had been a bondmaid, too, in this house, and even as Peony now watched, so had she in the days when she was young and pretty. Too kind, too old now to be envious of Peony, yet sometimes she stepped forward before the family.

Old Wang ran to the door and shouted and two servants came in with bowls of eggs boiled hard in salt water and peeled. Each one at the table took an egg, and in silence they ate.

"Signifying our tears and our hope," the old Rabbi murmured, and his deep voice echoed about the table.

When the eggs were eaten Ezra clapped his hands. "Now, now," he called, "let us have the feast!"

Wang Ma and Old Wang had gone out during the eating of the eggs and the other servants with them, and at this moment they pulled back the curtains and a procession of servants came in bearing dishes of all kinds of fish and fowl and meat, except pork, and set them upon the table in a wide circle. Taking up his chopsticks, Ezra waved them and urged all to begin, and he himself placed upon the bowls of the Rabbi and Leah those tidbits that he thought most delicious.

So all ate and Ezra ate and drank until the veins stood out red on his neck, the whole time talking and merry and pressing food on everyone. Of all of them, only Aaron sat silent and pale. Yet he ate voraciously and quickly, as though he had not for a long time had enough, and Leah looked at him reproachfully for his greediness, but he did not heed her. Once, catching her eyes, he made a sullen face at her, and this David saw with indignation, but he said nothing. He searched with his chopsticks and found a tender bit of flesh on his own plate, and he put it on Leah's plate for her. This Peony saw.

The feast went on its usual course. Ezra grew merry as he ate and drank, and even Madame Ezra laughed at his jokes and nonsense. The Rabbi smiled his dim high smile and Aaron snickered and David threw back joke for joke and Leah laughed with joy, until David began to crack his jokes only to make her laugh the more, while his parents admired him. This Peony saw.

She made no sign. A sweet fixed smile was set upon her lips and she busied herself, dismissing the servants at last. Alone she kept the wine cups filled and replenished the sweetmeats until the feast was over and the guests gone. Then she ran ahead and made ready David's bed, turning down the silken quilts and loosening the embroidered curtains from the heavy silver hooks. But she did not stay to greet him. She went away to her own room, and upon her narrow bed she lay long awake, remembering David's face as he had turned to Leah, and remembering, she could not sleep.

The next morning Peony woke early, and there upon her eyelids was still the memory of David's face when he had looked at Leah the night before. How foolish I am! she thought restlessly. She rose and washed and dressed herself and braided her hair freshly, and having made her room neat for the day she went into the peach-tree garden. It lay in the silence of the spring morning. Under the early sun the dew still hung in a bright mist on the grass, and the pool in the center of the garden was brimming its stone walls. The water was clear and the fish were flashing their golden sides near the surface.

The great low-built house that surrounded the garden was still in sleep. Birds twittered in the eaves undisturbed and a small Pekingese dog slept on the threshold like a small lioness. She had lifted her head alertly at the sound of a sliding panel, and when she saw Peony, she got up and moved with majesty toward her mistress, waiting in the path until Peony stooped and touched her head with delicate fingers.

"Hush, Small Dog," she said in a low voice. "Everyone is asleep."

The dog, receiving the caress without humility, lay down again, and Peony stood smiling and gazing about her with delight, as though she had never seen the garden before, although she had lived so many years in this house. Once again, as often before had happened, the oppression of the night vanished. The many joys of her life grew bright again with the morning. She enjoyed comfort, she loved beauty, and of both this house had much. If she were not in the main stream of its warmth and affection, yet the abundance of both overflowed upon her. She put aside her fears of the night, and then, tiptoeing along the stone path, she approached a peach tree about to bloom at last, and began to cut a branch with a pair of iron scissors she had brought with her. Her coat and trousers of pink satin were the same shade as the blossoms, and in the midst of pale pink and tender green, her black hair, combed in a long braid and coiled over one ear and fringed above her forehead, her large black eyes, and her ivory skin made her face as clearcut as a carving. She was slender and short, and her round face was demure. Her eyes were lively, the black pupils unusually large, the whites very clear, and her mouth was small, full, and red. Her hands, stretched above her head, were dexterous, and her pink sleeves, falling away, showed round pretty arms.

She had barely cut the branch when she heard her name called.

"Peony!"

She turned and saw David as he came from another part of the garden, and instantly all her hurt was gone. Did she not know him as none other did? He was tall, almost a man, but behind his new height she saw him the child she had always known. His height showed him foreign, she thought, and so did his full dark eyes and his curling dark hair, his skin dark, but without the golden tinge of a Chinese. This morning he wore a Chinese robe of thin dark blue silk tied about him with a white silk girdle, and she thought of him as her own. His handsome mouth was pouting and still childish.

"Why didn't you answer me when I called?" he demanded.

Peony put her finger to her lips. "Oh—you promised me you

wouldn't come into the garden after me!" she breathed. "Young Master," she added.

In a low voice he demanded fiercely, "You have never called me Master—why have you changed since yesterday?"

Peony busied herself with peach blossoms. "Yesterday your mother told me I must call you Young Master." Her voice was faltering and shy, but her black eyes, dancing under their long straight lashes, were naughty. "We are grownup now, your mother said."

It was true that yesterday morning Madame Ezra, beset by a gust of temper in the midst of preparations for the feast, had rebuked Peony suddenly.

"Where is David to sit?" Peony had asked, very carelessly.

"Dare to call my son by his name!" Madame Ezra had cried.

"But, Lady, have I not always so called his name?" Peony had asked.

"Let it be so no more," Madame Ezra had replied. "You should have been the first to know that you are not children now." She had paused and then had gone on, "And while I speak, here is more—you are no longer to go to his room, for any cause, if he is there—or he to yours. Do you hear me?"

"Yes, Mistress." Peony had turned away to hide her tears, and Madame Ezra had relented.

"I do not blame you, child, for growing up," she announced. "But I teach you this: Whatever happens is always the woman's fault."

"Yes, Mistress," Peony had said again.

"Oh, you know my mother," David now grumbled.

Peony darted a shrewd look at him. "She will scold you for wearing your robe tied around you like that. Only yesterday she told me I must help you to be neat—'a bondmaid's duty,' she said."

She put the peach blossoms carefully on the ground as she spoke and went to him. He laughed a young man's laughter, lazy, amorous, teasing, and standing beside her, he submitted to her nimble fingers. He was so tall that he shielded her from the house, but he threw a quick look over his shoulder.

"Whose bondmaid are you?" he demanded.

She lifted her long lashes. "Yours," she said. Then her lips twitched. "That's not to say I'm worth much! You know what I cost when they bought me for you—a hundred dollars and a suit of clothes."

"That was when you were a skinny thing of eight," he teased. "Now you're worth—let's see—seventeen, pretty, but very disobedient and still a handful of a girl. Why, you must be worth ten times as much!"

"Be still," she commanded him. "This button is almost off. Come with me and I will sew it on."

"Come to your room?"

She shook her head. "Your mother said that was to stop."

"You come to my room," he urged.

She shook her head, hesitated, and they heard a panel slide. Instantly he slipped into the twisting path behind a tall rock, and Peony stooped to pick up the peach blossoms. It was only Wang Ma, who came to sweep the threshold.

"I saw you," she said to Peony.

"What of that?" Peony replied with impudence. She went into the huge shadowy hall and began to arrange the peach blossoms in two blue hawthorn-flowered vases that stood on the wall table. This morning the great hall was, to the casual eye, a Chinese family room. After last night's feast the round table had been taken away and the other furniture had been placed again in the conventional Chinese way about the room. The long table was set against the wall facing the wide door into the garden, and against this table was set the square table of the same dark polished heavy wood. On either side of the square table were the two immense armchairs of the same wood. At intervals around the walls the small tables stood, each with a pair of chairs. Doorways were hung with red satin curtains and there were no windows except on the side toward the garden, which was set with sliding panels latticed with mother-of-pearl. Through the lattice the sunlight filtered, iridescent and pale upon the floor of smooth worn gray tile, on the white plastered walls, even on the high, beamed roof. Long ago the beams had been varnished an oxblood red, and the color had grown rich and dark with age.

To the discerning eye the room was not purely Chinese even today. Above the long wall table in the place of honor there hung an enormous satin tapestry. Upon its dull blue, Hebrew letters were embroidered in gold. Beneath this tapestry stood the two seven-branched candlesticks of brass, and in one corner of the room was an ancient Jewish prayer ark.

Peony stepped back to see the effect of the blossoms. With her usual skill she had arranged them in the vases in such a manner that they formed a composite as lovely as a painting. She smiled, her head lifted slightly to one side. A look of sensuous pleasure came over her exquisite small face.

"When the peach trees bloom then it is spring," she murmured to Wang Ma. "What a mercy of heaven that our spring festival comes after their sorrowful foreign feast!"

She shrugged, waved her little hands, and sat down on the edge of one of the great armchairs. "Wang Ma, I ask you, who have been in this house so long, what makes them love to grieve?"

Wang Ma pursed her full lips. "You'll grieve if our old mistress comes in and sees you sitting in her chair," she retorted. "Such impudence! I've never thought of sitting in one of those chairs. But then, I've only been here thirty years."

"Do not be cross with me, Wang Ma." Peony's voice was soft, and she rose from the chair and opened the red lacquered sweet box that stood in the center of the square table. It was full of small sesame cakes. She took one and began to eat it.

"Nor would I help myself to their cakes," Wang Ma said.

Peony went on eating.

"Those cakes smell of pigs' fat," Wang Ma said severely. She reached for one and smelled it. "Pigs' fat, it's certain! I told you all cakes must be bought at the Buddhist sweetshop!"

"I told your Old Wang so, too," Peony replied. "He bought them, not I."

"You!" Wang Ma cried. "Telling him!"

Peony smiled and did not answer. She opened the tea basket that stood beside the sweet box and felt the pot. It was hot and she poured tea into one of the rice-patterned bowls and sipped it, both hands cupped about its warmth.

"And I have never drunk from one of those bowls," Wang Ma said. She nibbled a cake. "Yes, it's pigs' fat," she murmured gloomily, and went on eating it.

"Why don't they like pigs' fat?" Peony inquired. "It's odd that I've lived with all their superstitions and still I don't know what they mean."

"It's their religion," Wang Ma said. She reached for another cake. "People do strange things when they are religious. I had an old aunt who went to be a Buddhist nun when her betrothed died, and she never ate meat again and she shaved her head and she slept on a bamboo bed with no quilt underneath her so that when she got up in the morning she was all wealed. Why? Who knows? But it made her happy."

"Yet our mistress is so sensible," Peony said.

She poured a bowl of tea for Wang Ma, who shook her head. Peony took the bowl in both hands and presented it. "Drink, good mother," she said. "You deserve it after all these years. Besides, they'll never know."

"Who knows what you'll tell?" Wang Ma said severely.

"I never tell anything I know," Peony said demurely.

Wang Ma put down the bowl. "What do you know?" she inquired.

"Now you want me to tell," Peony said, smiling.

"I know some things myself," Wang Ma retorted.

"What things?" Peony asked. Her innocence was flagrant in voice and wide black eyes.

"You and our young master," Wang Ma said.

"I and our young master! Don't think it's with us as it was with you and the old master," Peony said.

Wang Ma stared. Her neck grew red. "Dare to say it!" she cried.

Peony shrugged her pretty shoulders. "It's not I who say anything," she retorted.

Wang Ma pursed her lips and swept her eyelids downward. "*P'ei!* You ought to die!" she muttered.

Peony put her hand on Wang Ma's sleeve. "If we are not friends to each other in this house, who will be friends to us?" She paused and went on, "Yet I am only a servant. Well, what then? It has been my duty to care for him, to play games with him; if he were restless, to sing to him; if he were sleepless, to read to him; if he were hungry, to feed him—to be his slave in everything. Yesterday—" She shrugged her shoulders again.

Wang Ma came close. "You know what is to happen?"

Peony shook her head. Then she looked sad. "No, I won't lie. Of course I know. But he'll never be happy with Leah."

"He has to marry her, even as his father did before him marry one of their people," Wang Ma insisted. "This betrothal was fixed when the children were in their cradles. I remember—it was before you were born."

Peony said gently, "Do you think I have not been told that? Leah herself told me, when we were children playing together, David and she and I—'I'm to marry David,' that's what she said. 'Leah, stop talking about it'—that's what he always said."

"She's eighteen now to his nineteen." Wang Ma sighed. "It's time—"

"Hush!" Peony whispered. They listened. Steady footsteps approached, measured and strong. Quickly they moved together to replace the teapot, cover the sweet box, brush away the crumbs, wipe out the tea bowls. In an instant Wang Ma was sweeping the floor again with her short-handled broom, and Peony, taking a silk kerchief from her bosom, was dusting the table and the carved chairs.

The red satin curtain at the east of the room was pushed back by a dark strong hand covered with rings, and Madame Ezra stood there. This morning she wore a strange combination of garments, a Chinese skirt and robe of gray silk, a Jewish headdress of striped taffeta. The two women, young and old, stood and gave greetings.

"Old Mistress," their voices murmured. Both were careful, suspecting a tendency to temper after a feast.

"You two," Madame Ezra replied in a firm voice, "make haste with your tasks. My son's father will be here soon."

She moved across the floor slowly, her long silver-gray skirt swaying, and she sat down on the chair to the left of the square table, facing the garden. "He ought indeed to be here now," she went on. "But when was he ever on time?"

Wang Ma poured a bowl of tea and handed it to Madame Ezra with both hands. "Our master likes to linger in the teahouse over his early tea," she said. Her voice was easygoing, her manner half intimate, as befitted those of an elderly serving woman who had been long with the family. "Besides that, Mistress, he is every day hoping to hear of the coming of the caravan."

"That caravan!" Madame Ezra exclaimed. "It is made an excuse for everything."

"We all long for its coming, Mistress," Wang Ma said, laughing. "It is like a second New Year, bringing all these toys from foreign lands."

The caravan of which she spoke was one that Ezra sent every year under his trusted partner, Kao Lien. Although the route by sea from Africa and Europe was quicker than the land route to the north, yet for the bringing of goods the land route by camel was less expensive and more sure. This year the caravan had been delayed for reasons that, Kao Lien had said in his letter, he could not explain until he arrived, and he had wintered abroad. As soon as the turn of the year came and the days began to lengthen, he had set out. Now for a month Ezra had no message from him, and this led him to believe that Kao Lien must be near, and with him the longest caravan and the richest goods that Ezra had yet received. To distribute these goods to the best advantage was the anxiety of his life, and he had been long in negotiation with the Chinese merchant Kung Chen, whose shops were in every large city in the province and who talked now of opening a shop in the northern capital itself, under the very eyes of the ladies of the palace.

Madame Ezra did not hear Wang Ma. She lifted her head and sniffed the air searchingly. "Do I smell—yes, I do." She turned with determination. "Wang Ma, open the sweet box!"

But Wang Ma lifted the whole box and handed it to Peony, who stepped forward to receive it. "Now, Old Mistress," Wang Ma said firmly, "I had only this moment told Peony that there was a mistake about these cakes. We tasted them—she and I."

"Pigs' fat!" Madame Ezra exclaimed.

"It was that old man of mine," Wang Ma urged. "Lazy—too lazy to walk across another street to the Buddhist shop! But Mistress, you married me to him yourself with all his faults. What I've put up with all these years!"

"But to put them in the sweet box," Madame Ezra said reproachfully. "Take them away."

Peony took up the box and slipped silently toward a doorway, retreating gracefully and almost imperceptibly. With a sweet quick smile she disappeared altogether. Outside the door in the wide corridor she paused and looked behind the curtain and met Old Wang, a small gray-haired man, flattened against the wall. He put his finger to his lips and tiptoed after her down the passage and into the library. There she handed him the box of cakes.

"You heard?" she asked.

He nodded. "I was about to enter and say that Old Master is on his way when I heard her blaming me, and so I waited."

"You see what trouble you bring on your old woman and me," Peony went on gently, but her great eyes were dancing and her her red lips quivering with a smile.

He answered this mischief, wagging his head from side to side. "Someone always eats the cakes. Before Heaven, does it matter who, so long as it is a human being?" He held out the box to her and she pushed back her satin sleeve and delicately took a cake.

"Eat one, Old Wang," Peony commanded him. "You too are a human being."

They ate the cakes with a sort of solemnity, in common communion, and when she had finished she drew her silk kerchief from her sleeve and wiped her fingers. "After all, there is no sin among our people in eating cakes made with pigs' fat," she remarked. "Why do these foreigners refuse good meat and good fat from a pig?"

"How do I know?" Old Wang replied. "Believing in gods always causes confusion."

A door opened and they turned their heads.

"Old Master!" Old Wang cried.

Peony bent her head gracefully and Ezra came in. He looked handsome this morning even in his middle age, and as Peony discerned from under her smiling lashes, he was cheerful. She understood this very well. As each feast day approached he grew short-tempered and gloomy, and went half sulkily through all the rites upon which Madame Ezra insisted. The day after the feast was over, he was buoyant again, eager to be about his prospering business.

"Ah, Peony," Ezra said pleasantly. He stroked his beard. "You're looking very pretty, my child. Have you cut fresh peach blossoms this morning?"

"They are there in the vases, Old Master," Peony replied in a docile voice. "The forced ones faded after the feast."

"And where is my son?" Ezra went on.

"I have not seen him, Old Master," she replied.

"If you do, keep him away—there's a good child," Ezra said. He tightened the silk girdle about his substantial waist, fixed his turban on his head as though preparing himself for something to come. "I don't want David to overhear us this morning," he said to Peony in a low voice. "His mother wants me to agree to the marriage. David doesn't want to get married, does he?"

"I don't know, Old Master," Peony said faintly.

"Ha, no—why should you? How long has it been since he has seen Leah—until yesterday?"

Peony lifted fringed eyelids. "He sees her in the synagogue, Old Master."

"They don't talk together alone?"

"Not since she was sixteen."

"That's—ah—"

"Over two years, Old Master," Peony reminded him.

"Does he ever speak of her?"

"Not to me, Old Master."

"There is no letter writing?"

"No, Old Master."

Ezra's rolling eyes fell on the box of cakes Old Wang held as he stood, listening to all that was said. "What's this, eh? Cakes?"

Peony explained. "Old Wang is taking them away—they have pigs' fat in them."

"It's a pity," Ezra said absently. "Pigs' fat, eh? Of course I'm not orthodox—hmm—" He took a cake and ate it quickly. "Very good, too. Pity! Well, yes, it won't do in this house."

He hastened on and Peony and Old Wang looked at each other and broke into laughter. They parted, Old Wang to go to the kitchen and Peony to return to the great hall. She followed just behind Ezra and her entrance was not noticed.

"I have been waiting for you, Ezra," Madame Ezra said somewhat irritably.

"So have I been waiting for you, my dear," Ezra replied calmly. He sat down in the large chair opposite her and sipped the tea that Wang Ma offered him and then allowed her to light his pipe. She took a brown paper spill from a holder, blew the smoldering end into flame, and held it to the tobacco. A water pipe was a great resource in such a conversation as he knew waited for him now. It was necessary to fill and refill the tiny bowl of the pipe, to light the tobacco, to take two puffs or so, and then to blow out the ash and begin all over again. There was plenty of excuse for delay in answers, for pauses and repetitions.

"When I say I will be here midway between morning and noon meals, I am here," Madame Ezra said. "Even after a feast day," she added.

"No one doubts it," Ezra replied tranquilly.

He was an ample man, black-bearded and olive-skinned, and he filled the wide Chinese chair. This morning a long Chinese robe fell to his feet. It was of dark wine-colored satin, brocaded in a design of circles, and over it he wore a sleeveless jacket of black velvet. On his head he had wound a vivid turban of silk, and the fringed ends spread above his right ear, where he wore a heavy gold earring. The other ear was bare. His feet too were bare, and he wore leather sandals studded with gold. Feet and hands were large, to match his heavy frame and his big-featured face. With his size he moved in a slumberous fashion, yet he was not languid so much as indomitable.

Madame Ezra gazed at him with mounting impatience. They were a well-matched pair and she knew it. She loved him heartily, but he could make her more angry than anyone else.

"Have you seen David?" she now demanded.

"I seldom see him in the morning," Ezra replied. "Moreover, I have been at the teahouse since I rose from my bed. I had promised to meet Kung Chen there."

He coughed behind his large smooth brown hand. "What a clever merchant!" he said with admiration. "He and I—we're a pair. We respect each other. One day he has the best of me and the next day I have the best of him. But the end is coming now—we are almost agreed. Naomi, if I bring this contract to conclusion, as surely I will after the caravan comes, I shall have an outlet through the House of Kung for all my imports of ivory, porcelain, peacocks, western trinkets, and musical instruments—in short, for all foreign goods. Through their shops I shall pour my merchandise."

The two bondmaids, Wang Ma and Peony, had taken their usual places. Wang Ma stood behind Madame Ezra and Peony behind Ezra. They were as little noticed as though they were pieces of furniture, but this they took as a matter of course. Ezra leaned on the table. "Naomi, I have something to propose to you. Now be patient—"

"Well?" Madame Ezra's voice was edged with impatience.

"Kung Chen has a daughter, sixteen, very pretty—"

"How do you know?" Madame Ezra demanded.

"Well—hm—I saw the child, quite accidentally, the other day. He had asked me to come to his house—very unusual. But we wanted to talk privately about the contract. She was there in the main hall. Of course, she left instantly. But Kung said she was his daughter."

Madame Ezra contained herself with difficulty. She pressed her lips together and gazed furiously at her husband. "I suppose you are about to suggest that I accept this Chinese girl as my daughter-in-law?" she asked bitterly.

Ezra shrugged and spread out his big hands, palms upward. "Well, my dear, you see the advantages. I am an importer of foreign goods, he is a merchant with shops in a dozen big cities, you see After all, we are living in China."

"I see nothing except that you are asking a monstrous thing!" she cried.

"Eh?" Ezra lifted his shaggy eyebrows.

"You know that David must marry Leah!" Madame Ezra's rich voice threatened tears.

"Now, Naomi," Ezra began. "You can't mean that you are going to insist on that, after all these years!"

"I do insist!" Madame Ezra retorted. "All the more after all these years!"

Ezra spoke with persuasive gentleness. "But a foolish promise, Naomi, made by two sentimental women over their children's cradles!"

"A sacred promise," Madame Ezra declared, "made before Jehovah, to preserve our people pure!"

"But Naomi—"

"I insist!"

"It's a little late to talk about purity. My own mother was Chinese," Ezra said.

"Don't remind me of her!" Madame Ezra screamed.

Ezra lost his temper suddenly and completely. His face purpled. He rose to his feet. But Wang Ma was quicker. She stepped in front of him and she pushed him to his chair, her hands on his arms.

"Master, Master," she remonstrated.

He sank back. Wang Ma poured a bowl of tea and gave it to him with both hands and glanced at Madame Ezra. Ezra took the bowl and set it down abruptly before his wife.

"Drink tea, Naomi," Ezra said shortly.

Now Wang Ma filled Ezra's tea bowl and presented it to him. Peony drew a white silk fan from her wide sleeve and began to fan him gently. He sighed, relaxed in his chair, and lifting his turban, he wiped his face and head with his silk handkerchief and put the turban on again.

"Perhaps we had better send for David," he suggested at last.

"There is no use in sending for him until you agree with me," Madame Ezra said.

"But perhaps he will help us to agree," Ezra retorted.

"I will not have you mention this Chinese girl to him," Madame Ezra replied.

"No, no," Ezra said, "that I promise! But we could find out how he feels about any marriage. That, at least—"

"Why at least?" Madame Ezra broke in. "It is the most important, not the least."

Ezra slapped his knees. "Peony!" he shouted. "Go and fetch my son!"

"Yes, Master," Peony whispered. She moved out of the room, noiseless and graceful. Wang Ma filled the tea bowls again.

Madame Ezra went on, "I will not grant that David can decide this matter."

"You wouldn't want him to marry a woman he hates, Naomi," Ezra said more mildly.

"Who could hate Leah?" Madame Ezra rejoined. "She is a beautiful girl—and so good."

"Certainly," Ezra agreed.

"What our old rabbi would have done without her—" Madame Ezra said.

"His son is good for little," Ezra said with sarcasm.

"Aaron is still a child."

"Only a year younger than Leah."

"She seems much older."

"Yes," Ezra agreed absently. He fell silent.

He had in fact told his wife a lie. It was not he who had seen the pretty daughter of Kung, but David. But how could he have explained to his wife that he had purposely sent David to the house of Kung? He had sent him with a message to Kung Chen at the exact hour when the ladies of a house are freshly dressed and wandering about the courts for change and exercise. When David came back he had said teasingly, "Why are your eyes so bright, my son? What have you seen?"

David had blushed as a young man should and had shaken his head. "Here is the answer, Father," he had replied shortly, and had put Kung Chen's letter on the table.

Now Ezra closed his eyes, sat back in his chair, and circled his thumbs slowly one about the other. Behind the veil of his eyelids his acute and restless mind worked busily, sorting out the threads of his emotions. He was not confused so much as complex. In his veins ran the blood of two hearty strains. Half of the blood was nearly pure, but his father had taken as a second wife a young Chinese woman of strength and beauty, and he was her son. Outwardly his mother had seemed to adopt all the ways of his father's house. But Ezra, her son, alone knew how untouched was her heart. In her own room, in the secrecy of her being, she had laughed at the foreigners with whom she lived. While she had enjoyed the pleasures of being a rich man's wife and had eaten until she had in her age grown immensely fat, her pretty features sunk in mounds of rosy flesh, she had actually given up nothing of her own ways, and had even influenced the man she had married. Old Israel ben Abram, as the years passed, had begun to neglect the feast days once carefully observed in the house, and compromise became his habit. But when his Chinese wife died, leaving his son Ezra a boy of fifteen, in an excess of remorse and smitten conscience he had betrothed him to Naomi, daughter of a leader of the little colony of Jews in the Chinese city.

Ezra, at that time indolent and romantic, had yielded. Naomi was handsome and there was something fascinating in her cool young strength. After their marriage, he found the habit of compromise, taught him by his Chinese mother, a practical weapon. Naomi was too strong. It was with compromise that his brain was now busy.

Madame Ezra spoke suddenly. "Ezra, open your eyes—you look foolish."

"Certainly, my dear," he replied. He opened his eyes.

"Not so wide, stupid!" Madame Ezra said impatiently.

He drooped his lids and his lips twitched with secret laughter. She threw him a sharp look and he caught it as though it were a glass ball and threw it back at her. She looked away.

"David is a long time in coming," she remarked.

"He may have been on the street somewhere, Lady," Wang Ma hastened to reply. Every servant in the house rallied to the defense of the young lord.

Before there could be an answer they heard his footsteps. Peony preceded him, drawing aside the scarlet satin curtain with delicate fingers. He stood there, tall and dark, his impetuous eyes searching the two faces now turned to him.

"You sent for me, Father—Mother—"

"Come in and sit down, my son," Ezra said kindly.

"Where have you been?" his mother asked at the same time.

He answered neither of them. He sat down near his father and Peony poured him a bowl of tea and silently set it on the table beside him. Then she took her usual place behind Ezra and drawing the fan again from her sleeve, she opened it and began to move it slowly to and fro. Her eyes were half hidden beneath her drooped lids. David looked at her and away again. It was impossible to discern from that smooth pearly surface what thoughts flowed beneath.

"David, it is time—" Madame Ezra began.

The young man whirled around on his seat. "Time for what?" he demanded.

"You know, my son," Madame Ezra said. She humbled herself, she made her voice pleading, knowing full well how easily this beloved only child could harden himself.

"I don't know, Mother," he retorted.

Madame Ezra pleaded, "Leah is eighteen, David. And you are a man. And I promised her mother."

"Your promises have nothing to do with me," he said shortly.

"But you have always known—" Madame Ezra reminded him.

"I do not know now," he interrupted her. "Besides, I don't love Leah."

"Shame on you!" Madame Ezra cried. "Last night you were friendly enough."

"This morning I remember her nose is too long," David said.

Madame Ezra spread out her hands and rolled her eyes from

one face to the other. "She is a good girl—pretty, too— and learned in our faith. She will be a light in this house after I am gone."

"Still her nose is too long," David insisted.

It had become a habit for him to oppose his mother, and he did so unreasonably now. He knew well enough that Leah's nose was a handsome one, and had his mother kept silent, he might have remembered only Leah's beauty. But he was still childish enough to want to be free at all costs, and now he glared stubbornly at his mother and then laughed.

"Don't marry me off so young, Mother," he cried gaily.

Ezra laughed out loud. Peony allowed herself the smallest of smiles. Wang Ma's face was expressionless. Madame Ezra felt no support. She bit her lip, sighed, and summoned all her adoration of her son. When she turned to him again her full dark eyes were moist and her lips quivered.

"David, my son," she began in her richest, softest tones, "do not break your mother's heart. No, wait, I do not ask you to think of me, David. Think of our people! You and Leah, David—together—your children—carrying on the blood of Judah, in this heathen land! Such a good girl, David—a good wife, always loving you and the home, teaching the children about God! When the time comes for us to go back to our own country, our promised land—"

David broke in, "But I don't want to go away. This is where I was born, Mother—here, in this house."

Madame Ezra dropped her persuasion. Honest temper blazed in her full face. "Dare to speak so to your mother!" she shouted. "God grant us the chance to go back to the land of our fathers before we die—you and I and your father and all our house!"

Ezra coughed behind his hand. "I couldn't leave my business, Naomi."

"I am not talking about tomorrow!" Madame Ezra shouted. "I am talking about God's good time, when the prophets lead us."

"I may as well speak," David said suddenly. "Mother, I want to tell you something." He rose and they looked at him as he stood, tall and beautiful, before them. "Mother, I won't marry Leah, because I love someone else."

Madame Ezra's firm jaw dropped. Ezra lifted his tea bowl. Peony stood, her eyes on David. The little silk fan was motionless in her hand. Wang Ma turned away her head.

"Who is it?" Madame Ezra demanded.

David faced his mother, his cheeks scarlet. "I saw someone—in the Kung house—"

"When?" Madame Ezra demanded with passion. Her strength returned.

"Two days ago," David said simply.

Madame Ezra turned upon her husband. Her black eyes blazed at him. "You said—it was you who—"

Ezra groaned. "My dear, you compel us all to lie to you," he remarked sadly. He lifted his heavy-lidded eyes to his son. "Go on," he commanded him. "Now you have begun, finish! You saw a pretty girl. Did you speak with her?"

"Of course not," David cried. "She—she said something—'Oh, oh' —something like that—and she ran out of the room as fleetly as—as a—"

"As a fawn?" Ezra suggested dryly.

David looked astonished. "Father, how did you know? Have you seen her, too?"

"No," Ezra replied. "Not this one. But I believe 'fawn' is the usual term."

"What folly!" Madame Ezra said in a loud voice. "Ezra, I am shocked!"

Ezra rose suddenly. "I'm sorry, Naomi. Really, I can't stay—Kung Chen is waiting and he is not the sort that does wait, you know."

"Sit down, both of you," Madame Ezra said imperiously. "David, you shall be betrothed on the tenth day of the eighth month. It is the anniversary of the day upon which Leah's mother and I made our promise."

She met her son's eyes full and they looked at each other. His eyes fell. "I wont—I won't," he muttered. "I'll kill myself first." He turned and strode from the room.

"Go after him, Peony," Ezra commanded.

Peony needed no command. She was already halfway to the door and she disappeared behind the satin curtain.

To this revelation David had made she had listened with astonished ears. And she had dreamed that she knew all his heart! More than she had suffered last night for Leah's sake she now grieved that David had hidden this from her. She ran across the corridor and out upon the long verandas that lined the courts. Where had he gone? She paused, finger to lips, her eyes closed, pondering. He would want to escape, and where could he escape except into the streets? She turned and ran swiftly and lightly toward the gate.

In the silence of the great hall the two elders sat. Wang Ma sighed and filled the tea bowls again. Ezra's face was grave and Madame Ezra touched her eyes with her handkerchief. After a moment Ezra spoke, and his voice was very gentle. "Naomi, we waited a long time for this only child."

But she was not to be moved. "I had rather he had never been born than to see him lost to our people," she said heavily.

Ezra sighed, got to his feet, prepared to go. But he could not leave her so easily. He knew her heart after all these years, the great stubborn hot heart of a Jewish wife and mother. "Ah, Naomi," he said sadly. "If only you women could let us be what we are!"

She did not reply. She turned her face from him and held her handkerchief to her eyes, and he motioned to Wang Ma. "Take care of her," he murmured, and went away.

When he had gone Madame Ezra broke into loud sobs, as though she were alone. As though, too, it were the habit of years, Wang Ma moved to her side and took her hand and patted it softly, massaging the fingers and the wrist, pinching the firm flesh gently. One hand and the other she so comforted, and then she pressed Madame Ezra's temples again and again between her palms, and Madame Ezra was quieted and she leaned back against her chair and closed her eyes. Thus was she soothed.

But under her fingers Wang Ma felt the busy stubborn brain still working. "Ah, Lady," she murmured. "Let men have their way! What does it matter to women? To sleep—to eat—to enjoy our own lives—that is best."

They were the wrong words and instantly she regretted them. Madame Ezra's fiery black eyes sprang open. She sat up and turned on her serving woman. "You Chinese!" she said with bitter contempt. "You Chinese!" She rose as she spoke, and pushed aside Wang Ma's hands and left the room with imperious speed.

Wang Ma stood watching, then she felt the teapot and found it hot. She filled the bowl from which Ezra had drunk, and taking it in both hands she went and sat down on the high doorsill. There, warmed by the hot sun, she continued to sit, drinking the tea slowly and gazing reflectively into the sunlit court.

挑筋教

II

PEONY faced David.

"You!" she cried with soft ferocity. "Not to tell me!" He was fleeter of foot than she, and wile had to get her first to the gate. Once he had looked back and had seen her, and instantly she seemed to give up the chase and had slipped into a side alley of the immense compound. He looked behind him again, and not seeing her, he had smiled triumphantly and had slowed his steps. Then suddenly she was ahead of him in a passageway, and he knew he was outwitted. She stood, her hands outspread to catch him and hold him. He stopped just short of her, folded his arms, and looked down into her reproachful eyes.

"I am not bound to you!" he declared.

Her small lovely face quivered, flushed, and wilted before his gaze like a smitten flower. "No," she said in a little voice. "It is only I who am bound to you. And—and—you are quite right. You need not tell me—anything."

He was instantly remorseful. "Now, Peony," he argued. "I will tell you—but only if I am not forced."

"It is wrong of me," she agreed. "I will never do it again. See—you are free!"

She locked her hands behind her back. He put out his arms but she evaded them and stepped aside, and then turned and ran from him. Now it was he who pursued and she who fled. . . . How she loved to run! It was her luck to be bondmaid in this house of foreigners. Had she been in a Chinese house her feet would have been bound small as soon as it was sure she was to be pretty, so that if a son of the house were to love her and want her for a concubine, she would not shame the family by having feet like a servant's. She ran on, laughing at the sound of him running behind her. He was laughing, too, but they muted their laughter in the secret way of their childhood. He caught her, as he always did, as she knew he would, and she pushed him and twisted herself free—almost, but not quite. His arms were strong. Then her acute ear, quick to hear footsteps and voices, warned her that they were seen.

"Young Master," she cried loudly. "You must not take your life!"

He dropped his arms, but it was too late. Madame Ezra had seen them.

"Peony!" she said sharply. "You forget yourself!"

"I was holding him lest he throw himself into the well," she faltered.

"Nonsense!" Madame Ezra retorted. But she wavered. Did the girl lie or was she indeed holding him against death?

David laughed "She's lying, Mother," he said robustly. "We were only playing a game."

Madame Ezra was not pleased. "It is time you stopped playing games with Peony," she said coldly. She was less pleased than usual to see how beautiful her son looked at this moment. The high color and bold bearing in which she took her secret delight now alarmed her. And Peony, too, was growing dangerously pretty.

"Make yourself ready," she said shortly to the girl. "You must accompany me to the house of the Rabbi. And you, David, should be at your books."

She walked firmly down the passageway toward her own rooms. David made a grimace and shrugged his shoulders, and Peony answered with lifted eyebrows and a sigh. Then her little face took on its look of sweetest coaxing. She glanced at Madame Ezra's back and lingered to put a small hand, flower light, upon David's arm.

"You will tell me all about her?"

He smiled gloriously, and she smiled back, a tender smile, the same smile, or so it seemed, that he had seen so often upon her face when she looked up at him.

"Everything," he promised.

They parted and Peony went to her room to prepare for the duty of going with Madame Ezra. It was a small room, set in a tiny court of its own, but opening into Wang Ma's court, which in turn opened upon a dim mossy passage into Madame Ezra's own rooms. This little room in which Peony lived had once belonged to a concubine, three generations back, a secret love, scarcely acknowledged, of Ezra's own great-grandfather. Here, too, Wang Ma herself had lived before she was married to Old Wang by Ezra's own father. The room had stood empty while Peony was a child, too young to be alone, but when she was fifteen it had been given her. It was a pretty little room, the walls whitewashed and the gray tiles of the floor scrubbed silvery clean. Upon the facing walls on either side of her bed Peony had hung two pairs of scrolls, pictured with the flowers of spring and summer, the bright leaves of autumn, and the snowy pines of winter. These she had painted herself. She had sat in the schoolroom with David and his tutor for many years, her duty to fetch them hot tea and to clean their brushes and grind ink, and she had learned to read and write. This learning, added to her own graceful talent, had made her able to turn a verse as well as David could himself. Thus on the scroll for spring she had written in two long lines of brushed tracery:

The peach flowers bloom upon the trees,
Not knowing whether the frosts will kill them.

Upon the mimosa branches of the summer scroll she wrote:

The hot sun burns, the thunder drums across the sky.
The cicadas sing endlessly, unheeding.

Under the scarlet maple leaves she wrote:

The red leaves fall, and all the court is still.
I tread the leaves and under my feet they die.

Beneath the snow-covered pines she wrote two more lines:

Snow covers the living and the dead,
The green pine tree, the perished flowers.

These four poems she read very often, wondering how she could improve them. Whether she would ever be able to make them better she did not know. But at present they reached to the bottom of her heart and made her want to cry.

She moved now in haste to put on a plain dark coat and trousers, to take the peach blossoms from her hair, to put off her gold bracelets. She looked into the small old mirror of her dressing case and rubbed a little rice powder into her skin and touched her lips faintly with red cream. Her hair she made always in a long braid, as all bondmaids wore their hair, signifying that they were not daughters of the house, but at home she kept the braid twisted into a knot over her ear. Now she let it down and brushed the straight black fringe above her eyebrows.

This done, she made haste through the passageways until she came to Madame Ezra's court. Wang Ma was putting the last touch upon Madame Ezra's costume. It was rich and individual, and Madame Ezra thought it was entirely Jewish. She did not know that in the generations during which her family had lived in China touches of embroidery at sleeve and throat, folds in the skirt, the twist of buttons and braid, had crept into the costume of her grandmothers.

Peony paused at the door and gave a slight cough and prepared her smile. Madame Ezra did not turn. Usually she was voluble and kindly to her serving maids, but in the last few days, while her mind had been busy with the Passover and all her being was renewed in the faith of her ancestors, she had not been pleased with the intimacy she perceived between Peony and David. True, the girl had been bought as a companion as well as a servant for the solitary little boy he had been, but the years had passed too quickly. She reproached herself that she had not taken heed earlier that they were now grown, her son a man, and Peony a woman. She was inclined at this moment to feel aggrieved and to be harsh toward Peony, who should have understood the change by instinct.

All of this Peony perfectly comprehended, and she stood with patient grace, silent until Madame Ezra might choose to speak. When a gold hairpin slipped from Wang Ma's fingers she sprang forward as lithely as a kitten, picked it up, and herself put it into Madame Ezra's hair. In so doing she caught her mistress's eye in the mirror and smiled. Madame Ezra gazed severely into the wide black eyes of the little bondmaid, and then after a second or two she yielded her own smile.

"You are a naughty child," she said. "I am very angry with you."

"Ah, why, Mistress?" Peony asked sadly. Then with her quick frankness she went on, "No, do not tell me—I know! But you are quite wrong, Old Mistress. I know my place in this house. I want only to serve you, my lady. What you bid me do, I will do. What home have I except this house? Can I dare to disobey you?"

She was so pretty, so pleading, so yielding, that Madame Ezra could not but be mollified. It was true that Peony was entirely dependent upon her, and though she knew as well as ever that underneath all the gentleness and sweetness there was something hard and prudent, yet, she reasoned, Peony could scarcely destroy her own welfare. If indeed there were a youthful attachment between the bondmaid and David, Peony would not yield to it if it meant the loss of everything else—as it would, Madame Ezra said firmly to herself. If ever she saw proof that there was more between David and Peony than there should be between a young man and a serving maid, that day she would marry Peony to a farmer.

As well as though she had spoken, Peony knew the thoughts inside Madame Ezra's handsome head. She had learned so thoroughly the habit of such discovery that she had only to be still, to empty her own mind, to wait, and to receive, and soon into her brain would come on little creeping mouse feet the thoughts of others. To be married to a farmer was the common fate of bondmaids who went beyond their station. She had even less hope in this house than in a Chinese home. The Jews did not take concubines, Madame Ezra had often declared—not the good Jews, at least. Their god, Jehovah, forbade it.

When Madame Ezra did not answer her, she slipped back quickly, and then followed her mistress to the gate. A few minutes later she was in her plain sedan, riding along the street behind Madame Ezra's own satin-curtained one. She looked through the little pane set into the front curtain and saw a small square block of the street straight ahead. The street was as it had always been, through her life and through the centuries before she was born. It was a wide street, but however wide it might be, it was always crowded with people. On both sides low buildings of brick and stone stood open. They were shops of many kinds, but behind them were homes where men and women and their children lived together, happily or not, but in security. The street was shadowy and cool, for the shopkeepers had stretched mats over their thresholds woven of slit reeds over a framework of bamboo. Water carriers had slopped their wooden buckets as they went, and the wet stones of the cobbled street threw off coolness. Children ran and crawled everywhere, weaving between the people. Housewives bargained with vendors of fresh vegetables and lifted live fish from great tubs, and men went their way to teashops and business. Everywhere there was life, good common life, but she had no part in it, Peony thought sadly.

While her eyes watched the scene she knew so well, her thoughts were busy with herself. The years had passed too quickly, even for her. They had been happy years and good ones, and she had dreaded womanhood and change. She had felt almost a daughter in the house, but not quite, and in the last few days, during the strange foreign feast, she had realized she was alien to this family that had bought her. Compel her mind as she might, she could not remember her own mother's face or her father's voice. A castaway child, stolen perhaps from her home, or sold, she had been sold again.

"Who sold me to you, Lady?" she had once asked Madame Ezra.

"A dealer in children," Madame Ezra had replied.

"Had he many like me?" she had asked next.

"He had twenty little girls, and two boys," Wang Ma had put in. "I wonder, Lady, that you did not get a boy for our young master."

"My son's father wanted the girl," Madame Ezra had replied. "I believe he took a fancy to Peony because she had such big eyes. You were very thin, child. I remember you ate until we were frightened."

Riding along in the crowded street, high on men's shoulders,

Peony considered her fate. Outside the house of Ezra she knew no one, she had not a friend. All were strangers to her as were these passers on the street. Tears brimmed her eyes. Where could she ever go to find friends or family? Therefore must she stay where she was and cling to the only house she knew.

I have no one, she thought plaintively.

And then she denied this with the hard truthfulness that was her secret heart. She was lying to herself. She wanted to stay in the house of Ezra because she could never bear to leave David. "David" she called him in her heart and would always so call him, however she taught her lips to say "Master."

I love him, she thought. I would not go, no matter what was given me in exchange for him.

Thus she declared herself to her own heart. With truth, a clear peace descended upon her. She knew now what she wanted and would have. There remained only the matter of how to get it and keep it.

The house of the Rabbi was next to the synagogue on the Street of the Plucked Sinew. Long ago the street had been so named because of the mysterious Jewish rite of plucking the sinew from flesh before it could be eaten. The Chinese called the synagogue The Temple of the Foreign God. But the Jews called it The Temple of God. Once passers-by had wondered at the sounds of weeping that came from within. The weeping had almost ceased as the years went on, and then the only sounds that came from the synagogue were the long, slow, wailing chants one day in seven. Even the sound of the chanting had grown weaker as more years passed, and now those who passed by had to stop and listen, if they were to hear the voices within the heavy closed doors. The very building was falling into slow ruin. The typhoons of each summer tore at the cornices and the eaves, and when stones fell they were not replaced.

The same decay was creeping into the house of the Rabbi, which was near the synagogue. Moss grew between the flagstones of the court through which Madame Ezra and Peony walked while their sedans waited at the gate. Old Wang had been sent ahead to announce Madame Ezra's visit, and now he met them at the door of the guest hall.

"The Teacher was asleep, Mistress," he explained. "The young lady, his daughter, was in the kitchen alone, and she ran to comb her hair and change her garments. She begged me to ask you to seat yourself. She will come quickly with her father."

Madame Ezra inclined her head and stepped over the rotting doorsill and into the guest hall. It was called a hall, although actually it was only a small room set with common furniture. But it was clean and Leah had put some white scented lilies into a brown jar on the table. No tea was served in this house, for it was a Chinese fashion. Madame Ezra sat down and motioned Peony to a stool.

"Sit down, child," she said. "You need not stand while we are alone. And you, Old Wang, may return home to your work."

Old Wang bowed and went away, and Madame Ezra waited in the silent little room. Since she did not speak, Peony did not either. The young girl sat gracefully erect upon the wooden stool, her small hands clasped in her lap. She knew perfectly how to sit at ease, waiting, her look pleasant and yielding. There was no impatience or urgency in her bearing. When in a few minutes they heard shuffling footsteps, she rose and took her place behind the chair on which Madame Ezra sat.

Thus they were when the faded blue linen curtain in the doorway was pushed aside and Leah came in leading her father, the old Rabbi. He walked with a long staff in his right hand, his left arm leaning upon Leah's shoulder. The Rabbi had been tall in his youth, far above the height of the average man, and he was still tall, in spite of his aged stoop. He wore the robes of his people this morning as he always did, and though they were patched, they were clean. Snow-white, too, was his long beard, and his skin was clean and fair, in spite of his wrinkles.

"My daughter," the Rabbi said to Madame Ezra.

"I have waked you, Father," Madame Ezra replied. She rose and went forward to meet the old man, and he touched her hand delicately and quickly and then her head, in blessing. Leah led him to the chair opposite that in which Madame Ezra had been sitting.

"Please sit down, Aunt," Leah said, and when Madame Ezra had sat down, she moved a high stool near to her father. Then doubtfully she looked at Peony. "You—will you sit down?" she asked.

Peony inclined her head sweetly. "Thank you, Young Lady, I must be ready to serve my mistress," she replied softly.

Leah sat down. Nothing could have marked more clearly than this the change from her childhood, when she and Peony had been two little girls, playing children's games with David, and now, when one was a bondmaid and the other the young mistress of her father's house.

"I should have waked long ago," the Rabbi said in a voice surprisingly strong for his age. "But the truth is, daughter, that our Passover feast rouses sad memories in me and I lie awake in the night, sorrowing. These poor eyes—" he touched his blind eyes, "can still weep, even though they can no longer see."

Madame Ezra sighed. "Do we not all weep together in our exile?"

"I grow old," the Rabbi went on, "and my son is too young to take my place. Where is Aaron, Leah?"

"He went out early this morning, Father, and he has not come back," Leah replied.

"Did he say where he was going?" the Rabbi asked.

"No, Father."

"But you should have asked," the Rabbi insisted.

"He did not want to tell me, Father," Leah said gently.

Against the spare faded figure of the old man, the beauty of Leah was startling. The pure spring sunshine fell upon the tile floor in a square of pure light, and it lit her beauty into vividness. She was slender but rounded, strong in her looks, and rich in her coloring, and yet a vague timidity lent a modesty to her bearing that was almost childlike. Her full lips were red this morning, and her eyes were nearly perfect in their shape and in their deep brown coloring, the lashes long and curling, and the brows dark. Her hair was curling, too, and today she had tied it back from her face with a strip of narrow red satin at the nape of her neck. Her dress was a simple robe of coarse white linen. It fell to her feet and was girdled about her slender waist with a wide red strip of the same satin that bound her hair. The sleeves were short and her creamy arms were bare.

Peony under the cover of her straight lashes watched this beauty with appreciation and wonder. Her mind played now about the beautiful foreign girl with question and doubtful answer. When—or if—Leah came into the house of Ezra, as David's wife, would she be shrewd to see all that went on under that ample roof? Would she protest and forbid, would she lead David away again into the dreams of his own people?

"Aaron should not leave without telling you where he goes, Father," Madame Ezra was saying.

"He is young," the Rabbi sighed.

"Not too young to remember his duty," Madame Ezra said firmly. "He is the only one to follow after you, Father, and he must remember his duty to his people. If he fails, there will be none left to lead us home when the time comes."

"Oh, that it might come in my lifetime!" the old rabbi mourned.

"But we must remain ready, even though it does not," Madame Ezra said earnestly. "The synagogue should be repaired, Father, and we should revive the remnant of our people. As it is, our men are forgetting and our children never know our heritage. You should give Aaron the task of collecting the funds for the repairs. A good idea, Father—and I will promise five hundred pieces of silver as the beginning."

"Ah, if all our people were like you," the old rabbi replied. "But it is a good idea, eh, Leah? Aaron could busy himself with it and it would give him something to do."

"Yes, Father," Leah said doubtfully. She looked down into the pool of brightness about her feet.

These strange foreign people, Peony was thinking, the beautiful old man, the beautiful girl, even Madame Ezra handsome and stately, all burning from within! And why did their eyes glow and their faces grow rapt and their voices so grave while they spoke? Some spirit came out of them and enveloped them in a mystic unity that shut her out. Her downcast eyes fell on Leah's hands clasped loosely over her knees. They were like a boy's hands, the fingers square at the ends, strong and rough. Peony looked down at her own little hands as they rested on the back of Madame Ezra's chair —soft, small, narrow hands, the fingers pointed as a girl's fingers should be. Leah's hands were like Madame Ezra's, except that Madame's were not workworn. They were smooth and plump and she wore rings on the first fingers of each hand and on each thumb. Leah wore no rings.

"Yet I did not come to talk about the synagogue," Madame Ezra was saying.

The Rabbi inclined his silvery head. A small black skullcap covered the crown of it, but his hair curled about its edges.

"What then, my daughter?" he asked courteously.

"I do not know whether Leah should stay or go while I speak," Madame Ezra said, looking at the girl kindly.

Leah rose. "I will go."

"No," Madame Ezra decided abruptly. "Why should you? You are not a child and we are not Chinese. It is quite permissible to speak before you of your marriage."

Leah sat down again hesitating. Peony watched her sidewise from under her lashes. At the word "marriage" a dark rich red flooded up from Leah's straight neck and shoulders; it crept up her cheeks and into the roots of her hair. Seeing it, Peony felt the blood drain down from her own face and her heart began to beat slowly and heavily. The talk would go on before her, as a matter of course, for who would consider whether a bondmaid had a heart? Madame Ezra, in her shrewdness, might think it well for her to hear of David's marriage. Peony dropped her head low and stood like a small image of marble, her hands folded together upon the back of Madame Ezra's chair.

"Marriage," Madame Ezra repeated. "It is time, Father, to speak of our children. My son is no longer a child."

"Leah is only eighteen," the Rabbi said doubtfully. "Besides, what would I do without her?"

"To be eighteen is to be a woman," Madame Ezra retorted, "and you cannot keep her forever. We can hire a good Jewish woman to take her place. I will see to it. I know just the one—Rachel, the daughter of Eli and that woman he married—"

"A Chinese," the Rabbi said still more doubtfully.

"Only partly," Madame Ezra said firmly. "It is hard to find servants now who are purely of our people. I myself use only Chinese. It is better not to mix them. But to take Leah's place here, of course, we must have a woman who understands the rites and can help you. Rachel knows enough for that. And her husband is dead."

"He was a Chinese," the Rabbi said plaintively.

"It is as much as we can do to get our sons married to women of our people nowadays," Madame Ezra replied. "That is why I want my son married now. Leah, you must help me!"

A look of trouble came into Leah's deep eyes. "How can I help you?" she murmured.

"You must come and visit me," Madame Ezra said. "It is natural and right that at this age, when you are entering womanhood, you should come and stay with me, your mother's friend. We were like sisters, she and I, and I have long had it in my mind that you should come to me."

They were interrupted by a sound at the door. Aaron came in impetuously and then stopped, confounded by their unexpected presence. He gave a snigger of embarrassment.

"Aaron!" Leah whispered distressfully.

"My son!" the Rabbi cried. "How fortunate! Now we can talk with you. Aaron, sit down here, my son, near me."

The Rabbi felt for a chair, but Aaron did not move toward him. He took off his turban and wiped his hot forehead. It was Leah that rose and moved a chair near to the father and motioned to her brother. He sat down, trying to control his rapid breathing.

"Why have you been running?" the Rabbi asked.

"Because I wanted to," Aaron answered sullenly. He was a slight pallid young man and his eyes were small and black and set close on either side of a thin hooked nose. His curly black hair hung untidily from under his turban.

Madame Ezra gazed at him with dislike. "You do not look as the Rabbi's son should," she now said majestically. "You look as common as anybody's son."

Aaron did not answer. He threw her instead a shrewd peevish glance, sharp with hostility.

"Aaron!" Leah murmured again.

"Be quiet!" he commanded her in a fierce whisper.

"My son, do you not give greeting to our guests?" the Rabbi asked.

"Let us go on with our conversation," Madame Ezra said.

"Yes, yes," the Rabbi murmured. "Aaron, Madame Ezra wants Leah to come and stay with her for a while."

"Who's to look after us?" Aaron inquired rudely.

"Rachel will come," Madame Ezra replied.

"Do you mind if I go, Aaron?" Leah asked half timidly.

"Why should I mind? Do as you like," he replied. His eyes, roving about the room, now fell upon the silent Peony, and there they fastened themselves. She felt his coarse gaze and did not lift her eyelids.

Then Madame Ezra saw it and was angered. She rose, interposing herself between the two. "Let us decide it so, Father. Leah can come to me tomorrow. I will send a sedan for her, and at an earlier hour Rachel will come. Leah, you can tell her everything to be done. And do not set a day for your return—I may keep you for a long time."

Madame Ezra smiled and nodded to Leah, who had risen when she rose. Then bowing her farewell to the Rabbi, she left the room without giving heed to Aaron. The Rabbi rose too, and leaning upon Aaron's arm, he followed Madame Ezra to the gate.

Leah walked on his other side, and Peony went ahead to prepare the chair carriers.

Thus Madame Ezra returned to her house. She was ill pleased with her own thoughts, that Peony could see. She was very silent when she had reached her own rooms, and she gave brief commands for the preparation of the small east court for Leah. Peony stood to receive these commands, and when she had heard them she turned and went to fulfill them, only to hear Madame Ezra call her again from the gate of the court.

"Young girls have natural instincts," Madame Ezra said to Peony. "Do you prepare those two rooms as you can imagine Leah would like to have them prepared, with the scrolls and vases, flowers and perfumes, that she will most enjoy."

"But Madame, how do I know what a young foreign lady will most enjoy?" Peony inquired. She met Madame Ezra's fixed stare with a wide and innocent gaze.

"Try to imagine," Madame Ezra said dryly, and the innocent gaze flickered and fell.

Outside the gate, in the mossy passageway, Peony stood still for a full minute. Then she moved with decision. She went to her room and in a few swift movements she took off her somber street garments and put on her soft peach-pink silk jacket and trousers. She washed her hands and face in perfumed water and coiled her braid again over one ear and thrust a jeweled pin into the knot. In the other ear she hung a long pearl earring. Cheeks and lips she touched with vermilion, and she dusted her face with the fine rice powder. Then she slipped through the secret passages of the old house that went winding into the courtyards where David lived near to his father.

The house had been built hundreds of years ago for a great and rich Chinese family, and generations had added courts and passageways to suit their needs and their loves. Many of these were closed now, and left unused, but Peony in her exploring and David in his curiosity had found them, until, as the years of their childhood passed, all were familiar to them, and these ways underlay the upper surfaces of the house in a secret pattern for a secret life. The house was Peony's world, where she lived with the family to which she belonged, and yet where she felt that she lived most often alone, passing hours at a time in some forgotten overgrown courtyard, dreaming and musing. But she knew that until now she had never been really alone because there had always been David. Whether he was in her presence or not, he had been always in her dreams and musings.

As she went her secret way, she was bewildered with fear. Well she knew and had always known that someday he must be given a wife. But she had not believed that this wife could separate them. They would go on, the closeness of man and woman scarcely heeded, scarcely noticed, in the family life. But if Leah were brought here, would Leah allow this to be? Could anything be hidden from the foreign eyes of that young girl? Would she not demand the whole of David, body and mind and spirit? His conscience she would create in her own image, and she would teach him to worship the god of his fathers, and he would cleave to Leah only and there would be no room for any other in his heart. Now Peony feared Leah indeed, for she saw that Leah was a woman strong enough to win a man entire and hold him so. Peony's eyes swam with tears. She must go to David instantly, win him again, renew every tie. Impetuously, daring to disobey even Madame Ezra out of her fear, she ran silently upon her satin-shod feet into the library, where David at this hour should be at his books.

She found him at his writing table, his books pushed aside. When she stood in the doorway he was poring over a sheet of paper, pointing his camel's-hair brush at his lips. He did not see her and she waited, now rosy and smiling, ready for his lifted eyes. When he made no sign, she laughed softly and he looked up, his eyes thoughtful and far away. Then she went to him, and taking her white silk handkerchief from her sleeve, she leaned and wiped his inky lips.

"Oh, what lips!" she murmured. "Look!"

She showed him the stain on the handkerchief, but he was still far away. "Tell me a rhyme for 'lily,'" he commanded.

"Silly," she replied with prompt mischief.

"Silly yourself!" he retorted. But he put the brush down.

"What are you writing?" she inquired.

"A poem," he replied.

She snatched the paper, he snatched it back, and between them it was torn in two. "Now see what you have done!" he cried furiously. "It's the fifth time I have copied it!"

"For your tutor, I suppose?" she cried. She began to read the torn poem in a high, sweet voice.

"I came upon a garden unaware,
A flower-scented space,
But all the flowers did abase
Themselves before a lily. . . ."

"Why a lily?" she demanded. "I thought you said she looked like a fawn. The same girl cannot look like a fawn and a lily."

"She isn't exactly like a lily—she's too small. I wanted to say orchid, a small golden one, but there is nothing that rhymes with orchid."

Peony crumbled the paper in her hand. "There is no use in your writing poems to her, whatever she is," she declared.

"You wicked little thing!" he cried. He grasped her hand and forced the wad of paper out of it and smoothed it. Then he looked at her, remembering her words. "What do you mean?" he demanded.

She paused and then said firmly, "Leah is coming."

"Here?"

She was pleased with the horror in his eyes, and she nodded. "She is coming tomorrow—and she is really very beautiful. I never saw before how beautiful she is. Why not keep the poem? 'Lily' would suit her."

"What is she coming for?" he asked, biting his underlip.

"You know—you know," she answered. "She is coming to be married to you!"

"Stop teasing," he commanded. He stood up and seized both her wrists and held her firmly. "Tell me—did my mother say so—to her?"

Peony nodded. "I went with your mother to the Rabbi's house and I heard every word. They are going to rebuild that temple—the temple to your foreign god—and Leah is coming here to live."

"If my mother thinks—" David began.

"Ah, she will do what she likes," Peony declared. "She's stronger than you. She will make you marry Leah!"

"She cannot—I won't—my father will help me—"

"Your father is not as strong as she is."

"Both of us together!"

"Ah, but there are two of them, too," she reminded him triumphantly. "Leah and your mother—they're stronger than you and your father."

She felt a strange wish to hurt him, to make him suffer so that he would ask her help. Then she would help him. She looked up into his eyes and saw doubt creep into them.

"Peony, you must help me!" he whispered.

"Leah is beautiful," she said stubbornly.

"Peony," he pleaded, "I love someone else. You know it!"

"The daughter of Kung Chen. What's her name?"

"I don't even know her name," he groaned.

"But I do," Peony said.

She had him now in her power. He dropped her wrists. "What is her name?" he demanded.

"You were nearly right—to want to call her 'orchid,'" she said demurely. "Her name is Kueilan."

"Precious Orchid," he repeated. "Ah, it was my instinct!"

"And if you wish, I will take the poem to her myself—when you have finished it," Peony said sweetly. He opened the drawer of the table and drew out a fresh sheet of paper.

"Now quickly help me with the last line," he commanded her.

"Let's not have any flowers," she suggested. "Flowers are so common."

"No flowers," he said eagerly. "What would she like instead?"

"If it were I," Peony said, "I would like to remind someone—the one I loved—of—of a fragrance—caught upon the winds of night—or dew at sunrise—"

"Dew at sunrise," he decided.

He settled to his paper and brush, and she touched his cheek with her palm.

"While you write," she said tenderly, "I will go and do something your mother bade me to do."

He did not hear her, or know that she had left him alone. At the door she looked back. When she saw him absorbed, her red lips grew firm and her eyes sparkled like black jewels, and she went away to fulfill the task of preparing Leah's rooms.

How hard she was upon the two small undermaids she summoned to help her! Nothing she did herself, until the last corner under the bed was swept, until the silken bed curtains were shaken free of dust, and the bed spread with soft quilts, the carved blackwood table dusted. Then she waved the wearied maids away, and she sat down and considered Leah.

It was in her heart to leave these rooms as they were, clean but bare. Why should she put forth her hand to more? Then she sighed. She knew herself too merciful to blame Leah, who was good. She rose, unwillingly, and went about other rooms in the house and chose from one and another pretty things, a pair of many-flowered vases, a lacquered box, a pair of scrolls, each with its painted verse beneath flying birds, a footstool made of golden bamboo, a bowl of blooming bulbs, and these she took to Leah's rooms and placed them well.

When all was done, she stood looking about her; then, feeling duty done, she closed the doors. Outside these closed doors she paused in the court and considered. David would have his poem finished now, doubtless. Should she return to him to know his will? She went silent-footed through the courts again to David's schoolroom and looked in. He was not there.

"David?" she called softly, but there was no answer. She tiptoed to the desk. Upon the sheet of paper he had written only a single line.

Within the lotus bud the dewdrop waited.

Then he had flung down his brush. She felt its tip—the camel's hair was dry! Where had he gone and where had he stayed all these hours?

She looked about the empty, book-lined room, and all her perceptions, too sensitive, searched the air. Confusion—what confusion had seized him? She longed to run out, to look for him, to find him. But her life had taught her patience. She stood, controlled and still. Then she took up the brush, put on its brass cover, and laid it in its box; she covered the ink box, too, and set the slab of dried ink in its place. This done, she stood a second more, than took the paper with its unfinished poem, folded it delicately, put it in the bosom of her robe, and returned to her own room and found her embroidery. There the whole afternoon she sewed, and none came near, even to ask her if she were hungry or thirsty.

挑筋教

III

When Madame Ezra had gone, the Rabbi and his children stood in the small flowerless court. Leah turned to her father, her face imploring. But he was blind and could not see her. She turned to her brother.

"Aaron," she said tremulously.

But he was staring at the broken stone flags beneath his feet. "What luck you have!" he muttered. "To be getting out of this!"

The Rabbi listened intently, but his hearing was not sharp enough to catch the words. "What did you say, my son?" he inquired anxiously.

"I said, we shall miss Leah," Aaron replied, raising his voice.

"Ah, how shall we live without her?" the Rabbi said. He lifted his blind eyes to the sunshine that poured down warmly into the court. "Except we do the will of the Lord," he went on. He put out his hand for Leah, and she took it in both her own. "Even as Esther, the queen, went out to serve her people, so shall you, my daughter, enter the house of Ezra."

"But they belong to our people, Father, while Esther went to the heathen," Leah said.

"It is only here near the synagogue where I feel sure of sacred ground," the Rabbi replied. He sighed and lifted his face to the sun. "Oh, that I could see!" he cried.

"Let me stay with you!" Leah cried, and she took his arm and laid it across her shoulders.

"No, no," the Rabbi said quickly. "I do not complain. God leads us. He has His will to perform in the house of Ezra, and He has chosen you, my daughter, to be His instrument. Come, take me to my room and let me pray until I search out His meaning."

The Rabbi drew her along as he walked. It was he that led on the familiar ground, not she. She leaned her head against his shoulder. Behind them Aaron stood looking after them, then he darted out of the gate. The Rabbi felt for the high doorstep and then lifted his foot over it.

"My children," he began. Leah turned her head and saw that her brother had gone.

"Aaron is not here, Father," she said gently.

Usually she would not have told him that Aaron was gone. It was she that kept peace between them, urging the old father to remember that the son was still young. But now she needed to speak the truth.

"Gone!" the old man cried. "But he was here a moment ago."

"You see why I should not leave you," Leah said. "When I am not here he will always be away and you will be left alone with a serving woman."

"I must deal with him before Jehovah," the Rabbi said, and his face was moved with distress.

"Father, let me stay with you—to care for you both," Leah pleaded.

But the Rabbi shook off her hands. He stood in the middle of the floor and struck his staff against the stones under his feet. "It is I who have hidden the truth from you, my child," he wailed. "It is I who have been weak. I know what my son is. No, you must go. I will do my duty."

"Father, Aaron is young—what can you do?"

"I can curse my son, even as Isaac cursed Esau!" the Rabbi said with strange energy. "I can cast him out of the house of the Lord forever!"

Leah clasped her hands on his shoulder. "Oh, how can I go?" she mourned.

The father controlled himself. He hesitated, turned, fumbled for his chair, and sat down. He was trembling and there was a fine sweat on his high pale forehead. "Now," he said, "now—hear me—

I am not your earthly father while I speak these words. I am your rabbi. I command you!"

Leah stood hesitating, waiting, biting her red lips, her hands clenched at her sides. Her eyes were wide and burning, but she did not speak. There was a moment of silence and then the Rabbi rose, leaned on his staff, and spoke in a deep and unearthly voice: "Thus saith the Lord to His servant Leah: Go forth, remembering who thou art, O Leah! Reclaim the House of Ezra for Me! Cause them to remember, father and son, that they are Mine, descendants of those whom I led, by the hand of My servant Moses, out of the land of Egypt, into the promised land. There My people sinned. They took to themselves women from among the heathen and they worshiped false gods, and I cast them out again until they had repented. But I have not forgotten them. They shall come to Me, and I will save them, and I will return them again to their own land. And how shall I do this except by the hands of those who have not forgotten Me?"

The Rabbi's face was glorified as he spoke these words. His staff fell to the ground and he stretched out his arms. Leah listened, her head high, and when he was silent she bowed her head.

"I will obey you," she whispered. "I will do my best, Father."

He faltered. The strength went out of him and he sank upon the seat from which he had risen. "The will of the Lord be done," he said heavily. "Go, my child, and prepare yourself."

She went without another word, and that whole day she busied herself in silence. The little house next to the synagogue was always as clean and neat as she knew how to make it. But she cleaned it again, and prepared the noon meal for the three of them. Aaron did not come home, and she saved his portion and put it aside into a cool place. At the table she and the Rabbi ate almost in silence. He sighed when he heard that his son was not there, and then told her to bid Aaron come to him at once when he returned. After her father had eaten he slept, and while he slept, Leah put her few clothes together into a small leather trunk. Then she bathed herself and washed her thick curling hair. This was scarcely done when she heard a knock at the door, and she opened it. There stood Rachel, the serving woman, and a man with a wooden box holding her possessions.

"Madame Ezra bade me come here," she said simply.

"You are expected, Rachel," Leah replied. She led the woman into her own room. "Here is where you shall live," she went on. "It is near to my father. Have you eaten?"

"Yes," Rachel said. "I came early enough for you to tell me everything before I cook the night meal, for Madame Ezra said you were to go to bed early tonight and be ready in the morning soon after sunrise. You will sleep in your own bed this last night, and I shall sleep in the kitchen."

There was something very comforting about this strong, stout, dark-faced woman, and Leah sat down with her on the bed and told her all she could, what her father ate and did not eat, how he liked his things left upon the table untouched, and how often hot water must be brought to him for washing, and the care of his hair and beard. Then she told Rachel of the cleaning of the synagogue and of the dusting of the tablets and the ark, and of the velvet curtains, which were old and must be tenderly handled. Then last of all she told her of Aaron.

"He is not a good son," she said sadly. "I had better tell you, so that you will not lean on him."

"Leave him to me!" Rachel said firmly.

"You will be better for him than I have been," Leah said.

"I am older," Rachel replied. Then she leaned forward, her plump hands on her knees. "You poor lamb," she said, "led to the slaughter." She shook her head.

Leah gazed at her, not comprehending. "But it is a pleasant house," she replied. "I used to go there very often when David and I were children." Her clear skin flushed in spite of herself and she laughed. "There is nothing else for me to do, when my father and Madame Ezra combine to command me."

"She speaks for man and he for God," Rachel said humorously. Then she was grave again. "But never marry a man you cannot love," she said. "It's too hard in a house like that of Ezra, where they do not allow concubines. Marriage is not such a burden in a

Chinese house—if you do not like your husband, you can get a concubine for him without losing your place in the family. But to have to be a wife to a man you loathe—how disgusting!"

"No one could loathe David," Leah said gently. The flush was brighter.

Rachel looked at her and smiled. "Ah, in that case—" she said. "I had better see what you have in the house for supper."

In this last night in the small square room near her father's, Leah could not sleep. On the opposite side of the court was Aaron's room. He had not come to the evening meal, and it was after midnight before she saw a candle flicker against the latticed window. The pale beams glimmered upon the white curtains of her bed, and she rose and looked out of her window and saw him moving like a shadow about his room. Ordinarily she would have gone to him to ask if he were hungry or to know where he had been. But tonight she felt herself already separate from him. Her life in this house had stopped and tomorrow it would begin in another. She went back to her bed and lay quietly, her hands clasped under her head.

She tried for a while to think of what her father had said, how she was to be God's instrument, but she doubted that this could be, however much she longed for it to be true. She had been too busy since her mother died to read the Torah as much as she should. It was long ago that she had been left, so long that she could not remember her mother's face unless she put everything else out of her mind. Then against the gray curtain of the past she thought she could see a pale thin face, the eyes too large and too black, and the thin mouth sad. But she could remember very well this one thing her mother had told her, when she called her in the last night she lived.

"Take care of your father, Leah—and Aaron."

"Yes, Mother," she had sobbed.

"Oh, child," her mother had gasped suddenly, "think of yourself —for no one else will."

Those were her mother's last words, and Leah did not know what they meant then or now. How could she care for others if she thought of herself? She sighed and put away this question that she had never answered, and she began to think instead of David.

Her mind roamed, remembering him as far back as she could, when perhaps once in a month Wang Ma had come for her and had taken her to Madame Ezra, to be looked at, to be questioned, and then to be given sweets and fruit and released to play in the courts with David, the beautiful little boy, always so richly dressed, so gay, so charming. Her memory of him was one of laughter so continuing that wherever he was, the very air was bright with his presence. Her own home had been always sad, her father absorbed in scriptures and prayers, and Aaron whining and half ill, dependent upon her and cruel to her at the same time. And they were poor, always poor, and she had had to patch and mend and save and learn as best she could how to cook and clean. There had been a servant woman in her childhood, but she had gone away when Leah was not more than twelve, and since then she had been alone except for an old Chinese man who did the marketing and made a small kitchen garden in the back court and took out garbage and the waste from the household. He was a deaf-mute and lived out his days in silence.

The house of Ezra was therefore the one happy place of her childhood, and she could not but be glad that it was God's will, and her father's, that now she return to it. But I shall come home often, she thought, and I shall make everything here much better than it has ever been. And if I really do marry David—

Here her thoughts grew shy and humble. If she did, if such heaven were granted to her, she would thank God all her life and be so good that He would never regret it. She would move David's heart to rebuild the synagogue and to fulfill all her father's dreams. The remnant of their people, who were so scattered, would be brought together again in the new synagogue, and David would be the leader of them, and Aaron would be looked after and helped, and perhaps he would grow better than she feared, and all would be well—with everybody, she thought fervently.

Somewhere on the edge of her dreams there stood the shadow of a young Chinese girl, the little girl who had played near David, a pretty child with big almond-shaped eyes and a small red mouth. This child gradually became a slender young girl, still more pretty, who served David and her with tea and plied them with cakes, and was always near. Peony—Peony! But Peony, Leah reminded herself, was only a bondmaid.

And so near dawn Leah fell asleep, her cheek on her folded hands, and Rachel, stealing in, had not the heart to wake her. The good woman went into the kitchen and started the fire in the charcoal stove and heated water and set rice to boil for breakfast, and cracked three eggs into a bowl.

She did not waken Leah, indeed, until she heard the clatter of someone at the gate, and when she opened it there stood Wang Ma, and behind her chair bearers carried an empty sedan.

"Come in, Elder Sister," Rachel said. "No one is awake yet here."

Wang Ma came in, looking almost like the mistress of a house herself. She wore a dark blue coat and trousers of homespun silk, and there were gold earrings in her ears and gold rings on her middle fingers. Her oiled black hair was brushed into a round knot on her neck and held by a fine black silk net, and she had plucked and darkened her eyebrows, and rubbed her cheeks so clean that they were still very red.

"Not awake!" she echoed. She knew Rachel and they were good friends in the solid fashion of women who are respected in whatever households they serve. Both of them obeyed Madame Ezra above all others, Rachel because Madame Ezra had given her money at times when her husband was ill or idle, and Wang Ma because she knew that Madame Ezra ruled the House of Ezra.

"The Rabbi is old," Rachel said, "and the young man did not come in until after midnight, and Leah, doubtless, the poor young thing—"

Wang Ma's black eyebrows went up. "Why poor young thing?" she demanded. "She is lucky to come into our house."

"Of course—of course," Rachel said peaceably. "Come in and drink some tea, Elder Sister. I will wake her."

"I will wake her," Wang Ma said firmly. "Do you attend to the two men. We had better make haste, lest today the caravan comes.

The gateman told me when I passed that a runner reached our house the second hour after midnight, to say the caravan had reached the Village of Three Bells. But say nothing to the young lady. Our mistress does not wish her distracted."

"Has the caravan come indeed?" Rachel exclaimed. "How lucky are you, Elder Sister, to be in that household!"

"So I am, in some ways," Wang Ma replied. "In other ways—well, let us do our duty!" She shrugged her shoulders. Rachel nodded and led her to Leah's room.

So it happened that when Leah opened her eyes, they fell first upon Wang Ma's handsome rosy face. She was half bemused with her dreams, and she faltered.

"Why—why, but I am still at home—"

"Up with you, Young Lady," Wang Ma said briskly. "I am sent to fetch you."

Leah sat up and brushed back her long hair. "Oh—oh," she whispered in distress. "Today of all days to oversleep!"

"Never mind," Wang Ma said. "Put something on and come along. Our mistress has new garments ready for you. You need bring nothing."

"Ah, but my box is packed—I am ready!" Leah exclaimed.

So saying, she got quickly out of bed. Then she looked shyly at Wang Ma. Never in her life had she taken off her clothes before anyone, and she could not now. But Wang Ma would have no shyness.

"Come, come," she said, "no silliness, Young Lady! If you are to stay in our house, I shall have the washing and tending of you, at least until our Peony learns, and you have nothing that old women like me cannot see."

So with her back turned to Wang Ma, Leah undressed and washed herself at a basin and ewer, Wang Ma all the time telling her to make haste.

"You need not be too careful," Wang Ma urged her. "I shall wash you again and perfume you before we put you into new garments."

Then Rachel brought a bowl of hot rice soup, and so between

them Leah was ready. But there were the farewells to be said. No one could help her with those. She went tiptoe into Aaron's room, and he lay still asleep. She stood looking down at him, the tears gathering under her eyelids. Her brother lay before her in his weakness and in his too slender youth, and his pale ugly face touched her heart. Who would love this brother of hers? There was nothing in him to love. Her own rich love, always ready to well up at the sight of someone needy and weak, came up now, and she bent and kissed his cheek. His breath was foul and his hair smelled unwashed.

"Oh, Aaron," she murmured, "what shall I do for you?"

He opened his small dark eyes, recognized her, and pouted at her. "Don't wake me," he muttered.

"But I am going away, dear," she said.

He lay, half uncomprehending, staring at her.

"Take care of Father, Aaron," she begged him. "Be good, won't you, dear Aaron?"

"You'll be back," he said thickly.

"Every few days, if I am allowed," she promised. "And Rachel is here."

"Well, then," he retorted, and turned and burrowed into his bed again.

So Leah left him, closing the door softly, and then she went into her father's room. The Rabbi had got up and dressed himself, and was at his prayers.

"Father," she said, and he turned. "They have come for me, Father."

"So early?" he answered. "But let it be so, child. Are you ready?"

She had come near him and he touched her, head, face, shoulders, her hair and dress, his delicate fingers telling him how she was. "Yes, you are ready. And have you eaten?"

"Yes, Father, and Rachel is ready for you to come and eat."

She wavered and then laid her head against his bosom. "Oh, Father!" she whispered.

He smoothed her hair. "But you will not be far away, child—you will be back every day or so, and think how much better everything will be for us all."

So he comforted her, and she lifted her head and shook the tears out of her eyes and smiled at him.

"Don't come to the gate with me, Father. Let me leave you here, and Rachel will come and fetch you."

So she left him. She did not look back, and with a last word to Rachel she went out of the gate. Yet when the curtains of the sedan were closed about her, she felt that she was going on a far journey, from which there might be no return.

At the house of Ezra Peony waited in the outer court. So Madame Ezra had commanded her through Wang Ma.

"Am I to be a lady's maid to this foreigner?" Peony had asked when the command came that early morning. She widened her eyes at Wang Ma.

Wang Ma had come near enough to flick Peony's cheek with her thumb and forefinger. Her sharp nails left a tiny spot.

"If you have any wisdom inside that head of yours, you will not ask what you will do and what you will not do," Wang Ma advised her. "Had I asked such questions I would not have been in this house today. Obey—obey—and do what you like. The two go together—if you are clever. And now mind that you hurry! The caravan is near. Our master left before dawn to meet it."

"The caravan?" Peony cried.

"Yes, yes," Wang Ma said impatiently, and went away. "But Leah is not to know—our mistress commands it."

Peony had been braiding her hair when Wang Ma came and went, and she finished the long braid. The excitement of the caravan filled her mind for a moment. Then suddenly she forgot it. What had Wang Ma said? "Obey—obey—and do what you like. The two go together—if you are clever." Strange words, full of meaning! She pondered them, and the meaning began to sink like precious metal into the deep waters of her soul. She smiled to herself suddenly until the two dimples danced on her cheeks.

Instead of coiling her braid over her ear, she let it hang down her back. But into the red cord that bound her hair at her neck she thrust a white gardenia from the court. An old bush grew there, and at this season it bore many blossoms each morning. Peony had chosen to put on a pale blue silk coat and trousers, and now she looked delicate and modest as she stood waiting, and hers was the first face that Leah saw when the curtain of the sedan was lifted. Indeed, Peony herself lifted it, and she smiled into Leah's eyes.

"Welcome, Lady," Peony said. "Will you come down from this chair?" She held out her arm for Leah to lean upon, but Leah stepped down without this support. She was a head taller than Peony, and she did not speak, although she answered Peony's smile.

"Have you eaten, Lady?" Peony asked, following a little behind her.

"I did eat," Leah said frankly, "but I am hungry again."

"It is the morning," Peony said. "The air is dry and good today. I will bring you food, Lady, as soon as I have settled you in your rooms. I made them ready for you yesterday, and I shall bring you some fresh gardenias. They should not be plucked early, lest they turn brown at the edges."

So the two young women went together, each very conscious of the new relationship between them and each trying to fulfill it. Wang Ma had gone ahead to tell Madame Ezra that Leah had come, and so Peony was left to lead Leah to her rooms.

"Am I to have this whole court?" Leah asked in surprise when Peony paused. The rooms were much more beautiful than any she had ever used. As a child she remembered having seen here David's grandmother, an old lady, lighting candles at sundown.

"There are only two rooms," Peony said. "One is for your sleep and the other for you to sit in when you are alone."

She guided Leah into the rooms and a man followed, bringing her box. When he was gone Peony showed her the garments that Madame Ezra herself had worn in her youth, the robes of the Jewish people. Straight and full and long they hung, scarlet trimmed with gold, and deep blue trimmed with silver and yellow edged with emerald green.

"You are to wear the scarlet one today," Peony said. "But first you must eat and then be bathed and perfumed, and here are jewels for your ears and your bosom. And my mistress says you are not to hide yourself away here alone, but you are to come out and walk about the courts and mingle with the family and enjoy all the house."

"How kind she is!" Leah said. Then she was shy. "I doubt I can feel so free in a day," she told Peony.

"Why not?" Peony said half carelessly. "There is no one here to hurt you." She opened a lacquered red box on the dressing table as she spoke, and Leah saw a little heap of gold and silver trinkets set with precious stones.

Leah looked up from where she sat beside the table and met Peony's smiling, secret eyes.

"It is marriage, is it not?" Peony asked in a light clear voice. "I think our mistress has made up her mind that you are to marry our young lord."

Leah's face quivered. "A marriage cannot be made," she replied quickly.

"How else, then?" Peony inquired hardily. "Is not every marriage made?"

"Not among our people," Leah said proudly.

She looked away, and reminded herself again that this pretty Chinese girl was only a bondmaid. It was not at all suitable that she should discuss with Peony the sacred subject of her marriage. Indeed, it was too sacred yet even for her own thought, something as distant and high as God's will. "I will have something to eat now, if you please," Leah said in a cool firm voice. "Then afterward I can dress myself—I am used to doing so. Please tell Wang Ma I will not have her help—or yours."

Peony, hearing this voice, perfectly understood what was going on in Leah's mind. She bent her head and smiled. "Very well, Lady," she said in her sweet and docile way, and turning she left the room.

A few minutes later a serving woman brought in food, and Leah ate it alone. When she was finished the serving woman took it away, and alone Leah brushed her hair and washed again and put on the scarlet dress. But she put no perfume on herself, and she took none of the jewels from the box. When she was ready she sat down in the outer room and waited.

Peony had gone to her own room and wept steadily for a few minutes because Leah was so beautiful. She looked at herself in the mirror on her dressing table, and it seemed to her that all her own charms were mean and small. She was a little thing, light as a bird, and although her face was round, her frame had no strength. Leah was like a princess and she like a child. Yet she could not hate Leah. There was something lofty and good about the Jewish girl, and Peony knew that she herself was neither lofty nor very good. How could she be good, even if she wished to be, when she must win all she had by wile and trickery?

I have nothing and nobody except myself, the small Chinese girl thought sadly.

She shut down the mirror into the dressing table and laid her head down and cried still more heartily until she had no more tears. Then her brain, refreshed and washed clean by her tears, began to work swiftly.

You can never be a wife in this house, this hard little brain now told her. Do not tease yourself any more with dreams and imaginings. You cannot even be a concubine—their god forbids. But no one knows David as well as you do. You are his possession. Never let him forget it. Be his comfort, his inner need, his solace, his secret laughter.

She listened to these unspoken words, and she lifted her head, a smile twisting her lips. She opened the mirror and she coiled her hair about one ear and she examined every look of her face and her eyes. After a moment of intense gazing at herself, she changed her pale blue garments for the warm peach-pink ones and put a fresh gardenia in her hair. Then plucking a handful of the flowers for Leah, she presented herself again to the guest. It took all her strength not to be dismayed by the radiance of Leah's looks, as she now stood arrayed in the scarlet robe. It fitted her well enough, and the golden girdle clasped it to her slender and round waist.

"How beautiful you look, Lady!" Peony said, smiling at Leah as though with delight while she handed her the flowers. "These are for you. And I will go and tell our mistress that you are ready."

She ran away on her little feet as though all she did for Leah was pure joy, and going to Madame Ezra's court she stood at the door and coughed her delicate little cough, trying not to weep.

"Come in," Madame Ezra's voice said.

Madame Ezra had finished her breakfast, and now she was making ready to survey the house and especially the kitchens to see that all the servants did their duty, and that nothing was left undone for the Sabbath, next day, which was the day of rest.

This morning Wang Ma had wakened her with the news that the caravan was so near that it might even reach here before the day was done.

"The day before the Sabbath!" Madame Ezra had exclaimed. After a moment she had added, "Do not tell Leah—let her not be distracted from what I have to say to her."

"Yes, Lady," Wang Ma had murmured.

Now Madame Ezra was about to step over the threshold on her task to see that the servants, excited by the news of the caravan, were not careless about the preparations for the Sabbath, when Peony approached, having swallowed her tears and made her face smooth and empty. Madame Ezra sat down again. "Come, come, child," she said impatiently.

Peony stepped into the sitting room that Madame Ezra kept for her own. It was a room unlike any other in the house. The walls were hung with striped stuffs from foreign countries and with scripts woven into satin. The furniture was foreign, too, heavy and carved, and the chairs cushioned. The space and emptiness that a Chinese lady would have needed for the peace of her soul and the order of her mind were not here. In the midst of her many possessions Madame Ezra lived content, and Peony could not but grant, though she heartily disliked the room, that there was beauty in it. Had it been smaller, it would have been hideous indeed. But the room was very large, for Madame Ezra when she came here as a bride had taken out two partitions and had thrown three rooms into one long one.

"Mistress, the young lady is ready," Peony announced.

"Where is my son?" Madame Ezra inquired.

"He was still sleeping when last I looked into his room," Peony replied.

She had not seen David last night. This was her own fault, for she had not gone in the evening, as her wont was, to take him tea and to see that his bed was ready for the night. Partly this was because of Madame Ezra's new command, but partly it was to test David. Alas, he had not sent for her, and when she went to bed she wept a while. In the morning she woke to reproach herself, and she had gone early to his rooms to take him tea, and if he were awake to ask him where he had been and why he had not finished the poem he had begun. But he was asleep and he had not waked, even when she parted the curtains of his bed and looked. He lay there, deep in sleep, his right arm flung above his head, and she had gazed at him a long moment, her heart most tender, and then she had gone away again.

"Bid Wang Ma wake him," Madame Ezra now commanded. "And where is my son's father?"

"I have not seen him, Mistress," Peony replied, "but I heard Wang Ma say that he expects the caravan today, and therefore he went out early to the city gates to wait for it."

"The caravan would come this day!" Madame Ezra exclaimed. "Now David will think of nothing else."

Peony looked sad, to please Madame Ezra. "Shall Wang Ma bid him come here to you before the caravan comes?" she asked.

"Let her do so," Madame Ezra said. "I will put off going to the kitchens, and meanwhile tell Leah to come to me."

She opened an inlaid box and took out some embroidery, and Peony left her. Outside the door she met Wang Ma, and she said, as though Madame Ezra had commanded it, "You are to take the young lady to our mistress, and I am to go and wake our young lord. Make haste, Elder Sister!"

She ran on, but not to David's room. She went to his schoolroom, now empty, and at the table in haste she took up the writing brush, put off its cover, and then made a little ink. She had kept the unfinished poem in her breast, and now she drew it out. Thinking fast and drawing her brows together, she quickly wrote three lines more upon the empty sheet.

"Forgive me, David," she whispered, and replacing pen and ink, she ran back to her own room. Opening a secret drawer in her desk, she took out a purse with money in it, the gifts that guests gave her and the coins that Ezra tossed her sometimes when he was pleased with her. Putting this too into her bosom, she slipped through passageways to the Gate of Peaceful Escape at the very back of the compound, that little secret gate which all great houses have, so that in time of the anger of the people, when they storm the front gates of the rich, the family itself can escape by it.

Through this gate Peony now went, keeping to quiet alleyways, away from the streets, until she came to another small gate like the one she had left. This opened into the compound of the Kung family, and here she knocked. A gardener drew back the bar and she said, "I have a message for the family."

He nodded and pointed a muddy finger over his shoulder, and she went in.

The house of Kung was an idle, pleasure-loving place, and no one rose from bed before noon. Chu Ma, the nurse, was only just stirring about her room, yawning and scratching her head with a silver hairpin, when Peony opened the door a little.

"Ah, you, Elder Sister!" Peony whispered.

Chu Ma opened the door wide. "You?" she said. "Why are you here?"

"I must make haste," Peony said. "No one knows I have left the house, except the young master himself, who bade me bring this quickly to your young mistress—and let me know if there is an answer."

This was a house that she knew a little, for once Ezra had sent her here with some treasure for Kung Chen that he dared not entrust to a servant only, and she had met Chu Ma, the eldest woman servant, and at New Year's time Chu Ma had gone to pay her good wishes and Peony had come here to return her own, in the careless easy fashion between two houses whose elders had some business together. Madame Ezra, it is true, had no friendships here, but Ezra and Kung Chen were very thick in trade.

"What does it say?" Chu Ma asked, staring at the paper.

Standing there in the untidy room, Peony read aloud the little poem she had written. "Dew at sunrise," Chu Ma echoed, sighing. "It is very pretty!"

She was a huge fat woman who, when she was young and slender, had come as wet nurse when the little third girl was first born, and she had lived on as her maid and caretaker. She had a large soft heart, ready to laugh or weep, and her whole life was bound up in the pretty child she tended.

"I will give the poem to her," she now said. "Your young lord is so handsome that I do what I know is wrong. But I cannot help it. I saw the young man myself—after my little one came running to me to tell me she had seen him. I ran to the gate and saw him—a foreigner and that is a pity, but after all, foreigners are humans like ourselves, and he is so handsome, a prince, I told my child—so strong, so straight! And as for his being a foreigner, she can persuade him to be Chinese. Does he love her very much?"

Peony nodded. "He asked me to give you this," she said. She drew out of her pocket the purse of money and gave it to Chu Ma.

"Oh, my mother," Chu Ma said, remonstrating and pretending to push the purse away. "This is not wanted. It would shame me to take it. What I do, I do for—" But she took the purse when Peony put it into her hand again, and she began to dress herself with energy. "I will give the paper to her myself and tell you how she looks. Come back again," she told Peony.

With that Peony went slipping through the alleyways again, and now she went straight to David's room. There he lay in his canopied bed, still soundly and peacefully asleep. She touched his one cheek and then the other with her two palms to coax him awake. She knew better than to wake him suddenly, for in sleep the soul wanders over the earth, and if the body is waked too quickly, the soul is confused and cannot find its way again to its home.

"Wake, my little lord, wake, my dear lord," Peony murmured, as though she were singing, and soon David opened his eyes. Then he sat up and stretched his strong arms and yawned mightily. Peony stood laughing quietly at him, and watching the light of his soul shine again in his eyes.

He gazed at her with dreams in his eyes, and she wondered what they were, and dared not ask.

"Come, Young Master," she said gently, "your mother sends for you."

"For what?" he asked. He was getting out of bed now, and she stooped and put his silk slippers on his one foot and then his other. He seemed not to notice that she had called him "Young Master," and not by his name, and he had forgotten that Peony should not be here.

"Leah is already here," she said simply, without reminding him.

He leaped down from the high bed.

"No!" he exclaimed.

"I tell you so," she replied. She moved to the other side of the room and poured water into a large brass basin from a brass ewer carved in delicate designs. She fetched a towel and some perfumed foreign soap.

"Still I will not obey my mother!" he exclaimed.

Peony turned and considered him, her pretty hands outspread on her narrow hips. Then she yielded to temptation within her own heart. "You cannot say you will not obey," she told him sweetly. "You can say, perhaps, that your father bade you hasten to meet him and wait for the caravan—and that you will hurry home."

"The caravan!" he exclaimed. "Peony, do you speak truth? Did my father tell you?"

"The gateman told Wang Ma our master was called soon after midnight, and she told me," she replied. "Now wash yourself before you dress. I will have your breakfast sent here. And I will take the message to your mother."

She went away, her head demurely bowed, and entered Madame Ezra's room once more.

"Alas, Lady, we are too late," she said sadly. "When Wang Ma went to our young master's room, he was up and gone. I have sent a man to search for him but he is not to be found at the teahouse.

At the city gate the watchman said he went out an hour ago, saying that he was going to The Three Bells to meet the caravan."

"How tiresome it is, on the very day before the Sabbath!" Madame Ezra exclaimed. "And Leah?"

"She is coming," Peony replied. She waited an instant and then said, "Has my lady any commands for me?"

"No," Madame Ezra replied, "go about your usual work. I wait for Leah."

"I will go and put fresh flowers into the great hall for the Sabbath tomorrow," Peony said in her small pretty voice, "and I will keep watch of the gate, so that when our young master enters, I can give him your bidding."

So saying she tripped away, her satin-shod feet silent upon the stones of the court.

When Wang Ma went to fetch Leah, she found the young girl eating her breakfast alone.

"Do not hasten," she said, sitting down on a stool near the door to rest herself.

Leah put down the porcelain spoon she held and looked alarmed. "Am I wanted, Good Mother?" she asked.

"Only when you are finished," Wang Ma said peaceably. "Then, if it pleases you, you are to come to our mistress. Eat, Young Lady."

Leah took up the spoon again, but she could not eat as heartily as before.

Wang Ma looked at her. Though Wang Ma did not care for the shape of the foreign nose, and though this girl was bigger than a woman should be, thin enough but too tall, yet if one granted these faults, she was very beautiful.

"You look as our old mistress did when she came here a bride," Wang Ma said.

Well she remembered that day, and how she had wept the night before it, thinking that now she would never serve her young master any more. Ezra had been handsome, too, in his half-foreign way, but not so handsome as his son was now, and the young Chinese girl who had been Wang Ma was comforted because the new bride was half a head taller than the young groom of those days. He will never love such a big woman, she had thought secretly. It was that extra half head of height that had made her willing to stay in the house and to marry Old Wang, the gatekeeper. But Madame Ezra, even when she was only seventeen, had seen to it that the young Ezra came to his own rooms at night and did not idle about the courts. Not until she was forty and his son twelve years old did she agree to let him have his own court. By that time Wang Ma was fat and no one thought of her as anything but a bondwoman. She and Old Wang had had four children whom she had put into the village as soon as they could work on the land, while she continued to live in the house of Ezra. Long ago Wang Ma came to know that Madame Ezra was mistress in the house, and that Madame Ezra knew that she knew. Not a word had ever been spoken between the two women during the long secret struggle of the years. Now the struggle was over. Madame Ezra had won.

Thus while Wang Ma gazed at Leah, her mind ran back. "But you are more gentle than our mistress was," she said musingly. "You have softer lips, and your hair is more free."

"Oh, my hair!" Leah said sadly. She had tied her red satin band about it. "I can never bind it tightly enough."

Wang Ma looked at her. "The band should be gold," she said. "I remember there is a gold one with that dress."

She rummaged in the box Madame Ezra had bade her put in the room and found a rich gold band.

"When you have finished eating . . ." she began.

"I can eat no more," Leah said quickly.

"Then let me put this on your hair," Wang said.

With skilled fingers she put the gold band about Leah's head.

"These go with the dress also," she declared further, and she opened the jewel box and took out a gold necklace and gold earrings.

Leah submitted herself.

"Now come with me to our mistress," Wang Ma commanded. She grasped Leah's hand, and surprised at its strength, she lifted it and looked at it. "Why, this is a boy's hand!" she exclaimed.

"I have had to work," Leah said, ashamed.

Wang Ma turned the hand she held. "The palm is soft," she went on. "The fingers are cushioned, and the skin is still fine. I shall rub oil into your hands at night. After a few weeks here they will be pretty."

She pulled Leah gently along, and so they went to Madame Ezra, who while she waited was embroidering in close firm stitches the Hebrew prayer piece.

"Come in, my daughter," she said to Leah. "Come and sit with me."

So Leah came in and sat down, and Madame Ezra looked at her with keen eyes. "Why, you look very pretty," she said.

"Wang Ma decked me out," Leah said. "I had put on the dress but not these." She touched the gold she wore.

"I thought her too plain," Wang Ma said. "She is so big that she can wear plenty of gold."

"She is not as tall as David," Madame Ezra said quickly.

"David is very tall," Leah said shyly.

"He will be here soon to welcome you," Madame Ezra replied. She fell to her embroidery again, and Wang Ma went into another room.

Alone with Madame Ezra, Leah sat with idle hands and felt strangely ill at ease. She loved this friend of her mother's and was nearer to her in some ways than to any other human being. She knew Madame Ezra's longing to make her a daughter. But she did not know what Madame Ezra expected of her, and so she could only wait.

As though she discerned these thoughts, Madame Ezra looked up. The room was very quiet. In the next room Wang Ma moved about at her work. But no other sound came from the great house.

"You know why you are here, Leah," Madame Ezra observed.

"Not quite, dear Aunt," Leah replied.

"You remember the promise I told you that your mother and I gave each other over your cradle, before she died?"

Leah looked down without answering. In her lap her strong young hands clasped themselves tightly.

"I want you and David to marry," Madame Ezra said. Tears rose into her eyes. She lifted the edge of her wide sleeve and wiped her eyes on the silken lining, and watched Leah's slowly flushing face. The young girl looked back at her with honest miserable eyes. "Why should I not tell you exactly what I want?" Madame Ezra asked passionately. "It is the one hope I have. But not I alone, Leah!"

She moved her chair nearer to Leah's. "Child, you know—and no one so well as you—what is happening to our people here in this Chinese city—how few of us are faithful any more! Leah, we are being lost!"

"The Chinese are very kind to us," Leah said.

Madame Ezra made a pettish gesture with her right hand. "It is what Ezra is always saying!" she exclaimed. "Kindness—I grow tired of it! Because the Chinese have not murdered us, does that mean they are not destroying us? Leah, I tell you, when I was your age the synagogue was full on every seventh day. You know what a small remnant is there nowadays."

"Still, that is not the fault of the Chinese," Leah said doubtfully.

"It is, it is," Madame Ezra insisted. "They pretend they like us—they are always ready to laugh, to invite us to their feasts, to do business with us. They keep telling us there is no difference between our people and theirs. Now, Leah, you know there is unchangeable difference between them and us. We are the children of the true God, and they are heathen. They worship images of clay. Have you ever looked into a Chinese temple?"

"Yes," Leah faltered. "When I was a child sometimes Aaron and I would go—just to see—"

"Well, then, you know," Madame Ezra retorted.

"Can we blame them"—Leah was gently stubborn—"just for being kind?"

"They are not kind for kindness's sake," Madame Ezra retorted. "No, no, I tell you, it's their trick to be kind. They win us by guile. They get their women to entice our men. And they pretend to be tolerant—why, they even say they are quite willing to worship our Jehovah as well as their own idols!" Madame Ezra's full face was red and handsome as she spoke thus earnestly to the young girl.

Leah continued to listen, her hands still clasped in her lap. "What do you want me to do, Aunt?" she asked at last.

"I want you to—to—persuade David," Madame Ezra said. "You and he together, Leah! Think how you could influence him!"

"But David knows me," Leah said in her straightforward way. "He would think it very odd if I were different—from what I have always been."

"You are grown now, you and he," Madame Ezra urged.

"We have always been like brother and sister," Leah said simply.

Madame Ezra pushed the embroidery from her lap and rose. She began to walk up and down the room. "That is exactly what I want you both to forget!" she exclaimed. "It was well enough when you were children, Leah—"

She paused and Leah rose.

"Yes, Aunt?"

"You know what I mean," Madame Ezra said harshly.

"I know, but I don't know how to do it," Leah said. Tears came into her large beautiful eyes. "You want me to—to—"

"Entice him—entice him," Madame Ezra said in the same harsh voice.

"I can't," Leah said steadily. "He would only laugh at me. And I would laugh at myself. It wouldn't be—me."

She put out her hand and took Madame Ezra's hand and held it between her own. "I have to be myself, dear Aunt, don't I? I know David, too." She felt her heart warm at the thought of David and she grew brave before this lady whom she loved and yet feared. "Perhaps I know him even better than you do. Forgive me, Aunt! You see, we are so nearly the same age. And I feel something in him—something great and—and good. If I can speak straightly to that part in him—which is also in me—"

They were gazing into each other's eyes while she thus spoke. Madame Ezra listened, her heart beating. Yes, Leah could do this!

Then suddenly, at this instant before Madame Ezra could reply, they heard a great noise from the outside courts. Voices shouted, gongs clanged, Wang Ma hurried from the bedroom.

"Mistress, it must be the caravan!" she exclaimed, and hastened away to find out. At the gate to the court she ran full into her husband, Old Wang.

"The caravan—the caravan!" he yelled. "Old Mistress—Master says—please come—it's the caravan!"

Madame Ezra pulled her hand from between Leah's hands. "We shall have to go," she said. "Better today than tomorrow, the Sabbath."

But Leah sat still. "Aunt, let me wait here—let me think—of what you have said is my duty."

"Very well, child," Madame Ezra replied. "Think of it—but come when you will."

"Yes." Leah's voice was a sigh. The next moment she was alone, and she folded her arms on the table at her side and laid down her head upon them. Then, after a few seconds, she rose and went to the corner of the room, and standing with her face toward the wall, she began to pray in a soft sobbing voice.

The coming of the caravan each year was an event for the whole city. The news of it ran from mouth to mouth, and when the long line of camels came padding down the dusty path at the side of the stone-paved streets, the doors of every house and shop were open and crowded with people. Upon a proud white camel at the head of the caravan sat Kao Lien, the trusted business partner of the House of Ezra. Behind him came guards armed with swords and old foreign muskets, and behind them plodded the loaded camels. All were weary with the long journey westward through Turkestan and back again through mountain passes, but for the final homecoming the men had decked themselves in their best, and even the camels held their narrow heads high and moved with majesty.

Last of all came Ezra in his mule cart. For days he had posted men along the last miles of the caravan route, watching and ready to set off to bring him word of the caravan. In the small morning hours of this day he had received the breathless runner, and had heard that the caravan was traveling by forced marches and would reach the city in a few hours. With forethought the runner had called the gateman, who had called for the mule cart, and into it Ezra had hastened, counting upon food at an inn. He had met the caravan at a village some ten miles outside the city, and then he had greeted Kao Lien with a great embrace, and the two had eaten a hasty breakfast, and had come on again toward the city, Ezra's mule cart following the caravan. He had ordered the blue satin curtains lifted, and now he rode smiling through the watching streets, waving his hands to all greetings.

Then at the gilded door of the teahouse that stood on the main street he saw his friend Kung Chen, smoking a long brass-tipped bamboo pipe, and he ordered the muleteer to stop the vehicle and let him down so that he could do this Chinese merchant the courtesy of passing him on foot. He paused to bow and to give greeting, and the caravan halted while he did this.

"I congratulate you upon the safe return of your partner and the caravan," Kung Chen said.

"The camels are laden with goods of the richest sort," Ezra replied. "When you have time, I beg you to come and see what we have, in order that you may choose what you want for your own shops. I give you first choice. Only what is left shall go to other merchants, until our contract is signed."

"Thank you, thank you," the urbane Chinese replied. He was a large, fat man, his brocaded satin robe a little short in front because of his full paunch. A sleeveless black velvet jacket softened the curves.

Ezra grew warm with fine friendliness. "Come tomorrow, good friend," he urged. "Take a modest meal with me, and afterward we can look over the goods at our pleasure. No!" He broke off. "What am I saying? Tomorrow is our Sabbath. Another day, good friend."

"Excellent, excellent," Kung Chen replied in his mellow voice. He bowed, he pushed Ezra gently again toward his chair, and the caravan went on.

Just before it reached the gates of his house Ezra saw his son, David, drop lightly over the brick wall of the compound and run beside the first camel, waving his right arm in greeting to Kao Lien. Then he darted ahead and through the gates.

The chair bearers laughed. "The young master will rouse the whole house," they said.

Ezra laughed proudly in reply. Now they were at the gate, and though he had paid wages to the muleteers, when they stopped the cart he reached into his wide girdle where his money purse was and drew out extra money for them.

"Wine money—wine money," he said in his loud cheerful voice.

They smiled, the sun glistening on their brown faces. "Our thanks," they replied, and drove the empty cart away.

One by one the camels knelt before the gates, blowing and sighing and puffing out their loose lips, and quickly their loads were taken off and carried in. Then the camel tenders led the beasts to their stables, and the gates were locked. So great was the curiosity of the people on the streets that many passers-by would have pressed into the courtyards to see the foreign goods, but the gateman would not allow them. "Stand back!" he roared. "Are you robbers and thieves?"

Inside his own walls Ezra led Kao Lien toward the great hall. On his other side David clung fondly to Kao Lien's arm.

"I want to hear everything, Elder Uncle," he said. There was no blood relationship between Ezra and Kao Lien, but they had grown up as boys together, for Kao Lien's grandfather had been Jewish, although his father had taken a Chinese wife, who was Kao Lien's mother, and Kao Lien had been useful to Ezra in his business with Chinese merchants. Kao Lien was a man who was Jewish with the Jews and Chinese with the Chinese.

Now his long narrow face looked weary as he walked over the sunlit stones of the courts. A kind smile played over his lips, half hidden by his somewhat scanty beard, and his dark eyes were gentle. His voice was low and his words came slowly and he shaped them with grace.

"I have much to tell," he said.

Ahead of them Madame Ezra stood at the door of the great hall, and Kao Lien saw her and bowed his head in greeting.

"We welcome you home," she called.

"God is good!" Kao Lien replied.

He entered as she stepped back and he made an obeisance before her to which she replied by bending her head, signifying that he was not quite her equal. A hint of amusement stole into Kao Lien's eyes, but he was used to her ways and it would have been out of his nature to mind her pride.

"Where shall we spread the goods, Lady?" he asked. He always asked her direction if she were present, but he knew, and Ezra knew that he knew, that for him the man was the true head of the house.

"I will sit here in my own chair," Madame Ezra replied, "and you may open the loads one by one before me."

She sat down and Ezra sat opposite. Wang Ma came forward and poured tea and a manservant offered sweet tidbits on a porcelain tray divided into parts. By now all the servants were crowding quietly into the room. They stood along the walls to watch what went on. David was pulling at the ropes of the first load, hastening to get it open.

"Gently, Young Master," Kao Lien said. "There is something precious in that load."

He stepped over bundles and stuffs and he worked at the knot that David had been tearing. It seemed to fall open beneath his long and nimble fingers. Within the coarse cloth wrapping was a metal box. He opened the lid and lifted out of the inner packing a large gold object.

"A clock!" David cried. "But whoever saw such a clock?"

"It is no ordinary one," Kao Lien said proudly.

Ezra looked with doubt at the golden figures of nude children, whose hands upheld the clock. "It is very handsome," he said. "Those golden children are fat and well made. But who will want it?"

Kao Lien smiled with some triumph. "Do you remember that Kung Chen asked me to bring a gift for the Imperial Palace? He wishes to present it when the new shops are opened in the northern capital. This I bought for the gift."

Ezra was much struck. "The very thing!" he exclaimed. "No

common man could use it. The Imperial Palace—ah, yes!" He stroked his beard and was pleased as he contemplated the great clock. "This should make the contract between Kung Chen and me easy, eh, brother?"

"I wish I could open the back of this clock," David now said. "I would like to know how it makes its energy."

"No, no," Ezra said hastily. "You could never get it together again. Put it away, Kao Lien, Brother—it is too valuable. Do not tell me what it cost!"

There was laughter at this, and the servants, who had been staring at the golden children with admiration, watched it put away with reverence in their eyes, thinking that when next it was open, it would be before the Peacock Throne. Only David was reluctant to see it put into the box again.

"I wish I could go westward with Kao Lien next time, Father," he said. "There must be many wonders in the other countries that we do not have here."

"Young Master, do not leave us," Wang Ma exclaimed. "An only son must not leave his parents until there is a grandson."

Madame Ezra looked somewhat majestic at this intrusion by Wang Ma. "Some day we will all go," she said. "This is not our country, my son. We have another."

At this Ezra in his turn was displeased. He waved his hand at Kao Lien and he said, "Come, come, show us what other things you have."

Kao Lien hastened to obey, well knowing that upon this matter of the promised land of their fathers Ezra and his wife could not agree, and he ordered the loads opened until their contents were spread about and the whole hall glittered with toys and stuffs, with music boxes and jumping figures and dolls and curiosities of every sort, with satins and velvets and fine cottons, with carpets and cushions and even furs from the north. All were bewitched by what they saw, and Ezra computed his profits secretly. When everything was shown, each of its kind, he chose a gift for every servant and member of the family. For Peony he put aside a little gold comb, and to Wang Ma he gave a bolt of good linen, and to Madame Ezra, his wife, he gave a bolt of beautiful crimson velvet, every thread of which, warp and woof, was of silk.

As for David, he moved in a dream from one thing to another of the riches spread before him, speechless with pleasure. The more he saw, the more he longed to know the countries from which these marvels came and the people who were so clever as to make them. It seemed to him that these must be the best people in the world. To conceive this beauty, such colors and shapes, to make the beauty into solid forms and shimmering stuffs and rich materials, into machines and energies, surely this must be the work of brave and noble people, great nations, mighty civilizations. He longed more than ever to travel westward and see for himself those men who could dream so high and make such reality. Perhaps he himself be longed more to those people than he did here. Had not his own ancestors come from west of India?

Ezra looked uneasily at his son. David was at the age when all his natural curiosities were coming awake, and his heart was impatient with unfulfilled desires. Were his mother to give him her constant longing to leave this country, which she insisted upon calling a place of exile, how could Ezra alone circumvent the two of them? David loved pleasure and Ezra encouraged him in friendships with the young men of the city, but what if these pleasures grew familiar and stale? As he watched his son, it seemed to Ezra that David was not today as he had been in other years. He did not exclaim over each toy and object and marvel, pleased with the thing itself. A deeper perception was in his son's eyes and apparent in his face and manner. David was thinking, his heart was slipping out of him.

"My son!" Ezra cried.

"Yes, Father?" David answered, scarcely hearing.

"Choose something for yourself, my son!" Ezra cried in a loud voice, to bring David back again into his home.

"How can I choose?" David murmured. "I want everything."

Ezra made himself laugh heartily. "Now, now," he cried in the same loud voice. "My business will be ruined!"

Everyone was looking to see what David would choose, but he would not be hastened.

"Choose that fine blue stuff," Madame Ezra said. "It will make you a good coat."

"I do not want that," David said, and he continued to walk about, to look here and there, to touch this and that.

"Choose that little gold lamp, Young Master," Wang Ma suggested. "I will fill it with oil and set it on your table."

"I have a lamp," David replied, and he continued to search for what his heart might most desire.

"Come, come!" Ezra cried.

"Let him take his time," Kao Lien begged.

So they all waited, the servants at first half laughing, to discover what this most beloved in the house should choose for himself.

Suddenly David saw something he had not seen before. It was a long narrow sword in a silver wrought scabbard. He pulled it out from under bolts of silks, and looked at it. "This—" he began.

"Jehovah forbid!" Kao Lien cried out.

"Is it wrong for me to choose this?" David asked, surprised.

"It is I that am wrong," Kao Lien declared. He went forward and tried to draw the sword from David's grasp. The young man was unwilling, but Kao Lien persisted until he held the sword. "I should not have brought it into the house," he said. Then he turned to Ezra. "Yet it is my proof. I told myself that if you saw this sword, Elder Brother, you would believe—"

But David had put out his hand and Kao Lien felt the sword drawn away from him again. David held it now in both hands, and he loved it as he looked at it. Never had he seen so strong, so delicate, so perfect a weapon.

"It is a beautiful thing," he murmured.

"Put it down," his mother said suddenly.

But David did not heed her.

Kao Lien had been looking at all this with horror growing upon his subtle and sensitive face. "Young Master," he said. His voice, always pitched low, was so laden with meaning that everyone in the room turned to hear him.

"What now, Brother?" Ezra inquired. He was astonished at David's choice. What need had his son of a weapon?

"That sword, Young Master," Kao Lien said, "it is not for you. I brought it back as a token of what I saw. When I have told its evil, I shall destroy the sword."

"Evil?" David repeated, his eyes still on the sword. His parents were silent. Had he looked at them, he would have seen their faces suddenly intent and aware and set in fear. But he was looking only at the beautiful sword.

Kao Lien looked at them and well he understood what they were thinking. "Before I crossed the western border, I was warned by rumors," he said. "They are killing our people again."

Madame Ezra gave a great shriek and she covered her face with her hands. Ezra did not speak. At the sound of his mother's cry David looked up.

"Killing?" he repeated, not understanding.

Kao Lien nodded solemnly. "May you never know what that means, Young Master! I went onward, thinking that the westerners would believe I was a Chinese. Yet had I known what I was to see—I would have gone a thousand miles out of my way!"

He paused. Not a voice asked him what he had seen. Ezra's face was white above his dark beard and he leaned his head on his hands and hid his eyes. Madame Ezra did not take her hands from her face. David waited, his eyes on Kao Lien, and he felt his spine prickle with unknown terror. The servants stared, their mouths hanging open.

"Yet it is well for you to know what I saw," Kao Lien said, and now he looked at David. "You do not know that in the West our people are not free to live where they choose in a city. They must live only where they are allowed to live, and it is always in the poorer parts. But even there they were driven out. I saw their homes in ruins, the doors hanging on their hinges, windows shattered, their shops robbed and ruined. That was not all. I saw our people fleeing along the roadsides, men and women and children. That was not all." Kao Lien paused and went on. "I saw hundreds dead—old men, women, children, young men who had fought rather than try to escape—our people! They had been killed by swords and knives and guns and poison and fire. I picked up that sword from a side street. It was covered with blood."

David dropped the sword and it clanged upon the floor. He looked down at it, and felt dazed and choked. In those countries of whose beauty he had been dreaming—even this sword was beautiful—Kao Lien had seen this!

"But why?" he asked.

"Who knows?" Kao Lien asked, sighing. How could he make this young David understand, who had all his life lived in safety and peace? What ancient curse was upon their people elsewhere that did not hold under these Eastern skies?

"What had they done?" David's voice rang through the great hall. He looked at his father and his mother and back to Kao Lien.

"Nothing!" Madame Ezra cried, and she lifted her face from her hands

"Even though we sinned," Kao Lien exclaimed, "are we among all mankind never to be forgiven?"

But Ezra was silent.

Now the servants, feeling distress in the air and being moved to pity by what they had heard, came forward to pour tea and to put away the goods. Only then did Ezra come to himself. He took his hand away from his face and he drank a bowl of tea. When Wang Ma had filled it again, he held it in both hands as though to warm himself.

"As long as we live here, we are safe," he said at last. "Kao Lien, take the sword, melt it into its pure metal. We will forget that we saw it."

Before Kao Lien could move to obey, David stooped and grasped the sword again by its hilt. "I still choose the sword!" he declared.

Ezra groaned but Madame Ezra spoke. "Let him keep it," she said to Ezra. "Let him remember that by it our people have died."

Ezra put down the bowl and rubbed his hands over his head, and sighed again. "Naomi, it is the thing he should not remember!" he exclaimed. "Why should our son fear when none pursue him?"

"Father, I will remember—forever!" David cried. He stood straight, the sword in his hand, his head high, his eyes passionate.

At this moment there was a footstep at the door and Leah was there. David saw her in her scarlet and gold, her dark hair bound back, her great black eyes burning, her red lips parted.

"Leah!" he cried.

"I heard what Kao Lien told you." Her voice was clear and soft. "I heard about our people. I was standing behind the curtain."

"Come in, child," Madame Ezra said. "I was about to send for you."

"I knew I should come," she replied in the same soft voice. "I felt it—here."

She clasped her hands together on her breast and she looked at David. He gazed back at her, startled out of himself, and as though he had never seen her before. At this moment she came before him, a woman.

Madame Ezra watched them, and she leaned forward in her seat, and everyone else watched her. She smiled, yearning toward those two. Ezra watched from under his brows, his lips pursed and silent, and Kao Lien watched, smiling half sadly, and Wang Ma watched and her lips were bitter.

But Leah saw only David. He stood so tall and he grasped the silver sword in his right hand. He was more beautiful in her eyes than the morning star and more to be desired than life itself. He was manhood to her womanhood, theirs was one blood, and she forgot everything except that he was there and that his face was tender, his eyes warm upon her. She came to him as to the sun, hesitating and yet compelled.

Madame Ezra turned to the Chinese. "Go—all of you," she commanded in a low voice. "Leave us to ourselves."

The servants slipped away. Even Wang Ma left her post and hurried out by a side door. Small Dog, asleep in the sun on the stone doorstep, awoke, lifted her head, whined, and getting up, she too went away.

Leah smiled at David. "Another David, the sword of Goliath in your hand," she said. Suddenly tears filled her eyes. She stepped forward, and stooping, she kissed the silver scabbard of the sword he held. He saw her bowed before him, the soft dark hair curled upon her creamy nape. Around them his father, his mother, Kao Lien stood, watching them.

Peony watched them, too, unseen. Wang Ma had hastened to her door, and finding it locked, she had beaten upon it. "Peony, you fool and child of a fool!" she shouted. "Open the door! Are you sleeping?"

Peony opened the door, frightened at Wang Ma's strange voice.

"Quick!" Wang Ma said between her teeth. "Go to the great hall —break in as though you knew nothing—drive them apart with a laugh."

Without one word Peony had flown thither on silent feet. Still silent, she had pulled the curtain aside and had looked in. There stood David, holding a sword, while the elders watched, and upon this sword Leah pressed her lips. What rite was this? Was it their foreign way of declaring betrothal? No, no, she could not speak—she could not laugh! She dared not break the moment. What did it mean? She dropped the curtain and fled back to her room, her soft eyes dark with terror.

挑筋教

IV

IN HER room alone Peony did not weep. She sat down and wiped her eyes on her undersleeves of white silk from habit although her eyes were dry, and she felt that she was in a strange house whose secret life excluded her. But she made little sighs and moans that she did not try to stifle, and in the midst of this Wang Ma came in.

The relationship between these two was a complex one. They were Chinese, and therefore united among all who were not Chinese. They were women and therefore they had a bond together among men. But one was old and no longer beautiful and one was young and very pretty. Each knew the other's life, and yet neither thought it necessary to tell what she knew. Thus Peony knew that Wang Ma had in her youth been the young bondmaid in the house, even as she herself now was, and yet how far she had been only bondmaid and how far something more, Wang Ma in prudence had never told and doubtless would never tell. Moreover, Peony did not wish to grant that she and Wang Ma were alike. Wang Ma could not read or write, and although she was shrewd and kindly enough, she was a common soul. This Peony was not. Peony had read many books, and Ezra had allowed her to talk with him sometimes, and she had listened long hours to the old Confucian Chinese teacher while he was teaching David. Above all, she had until now wholly shared David's mind and thought as Wang Ma could never have shared his father's. Peony had guided David into his love of music and poetry making, and they had read together in secret such books as *The Dream of the Red Chamber,* and when she had wept over the sad young heroine, scattering the flower petals, David had put his arm about her that she might weep against his shoulder.

Until now he had told her everything, this she knew, and she had met his every mood with delicate eagerness and welcome. Only one thing she did not know—she had not asked him why he had not finished the poem he had begun to write. Had he even missed it when she had taken it? She had been afraid to ask him lest he force from her the truth that she had stolen it and had finished it and taken it to the third young lady in the house of Kung. She feared his angry question, "And why did you that?"

Why indeed? She could never tell him. She had always been too wise to tell him all she thought and felt, knowing by some intuition of her own womanhood that no man wants to know everything of any woman. His heart was centered in himself, and so must hers be centered in him. Thus she had never told David the one continuing question that she put to herself without being able to answer it. Here was that question: Was life sad or happy? She did not mean her life or any one life, but life itself—was it sad or happy? If she but had the answer to that first question, Peony thought, then she would have her guide. If life could and should be happy, if to be alive itself was good, then why should she not try for everything that could be hers? But if, when all was won, life itself was sad, then she must content herself with what she had. Now this old question thrust itself before her, and she found no answer in her heart.

"I knew I would find you grieving," Wang Ma was saying calmly. She sat down, and planting a plump hand on each knee, she stared at Peony. "You and I," she went on, "we must help each other."

Peony lifted her sad eyes to Wang Ma's round and good face. "Elder Sister," she said in a plaintive voice.

"Speak what is in your mind," Wang Ma replied.

"It seems to me that if I could answer one question to myself, I could arrange my life," Peony said.

"Put the question to me," Wang Ma replied.

This was not easy for Peony to do. Never had she talked with

Wang Ma except about such things as food and tea and whether the rooms were clean and what should be done in house and court, and she feared lest Wang Ma laugh at her. But now her heart was ready to break because she did not know what would happen to her if David were to wed Leah.

"Wang Ma, please do not laugh at me," she said faintly.

"I will not laugh," Wang Ma replied.

Peony clasped her small hands in her lap. "Life," she said distinctly —"is life happy or sad?"

"At bottom?" Wang Ma inquired. Her face was entirely serious and it seemed she understood what Peony meant.

"At bottom," Peony replied.

Wang Ma looked grave, but she did not look surprised or bewildered. "Life is sad," she said with clear decision.

"We cannot expect happiness?" Peony asked wistfully.

"Certainly not," Wang Ma said firmly.

"You say that so cheerfully!" Peony wailed. Now she began to cry softly.

"You cannot be happy until you understand that life is sad," Wang Ma declared. "See me, Little Sister! What dreams I made and how I hoped before I knew that life is sad! After I understood this truth I made no more dreams. I hoped no more. Now I am often happy, because some good things come to me. Expecting nothing, I am glad for anything." Wang Ma spat cleverly out of the door into the court. "Ah, yes," she said comfortably, "life is sad. Make up your mind to that."

"Thank you," Peony said gently. And she dried her eyes.

They sat, the two of them, in reflective silence for some time. Then Wang Ma began to talk very kindly. "You, Peony, must consider yourself. If it is your wish to spend your years in this house, then inquire into what woman is to be our young master's wife. A man's wife is his ruler, whether he likes her or not. She has the power of her place in his bed. Choose his wife, therefore."

"I?" Peony asked.

Wang Ma nodded.

"Did you choose our mistress?" Peony asked.

Wang Ma rolled her head round and round on her short neck. "My choice was to go—or to stay," she said at last.

"You stayed," Peony said gently.

Wang Ma got up. "It is time for me to take our mistress her mid-morning sweetmeats," she said abruptly.

With that she went away, and Peony continued in long thought. Duties waited. At this moment through the door that she had left open Small Dog came into the room on her padded feet. She moved in habitual silence unless she saw a stranger, and now she came to Peony and looked up at her, pleading but silent.

"I have forgotten you, Small Dog," Peony murmured. She rose and found a bamboo brush, and she knelt on the floor and brushed Small Dog's long golden hair. The stiff bamboo was pleasant to the dog and she stood motionless, her bulbous eyes half closed, while Peony lifted each ear and brushed it smooth and carefully brushed the hair about the upturned black nose. Had she been a cat Small Dog would have purred. Being a dog, she could only move her plumy tail slowly to and fro.

Yet Peony did not make the mistake of considering Small Dog more than a little dog. When her task was done she rose from her knees and washed her hands, and sitting down again, she resumed her thoughts. Small Dog lay on the stone threshold and rolled her round eyes a few times, snapped at a fly, and went to sleep.

Peony gazed at her thoughtfully. In this house Small Dog, too, was entirely happy and everyone accepted her being. Even a dog could be part of the whole. So Peony pondered, and no one came to call her. On another day, any day, she would have been called many times, and this silence gave her further warning that something new and strange was happening in the house, something in which she had no share. Whatever it was, she had to live with it and within it, yielding to it, accepting it, becoming part of it. Whatever David was, wherever he was, she would be there. If he spoke to her sometimes, if he let her serve him, if she did no more than tend his garments, she would make it enough, a life for herself.

So motionless she sat, so many were the minutes passing, that at last the small creatures who hide behind furniture and curtains and doors began to stir. A cricket sang a long thin note from a cranny in the roof, and into a beam of late sunlight that fell across the tile floor a kangaroo mouse crept out, and standing on its hind feet, it began a small solitary dance. Peony watched, and then in sudden delight she laughed aloud. The little creature darted back into its hiding place again, and she sat on, smiling now instead of grave. There were these small pleasures to be had! Here in this house little lives went gaily on, hidden from the great ones. Let her life be one of these! Into her came some spirit too gentle to be force, too quiet to be energy.

Nevertheless, it revived her. She rose, smoothed back her hair, looked into her mirror; and seeing herself pale, she touched her lips with red. Then, after a moment's contemplation, she wound her braid again over her ear and thrust into it a jade hairpin. She had duties and she must do them. This was the day before the Sabbath and the usual evening meal must be served with special care. She must polish the silver candlesticks and the vessel for the wine, and she must place the loaves of braided bread upon the table. Then she sat down again, and sat on, knowing all that remained to be done and yet not moving. After a moment more she took brush and ink and some plain white rice paper from the drawer of the table, and quickly she wrote four lines of a poem. They had not anything to do with herself. They were in reply to the poem that she had taken to the house of Kung, and they had to do with the consuming warmth of the sun that drank the dew it found upon the flowers at sunrise.

This poem being finished, she put it in her bosom. Then only did she proceed to perform her duties for the Sabbath.

In the great hall Peony had not been seen. The three elders, Madame Ezra, Ezra, and Kao Lien, had gazed with different feelings upon David and Leah as the beautiful girl bent her head to kiss the shining scabbard of the sword. To Madame Ezra the act meant that Leah had dedicated herself to the task she had been given. Kao Lien, his narrow eyes on Madame Ezra's face, perceived by its expression of joy and devotion that some secret hope of her heart was about to be fulfilled, and he guessed easily what it was and grieved for David, whom he loved. That Leah was handsome to look upon he could see as well as any man, but he discerned in her that quality of spirit which he had so often seen in Jewish women, and which, or so he thought, had driven and compelled their men to the separatism that he feared and deplored. For a woman to love God too much was not well, he now told himself. She must not love God more than man, for then she made herself man's conscience, and he was the pursued.

Ezra was the most disturbed. More than ever now he longed to hide himself and all that he was in this rich and tolerant land to which his ancestors had come. He feared Leah and all her beauty, and he was afraid lest David yield to the spiritual quality it possessed. That his son was more the son of his mother than of himself Ezra well knew. David had not the consolation that he himself had had, of a rosy, warm little Chinese mother, ready to laugh at God and man, and judging all in life by her own sense of pleasure. No, although this small creature lurked in David's blood, the main stream of his being was from his own mother, and her sternly loving eyes had been always upon him.

Ezra stirred in his chair, coughed, pulled his beard, and in all his manner he showed his displeasure. "Come now," he cried loudly, "Leah, my dear—that dirty old sword! Has it not been in the hands of soldiers, who are the scum of any nation?"

His harsh practical voice bewildered Leah. She stepped back shyly and put her hands to her cheeks. "Oh—I took no thought," she faltered.

"Leah did right to kiss the sword," Madame Ezra announced. "The Lord moved her."

Now David spoke, repelled as usual by his mother and hiding behind his rebellion his unwilling and instinctive sympathy with her. "I shall hang the sword on the wall behind my desk," he declared half carelessly. "It will be a decoration."

"A good thought," Kao Lien said. "May it never again be wielded against a human life!"

Ezra rose. "Let these stuffs be gathered and put away," he commanded Kao Lien. He took up the comb he had put aside for Peony. He ignored Leah purposely and turned to Madame Ezra. "Wife, I am hungry. Let the evening meal be early." With this he left the room abruptly.

Leah stood, half awkwardly, half shyly. David, too, seemed to have forgotten her. He was testing the keenness of the sword's blade upon the coarse wrappings of the bales. So sharp was the damascene metal that the blade melted through the cloth.

"Look at this, Kao Lien!" he called in delight.

Kao Lien, about to summon the men, paused to look.

"Never test it against your hand, I beg," he said quietly. "Without half your strength it can cut through a human body. I saw it done."

He went out, and Leah stood irresolute, now looking at Madame Ezra, now at David. But Madame Ezra looked in silence only at her son, and he, feeling that deep grave look, continued willfully to cut the cloth.

"Leah," Madame Ezra said at last, still watching David, "you may go to your room."

Before she could move, David raised his head. "I will go, too, Mother, and hang my sword," he said, and quickly he left the room by the nearest door.

"Shall I still go, Aunt?" Leah asked timidly. She longed to cry out and ask what wrong she had done but she dared not, and she could only stand, tall and drooping, and wait for Madame Ezra's command.

"Go—go!" Madame Ezra said, not unkindly, but as though she wanted to be alone.

What could Leah do but go?

On the morning of the Sabbath David sat alone in his room. He had waked late from a strange exhaustion after yesterday.

For the first time in his life it seemed to him that he understood his mother and all that she had tried to teach him and all that had made her what she was. He lay now upon his bed in the silken dimness of the curtains, and in the solitude it came to him that he was not what he had supposed he was, a young man free to be himself, to live as he liked, to take his pleasure, to be only his father's son. He was part of a whole, a people scattered over the earth and yet eternally one and indivisible. Wherever a Jew lived, in whatever safety and isolation, he still belonged to his people.

This that his mother had taught him since he was born, to which hitherto he had been as impervious as stone to rain, he now comprehended, not with his mind, but with his blood. Why should his people be killed? A perverse anger rose in him. If the world outside sought to destroy his kind, then here inside the safety of this country where he had been born he would do all he could to keep them living. He would begin seriously to learn about his own people. For two years he had resisted his mother's wish that he take lessons in their religion from the Rabbi. He had no time, he had told her. There were still many books he wished to read, and his father pressed him for more hours in the business, and he wanted to travel. His mother would not let him travel, he knew, until he was married and his son born. His son! Until now the child had been a myth made by his mother. But now he perceived in some depth in him, having nothing to do with thought and reason, that he ought to have sons. If his people were being killed, more must be born. Birth was their retaliation for death.

Thus for the first time in his pleasure-filled life David began to think beyond himself. He felt his hidden roots through his mother and his father, but most strongly through her. He saw now that while it had seemed to him she had been trying to control him and deny him his independence, she had actually been trying to preserve him and save him.

And then from his mother his thoughts went to Leah. How beautiful she had looked last night! They had not been alone together, and yet they had been close, united by the same bonds of blood and heart and spirit. It was true—theirs was a people separate and apart, a people of destiny, appointed by Jehovah, the One True God. He felt now, with deep strange guilt, that he had denied God by his careless gay life in a heathen country. While his people had suffered and died he had laughed and played and wasted his days. He remembered the things he had loved most, the gambling in Chinese teahouses, the idle summer afternoons on the lake where he and his young Chinese friends floated in pleasure boats, the smell of lotus flowers, the music of violin and flute in a courtyard in the moonlight. Then he remembered his father's friend Kung Chen, and now Kueilan returned to his mind in all her innocent bloom. He knew her little face as though he had seen it a hundred times, the delicate curving eyebrows, the round black eyes, the little full red mouth, the pale beautiful skin, the willow slenderness of her small frame. But he knew her because Peony, too, was small and her mouth also was red, and her eyes were lit with laughter. How often they had laughed together! He checked his involuntary smile. While he had enjoyed his life, his people were being driven from their homes. In other cities, among other peoples, they lay dead in the streets. Impelled by guilt, he rose and went to find his mother and tell her he would go with her today to the synagogue. It would comfort her, after yesterday.

When he had washed and dressed himself his way led him past the peach garden, and as he passed the round moon gate, he saw the trees, in late bloom, reflected in the quiet oval pool. The morning was bright, the air warm, and in spite of his wish to be sorrowful, a surge of joy ran through him.

"Peony!" he called softly.

There was no answer. Yet often she did not answer him when she was in the garden. She was a teasing and mischievous little thing. He smiled and stepped inside the moon gate. It was still too early to go to the synagogue and he would not go to his mother.

Madame Ezra had scarcely slept for happiness. Her heart, so often solitary in this house, today was comforted. It was Leah, she had told herself in the night, Leah who had waked David's sleeping spirit, if only for a moment. It would wake again—yes, and Ezra's too. No, more than Leah, it was the mysterious way of Jehovah, Who had brought everything together at the appointed hour. The caravan had come on the day when Leah came. How blind and small of faith she had been to complain against that coincidence! It had been planned by God. For Kao Lien to bring the tidings of new persecution, for Leah to enter the room when David's heart was moved with sorrow, for Leah to have faith and wit to seize his sorrow and twist it into a weapon to stab his conscience—who but God could have done all this?

Last night Ezra, coming into this room in the night, did not lie down beside her. Instead he had sat by her bedside, holding her hand, and they had talked deeply and sensibly, as Jewish man and wife.

"Naomi, I am willing now that David should be taught the law and the prophets," Ezra had said.

Her heart sang before the Lord when he so spoke. Long ago the Rabbi had taught David, until the boy had rebelled and Ezra had not aided her to put down his rebellion. Instead he had said that David was old enough to help in the business and there was not time enough for everything. In triumph the boy had gone with his father and had made his own friends among the sons of Chinese merchants, and so he had gone even into the house of Kung and had seen the daughter there.

"Thank you, Ezra," she had replied, and had subdued her joy.

"There is nothing we can do about our kinsfolk abroad," Ezra had gone on. "The sensible thing for us is to stay here, where we at least are safe."

"Until such time as a prophet comes forward to lead us home," Madame Ezra had answered gently.

Ezra had coughed. "Well, my dear," he said. He patted her hand. "I sometimes wonder why we should ever leave China. Four generations we have been here, Naomi, and David's children will be the fifth. The Chinese are very kind to us."

"I fear such kindness," she had replied. She had pulled her hand away, and then alarmed lest he repent what he had promised, she put it back between his. They had not spoken again, and after a time he had returned to his rooms.

Now the Sabbath had dawned, a new Sabbath, wonderful for her, because they were all going to the synagogue together. The house was silent, no one was at work. Only from over the walls came the street noises and the voices of the heathen city. Here in her house God had come again, with sorrow, it was true, but here. He was always most near to His people in times of sorrow—"Out of death we cry to Thee, O Jehovah!" she murmured after Ezra had gone. She prepared herself for the day, putting on her richest garments, a brocaded satin of deep purple, the skirt and sleeves edged with gold.

And Leah, dear child! Did she know how obedient she had been to the will of God? Not one whit must be lost of what she had done yesterday, under the guidance of the Lord. Madame Ezra turned impulsively to Wang Ma, who had come to help her dress. "Go and fetch that dear child Leah!" she said. "I can wait no longer to bless her."

Wang Ma threw her a shrewd look and without speaking went to obey. Then Madame Ezra stopped her. "No," she said. "I will go to her, and see her for myself."

Wang Ma shrugged her firm shoulders and stood aside to let her mistress pass.

Thus it was that Leah on this Sabbath morning saw Madame Ezra approaching her door. The young girl had spent the night in healthy sleep, her spirit at ease. She had obeyed the will of the Lord. Yesterday when she had been left alone, she had felt impelled to go out and find the others. She had walked through passageways and courtyards and her feet were guided. She had reached the great hall at exactly the moment when David's heart was stirred and his soul bright with the anger of the Lord. When she put aside the curtain at the doorway she had seen him kneeling as before the altar, a silver sword across his knees. He had lifted his eyes to hers, and the Lord put words into her mouth and she spoke them. When she waked in the night she remembered David's face turned to her, his eyes upon hers, and she slept again, smiling in her sleep.

This morning she repeated to herself a few verses from the Torah and she wondered how her father was and whether Aaron was being good, and if Rachel could manage him. Then she wondered shyly if David would come to her, or send for her, perhaps, or whether Madame Ezra would bring them together. Last night at the evening meal he had been very silent, but that was natural—she had been silent, too. Whatever was to be, she was no longer afraid. God was with her.

Filled with such dreaming thoughts this morning, she had moved here and there, and had stood smiling and gazing into space. She walked in her little garden and came in and sat down, all in such a happy hopeful mood that now when she saw Madame Ezra she went to meet her.

"Ah, dear Aunt," Leah murmured.

"Dear child," Madame Ezra replied, touched by this warmth. "Today you look happy."

Leah lifted her head. "I am happier than I have ever been in my life," she declared. They walked into the house hand in hand, and when Madame Ezra had seated herself, Leah drew a footstool near her and sat down, and again they clasped hands. Leah looked trustfully at Madame Ezra. This look moved Madame Ezra so much that her throat tightened with tears. She felt an ecstasy well up from her heart and infuse her spirit.

"Bow your head, dear child," she murmured. "We thank God."

She bowed her own head and began to murmur the words of a psalm, and Leah joined her. When the psalm was over Madame Ezra paused in silence, and then, lifting her head, she opened her eyes and met Leah's.

"We have Jehovah's blessing," she said gently. "I feel it. Now we have only to follow step by step the way that God leads us. Dear child, my son's father is willing, quite of his own accord, to ask the Rabbi to teach David the Torah again! I have considered how this shall be done, and now it comes to me. The Rabbi must come here to our house—we must all be together."

"Oh, but what of Aaron?" Leah asked anxiously.

"Aaron will come too," Madame Ezra said firmly. "They can live in the little west wing."

"May I not live with them?" Leah asked.

"No, you will stay here," Madame Ezra replied. Actually she had thought of all this only within the last few minutes. But it came to her so clearly, it seemed so simple, that she was sure God guided her mind.

"I shall speak to your father before we worship," she went on. "But you will tell David now. No, I shall tell David myself, and you will come with me, and then you and he will talk together. After all, yesterday was yesterday and today is today, and each day must be managed separately so that we arrive at the goal."

Madame Ezra pressed Leah's hand and released it and rose. "What is the goal, dear Aunt?" Leah asked, somewhat timidly.

"David's marriage—and yours," Madame Ezra replied serenely. "Now is the time. I never saw him so stirred as he was yesterday."

"Now, dear Aunt?" Leah asked, alarmed.

"Yes, certainly," Madame Ezra replied.

She moved toward the door as she spoke. She did not want to go more deeply into what Leah might do, or should do. Let the two young creatures be together and God would do His work.

At the door she paused and looked back at Leah. The young girl had not moved. She sat, her long strong hands folded palm to palm between her knees, and her face anxious. "Talk to David about God," Madame Ezra said abruptly, and so saying she went away.

In a short while, even before Leah had finished pondering these words, Wang Ma appeared at the door.

"Our mistress bids you come to the peach garden," she said, and stood stolidly waiting while Leah rose, and then led her southward to that place.

The peach garden was David's favorite spot, as Madame Ezra knew, and thither she had gone when she left Leah. She saw him standing under a blooming peach tree, alone, a puzzled look on his face.

"David, my son," she said tenderly.

"Yes, Mother?" His reply was ready, but his mind was far away.

Death seemed remote here in the garden. The Sabbath air was quiet. The high wall of the great compound cut off even the noise of the streets. Usually David disliked silence. Not finding Peony here, he would on any other day have hastened out of the gate to find friends or to walk about the streets seeing what new thing had come into the city overnight. The city was halfway between north and south, and travelers stopped here to rest and refresh themselves and to enjoy the good inns. Fakirs and jugglers with all the tricks of India at their finger tips, or troupes of wandering actors from Peking, played at the temple grounds every day or wandered into the teashops to coax the guests.

But this morning he did not wish to see them. He wanted to stay in this house, encircled by walls whose great iron-bound gates were locked at night. How safe it was! Images of dead faces rose to the surface of his mind like drowned men.

"Your father and I have decided that you must begin the study of the Torah, my son," his mother was saying.

She had said this before and more than once, and he had always protested that he had enough to do. But now he did not protest.

"I am ready, Mother," he said. Inwardly he was surprised and even awed at the coincidence of his own will with that of his parents, but this he did not tell his mother.

"Today, after we leave the synagogue, I will invite the Rabbi to come here and stay with us for a while," Madame Ezra went on. "This will make it easier for you. He can attend to his duties quite as well from here." She looked up at the blossoming trees. "How lovely they are!" she exclaimed. "Leah enjoys them. I shall send for her."

She was about to say that David was to wait here, and then she did not. Let God bring these two together! She lifted up her heart in secret words: Let my son wait here, O God!

David caught the movement of her spirit without hearing its words. Sensitive and receiving, he felt impelled to stand where he was under the rosy peach trees, and there he stood while his mother, smiling at him, went away, and meeting Wang Ma, commanded her to bid Leah go to the peach garden. Thus David still stood as though his feet had roots into the earth when Leah came with her long swift step to the garden gate.

"Leah!" he said, and went toward her slowly. The morning renewed the magic of yesterday. The sunlight fell upon her, her clear pale skin showed faultless, and her eyes were dark. She had put on white this morning, a white Chinese linen that fell to her feet, and her girdle was gold and so was the band about her hair. She was beautiful, fairer than any lily. At the word he remembered the unfinished poem, and why he had not finished it.

Leah came toward him and put out her hands and he clasped them. "You look like the morning," he told her.

She lifted her eyes to him and her heart flew as straight as a bird from her bosom and nestled in him. From that moment she loved him altogether and him alone.

God bring his heart to me, Leah prayed. The prayer was so strong and so single that it sang through her body, and all her frame was tuned to it.

He saw her love in her eyes, and sensitive and still receiving, he felt her heart come into him, an overwhelming gift. Even had she been a stranger he would have been moved, and how much more when she was no stranger but one of his own blood and his own kind! They stood alone in the garden. Above them was the soft sky of the spring morning and against it were the tender hues of the peach blossoms and the small new green leaves. Against the memory, too, that Kao Lien had put into them yesterday, the terror of death and the cruelty of persecution, they felt a luxury of safety around them here in the garden.

David wavered, torn between some far past that he did not know and the pleasant childhood he had known. But he was no longer a child. That far past he shared with Leah. They were one in the bond of their people. He dropped her hands and upon the impulse of his blood he put his arms about her and held her to him.

She leaned against him, and bent her head against his breast and closed her eyes. Thus has God answered, she thought in gratitude.

And he, looking down on those dark curling lashes, wondered what he had done on this Sabbath day. Had he made a choice? Somehow he had, but what it meant he did not know.

Then suddenly he heard his mother's voice. "Children!" So she called.

They sprang apart as she appeared at the gate. "Come and eat before we go to the synagogue together, for it is time. David, your garments for worship—I have laid them upon your bed."

They followed her in silence, and somehow, to his own bewilderment, he was glad that his mother had come, and glad that the moment was broken in which he had held Leah in his arms. To his mother's questioning, smiling look he answered a smile, and wondered why he felt himself a liar.

In the house of Kung, while David was at the synagogue, Peony was talking earnestly to Chu Ma, rousing the pride of the old nurse, skillfully playing upon jealousy and anger.

In the night she had determined upon this visit. The evening meal before the Sabbath had been a strange one, silent and full of feeling in which she had no share. Even Ezra had been quiet, eating his food as if he did not care what it was. David and Leah ate little and only Madame Ezra had her appetite. Yet she too had said almost nothing, although she had looked often at David and then at Leah.

Peony, feeling herself excluded, had left the room early, and had spent the evening rewriting and polishing the new poem. She would take it with her tomorrow, as tender of some kind in the bartering she had to do in the house of Kung. Now in the service courtyard in this house she sat on a stool under a cassia tree, talking with Chu Ma.

"I ask to be forgiven," Peony said gracefully. Thus she began. Then she smoothed the straight fringe of her hair with her delicate fingers. The breeze had disarranged it.

Chu Ma, embroidering a small satin shoe, lifted her eyes from her work. "What wrong have you done?" she asked, and smiled.

"I did not come back yesterday as I hoped," Peony said. "But hear my excuse, good mother, and then forgive me."

So saying, she went on to tell Chu Ma how the caravan had come, and with the caravan the evil news that in foreign countries the kinsfolk of her master and mistress were being killed, and how mourning had filled the house and she feared it would be bad luck to the house of Kung for her to come here out of such mourning.

Peony looked sad and she dropped her pearly eyelids and went on, knowing that Chu Ma's sharp eyes were on her.

"And I fear I spoke too soon yesterday," she said very softly. "I fear I did not read my young lord's heart rightly."

She sighed and Chu Ma said stiffly, "Young woman, I cannot remember what you said."

Peony knew she remembered and she went on again, "I said my young lord thinks only of your young mistress. I gave her his poem—you remember? But now they have brought the Rabbi's daughter into our house, and I fear they have used God's witchery and they have made our young master forget even his love."

Chu Ma sniffed and got to her feet. She was very fat, and when she struggled upright scissors and thimble and silks tumbled from her. Peony made haste to pick them up.

"Let them lie," Chu Ma said peevishly. "You had better come with me and undo the damage you have done."

She went ahead and with her chin she motioned Peony to follow, and so Peony did, feeling that she was entering into a maze whose end she did not know.

The house of Kung was a large one, larger than the house of Ezra, and it was filled with generations of men, women, and children, all of whom drew their life from the same source. The women watched Peony from the corners of their eyes and the children stared, but she passed by them with her head bent modestly. So she came to the court where the young ladies lived who were the daughters of Kung Chen, the head of this great family. There were four daughters, but two of them were already married and away, and Kueilan came third, and after her had been born a child who was not the daughter of the same mother as she but of a young concubine whom Kung Chen took, and then was sorry he did because she fell in love with his head servant. After much pain, he had sent them both away, but his daughter he had kept.

Kueilan was playing cat's cradle with this little sister when Chu Ma came in with Peony following her. Now Peony had never seen this third young lady, and had only David's talk to make her know what she was. But she had no more to do than to look at the young lady, which she now did, without knowing that everything David had said was too little and that here indeed was the most beautiful female creature that anyone could imagine. Kueilan was childish in her looks, being only a little taller than the younger sister, whom Chu Ma now sent away.

"Nurse, why do you send Lili away?" Kueilan asked, and Peony heard what a sweet voice she had besides all her other beauties.

Chu Ma had no fear or reverence before her little mistress, and so she asked in a loud voice, not answering the question, "What have you done with the letter I gave you yesterday?"

"Here it is," Kueilan answered, and she took David's poem from her wide silk sleeve.

Chu Ma looked at Peony with reproachful eyes. "You see what hurt has been done!" she declared. "The child keeps his letter with her day and night." She turned to her mistress again. "Give it to me, child," she commanded. "It is worth nothing. I will throw it away."

Now Peony's quick brain had been working, and she saw very well that in this pretty girl she might have a friend and an ally to win David's heart. There was nothing here that was strong and fearless. No, Kueilan was a kitten of a creature, her little face itself was a kitten's face, the eyes wide and wondering and tinged with ready mischief, the mouth always ready to laugh. Just now she was looking half fearfully at Chu Ma. She clutched the paper and shook her head.

"I will keep it," she said willfully. "I will not let you throw it away. I won't—I won't!"

Chu Ma looked up to heaven and Peony saw she was preparing to be angry, so she spoke at once. "Young Lady, do not trouble yourself. I have only come for your answer." And to Chu Ma she said in a low voice, "I see how it is here. Do not be angry, Good Mother. Somehow I will mend the evil I have done."

So Chu Ma kept silent, only continuing to pout, and Peony went nearer and spoke coaxingly to Kueilan. "Have you written an answer, Little Mistress?" she asked. Kueilan looked down and shook her head.

"Shall I help you?" Peony asked next.

Kueilan looked surprised. "Girl, can you write?" she asked.

"I can," Peony said smiling. "If you tell me what you wish to say, I will write it down for you."

"I can write—but I don't know what to say," Kueilan faltered.

"Our young lady has never written to a man," Chu Ma proclaimed virtuously.

Peony was very gentle indeed. "You need not fear my young master," she said. "Why, he is the kindest and best young man. He never hurts anyone. I have been his slave all my life, and he has never beaten me or let others beat me."

Kueilan looked at her with surprise. "Even when he is angry?"

"He is never angry," Peony said smiling.

"Oh!" Kueilan sighed.

Then Peony took from her own bosom the poem she had written and she read it aloud in a soft sweet voice.

"Within the lotus bud the dewdrop waited.
At dawn the sun looked down and found her there.
He lifted her and set her on a cloud
And made her queen to rule the skies with him."

"Give it to me," Kueilan exclaimed. Her small face was lit with delight and she followed the four lines with the tip of her tiny forefinger. "I wish I had written it," she said wistfully.

"Lady, I give it to you," Peony said. "It is yours, as if you had made it."

"Will you never tell him I did not write it?" the spoiled child asked.

"Never," Peony promised. "But, Lady, copy it in your own handwriting," she suggested.

"Chu Ma, fetch my brush and ink and my silk paper," Kueilan commanded.

She sat in silence like a small reigning queen, allowing Peony to stand. When Chu Ma had brought the brush the young lady with much ado and ceremony made ready to write and then did write, her pink tongue between her lips, until she had copied the poem upon the silken paper, and had folded it intricately. Then she gave it to Peony.

"Take this to him," she said, and waved her hands in dismissal.

Peony bowed her head, exchanged looks with Chu Ma, and went away.

Now had she gone the way she came she might have passed through this house unseen by any except Kueilan and Chu Ma. But Peony had curiosity as well as wit, and so she did not go as she came. Instead she told herself she would see this famous house while she was here, and especially the great lotus pool that was said to be in the central court. There she went, stopped only now and then by a servant who asked her what she did. She answered coolly that she had brought a message to the young mistress and was looking for the front gate. "This place is so vast I am lost," she said laughing.

So she went on until she saw a round moon gate, and there she guessed was the central court. She tiptoed to the gate and looked in and saw a most beautiful garden. It was floored with green tiles and in the center was a long pool, and in this pool lotus leaves were pushing up their pointed buds. Around the walls stood peach trees and plums and the scarlet flowers of the pomegranate were in full bloom. Among them bamboos waved their fernlike fronds and little birds flew here and there, and looking up Peony saw far above her, over the high walls, a fine net spread to hold the birds.

She forgot everything, and stepping inside the gate, she walked softly to the pool and gazed into it. The water was clear between the lotus plants and gold and silver fish played among them. In the midst of her pleasure she heard a man's voice.

"Little Sister, where have you come from?"

Peony was startled and she looked up, and there stood the master of the house, Kung Chen himself. Now she must explain why she was here. She smiled deeply enough to make the two dimples in her cheeks appear and she said, "I was sent from the home of Ezra to fetch a pattern for embroidery, and then, wicked one that I am, I could not resist the temptation to come and see this court, of which I have often heard. Indeed, everyone has heard of it. Please, sir, forgive me."

Kung Chen stroked his chin and smiled. His face was round and kind and his small eyes were pleasant. He had thick placid lips and a broad flat nose. On this spring day he wore a gray brocaded silk robe, and since he was at ease in his home, he had no jacket or hat. On his feet were white silk socks and black velvet shoes. On his two thumbs he wore heavy jade rings and in his left hand he carried a silver water pipe. His eyebrows were scattered and scanty and his face was shaven, and this smoothness gave his full face a bland and open look.

"There is nothing to forgive," he said kindly. "Enjoy the garden and the pool as long as you like. I come here at this hour every day when I have eaten, so that I may look at my fish."

He pointed the mouthpiece of his pipe toward the water, and she looked into the clear depths where the fish swam serene and gay.

"How happy they are!" she said plaintively. "Here in your house even they are safe and well fed."

"Have you fish at your master's mansion?" he asked.

It seemed an idle question, but Peony recognized it for what it was, the beginning of other questions.

"Oh, yes," she answered at once, "we have pools and fish and we feed them. We have also Small Dog."

Kung Chen filled his pipe and took two puffs. "Birds are the best," he murmured. "They are beautiful to look at, they sing pleasantly, and when one takes them into the bamboo grove, they attract other birds. Every evening at sunset I bring my singing thrush to the bamboos, and after I have fed it fresh meat it sings and other birds gather on the net. I sit so still they think I am a stone."

"How pleasant!" Peony said.

"It is at such moments that the best of life is lived," he replied simply.

She waited. Between them was all the distance of their differing sex and age and station. But there was no embarrassment. She felt his ageless simplicity, his complete hard wisdom, and suddenly she trusted him. She said, still gazing into the pool, "I did not tell you the truth, Honored One."

His small eyes sparkled with laughter but he did not laugh aloud. "I know you did not," he replied.

She stole a glance at him and laughed with him.

"Tell me now," he suggested. "After all, you and I—are we not Chinese?"

She could not approach truth directly. "Sir, have you hatred against the foreigners?"

He opened his eyes. "Why should I hate anyone?" he asked in surprise. He paused and then proceeded amiably. "To hate another human being is to take a worm into one's own vitals. It consumes life."

"I will ask another question," Peony said.

"Why not?" Kung Chen asked, still very amiably.

"Would you give your daughter to a foreign house?" she asked.

"Ha!" Kung Chen said. He took two more puffs of his pipe. "Why not?" he asked again. He knocked the ash from his pipe. "Now let me proceed for you," he said. "Your house has a young master, and I have plenty of daughters. I take it my Little Three is nearest his age. I have good business with your elder master. He brings me goods from abroad that others cannot buy. My shops alone carry the goods. I shall soon have an exclusive contract—for which I shall pay much money, it is true. Were we related even in the outside fashion through my daughter, it would be good business. But—I am not a man to sacrifice my daughter for business. Therefore let us speak of rectitude and philosophy. When foreigners come into a nation, the best way is to make them no longer foreign. That is to say, let us marry our young together and let there be children. War is costly, love is cheap."

Now Peony cast aside all modesty. She admired Kung Chen very much and she felt proud to think he was her countryman. What he had said was wise and good. So she went on: "My young master saw the Third Young Lady a few days ago and he has not been able to eat or sleep since."

"Good," Kung Chen replied easily.

"He has written her a poem," Peony went on.

"Naturally," Kung Chen said.

"She has also written him a poem," Peony said.

At this Kung Chen looked astonished. "My Little Three cannot write poems," he declared. "When I bade the tutor teach her to write poems with the others, he complained that her mind was only a butterfly."

Peony blushed. "I helped her," she confessed.

Kung Chen laughed. "Ah-ha!" he exclaimed. "Do you have the poem with you?"

Upon this Peony produced the poem, and he spread it out on his soft fat palm and read it aloud, in a half singing voice. "Very good—for the purpose," he announced. "But I see you have not written the proper radical for the word 'rule.'" He pointed out the word with the stem of his pipe.

"Forgive me," Peony said gently.

"Leave it," Kung Chen bade her. "If it is too perfect he will suspect her. Now you had better deliver it to him. Love must be taken on the tide, before it ebbs."

So Peony took the poem and made her little bow and went away.

She felt so much more happy than she had when she came that she examined herself to find why this was so, and she found it was because Kung Chen had somehow made her feel one with him and with all who were Chinese. She was not solitary or alone. In the great sea of her people she was only one, but she belonged to the sea, and her life was not separate from the lives of all around her.

Oh, that David would join himself to us! she thought. Her mind grew clear. She would take him away from the dark, sorrowful people to whom he had been born and bring him into the pleasant sunshine in which her people lived. He would forget death and learn to love life.

Thus lighthearted, she went home again and to her duties. Ezra and David returned from the synagogue, and soon Madame Ezra and Leah came too, and the Sabbath day proceeded in the rites that Peony knew so well, and in which she did not share. But her part was to serve, and even as the night before she had set the great candlesticks before Madame Ezra that she might light them and usher in the sacred day, so now when they gathered for the Sabbath meal Peony brought the wine to Ezra and stood while he blessed it and spoke the Sabbath prayer. She directed the washing of the hands and then the serving of the food. When a servant newly hired was about to bring Ezra his pipe she shook her head and frowned, knowing that no fire must be lit on this day. In his own room alone Ezra might take the comfort of his pipe, but not here.

So went the day, and Peony would not let herself see how often David spoke to Leah and that even when he did not speak he looked at her long and thoughtfully. When evening came it was Leah whom David led into the court to find the first three stars of night, and he bade Leah declare the Sabbath was over.

Peony ran to light the candles and the lanterns, and never was she so glad as now to hear their greetings for another day, a good day, she told herself, a pleasant common day belonging to humans and not to a foreign god. She had spoken no word with David this Sabbath long, but she was not downcast. She could wait.

挑筋教

V

After Peony had left him, Kung Chen stayed on alone in his garden. By habit he worked long and steadily in the big room in his main shop, going early and coming home late. His fortune grew under his hands and he was a rich man. He enjoyed his riches, but he was not corrupted. When he felt his mind grow too single in pursuit of money he stopped, and for a whole day he did not go near his shops. Instead he sat here in his private garden, idle, his mind wandering where it would.

Upon such a day he had found Peony in his garden, and after she had gone, he sat down upon a green porcelain seat to watch the fish. Whenever he sat thus no one disturbed him. Time and again someone looked in the gate, hesitated, and stole away. In the midst of his crowded household Kung Chen's life was full of many cares and responsibilities, and here was a center of peace. But he was reconciled to all that was, and he considered himself to be, and indeed he was, a happy man. For him happiness was reasonable and attainable. On earth he desired wealth, the respect of his associates, satisfaction in women, and sons enough so that he need not be anxious if one or two died. He had all these.

Of Heaven he asked nothing. While he was content to believe in no gods, he knew he would be surprised at nothing that after his death he might find to be true. Thus he saw no necessity for the immortality of his being, but if he found immortality to be the lot of the human soul, he would meet the future as he met the present, with smiling certainty that he himself, as a good man, need fear neither god nor devil, did these exist. Ezra had inquired once as to his faith in God, and Kung Chen had replied calmly, "If there is a God and He is what you say, He will be too sensible to ask me to believe in what I have not seen."

To do good, to love justice, to grant that all men had an equal right to a pleasant life, these things Kung Chen believed in, and believing, he did all he could to perform his belief.

Now alone in his garden, greatly enjoying the beauty of the morning, the clearness of the pool, and the colors of the flashing fish, he made his mind empty and rested himself. Yet today the emptiness was invaded by the necessity to decide the life of his third daughter. If it were true that she had begun to think of the young man who was the only son of the house of Ezra, there could not be long delay. He must decide first of all whether he himself were willing for such a union. It was no small decision for a man to give his daughter to a family not of his own kind, whose name was not among the Hundred Names of Antiquity. But knowing the history of his people, Kung Chen remembered that others before him had done this thing, believing that only thus could all blood be made one, and he knew this was right. Nevertheless, he was a loving father even to his daughters and he did not wish to make the burden of life too heavy upon his Little Three.

While he mused something pretty happened in the pool before his eyes. A day or two before this he had observed that the female of a species of Siamese fish was heavy with eggs. He had directed, therefore, that a male be bought from the toy fish market, and yesterday it had been done. Now he saw the new fish swim proudly in the pool. He was a handsome creature, and as he swam he was surrounded with a cloud of floating iridescent fins. He swam near the surface, and the sunlight caught in his fins as in a tiny net. At this moment the small female saw him also, and she darted toward him with joy.

Now Kung Chen knew what was about to happen. He watched, smiling half tenderly at the small love scene that unfolded before his eyes. The male fish, when he saw the female, blew out a nest of bubbles that rose to the surface of the pool. The female came near to him, and he met her and curled his body around hers. In this embrace he turned her gently over and wrapped her in his golden fins. There was an instant of ecstasy, then they parted, and the little female scattered her eggs. The male caught each egg in his mouth as it sank, and soaring upward he thrust them one by one into the nest of bubbles. Again and again the fish met, mated, and parted, until the little female could endure no more of such ardor. But the male grew angry when she evaded him, and he pursued her to force her. When Kung Chen saw her distress he laughed silently, and he slipped his smooth hand into the water and lifted her into the palm of his hand and he put her into a porcelain jar of water that stood near to hold fish when they began to fight in the pool. When the male fish searched and could not find her, Kung Chen laughed again. "Do not be angry, little man—she has had enough of you!"

He sat down again, and the parted lovers went their separate ways. But the tiny play had set his mind to work. He remembered Peony's pretty face and he thought of her in the household of his foreign friend Ezra, and he thought to himself that it must be a strange place for so young and beautiful a girl. Then he remembered Ezra's son and smiled. Then he thought of his own Little Three and was grave again. He would not have considered such a marriage had she been his only daughter, or had she been Lili, his Little Four. Lili was his favorite, for she was the child of the woman he had loved. The wound this woman had made in him was healed after a fashion, but the scar would always remain. Kung Chen was not a lustful man. He had not gone after many women. He had accepted the wife his parents had given him for his youth, and he had lived with her well enough, but without great happiness, except in the children she had given him, four sons and three daughters. Then a few years ago he had suddenly loved a girl he had seen in a pleasure house, and he had brought her into his own home, with his wife's consent, and then it had seemed to him that his personal life was full.

A year ago he had discovered the girl with his own head servant, and when anger was spent and he came to full measure of sorrow, he comprehended that sorrow, too, is part of love. At first he had thought of punishment for the two who had betrayed him, but then he understood that punishment cannot win back a woman's love or a man's loyalty, and that it could therefore be only self-indulgence for himself. This he would not allow, and so he had called the two before him, and with a smiling face and kindly words he had told them to go away and set up their own family, and he gave them money and dismissed them, keeping only his daughter. When the pretty woman looked back longingly, thinking of what she must do without, now that she had chosen the servant instead of the master, Kung Chen's face was inexorable in its calm, and she knew that what she had lost she had lost indeed, and so she went away.

Now, although Kung Chen had ceased to think of love, the little romance of the fish brought it back to him for a moment, a forgotten dream, and he sighed. Love passed swiftly and no man could put off its end, and marriage had nothing to do with love. If his daughter fancied the young foreigner, and if the family welcomed her, as assuredly any family would welcome a daughter of his, then it remained for him a matter of business. If he denied his daughter to Ezra's son, it would be painful to do business with Ezra thereafter. The contract pending between them could never be signed. Ezra would take it to another merchant, and of good merchants there was a plenty in the city, though none so rich as he. It would be very irksome to see one of them benefit from Ezra's foreign goods. Yes, marriage could be a good connection for him to make with the House of Ezra. It would make their partnership something more than business. All business should have its human connections. The more human every relationship could be, the more sound it was, the more lasting. Kung Chen did not altogether trust Ezra as an honest man any more than he trusted himself. Where large sums of money were concerned, no man could be sure of any man. But if Ezra and he poured their separate bloods into one, then they were one, and dishonesty became absurd.

"Call it only shrewdness," he murmured to the fish.

Well, his Little Three would be happier in the foreign house if Peony were there, a young Chinese girl, to be her playmate. He must talk with Little Three, if the marriage was to be arranged. But first he should talk with her mother.

Upon this Kung Chen rose reluctantly and sauntered toward his wife's court, and he clapped his hands at her door. A maidservant came running, and seeing him invited him to enter.

"Is my son's mother at leisure?" he inquired.

"My mistress is sitting in the sunshine, doing nothing," the maid told him.

So Kung Chen went in and found his fat, middle-aged wife sitting in a large wicker chair, a tortoise-shell cat before her tossing a mouse it had caught. She looked up when he came, her face covered with smiles.

"Look at this clever cat!" she exclaimed. "It has caught two mice today."

"I thought you were a Buddhist," he said teasingly.

"I kill no mice," his lady retorted.

"You are not a cat," he said.

"No," she agreed.

"Nor the cat a Buddhist," he went on.

To this pleasantry she made no reply, only continuing to watch the cat. But Kung Chen did not mind. Long ago he had comprehended that hers was a pleasant little mind, not deeper than a cup, and he must not pour it too full. He had measured it exactly and they never quarreled. Now he sat down so that he could not see the cat, who was daintily crushing the mouse's bones.

"I have come to ask your advice about our Little Three," he began.

His wife made a gesture of impatience with her plump gold-ringed hands. "That naughty girl!" she exclaimed. "She will not learn her embroidery and I am sure Chu Ma does it for her."

"Little Three takes after me—I never liked to embroider," Kung Chen said. His face was grave but his eyes twinkled.

His wife looked up at him in simple surprise. "You were never taught to embroider!" she exclaimed.

"No," he agreed. "Had I been, I should have hated it. She is my daughter—forgive me!"

Madame Kung smiled, perceiving that he was joking again, and fell silent, enjoying the cat. Her plump hands lay on the lap of her pearl-gray satin robe like half-open flowers of yellow lotus. She had been so pretty when she was young that it had taken Kung Chen some years to discover that she was stupid.

"Well?" she asked after a long silence.

"I am about to have another proposal for our Little Three," Kung Chen said.

"Who wants her now?" Madame Kung asked. There had been many proposals for each of their daughters. Any rich family with a son thought first of a daughter of Kung.

"The foreigner Ezra is considering her for his son, David," Kung Chen said.

Madame Kung looked indignant. "Shall we consider him?" she asked.

Kung Chen replied in a mild voice, "I think so. They are very rich and Ezra and I have planned a new contract. There is only the one son, and Little Three will not have to contend with other sons' wives."

"But a foreigner!" she objected.

"Have you ever seen them?" Kung Chen asked.

Madame Kung shook her head. "I have heard about them," she said. "They have high noses and big eyes. I do not want a grandson with a big nose and big eyes."

"Little Three's nose is almost too small," Kung Chen said tolerantly. "Moreover, you know our Chinese blood always smooths away extremes. By the next generation the children will look Chinese."

"I hear the foreigners are very fierce," Madame Kung objected.

"Fierce?" Kung Chen repeated.

"They have religious fever," Madame Kung said. "They will not eat this and that, and they pray every day and they have no god that can be seen but they fear him very much and they say our gods are false. All this is uncomfortable. Our Little Three might even have to worship a strange god."

"Little Three has never done anything she did not want to do," Kung Chen said, smilingly.

"With many young men wanting her, why should we choose a foreign husband for her?" Madame Kung asked.

The cat had now consumed the mouse, except the head, and she took this and put it neatly behind the door. Madame Kung was so diverted that she laughed and forgot what they were talking about.

"Aside from business," Kung Chen said with patience, "I do not believe in separating people into different kinds. All human beings have noses, eyes, arms, legs, hearts, stomachs, and so far as I have been able to learn, we all reproduce in the same fashion."

Madame Kung was interested when he mentioned reproduction. "I have heard that foreigners open their stomachs and take their children out of a hole they have there," she said.

"It is not true," Kung Chen replied.

"How do you know?" she asked.

"My friend Ezra and I attend the same bath house and he is made as I am, except that he has much hair on his body."

Madame Kung showed still more lively interest. "I have heard that this hairiness is because foreigners are nearer the monkeys than we are." Then she looked concerned. "Suppose our Little Three does not like a hairy man?"

"Our Little Three will never see any man except the man she marries," Kung Chen said. "Therefore she will not know she does not like his hairiness."

They had now come to the crux of the matter and Kung Chen put the question to her. "Then if I receive the proposal?"

"If?" Madame Kung interrupted.

"When I receive the proposal," he corrected himself, "I shall accept it?"

It was partly affirmation, and she nodded indifferently. It was easier to yield to him than not.

"We have so many girls," she murmured and yawned, and he saw she was ready to think of other things and so he went away. From the gate of the court he looked back. She had composed herself for sleep and her eyes were closed.

For a moment he was half angry. It was in his mind to go to his daughter and speak to her, since her mother cared so little what she did. Then he decided against it. It was too soon. Better it would be to wait until he had the proposal in his hand. Better even then to consider a while longer—his Little Three was very young. Nevertheless, he felt himself so disturbed that he knew his day of rest was ended. He turned his footsteps and moved in his slow stately fashion toward the great gate that opened to the street. His satin-curtained mule cart waited always ready for his coming. The gateman shouted and the muleteer sprang to his feet. Kung Chen stepped into his cart.

"Take me to my countinghouse," he commanded. The muleteer cracked his whip and Kung Chen was on his way.

At the synagogue on that Sabbath day Madame Ezra planned while she worshiped. Her busy mind ran hither and thither about her plan. Purposely she had not told Ezra that she would invite the Rabbi to be her guest for a while. For how long? Who knew? Perhaps a week, even a month—at least until David spoke his willingness to take Leah for his wife. Had she told Ezra, he would have exclaimed that David must not be forced. Yet it was not force she planned—it was the will of God.

The will of God—the sweet peace of these words filled her spirit. But the synagogue was a place of peace. Ruin was not too evident—not yet. The curtains were old, but they were still whole, thanks to the women who mended them tenderly. Most of the Jews were poor, and their homes were clustered about the synagogue. Madame Ezra felt guilty sometimes that she did not share the poverty of the small community, all that was left of the once large one.

Where had the Jews gone? It was a matter to puzzle them all. Without persecution or any sort of unkindness from the Chinese, they had disappeared, each generation fewer in number than the one before. Madame Ezra was angry when she thought of this. It was, of course, easier to sink into becoming a Chinese, easier to take on easygoing godless ways, than it was to remain a Jew. All the more reason, therefore, for her to live strictly, in spite of her wealth—perhaps, indeed, because of her wealth. A poor Jew might be constrained to choose between God and money. She had no such compulsion. With such thoughts she renewed her determination. As soon as the worship was over, she would stay behind and go to the Rabbi. When her plan was secure, she would tell Ezra. It was not difficult to stay behind, for in the synagogue a high carved wooden partition separated men from women, and it was her habit to worship separately from Ezra. Leah was at her side, and David was with his father. She would send Leah home with Wang Ma while she herself went to the Rabbi.

Peace descended upon her as she saw her way clear, and she lifted her eyes to look at the Rabbi as he stood beside the Chair of Moses upon which the sacred Torah was placed. He wore long black robes and about his black-capped head was wrapped a fine white cloth that streamed down his back. He was reading aloud, while Aaron, dressed in the same fashion, except that his cap was blue, turned the pages. The Rabbi seemed to read, but actually he recited from memory, page after page. If he faltered, which was seldom, Aaron prompted him in a loud voice.

When the service was over, Madame Ezra discovered that the Rabbi did not come easily to the house of Ezra. When she explained, when she begged him to come at once, he shook his great bearded head. "Let your son come here to me to learn from the Torah," he said firmly.

Madame Ezra wailed aloud at this. "Father, why should I hide anything from you? What if he does not come? Just now, yes, he is very eager. He is moved by what Kao Lien said of the murder of our people. But he is young. There will be days when he does not want to come. He will make an excuse of a game or of sleep or of playing with birds or the dog or writing a poem—anything! But if you are in the house, he cannot escape you."

The Rabbi considered this. "I am a servant of the Lord," he declared at last. "It is of Him that I must inquire."

Now Madame Ezra, being a woman of impetuous nature, felt that she must say more. The will of God was clear to her and it must be made equally clear to this stubborn good old man.

"You know, Father, I say without any vanity that ours is the leading Jewish family," she now told him. She saw a certain smile flicker about the blind Rabbi's mouth and she hastened on. "Yes, yes, I know that Ezra is a man divided in heart, and I can tell you with truth that many a night I have wept because of his pleasure-loving ways. But I have tried the more, Father, to do duty for us both, and you know that is true."

"I know," the Rabbi said gently.

"Yet I cannot live forever," Madame Ezra went on, "and I must see my only son set in the way of his fathers. If he marries Leah—"

The Rabbi looked surprised. "Is he not to marry her?" he asked.

"Of course he is," Madame Ezra said with some impatience. "But we cannot say he is married to her until the act is done. You do not understand young men and women these days, Father. I assure you that David, left to himself, would be the best of sons, but Chinese girls are always looking at him. I shall not be sure until—"

"Does David look at them?" the Rabbi interposed.

Madame Ezra evaded this. "He will not look at anybody after he is married to Leah."

"Why does he not marry Leah at once?" the Rabbi asked innocently.

Madame Ezra sighed. "Father, to speak plainly, David must first want to marry her."

At this the Rabbi looked very grave indeed. "Does he not want to marry her?" he asked.

"A young man often does not know what he wants until it is pointed out to him," Madame Ezra retorted.

The Rabbi considered this for some time, sitting with his head bowed and his hands clasped on his staff. Then he lifted his head as though he could see. "What have I to do with this?" he asked.

"Nothing," Madame Ezra said quickly. "It is entirely my duty—and Leah will help me. But what you must do, Father, is to guide David into the way of Jehovah. Instruct him, Father, teach him the Torah, incline his heart to the Lord—and we will do the rest."

The Rabbi considered this. Then he said, "Still, I will go before Jehovah and inquire of Him. Leave me, my daughter."

Madame Ezra rose with vigor from her chair. "I will obey you, Father." Her rich voice was angry. "May it be soon that you come to us!"

She returned to her home and the Rabbi returned to the synagogue through a covered passage from his house. He knew every step of his way, and his feet fitted into the slightly worn hollows in the stones of the floor. It had been many years since he had seen the synagogue with his eyes, but he had other senses. Thus now he could smell mildew on the hangings, and he touched doors, table, altar, and he felt dust like sand between his too sensitive finger tips. By the soles of his feet he knew the floors had not been swept, even for the Sabbath. But it seemed to him that someone was here and he listened. Yes, he heard a slow deep breathing.

"Who is asleep in the house of the Lord?" he asked loudly.

The breathing ended in a snort. A half-strangled voice answered out of sleep, "Eh? It's only me, Teacher—Old Eli! I fell asleep. Is the worship over?"

It was Rachel's husband, whose duty it was to keep the synagogue clean.

"You should not sleep here," the Rabbi said. "The worship is long over."

"It is so quiet here," Old Eli said in apology. "Except on holy days there is no one here but you, Teacher, and this is not your hour."

"Come here," the Rabbi commanded him suddenly. He waited until he heard the man's shambling footsteps come near. Then he said, "Tell me—what of the silver vessels?"

Old Eli coughed the tinny cough of the aged. "Those vessels," he muttered. "Well—"

"Tell me!" the Rabbi said sharply.

"They're pewter now," Eli said.

"I felt the difference," the Rabbi muttered. "I knew it when I held them this morning." He lifted his head and upon his face there was inexpressible pain.

"Why do you trouble yourself, Teacher?" Eli asked in pity. "Young priests are always—" he broke off.

The Rabbi began to tremble. "Tell me what my son has done," he commanded.

Old Eli coughed and delayed and wiped his head and face with his sleeve but he could not disobey. He laughed painfully to show nothing was sorrowful and then he said comfortingly, "The pewter vessels are silver-washed and they look just as the old ones did. You know the Chinese pewter workers are clever and when the young teacher told them—"

"My son has sold the silver vessels from the synagogue!" the Rabbi muttered.

"But do not let him know I told you," Old Eli said in a small voice.

"And only I knew the difference!" the old Rabbi muttered. "Those who came to worship—"

"Not many come now, Teacher," Old Eli said to comfort him.

The Rabbi wavered and Eli tottered forward and put his hands under the Rabbi's elbows. "Come with me, Teacher," he said. "Come and rest. You are too old to grieve. Old people should be happy, like children. Now is your time to sleep and sit in the sun and eat good food and let all serve you."

"You talk like a Chinese," the Rabbi said.

He spoke bitterly but Old Eli laughed. "Eh, yes—but of my seven parts six parts are Chinese! Outside the synagogue they call me Old Li. I answer to the name."

As he spoke he guided the Rabbi tenderly out of the synagogue and into his house again, and there he sat him down and busied himself with everything to make him comfortable. He went to the kitchen and bade Rachel bring a bowl of broth, and the Rabbi let him do what he would. He sat like one stunned by a stone fallen upon his head. Only once he spoke while he supped his broth, and it was to say in the voice of a broken heart, "You are kinder to me than my own son is."

"Now, now," Old Eli said, "young priests—it's hard for them."

After Eli had gone, the Rabbi took these words and turned them over in his mind. "Yes," he murmured after a long time, "yes, it is hard for my son. O Jehovah! If another is to take his place, Thy will be done. I will go to the house of Ezra."

Thus it was the Rabbi found the will of God. The next day after this Sabbath, taking with him Aaron, he went to the house of Ezra. But he bade Rachel stay in his house and keep it ready for their return. To Aaron, his son, the Rabbi said nothing, either in reproof or in sorrow.

For three days Peony kept in her table drawer the poem that Kueilan had bade her give David, awaiting a proper time to give it to him. Such a time did not come. For after the Sabbath he withdrew himself, spending much time with his father in the counting-house. He was little at home, indeed, and when he came late in the evening, he avoided all women and sat alone in his rooms, reading. Peony waited for this mood to pass, knowing it useless to force his heart out of its hermitage. Then before she could find the moment she sought, the Rabbi came with his son, Aaron, and they were put into the court next to Ezra's.

Now David was cut off from her indeed. She served him in her usual ways, but more quietly than she had before, and her eyes were pensive. He did not seem to see her. He spent his mornings with the Rabbi and the old man commanded Aaron to sit with them too. Aaron, somewhat afraid in this great house where everything was under the eyes of Madame Ezra, did not rebel. Peony took care to be the one sometimes to bring hot tea to the room that she might see how it went with David, and she saw him poring over the books unrolled and open upon the table before him, and Aaron fidgeting and always ready to look up and out the door. This Aaron had learned to be silent whatever he did, so that his blind father could not know how his eyes roved and how he yawned. Then after a few days Leah came, too, to read the books. This was because David had told his mother how troublesome was Aaron and Madame Ezra grew alarmed lest Aaron anger David, and so she bade Leah be present, and if Aaron were disobedient, Madame Ezra declared, she herself would come. This Leah was to tell Aaron to frighten him, and she did.

When Peony saw that every day Leah was to be there at David's side she knew that she could not wait for an opportune time. One night when she took the last pot of hot tea to David's sitting room as she used to do until this change had come into the house, she paused and coughed. He was in his bedroom, and some new delicacy now forbade her to go in as freely as she had.

He came to the door at once to inquire what she wanted. He had taken off his outer robe and he stood in his white silk inner coat and trousers, his eyes clear, his cheeks red, and seeing him, Peony's ready heart melted with love.

"I bring you tea," she said softly.

"Why do you tell me?" he asked in surprise. "Why do you not bring it in as you always did?"

Then she came in, and after she had set down the tea she put her hand into her pocket and drew out the folded paper and held it toward him. "I have waited to give you this," she said, "but no good time seems to come because you are so busy now."

He took it and sat down and she stood while he read the poem, and he looked up and saw her standing. "Sit down," he commanded her. So she sat down and he read the poem over again. Then he lifted his eyes to hers. "It is very pretty," he said. "Did she write it?"

"With her own brush I saw her write it," Peony replied. Then she confessed to him, "I took her your poem—the unfinished one."

"You saw her?" he repeated, not seeming to care what Peony had done.

She nodded.

He leaned upon the table. "How did she look?" he asked.

Peony shook her head. "It is better not to speak of her."

"And why?" he asked. His eyes were inscrutable, and he continued to hold the poem.

Peony looked sorrowful. "She is gentle, young, pretty—so soft—she must not be crushed."

David flushed somewhat. "I do not know what you mean," he argued.

Peony looked steadily grave. "Ah, yes, you know," she retorted.

"Having seen you, she is ready to love you, poor little beauty, and when she knows—" She paused.

"Knows what?" David prompted her.

She shook her head and was silent and he grew angry. He threw the poem on the table. "Now, Peony, I command you to tell me what you mean. If there is one thing I hate above another it is a woman who hints in and out and around something that she has in her mind and will not speak it out."

At this Peony grew angry too, and she put her eyes full upon him and spoke passionately. "You must not see her—that is what I mean! She is beginning to think about you, and she must not!"

"This is not for you to say," he retorted. "Why do you want to part me from her?"

Secretly David was amazed at his own guile. Had he not allowed Leah to think he loved her? The memory of that moment in the peach garden when Leah had stood in his arms came back to him, as it had many times in these few days. It was welcome and unwelcome. Sometimes his blood ran swifter at the thought of her. When he saw her face, earnest and lovely, bent above the Torah, or lifted to look with devotion at her father, he was moved. And yet David was coming to understand that his marriage was no ordinary one. When he chose, it would be for more than himself. However he might wish he were like other men, he knew he was not.

"I am not thinking of you," Peony said, "I am thinking of Kueilan."

He felt suddenly angry with Peony. "You used to think of me!" he cried.

"Why should I any more?" Peony asked.

Her voice rang with a harshness he had never heard before and her face was smooth and cold. He was shocked. "Peony!" he said. "What has happened to you?"

She bent her head. "Nothing has happened to me," she said. "It is you—"

"But I am just the same," he insisted.

She shook her head. "Not now."

He put out his hand across the table and caught hers. She tried to pull hers away.

"Let me go!" she cried.

"No!" he cried back. "Not until you have told me how she looked!" This he said to cover his confusion.

There was a long pause. He held her hand, locking his fingers into hers, and she could scarcely keep hers from trembling. She wanted to pull her hand from his and she wanted him to hold it. She was about to weep and her heart beat hard against her breast. Then she began in a small voice, not looking at him:

"She—she wore a—a fern-green—"

"Her face," he commanded.

"But you know she is very pretty," she said.

"Tell me how pretty," he commanded.

So she began again. "Well—well—her mouth is small, the lower lip a little more full than the upper, red as pomegranate—such small white teeth—a small tongue—when she wrote the poem I could see her tongue like a kitten's, touching her lip." She paused.

"What else?" he demanded.

"Her eyes—very black—and shaped like apricots—eyebrows like willow leaves, you know—and her face more long than round, perhaps—tiny pale ears—she had a rose in her hair."

"Go on," David commanded.

"I leaned over her while she wrote—her breath was as sweet as a flower—and her little hand—it is even smaller than mine."

He opened her hand upon his. "You have a small hand," he said.

She looked at him. "Do not make her love you," she said pleadingly.

Now he dropped her hand and she let it lie there, lonely on the table. "How do you know she thinks of me?" he asked.

Peony withdrew her hand, and folded both hands into her wide sleeves. "I know," she said in a low voice, and drooped her head.

"Tell me!"

"That I cannot. I only feel it."

Now silence fell between them and David rose and went to his shelves of books and stood looking at them. He was not thinking of them, she knew.

"I wish to see her again for myself," he said, not turning.

She hid her smile behind her sleeves. "No," she said.

He strode to the table and struck it with the palm of his hand. "Yes!" he cried.

"You are very wicked," she declared.

"How do I know what I must do unless I see her again?" he asked.

She considered. "If I arrange it, will you promise me that you will not write her any more or ask to see her any more or do anything to break her heart any more?"

His eyelids wavered and he smiled. "I promise you this: After I have seen her I will make up my mind whether I want to write her or see her any more."

Their eyes met, full and long. Then she rose in her graceful fashion.

"Let it be a promise between us," she said firmly. She put her hand to the teapot, and feeling it still hot, she bade him sleep and went away, well pleased with herself.

In the midst of all that went on in his house Ezra remained in unwonted silence. He had been too shaken by Kao Lien's story to become indifferent to it, even though his bustling cheerful days dulled the edge of memory. In a strange way his wife was his conscience, and however he rebelled, he always feared lest she might be right in some fashion that he could not discern. Where business was concerned, all was clear to him. Where God was concerned, he was in waters deeper than his soul. Naomi made him remember his Jewish father, whom he loved and feared, a sad man, gentle in all things, but incurably sorrowful, for what reason Ezra never knew. When he was a child his father's sadness had made Ezra feel guilty, and yet somehow it was not his own guilt, but his Chinese mother's, which he shared. Yet he heard no word of blame, and certainly his mother felt neither sin nor sadness, nor, when he was with her, did Ezra.

After his mother died, however, the old sense of guilt rested on him alone, and partly because of this he had been willing to marry the young Naomi at his father's wish. He went very gravely for a while after his marriage, anxious to please his handsome bride; then, feeling that whatever he did he could not please her enough, he began to live as he had before, and he grew cheerful again. Cheerful he was, that is, unless the dark pool of old unexplained guilt in his soul was stirred, and Kao Lien had stirred it when he told of the massacred Jews.

Part of what went on now in his household Ezra saw, the rest his Chinese servants told him. He kept silent, comprehending everything because he was divided in himself. Thus he knew through Wang Ma's shrewd eyes that the Rabbi was dreaming a great dream and it was that if his own son, Aaron, should fail as the leader of the Jews, David might take his place. This indeed was true. The old man could not see David, but after he had taught him for many days, he said one day, "Come here, my son, let me know your face."

So David came near.

"My son, kneel as before the Lord," the Rabbi commanded him.

So David knelt, and the Rabbi touched his young face with the tips of his ten fingers, each finger so knowing, so conveying, that David felt as if a light played upon him. Then the Rabbi felt his strong shoulders and his broad chest and his slender waist and narrow thighs and, bidding the young man stand, he felt the straightness of his knees and his firm ankles and well-knit feet. He took one of David's hands and then the other, and felt its shape and grasp. Then he stood up and felt the top of David's head.

"You stand higher than I do, my son," he said wondering.

While this was going on Aaron sat sullenly looking on.

"Ah, that you were my true son!" the Rabbi murmured to David. "Then would I praise the Lord."

At this David felt pity for the pale ugly boy who glowered at them and he said, "It is not how a man looks, I think—or so my Confucian tutor has taught me."

"Is that man still your tutor?" the Rabbi asked jealously.

David hesitated, then he replied, "My mother sent him away when you came."

So Madame Ezra had done without asking anyone, but David hesitated because he did not wish to tell the Rabbi that he still met his tutor. But Ezra knew, for Wang Ma told him this, too, one night, chuckling as she did so.

"The young lord, your son, meets his old teacher in the late afternoon at his own house on the Street of the Faithful Widow," she told Ezra. It was her habit to take Ezra every night before he slept a bowl of thin rice gruel, which he drank slowly, so that she could gossip to him. In this fashion he learned much that no one thought he knew. He looked a little grave when Wang Ma told him this and she made haste to say, "Should your son not learn of our teachers, also?"

Ezra considered while he drank the hot fragrant rice, the bowl held between both hands. "I cannot decide," he said at last. "I think he should not, in honor to his mother, lest the Confucian undo all that the Rabbi does."

"How is it that you are so harsh?" Wang Ma exclaimed pettishly. Long ago their youthful intimacy had made her free with Ezra as she was with no other.

"Our God is a jealous God," Ezra replied.

"Gods are what men make them," Wang Ma retorted. "It is the Jews who have made their own God."

"Not me," Ezra said, suddenly smiling.

His smile was so fresh and frank in his black beard that Wang Ma, remembering the young man he had once been, smiled back at him. Then she leaned toward him and began to whisper.

"Do not let your fine son be unhappy," she said. "Yes, yes, you are a Jew, I know—you have to be—but tell me— No, you need not tell me—I know. When you remember your father was a Jew you are unhappy and sad, and when you remember your mother was Chinese you are happy and life is good."

Ezra could not quite allow this all at once. "Perhaps I am unhappy sometimes because I know I am not a good Jew," he said.

Wang Ma laughed at this. "You are happy when you remember

that you are a good man and a rich man and a clever man," she declared, "and what else matters?" She came closer. "Why, here in this city, everybody respects you for what you are. Who cares what your father was?"

She could always move him when she gave him her affectionate and robust praise. The approval that his wife never gave him this good Chinese woman gave with her whole heart and had given him since they were young together. He loved to be happy and she made him happy because she gave him courage in himself.

"Now then," she argued, "ought you not to be doing business again with Kung Chen? Ever since the caravan came you have been doleful. You are at home too much. Men ought not to linger about a house. Leave that to women and to priests. Kung Chen will be wondering what has become of you. He is impatient to put the new goods on his counters."

"You are right," Ezra declared. "In the morning I will go early to his countinghouse."

He got up and began to undress for bed and she took the bowl away. At the door he called her and she paused.

"Eh?" she asked.

"Let David visit his old tutor," Ezra commanded.

"Why not?" Wang Ma returned amiably, and so they parted.

So David continued to do in secret what he had begun to do one day when the Rabbi had demanded that he learn by heart the curses that Jehovah put into the mouths of the prophets against the heathen: "Thou shalt surely kill him, thine hand shall be the first upon him to put him to death and afterwards the hand of all the people. And thou shalt stone him with stones that he die, because he sought to thrust thee away from the Lord thy God."

Such words David learned, and he hated them even while he knew them to be the words of Jehovah. He dared not speak his hatred, and he found comfort by going to the little house of his tutor and sitting with the mild old man in his quiet court. There he listened to other words that the gentle Chinese read all day:

"To repay evil with kindness is the proof of a good man; a superior man blames himself, a common man blames others.

"We do not yet serve man as we should; how then can we know how to serve God?

"There is one word that can be the guide for our life—it is the word reciprocity. Do not unto others what you would not enjoy having them do to you."

While the Rabbi sharpened David's soul, these words comforted his heart, and at night he was able to sleep.

In the morning after he had talked with Wang Ma, Ezra woke filled with new energy and zest for his life. He loved to bargain in amiable and lively talk over a feast, and now he made up his mind that he would invite Kung Chen to a fine dinner at the teahouse on the Stone Bridge, which was the best in the city. Kao Lien must come too, and the three of them would talk together of new and better business. The times were good. There had been no famine in nearly a decade and they had a good governor and taxes were low, so that people had money with which to buy goods. Now was the time for trade.

He went out that morning without seeing any one of his family. Wang Ma and Old Wang served him together and there was no need for talk. Wang Ma, pleased with what she had done the night before, was all smiles and calm, and Old Wang was full of usual zeal to please his master, and the gateman was awake and clean and at his place, and Ezra's mule cart waited outside. It was a bright gay morning in summer, and upon the street the people looked lively and well fed and ready to be amused. Riding among them, Ezra told himself it was folly indeed to cling to the dream of that narrow barren land of his ancestors. A good thing they did leave it, Ezra told himself. He was learned enough to know that Palestine was a small dry place, and had now been possessed for hundreds of years by nomads and heathen. Should we go back, he mused, would they let us come in? What madness not to stay here where we are welcome!

He asked himself if ever there could be hatred against him here, and he could not imagine it. No people had ever been killed in China because of their kind. True, these Chinese could be cruel enough against a man they hated, but because of what he himself did, not because of his kind. Once when Ezra was a boy he had seen a man from Portugal torn in pieces by angry people on the street, because he laid his hands on a young girl who had come with her father to the city to sell cabbages from their farm. Ezra had run out to see the sight, but all that was left of the man was his head, wrenched from his neck. The rest of him was mangled meat. The head was plain enough, a big thing with matted curly black hair and big black eyes still open and coarse lips once red, now white, set in a thick dark beard. But the man's death had been his own fault, and all felt that only justice had been done. Had he been courteous as a stranger in their city, all would have welcomed him and none would have harmed him beyond staring at him with curiosity and perhaps with a little laughter at his coat of hair.

Ezra had already sent word of his coming to Kung Chen, and so the Chinese merchant was ready for him. He sat in the great room in his countinghouse, which was his place of business. The room was furnished with the most expensive goods, the floor of polished pottery tiles, the desk and tables and chairs of fine blackwood, carved delicately and without excess and inlaid with marble from Yünnan. The seats of the chairs were made comfortable with red satin cushions and at the windows there were shades made of slit bamboo woven with scarlet silk cord. Indeed, everything was shaped for comfort, but Ezra knew from the past that there was everything here, too, for business, cleverly concealed but near.

Kung Chen rose when Ezra entered, and bowed in the most friendly fashion. "How long has it been since we met?" he said kindly. "I sent my servant to inquire of your gateman if you were ill, but beyond that I did not wish to disturb you."

"I must ask your forgiveness," Ezra replied.

Each took his seat, and a door opened and a servant brought tea and a tray of sweetmeats of the best kinds and then he went away again.

"I hope there has not been a misfortune in your household," Kung Chen said after they had sipped tea and eaten cakes.

"No," Ezra said and hesitated. How could he explain to this

urbane and good man what had been going on in his house? Then suddenly he decided that he would try to explain and see what this friend would say. Could it be that the Jews were wrong to all eyes except their own? Perhaps this good man would help him to understand why they were hated in so many lands, and if Jews were wrong, then why were they not hated here, too?

So Ezra began in the simple brusque fashion that was the only way he knew to talk. "Now, my friend," he said, "I would ask you something but I do not know if I can make even you see what it is."

"Try me," Kung Chen said.

He looked so wise, so understanding, as he sat there in his handsome gown of dark blue satin, his smooth face smiling and his eyes content, that Ezra's heart went out to him as to a brother.

"My father came of a strange people, Elder Brother," he said. "I do not understand them altogether myself. Yet in one part of me I do understand them. You must know our history, perhaps—"

"Tell me," Kung Chen said gently.

"A small people, a few among many," Ezra said. "We were enslaved in Egypt—"

"How came you to be slaves?" Kung Chen inquired.

"How do I know?" Ezra returned. "The tradition is that we made Jehovah angry—somehow."

"Jehovah?"

"The God of the Jews."

A veil of gentle laughter passed over Kung Chen's face, but he spoke courteously and with respect. "This is the tribal god of your people?" he suggested.

Ezra hesitated. "My father considered him the God of the Universe—the One True God."

"We have never heard of him here," Kung Chen said, "but go on, Elder Brother."

"My father's people were delivered from slavery by the hand of one of our leaders. He promised us—that is, God promised—that if we obeyed Him perfectly we might return to the land of our fathers."

"And did your father return?" Kung Chen asked with interest.

"No, but some did," Ezra said hesitating.

"Then how is it that you are scattered again?" Kung Chen inquired.

"Our people disobeyed God—mixed with the heathen and so on." Ezra found it difficult to explain all this before the clear, tolerant Chinese eyes. He gave up abruptly. It was impossible. It did not sound reasonable.

"But what has all this to do with you now, my friend?" Kung Chen asked when Ezra was silent.

"I could say it has nothing to do with me," Ezra replied, "except that Kao Lien brought evil news that now our people are being killed—thousands of them—across the mountains."

"What evil did your people in those lands?" Kung Chen inquired.

"None," Ezra said with energy. Of this he was sure.

"Then why do they suffer?" Kung Chen asked.

"That is what I should like to ask you," Ezra said. "Judge of us who are here."

Kung Chen shook his head. "I have no answer," he replied. "I have never heard of such a thing. I should like to inquire of Kao Lien myself."

This was Ezra's opportunity. "I was about to invite you to feast with me this night," he said. "I will bring Kao Lien also."

"Thank you for your kindness," Kung Chen replied.

"At the Stone Bridge?" Ezra suggested.

"The best place," Kung Chen replied.

"When the moon rises?" Ezra said again.

"The best time," Kung Chen replied. "But do me this further kindness, that I be host."

After some polite argument Ezra agreed, and since business should not be discussed before a feast, after a little more talk he rose and bowed and the two friends parted, promising to meet again in the evening.

Each spent the day in his own fashion, but Kung Chen sent for some of the men in his countinghouse whom he trusted and he put certain questions to them concerning the small colony of Jews remaining in the city from ancient times. Two of the men were older than he and one was a partner of his father's time, long past his seventieth year and at his desk only because he was loath to leave it. His love of work shamed his children very much but they could do nothing with him, and so every noon his eldest son, disapproving and silent, brought him here, and before sunset the son came and fetched him again, to show that however stubborn the father was, the children were filial.

He was an old man, Yang by surname and Anwei by name, and Kung Chen talked with him and from him he found out about the Jews.

Yang Anwei said, "These people from the country of the Jews have from time to time taken refuge in our country and especially here in our city because it is near the great river. I remember that my great-grandfather said that once or twice hundreds of them came together into this city and our elders met in the Confucian temple to decide whether they were to be allowed to stay in such numbers. So many of them, our elders thought, might change our ways. But some of these Jews spoke our language, having been here before as traders, and they told the elders that their people asked for nothing except to live here quietly and according to their laws and traditions. They have a god of their own, but they do not ask others to believe in him, and only to be allowed themselves to continue their own traditions and laws."

"Why did they leave their country?" Kung Chen asked with lively interest.

To this Yang Anwei replied, "As I can remember, and I have not thought of these things for many years, it was because a warlike savage nation attacked them. Some of the Jews resisted, but others were for compromise." The ancient man paused here and shook his head. "I can remember no more," he said.

"One more question," Kung Chen urged. "Was it the compromisers or the resisters who came to our city?"

But Yang Anwei could not answer. Yet after a little while he said with his wrinkled smile, "I daresay it was the compromisers, for see how they have settled into our people! You have only to look at their ruined temple. Who goes there now to worship on their sacred day except a handful of them?"

"The Jews are being killed again in the countries west of the mountains," Kung Chen said.

Yang Anwei's old jaw dropped. "Why now?" he asked.

"That is what I ask and no one can tell me," Kung Chen replied. Then he went on in a different voice, "None of this matters to me, except that I am considering allowing my Little Three to join the family of Ezra. If there is something strange in the Jewish blood, then I must ponder for a few moons before deciding."

Old Yang Anwei heard this. "There is something strange in them," he declared. "It is not in all of them but it is in some of them. Ezra himself is a man like us, and indeed he carries our blood in him. But there are others who are different."

"What is the difference?" Kung Chen asked.

The old man hesitated and then he said shrewdly, "If they worship their god they are strange; if they do not worship him they are like other men. In my long life in this city I have seen that the worship of a special god makes a special people."

Kung Chen listened to this with the utmost silence and respect. There was deep wisdom in this old man, wrinkled and dried with age until his body was like a preserved fruit. But his mind was clear, and indeed he had become all mind.

"Then what we should do," Kung Chen now declared, "is to steal them away from their god, so that they will become like us."

Yang Anwei laughed noiseless old laughter. "Or else destroy their god," he retorted.

"How can we do that?" Kung Chen asked. "This god cannot be seen, he is not of stone or clay, as the gods of our common people are. He is a subtle god who lives only in their minds."

"Then destroy the god in their minds," Yang Anwei said.

The two Chinese looked at one another.

"It is not hard to destroy that god," Yang Anwei went on. "Let us be kind to this Ezra, let us grant him his wishes, heap him with favor, help him to grow rich, remove all his fears, teach him to enjoy our city with all its pleasures, urge him to know that however they ill-treat Jews elsewhere, here there will never be anything but kindness for him and his people."

"What wisdom!" Kung Chen exclaimed in admiration. "I pray you, Elder Brother, never leave our house."

"I thank you," Yang Anwei replied modestly, and getting up he took his leave and returned to his desk, where by the light of a small latticed window he spent his days copying entries of goods into a large ledger. His characters, which he brushed slowly one by one, were exquisite in their perfection. The work demanded about one tenth of his mind, and with nine tenths he thought about everything of which he had ever heard in his long life.

Kung Chen, left alone, sitting as motionless as a stone lion, for a long time considered what the old man had told him. He still wished to know why it was that Jews were killed, for he did not want to put his Little Three into the danger of becoming a widow. But even more than that, he wanted to know whether there were something hateful in these people, something that he did not see. He thought about Ezra, and he could not find anything in that hearty, good-natured, clever merchant that could be hated. Somewhat coarse, perhaps, not very learned, laughter too loud, but otherwise Ezra was a man as common as other men and as easily understood.

But was Ezra like his people? What of his wife and son? What of the strange old priest, blind, and yet able, the city gossips said, to see with the eyes of his inner ghost? This old man and his evil son now lived inside the house of Ezra, and what would they do to Ezra's son? Some Jews indeed were strange, Yang Anwei had said.

And then Kung Chen fell into one of his musing, perceiving fits of thought. How was a man called strange? A strange animal among other animals was feared and hated for his strangeness. He was a thing apart, one marked in some fashion different from others. Was this also true of the Jews?

He made up his mind that before he decided to let his daughter marry the son of Ezra he would know what a strange Jew was, the old Rabbi and his children, and he would talk with David himself.

Until then he would keep his Little Three safely in his own house. He would not marry her to make his business better.

That evening Kung Chen, Ezra, and Kao Lien met in the Stone Bridge Teahouse. The moon rose over the canal, and though the waters were foul, the moonlight turned them pure and beautiful as they flowed beneath the ancient and mighty bridge of white marble. The teahouse was so full of guests that talk was impossible, and Kung Chen called the proprietor and asked for a separate room that overlooked the canal. The man said every room was full, but when Kung Chen put a sum of money into his hand, he went away and took guests out of the best room, saying that those who had ordered it before and had delayed coming were now here.

So the three men found themselves alone in a small but cool and pleasant room just at the edge of the canal. The table was put before the wide-open window and they could look along the canal and see it winding its way among the overhanging houses.

"Will you have singing girls to amuse you?" the proprietor asked. He was a fat busy man, sweating and panting, bawling here and there and everywhere at once.

"No, for we must talk of important affairs," Kung Chen said. Then seeing the proprietor's downcast look, he remembered that these small pleasant rooms were used for the girls and so he said, "But you may choose three who sing well and let them sit in a little boat under the window and do their singing, and we will pay for their food and wine to the same amount that we would if they were here with us."

The proprietor thanked him and went away, and the waiter brought in the dishes that Kung Chen had ordered earlier in the day, first the cold small dishes and then the hot small dishes, and so in order to the sweet rice in the middle and then the meats and vegetables and hot rice at the end.

Ezra loved this food. In his own house beneath his wife's eyes he was scrupulous as to food, but when he was alone and free he ate whatever was praised by his host, and tonight his willing belly was warm and waiting.

Kung Chen was too wise to begin the evening with serious talk. He talked of the food, praised or judged the flavor of the dishes, discussed the wine, and when the sound of girls' voices, very sweet and clear, rose from beneath the window, he lifted his hand smiling, and the three men listened.

Kung Chen watched the faces of his guests without seeming to do so. Ezra's round face was plump and melting, his eyes were filled with swimming pleasure, and his full lips smiled. But Kao Lien's long narrow face did not change. He sat straight, his tall lean figure unbending, and he ate sparingly of the food that Kung Chen put upon his plate. He did not join in the talk, and in proud acknowledgment that he was not quite the equal of the other two he had taken the lowest seat opposite the window. But upon his face the moonlight shone most clear, for Kung Chen had commanded the waiter to put the candles in a corner so that they would not spoil the moon.

So through the evening; and as the courses came and went, skillfully Kung Chen led the talk. Each time the songs floated up from the canal, he fell silent and listening, and after every song Ezra was more open and more ready for warm friendship. But Kao Lien stayed always the same.

At last, when the feast was nearly over and fresh hot wine had been brought, a small pewter jug for each, Kung Chen told the waiter that the girls should be silent for a while, but that at midnight they might come into the room and sing their last song for the sake of kindness. He gave the waiter money for more wine for the singers, and then the door was closed and the room silent.

Kung Chen turned at once to Kao Lien. "On your travels, Elder Brother, I hear that you met war in some parts of the West."

Kao Lien answered readily in his soft composed voice, "Not war, only the persecution of my people."

"Can you tell me why this was so?" Kung Chen asked.

Kao Lien glanced at Ezra, and Ezra, warmed with good food and delicate wines and melted with the songs, exclaimed, "Tell him anything, Brother! This good Chinese brother is our true friend."

So Kao Lien said, "I cannot tell you why again and again through the centuries the Jews, my people, are killed. There is something strange about us."

Something strange! These were the very words of Yang Anwei.

"Can you describe this strangeness?" Kung Chen inquired.

Kao Lien shook his head. "I am a trader and I am not a learned man. We are a people bemused with God."

"Can you describe this god?" Kung Chen asked again.

"I sometimes wonder whether He is," Ezra broke in. "He cannot be seen, He cannot be heard—"

"Then why do you think he exists?" Kung Chen asked.

"Our old rabbis tell us so," Ezra said violently.

"Elder Brother," Kao Lien said in a low voice of remonstration.

By now Ezra was a little drunk. "Let me speak, Brother!" he exclaimed. "This is my best friend, yes, though he is Chinese—ah, because he is Chinese! When I am with him I feel happy and I am not afraid—I tell you, a man's wife can make him feel always sinful. Sin—sin—what is sin, Elder Brother?" The wine had come up in Ezra's head and his eyes were beginning to glaze as he turned to Kung Chen with this question.

The Chinese laughed his mild, rolling laughter. "We do not have this word," he replied.

Kao Lien said, "For us sin is to forget our God and our law."

"Let me be as other men!" Ezra cried. He began to weep. "I have always wanted to be as others are," he babbled. "When I was a little boy, they laughed at me—the other boys—because I was strange. I am not strange."

"Indeed you are not," Kung Chen said, comforting him. He perceived now that talk of business would be impossible, and he turned to Kao Lien. "Let us comfort our brother. You see how the wine has revealed to us the trouble in his heart. Shall we call in the singing girls?"

"Look at him," Kao Lien said. They looked and saw that Ezra, always volatile and ready to change, was now beginning to sleep, his head rolling on his shoulder. There was a couch in the room, and Kung Chen rose and Kao Lien also, and together they laid Ezra on the couch. There he fell fast asleep.

"Now," Kung Chen said, "let us talk together, you and I."

"Nothing that I say can be binding," Kao Lien said, somewhat troubled.

"That is understood," Kung Chen said.

Little by little skillfully he led Kao Lien along to telling, until by midnight he understood exactly what Kao Lien had seen, how cruel was the plight of the Jews, and how in Ezra's own house there was division between the Rabbi and Leah and Madame Ezra on the one hand and Ezra on the other. Between these two sides David stood undecided, and in his shadow was the weak and useless Aaron.

"Nor are these two sides unusual to our people," Kao Lien said thoughtfully. "Everywhere I find them, the Jew of the Covenant and the Jew who wishes only to be human and like any other man."

"What is this covenant?" Kung Chen asked.

"It is the covenant that we made with God in the beginning," Kao Lien said half sadly. "A covenant that we would be His people if He would be our God."

"You believe in such superstition?" Kung Chen asked in surprise.

Kao Lien looked apologetic. "I believe and I do not believe," he acknowledged. "I was taught the law and the prophets, and it is difficult to forget them. I deny them often and sometimes for years together. But I remember them, and I know that it is as a Jew that I shall die." He sighed. "Let us have in the singing girls," he said abruptly. "It is nearly midnight."

So the girls came in, three of them, all pretty and gentle and trained in the art of pleasing. Ezra woke when their music began and he lay there, his head pillowed on his hands, and he listened and looked at them. When their singing was over the girls hesitated, not knowing whether they were wanted further, but Kung Chen shook his head.

"Nothing else," he said laughing. "We are old staid men and we must go home to our wives."

He put money into each little palm and the girls laughed and went away and Ezra got up, sighing, and so they went each to his home.

Kung Chen did not sleep well that night or for several nights to come. The end of his sleeplessness was that he decided that he would not give his Little Three to the House of Ezra and he decided to call her to him and find out how much it mattered to her when he told her so.

After he had eaten his breakfast one morning, therefore, he sent a servant to invite her to come to him, and she sent back word that she would come immediately, as soon as she had brushed her hair.

Hearing this, he settled himself for an hour or two, and toward noon she came led by Chu Ma. He knew this little daughter of his was pretty, but each time he did not see her for a while, he forgot how pretty she was. Now he gazed at her with such pleasure that she blushed, seeing in his eyes the admiration of all men, even though he was her father.

"My father!" she called in greeting from the door.

"Come in, my Little Three," he said, and she sat down on a chair near him and Chu Ma stood behind her.

He asked her his usual fatherly questions, how she did and what she did, and he admired her silk garments and he asked her whether she had read any books, and how her pet birds were that he had given her, and all such small questions. She answered in a pretty voice, shy and smiling, child and woman together, and he told himself that this little creature must be wed only into the safest and kindest of homes.

So he brought himself to what he wanted to say. "My Little Three," he began, "the time has come to talk of marriage for you. There is your younger sister, Lili, to think of, and I must have you bethrothed first. I should have done so before, had I been a good father, but I dislike these early betrothals. Who knows what a boy will be when he grows up? So I have betrothed all of my daughters late, that I might see my sons-in-law as men. Now it is your turn."

At this Kueilan turned a deep rosy pink and she took her handkerchief from her sleeve and put it to her face and leaned her head against her nurse so that he could not see her. All this was as she should do.

"Master, you put her to shame!" Chu Ma exclaimed. "These things are not to be mentioned before a young lady."

"I am very forward, I know," Kung Chen said smiling, "but I prefer to find out from my daughters themselves how they feel."

So he went on. "Tell me, child, what sort of husband I shall find you. There is a fine young man in the house of Wei, just a year older than you. I hear good things of him."

"No," Kueilan said faintly.

"No?" Kung Chen asked in seeming surprise. "Well, then, I hear the youngest son of the Hu family is handsome."

"No, no!" she said more strongly.

"This young lady is hard to please!" Kung Chen exclaimed to Chu Ma. He went on somewhat gravely, "I hope you have done your duty. I hope you have not allowed her to see any young man."

Kueilan began suddenly to sob and Chu Ma looked terrified.

"Ha—what is this?" Kung Chen demanded, pretending to be angry.

Chu Ma fell on her knees before him and knocked her head on the floor and began to babble. "How could I help it? The young man saw her here in this house. She was going to the temple with our lady, her mother, and she sent me to fetch her a handkerchief."

"It was my fan, stupid!" Kueilan wailed.

"Her fan," Chu Ma babbled. "And while I was gone the son of the foreigner Ezra came into the hall."

"But I didn't stay!" Kueilan cried.

"I swear to my ancestors that she did not stay," Chu Ma said.

"Get up," Kung Chen said very sternly to Chu Ma. She got up and stood wiping her eyes. "How much has happened?" he demanded.

"Nothing," Chu Ma said. Then his eyes frightened the truth out of her. "Well, only a poem or two."

He turned to his daughter. "How dare you think of a young man?" he demanded.

Now Kueilan had a nice lively temper of her own, and it was her way to weep first and then be angry. So she stamped her foot and said, "I dare anything!"

"I will not have you marry a foreigner," Kung Chen said.

"I will marry him!" Kueilan cried.

"Oh, hush, hush," Chu Ma wailed. Kung Chen lit his pipe. "You say that because you are angry," he told his daughter. "But when you have considered what it means, you will not want to marry into that house. They are a strange people, not like ours. They are a sorrowful people, and they worship a cruel god."

Kueilan pouted. "I am not afraid," she declared.

Kung Chen did not answer his willful child. He had found out what he wanted to know.

"I command you to obey me in this one thing," he said after a long silence. During this silence Kueilan's anger had been cooled by fear and Chu Ma was frightened pale.

"You are to wait until I have seen for myself this young man," he told his daughter. "When I am ready, I will tell you what my will is." He turned to Chu Ma. "And you, woman, if you allow her to disobey me, I will send you out of this house and you shall not come back to it as long as you live."

Chu Ma trembled. "I will stay with her day and night," she promised. And she took Kueilan's hand and led her away.

挑筋教

VI

IN THE house of Ezra the Rabbi lived in blind ecstasy. Never would he have acknowledged it, yet it was true that the quiet comfort of the house, the ample food, the space and stillness of the courts comforted him and gave him the surroundings of pleasure.

Because he was there, Madame Ezra was careful that every rite of Sabbath and feast day was performed. She took care, too, to come in when David was with the Rabbi and inquire whether each rite was performed according to the Torah. For through so many years and generations in this heathen land she declared that even she had grown ignorant. Thus the rites of Passover and of Purim had mingled with the Chinese Festival of Spring, and the Feast of First Fruits with the Feast of the Summer Moon, and the sacred ten days of penitence before Yom Kippur came often at the Feast of the New Moon Year, so that even David escaped too easily from the penitence to pleasure.

The Rabbi answered her every question with zeal and care. Shut off from the sight of human beings, he perceived them only through the mist of his own feelings and longings. Thus it seemed to him as day followed day that David was living with him in his ecstasy, walking with him near to God, as he expounded the meaning of the Torah. True, he felt about him the atmosphere of something burning and strong, the presence of a spirit that he himself scarcely understood. What could it be except the brooding spirit of the Lord? He could not know that the conflict that he felt in the air about him when he taught the Torah to David. Leah, and

Aaron was their conflict. The Rabbi, accustomed to the blindness of his eyes, had other ways of perception. Thus he knew that when these three were not near him, the room in which he sat was empty with peace, but when they came in, whether quietly or with laughter, peace was gone.

He told himself that of Jehovah and His words he did not expect peace. "Before Jehovah our God there can be neither slumber nor sleep," he told David. "We are a restless people, O my son! It is our destiny to keep the world restless until all know who is Jehovah, the One True God. We are sojourners, transient between earth and heaven." He paused and then lifted his head high and held up his clenched hands above his head. "Hear, O Israel! The Lord our God, the Lord is One!"

The sonorous familiar words of the Shema rolling from the lips of the blind old man haunted David's soul. He himself was often divided between heaven and earth, and his soul was rent in two. It was impossible to answer the Rabbi. He could only listen, and listening receive into himself the meaning of the faith of his people. He was beginning to understand it now. What his mother expressed in her own practical way in her careful observance of feast days and worship days, in rites and rituals, in her refusal to accept the Chinese name of Chao even in this community where nearly all the Jews were known also by Chinese names—all this was the outward manifestation of the burning spirit of the Rabbi. These two believed that their people were a special people, set apart by God, to fulfill a destiny in the world. To their people, his mother and the Rabbi believed, God had entrusted a mission, the sacred mission of persecuting the souls of human beings until they turned to God.

Now the conflict among the three, David, Leah, and Aaron, came about thus. As the Rabbi perceived that David grew in understanding, unwittingly he put aside Aaron, his own son. At first he had asked each morning if Aaron were in the room, but now he asked no more. When David entered he turned only to him, and he put out his hands, restless and trembling, until he felt for himself the clasp of David's hands and until he felt his head and cheeks and brow. He must always have David sit near enough for him to touch. Aaron grew sullen as he perceived himself forgotten, and since he dared not complain to his father, he vented his temper on Leah.

"You are plotting against me," he declared when they were alone. "It is your plan to put up David as the rabbi instead of me, when our father dies, and he will be the head of our people. But you will be the true head, for you will rule David as that old she-Ezra rules Ezra."

Leah was so soft at heart, so purely good, that she could not answer this wickedness from her brother. When even as their father taught them the Torah Aaron silently mouthed his charges at her, her great eyes filled with tears, and still she did not speak. Aaron took care, or thought he did, to hide his persecution, but David was too shrewd not to see it. He loathed Aaron and paid no more heed to him than he would to a cur in the house. When Aaron came fawning on him and wheedling to go with him among his friends and share his pleasures, David pretended not to hear him or know his meaning. Aaron shrank back rebuffed, and with all the strength of his human nature he hated David for his pride and for the air of freedom in which David walked.

When David saw, now, that Aaron was oppressing his sister in some secret way, he stopped Leah one morning as they met near the threshold, and he said, "When Aaron makes his silly faces at you, why do you weep?"

"Because I know what he is thinking," Leah replied.

They stood in the sunlight, and David saw how smooth was her rich-colored skin, and how her dark hair gleamed. He had never renewed the signs of love since the day in the peach garden, for his soul had been more confused every day since. Her warm and loving eyes now upon him increased his confusion, and he could only stammer, "What is Aaron thinking?"

"I am ashamed to tell you," Leah said honestly.

Now had David been clear in his soul he would have demanded her meaning, but he was afraid to press her lest she tell him that Aaron was teasing her about love.

"Aaron is a fool," he said abruptly.

At this moment Aaron lounged through the gate, and David went in, and Leah followed.

Even Leah the Rabbi forgot. Every morning she came in quietly, and if the Rabbi did not hear her she gave greeting to him, and he answered as if he scarcely heard. Indeed, the Rabbi thought only of David. He spent the hours of the night in prayer and he woke from brief sleep feverish with eagerness. He told himself that he could not sleep until David declared himself for the Lord. He longed and yet he did not dare put to David the direct question. Yet after the two and three hours of expounding the Torah the question hung on his very beard: "David, will you be rabbi after me? Hear the word of the Lord, O my son David!" He could hear himself bidding his own son and daughter leave him in order that he might speak to David, and yet he determined that he would not speak until he heard the command of God ringing in his ears.

There came a day in late summer when it seemed to the Rabbi that until this command came he could not go on. It was in the eighth month, the month of storms, and the morning was still and hot. The air was heavy and it weighed upon the blind man with the wet heaviness of a fog. He was exceedingly restless. His old bones quivered and his blood ran through his veins with such speed that he felt giddy.

David came early that morning and alone. Leah had sent word that she was ill and Aaron sent no message but he did not come. The Rabbi, alone with David, felt his heart tremble. Was not this the day? He began to expound the book with care and tenderness, pressing near the young man in his zeal. David too was restless with the heat, and he could not bear the smell of age and decay that clung to the old man. As the lesson went on the Rabbi heard him rise and move about and sigh, and he grew frightened. Why did the Lord not speak? He lifted his head to listen, but the very air was silent. In his fear he made a mighty effort for calm.

"My son," the Rabbi said, when he felt David did not hear him, "let us go into the house of the Lord. The day is strangely hot, but in the shadows of the synagogue the air will be cool."

"As you wish, Father," David replied.

"Let me put my hand upon your arm," the Rabbi said. "We will go on foot."

The synagogue was not far. The houses of the Jews were clustered about it, and they had only to walk along a few streets to come to the narrow one that the Chinese called the Street of the Plucked Sinew. The path was familiar enough to David, and so was the synagogue, and yet he felt strangely that this was the first time he had ever entered it. Until now it had been a temple that he had often entered reluctantly, torn from play at the command of his mother. Now he came of his own free will—yes, it was his will today to meet God face to face. He had been putting off decision, but it must be no longer delayed. Slowly he paced his step to match the long slow step of the Rabbi. If he felt today the call of Jehovah, choosing him, commanding him to restore the remnant of his people, he would answer firmly yea or nay, out of what his heart said when he heard the Voice.

"You have put on your cap?" the Rabbi murmured.

"Yes," David replied. "I put it on when I come to you each morning."

"I know," the Rabbi said. "Why did I ask? You are faithful to the commands of the Lord."

Nevertheless he reached up his hand and touched the blue cap on David's head.

"You doubt me?" David asked, smiling.

"No, no," the Rabbi said quickly.

They entered now the gate to the outer courts of the synagogue. When the Rabbi came here alone, he went at once into the inner courts at the back of the compound, near which his own small house stood, but today he wanted to lead David through the wide front gate, which was opened to them by an old man who belonged to the Jewish clan of Ai. The gate faced the east, and immediately inside was a great and beautiful archway. Beyond it was still another gateway and beyond this another archway. On either side stood two stone tablets, each upon a stone base carved in lotus leaves, and upon the tablets were cut in ancient letters the story of the Jews and how they had been driven from their land. Beyond the tablet was the immense platform upon which the great tent was raised at the Feast of Tabernacles, and still beyond was the Ark Bethel in the most sacred and inner part of the synagogue.

All of this David knew, and yet this day he looked with eyes that saw for the first time the meaning of this place, set for a palace of God in the crowded heathen city and its many temples to other gods. The air was cooler here than elsewhere, and he felt it cool upon his flesh. Olive trees lined the courts, and the silence was sweet. The place was empty of man but it was filled with the high spirit of Heaven. Upon a tablet over the main arch were carved these words, "The Temple of Purity and Peace." Such indeed it was.

So they went slowly step by step, the Rabbi murmuring the Scriptures until David paused before a great stone tablet.

"How is it that the letters I see carved upon many of these stone tablets are Chinese letters and not Hebrew?" David asked suddenly.

The Rabbi sighed. "Alas, our people have forgotten the language of our fathers! When I die, there will not be one left who can read the word of the Lord."

He paused, waiting for David to speak, to offer himself. The Rabbi had hoped each day that David would ask to learn the Hebrew language, but he had not asked and he did not now.

"Yet the story of our people is very plain upon this stone," David said instead. And he began to read aloud the Chinese letters:

> *"Abraham, the patriarch who founded the religion of Israel, was of the nineteenth generation from P'anḵu Adam."*

"You see," the Rabbi broke in. "P'anku is the Chinese first man. Yet even those who carved these tablets put his name with Adam."

David smiled and read on:

> *"From the creation of Heaven and earth the patriarchs handed down the tradition that they received. They made no image, flattered no spirits and ghosts, and believed in no superstitions. Instead*

they believed that spirits and ghosts cannot help men, that idols cannot protect them, and that superstitions are useless. So Abraham meditated only upon Heaven."

David's strong young voice fell silent. But to meditate upon Heaven was what his Chinese tutor also taught him! For some weeks now he had not gone to the Confucian, but the last time he had gone was on the midsummer feast night. The sky had been full of stars, and the old man had lifted his face to them.

"We can meditate upon Heaven," he had murmured, "but we cannot know it."

"The synagogue has twice been swept away by flood from the Yellow River," the old rabbi said, not knowing David's thoughts. "Yet these great stones have been preserved. Our God does not allow the name of His people to perish."

They walked on slowly. The sky had darkened, and looking up, David saw hovering above the walls black clouds edged with silver.

"It will rain and then the air will be cooler everywhere," he answered.

The Rabbi paid no heed. "Come with me into the Holy of Holies," he said with solemn excitement. "I want to put the Torah into your hands, my son."

They stepped over the high threshold and into the dim innermost chamber of the synagogue, and crossing the smooth tiles of the floors, they went toward the Ark. Before it stood a table, and above it was an archway, made in three parts, upon which was written:

Blessed be the Lord,
The God of Gods, the Lord of Lords,
The Great, the Mighty and Terrible God.

These words the Rabbi spoke aloud in a deep voice, and suddenly, like an echo from heaven, thunder rolled through the synagogue. The Rabbi stood still, lifting his face until his beard was thrust high. Then in the silence after the thunder he parted the curtains, and David saw the cases that held the Torah. They were gilt-lacquered, and the hinges were gilded, and there was a flame-shaped knob on each cover.

"These are the sacred books of Moses," the Rabbi said in his grave voice, "and there are twelve, one for each of the tribes of our people, and the thirteenth is for Moses."

So saying, he opened the thirteenth box, which like the others was in the shape of a long cylinder, and he set it upon a high carved chair, which was the Chair of Moses. Then he opened the cylinder and he took out the book.

"Put out your hands," he commanded David.

David put them out and the Rabbi placed upon them the ancient book, shaped like a roll of thick paper.

"Open it," he commanded, and David opened it.

"Can you read it?" the Rabbi asked.

"No," David said. "You know the letters are Hebrew."

"I will teach them to you," the Rabbi declared. "To you, my true son, I will teach the mysteries of the tongue in which God gave the law to Moses, our ancestor, who carried the law down from the mountain to our people, who waited in the valley."

The thunder was rolling again around the synagogue and the Rabbi bowed his head. When there was silence he spoke on. "It is you who will speak to our people in the words of the law, a second Moses, O my son."

Then lifting his head and raising his hands high above it, the Rabbi cried out words that were used by the people when they worshiped in the synagogue.

"Hear ye, O Israel! The Lord our God, the Lord is One!"

His great voice drew out the solemn word One into a long wail, and again the thunder roared.

Who can say how this thunder, echoing the Rabbi's voice, might have sealed the soul of David, the son of Ezra? But even as his soul trembled, even as he waited for the still small voice of God to come out of the storm, his eyes fell upon an inscription carved into a little tablet. There were many such inscriptions set into tablets, the gifts of Jews who had wished through hundreds of years to leave something of themselves in the synagogue. This tablet was less than any other, a dusty bit of marble without ornament. But upon its face a Jew, now forgotten and dead, had put this part of himself into these words that now fell under David's eyes:

> *Worship is to honor Heaven, and righteousness is to follow the ancestors. But the human mind has always existed before worship and righteousness.*

The wickedness in these last words shook the soul of David as though he had heard laughter in this sacred place. Some old Jew whose blood was mixed too strongly with ribald Chinese blood had written those words and had commanded them to be carved upon stone and set even into the synagogue! David laughed aloud, and he was not able to keep back his laughter.

The Rabbi heard it and was shocked. "Why do you laugh?" he demanded, and his voice was very sharp.

"Father," David said honestly, "I see something that makes me laugh."

"Give me back the Torah!" the Rabbi said angrily.

"Forgive me," David said.

"May the Lord forgive you!" the Rabbi retorted. He took the Torah from David's hand and fastened it into the case and put it into its place in the Ark. He felt confused and wounded. All his ecstasy was stopped, giddiness seized him, and he leaned upon the chair.

"Leave me," he said shortly to David. "I will pray for a while."

"Shall I not wait for you?" David asked, ashamed but still smiling.

"I will find the way alone," the Rabbi said, and so stern was his voice and look that David left him.

A clear cool wind swept through the synagogue as David walked away, and he breathed it in. He was dazed by the sudden change in the air, in himself, and he scarcely knew what had happened. *The human mind has always existed before worship and righteousness*—the human mind, his mind! He stood at the gate of the synagogue, at the top of the steps, and his spirit, held taut and high for so many days, was suddenly loosed like a stone from a sling. The storm had passed over the city and the air was cool and bright, the sun was shining down on the wet roofs and upon the wet stones of the streets, and the people looked gay and cheerful and busy.

At this moment as the sun poured into the streets after the storm he chanced to see Kung Chen. The merchant had been held in the teashop by the rain beyond his usual hour for drinking his mid-morning tea, and now he was choosing his path over the wet cobblestones toward his countinghouse. He was his usual calm and satisfied self, and in the new cool air his summer robe of cream-colored silk was bright and his black silk shoes were spotless. In the collar of his robe he carried his folded black fan, and his dark hair was combed smoothly back from his shaven forehead and braided in a queue with a black silk tasseled cord. A handsomer man of his age could not have been found in the city, or one more pleasant to look upon. His all-seeing eyes fell upon David and he paused to call his name.

"How is my elder brother, your father?" Kung Chen inquired.

"Sir, I have not seen my father this morning," David replied. He ran down the steps, drawn to Kung Chen as inevitably as a child is drawn to a smiling and cheerful adult. Indeed, it was comforting to allow himself to feel young and even childish before this powerful and yet kindly man. In these days when he had been so closely with the Rabbi he had been stretched and lifted beyond himself.

"Have you been worshiping your god?" Kung Chen asked in the same voice that he might have used in asking if David had been to a theater.

"The Rabbi has been teaching me," David replied.

Kung Chen hesitated. Then he said in a voice of curiosity, "I have always wanted to see inside your temple, but I suppose it would not be allowed."

"Why not?" David replied. "If it is your wish, please come in now."

He had no desire to return to the synagogue, and yet he was glad of a reason to stay with Kung Chen, and so half proudly he led the way up the steps again, and the old gateman, looking doubtful, opened the wide doors and let them pass in.

How different did the synagogue now look! The sun was pouring down upon it out of a bright sky, and Kung Chen did not feel fear or reverence but only courtesy. He looked at everything with lively eyes and he read the inscriptions in a loud cheerful voice, approving all.

Thus he read aloud from the vertical tablets such lines as these:

> *Acknowledging Heaven, Earth, Prince, Parent, and Teacher, you are not far from the correct road of Reason and Virtue.*
>
> *When looking up in contemplation of what Heaven has created, I dare not withhold my reverence and my awe.*
>
> *When looking down, in worship of our ever-living Lord, I ought to be pure in mind and body.*

These sayings were hung on the pillars of the central door of the Front Great Hall, and Kung Chen admired them very much. He turned to David and said with surprise and pleasure, "Why, young sir, your people and mine believe in the same doctrines! What is there different between us?"

And before David could answer he read aloud another that said this:

> *From the time of Abram, when our faith was established, and ever after, we the Jews of China have spread the knowledge of God and in return we have received the knowledge of Confucius and Buddha and Tao.*

Kung Chen wagged his big smooth head in approval, and so he went from one tablet to another, increasing his approval of each. But the one that he liked best was one that said:

> *Before the Great Void, we burn the fragrant incense, entirely forgetting its name or form.*

Side by side David and the great Chinese walked through the synagogue, and the heart of each pondered its own desires. Kung Chen said to himself that he need not fear to give his daughter to a house where the wisdom was so nearly that of the Sages, and David felt that the weight that had descended upon him in the days since Kao Lien came back from the West was somehow gone. The very presence of Kung Chen was cheering and enlightening, and the bands about David's spirit loosened. Surely this good man could not be altogether wrong, and perhaps the Rabbi was not altogether right. Small glints of hope and comfort began to creep into the crevices of David's being, and after these many days without pleasure he longed for it again. He longed suddenly to go out into the sunlit streets, where the dust was laid by the rain, and wander about in his old idle fashion. He felt as if he had been away on a journey into a dark land and that he was home again. And he knew that it was Kung Chen who made him feel so, this ample, slow-moving, kindly figure at his side.

Now as they walked, Kung Chen admired all he saw, stone monuments and memorial archways, the big lotus-shaped stone bowls placed in the courtyards, the bathing house, and the slaughterhouse. Of these last two he inquired of David, wondering that in a temple these should be found. When he heard that the Jews believed the body must be clean before the rites were observed, he nodded his head, approving, but he wondered when David said that their faith demanded that the sinews be plucked from an animal killed for sacrifice, and he asked why this was. When he heard the story of one called Jacob who wrestled with an angel, he smiled his unbelieving smile. "For myself," he said, "I am inclined against taking life even for worship." Then he laughed aloud. "So I say, and yet when a dainty dish of pork is set before me, I eat it as eagerly as the next man does! We are all human."

By this time David was beginning to be troubled lest the Rabbi had not left the inner chamber. What if he were there, and what if he were angry that David returned bringing a Chinese with him? He walked slowly and delayed at every possible place, but he was compelled at last to come to the door of the Holy of Holies, and there indeed he saw the Rabbi before the Ark, in prayer. To his shame he was glad for this moment that the old man was blind, so that if he lifted his head he could not see. Kung Chen stopped on the threshold and looked at David.

"The old teacher!" he whispered.

"He is praying," David whispered back.

They were about to withdraw, but the Rabbi lifted his head. His hearing was very acute and he had heard both footsteps and whispering voices.

"David, my son," he called in a loud voice, "you have come back!"

The Rabbi had regretted his anger and he had stood before the Lord, praying that David come, and he thought now that his prayer was answered. He went toward the door, his hands outstretched. David would have drawn back, but Kung Chen's ready mercy overflowed and he stepped forward.

"Old Teacher, please be careful," he said.

The Rabbi stopped and his hands dropped. "Who is here?" he demanded.

Kung Chen felt no wrong, and so he answered at once. "It is I, Kung Chen the merchant. I saw my friend Ezra's son at the gate, and being curious, I asked him to bring me inside your temple."

At this the Rabbi was suddenly overcome with rage. He cried out to David, "How is it that you bring a stranger into this place?"

Kung Chen might have let this go as the superstition of an old priest, but he felt it only just to defend David, and so he said in an amiable voice, "Calm yourself, Old Teacher. It was not he who asked me to come. Blame me."

"You are a son of Adam," the Rabbi said with sternness, "but he is a son of God. The blame is on him."

Kung Chen was much surprised. "I am no son of Adam," he declared. "Indeed, there is no such name among my ancestors."

"The heathen people are all the sons of Adam," the old Rabbi declared.

Now Kung Chen felt his own wrath rising. "I do not wish to be called the son of a man of whom I have never heard," he declared. His voice was mild, for he would have considered it beneath him as a superior man to show his anger, especially to an old man. But it boiled in him, and he had much trouble to hide it as he went on. "Moreover, I do not like to hear any man call only himself and his people the sons of God. Let it be that you are the sons of your god if you please, but there are many gods."

"There is only one true God, and Jehovah is His name," the Rabbi declared, trembling all over as he spoke.

"So the followers of Mohammed in our city declare," Kung Chen said gravely, "but they call his name Allah. Is he the same as your Jehovah?"

"There is no god beside our God," the Rabbi said in a loud high voice. "He is the One True God!"

Kung Chen stared at him. Then he turned to David. "This old teacher is mad," he observed. "We must pity him. So it often happens when men think too much about gods and fairies and ghosts and all such imaginary beings. Beyond this earth we cannot know."

But the Rabbi would not have his pity. "Beyond this earth we can know!" he cried in a loud firm voice. "It is for this that God has chosen my people, that we may eternally remind mankind of Him, Who alone rules. We are gadfly to man's soul. We may not rest until mankind believes in the true God."

All the anger faded from Kung Chen's heart and he said in the kindest voice, "God—if there is a God—would not choose one man above another or one people above another. Under Heaven we are all one family."

When the Rabbi heard this he could not bear it. He lifted up his head and he prayed thus to his God: "O God, hear the blasphemy of this heathen man!"

David had stood with bent head and clasped hands while the two elders argued, and he said nothing. His soul hung between these two men.

Now Kung Chen turned to him. "Let the Old Teacher pray thus, if it eases him. I believe in no gods and so none can hurt me or mine. . . . I bid you both farewell."

He moved with great dignity to the door and then eastward toward the gate. David was torn between pity and shame, and he ran after Kung Chen and caught him at the gate.

"I beg your forgiveness," he said.

Kung Chen turned his benign face to the young man. There was no trace of anger left in him. He spoke very gravely. "I feel no wrong and so there is no need to forgive. Yet for your sake I will say something. None on earth can love those who declare that they alone are the sons of God."

With these words Kung Chen went his way. David hesitated on the threshold, and the words burned themselves into his brain. He could not to save himself return to the Rabbi. Yet the desire for careless pleasure was gone from him, too. The weight of his people fell on him again with the heaviness of all the ages.

He felt a sob come into his throat, and turning back into the synagogue he hid himself inside an archway and wept most bitterly.

On that sultry summer morning Peony saw David go away with the Rabbi, and she ran to peer through a window and see if Leah was with them. But Leah sat working upon her embroidery, and so Peony went away again unseen. Late in the day David came home again, and she went to him to ask if he wished anything, but he sent her away, wanting to be alone.

Everybody in this house wants to be alone, she thought half angrily. She felt a strange impatience fall upon her. Since she had given him the poem, David had said no more to her. He had not sent for her once, nor had he written any poem. All that Peony knew was this: The poem he thought Kueilan had written was in the drawer of his desk. Each day when he was gone, she opened the drawer and saw it there, under a jade paperweight. She could only wait until the day was over.

Now Peony had clever skill in her fingers to smooth away an ache in heart or muscle. Wang Ma had taught her this, and she taught her the centers of pain in the body and the long lines of nerves and veins. Sometimes Peony smoothed out a pain for Madame Ezra and sometimes for David. To her surprise Ezra, on this hot day, although the storm had cooled the air, sent for her to press his temples and soothe his feet. Never before had she known this stout hearty master of hers to have pain anywhere. But this night when she entered his room he sat in his chair, and when she stepped behind him to begin her work she felt the fullness of blood in his temples and the hard knot of pain at the base of his skull.

"Your spirit is distressed, Master," she murmured. She could discern the kinds of pain there were in a human body, some the pains of flesh and some the pains of spirit and still others those of the mind.

"I am distressed," Ezra answered. He leaned his head back and closed his eyes and allowed her to do her work.

She did not speak again, nor for a while did he, and she stroked the nerves and pressed the veins in his head and persuaded the blood to recede.

Then he said suddenly, "What soft power there is in your hands! Who taught you this wisdom?"

"Wang Ma taught me some, but some I know of myself," she replied.

"How do you know?" he asked. His eyes were still closed, but his lips smiled slightly.

"I am sometimes sorrowful, too," she said in her cheerful little voice.

"Now, now," he said playfully. "You, here in this house where we all are kind to you?"

"You are kind," she said, "but well I know I do not belong in this house. I am not born here, nor am I of your blood."

"But I bought you, Peony," Ezra said gently.

"Yes, you paid money for me," she answered, "but that does not make me yours. A human creature cannot be bought whole."

He seemed to muse on this while she stroked the strong muscles of his neck. Then stooping she took off his shoes and began to heal his feet. He sat up refreshed while she did this and he said, "Yet you are like my own daughter. See, if I did what was right, I would not let you heal my feet. Your people would think it strange. But in the country of my people a daughter may do what you do.

Yes, and in India too. When I once went with the caravan through India, I saw this healing for the feet."

"The feet bear the burden of the body, the head the burden of the mind, and the heart the burden of the spirit," Peony answered sweetly. "And it does not matter what my people say. What would they say? Only that it is a foreign custom. You know how kind my people are. They allow all."

"I know," Ezra said. "They are the kindest people in the world, and to us the best."

He sighed so deeply that Peony knew his thoughts. Nevertheless, she asked, "Why do you sigh, Master?"

"Because I do not know what is right," Ezra replied.

She laughed softly at this. "You are always talking of right and wrong," she said. Now she was pressing the soles of his feet. They were hard and broad, but supple. She went on in her cheerful way. "Yet what is right except that which makes happiness and what is wrong except that which makes sorrow?"

"You speak so because you are not confused between Heaven and earth," he said.

"I know I belong to earth," she said simply.

"Ah, but we belong to Heaven," he rejoined.

Now she had finished her task and she put his shoes on his feet again. "You and I speak of Heaven and earth," she said, "but we are thinking of something else."

"Of what?" he asked. But he knew.

She sat back on her heels and looked up at him. "We are thinking of David," she said softly.

"You think of him, too," Ezra said.

"I am always thinking of him," Peony replied. Then kneeling and looking at him she decided that she would tell him everything. "I know that it is foolish of me, Master, but I love him," she said simply.

"Of course you love him," Ezra said, in his usual hearty voice. "You have grown up as brother and sister."

"Yes, but we are not brother and sister," she said. "It is not thus that I love him."

Ezra looked uncomfortable indeed. Had he taken thought he must have known that a young, soft, pretty girl could not live and serve David without love. He remembered his own youth, when he had felt a fancy for Wang Ma. It made him blush to think of it now, for so long had she been no more than a serving woman. But he could remember very well himself about sixteen and she the same age, when she had been beautiful enough to make him tell his father that he would have no other woman. Flower of Jade had been her name. Flower of Jade! When he remembered this name something long dead stirred again. She had been prettier than Peony, her skin more fair, her frame taller, her nose straighter, and her lips more delicate.

His father had roared with laughter. "But the girl is a bondmaid!" he had shouted. "My son cannot marry a servant!"

"She will not be a servant if I make her my wife," young Ezra had said hotly.

His father had suddenly stopped laughing. "Do not be a fool," he had commanded his son. "What you do with a bondmaid is not my business if I do not hear of it. But your wife will be Naomi, the daughter of Judah ben Isaac."

He had been startled. Naomi was known then among the young men of their community as the most beautiful Jewess in the city. He had been susceptible enough, vain enough, to imagine the envy of his friends when he told them. And Judah ben Isaac belonged to a family so rich that its wealth had rebuilt the synagogue after the flood in the last century. True, they had taken a Chinese surname, Shih. But Judah said it was only for business.

Ezra said to Peony, still on her knees and looking up at him, "Keep your love to yourself, my child, let there be no confusion in the house. One thing at a time, I pray."

Thus in his own way he repeated what his father had said in his youth. To Peony it would have been folly to use the word "concubine," for Madame Ezra would never allow her son a concubine. But Peony understood all his meaning and she remained as still as a small image, looking at him with her clear eyes, which could be so gay and which now were sad.

"David will be very unhappy if he marries Leah," she said in a small voice.

Ezra shrugged his heavy shoulders and spread out his hands. "You will bring on my headache again," he complained. "Go away, good child, and leave me alone."

She saw that he would say no more. Although he would be always generous and indulgent as a master, he would refuse to remember that she was more than a bondmaid, a pretty comfort in his house. Her heart grew hard in her. She rose and bowed and was about to go, when Ezra's kind heart smote him. He lifted his hand. "Stay, child. I have a little gift the caravan brought for you. The house has been in such turmoil that I have forgotten to give it to you. Open that box and see what is in it."

He nodded toward a lacquered box on the table and Peony went to it and lifted the lid of the box. Within it lay a gold comb.

"For me?" she asked, opening her eyes prettily.

"For you," Ezra said, smiling. "Put it in your hair."

"Without the mirror?" Peony exclaimed, pretending to dismay.

Ezra laughed. "Well, well, take it and be happy."

"Thank you, Old Master," Peony said. "Thank you many times."

"There, do not thank me," Ezra replied, but she saw he was comforted. He loved to give gifts and he wanted everyone happy. It pleased him to see Peony's smiles, and she took care to show delight. It was a pretty comb indeed, and well she liked every pretty thing. But she was no longer a child, and a toy could not content her. She went away and her heart continued hard.

After she had gone Ezra sat in most uncomfortable thought. He sighed many times, heavily and restlessly. He had already been so foolish as to make one or two meaningful jests with Kung Chen about his third daughter and David. Without being so discourteous as to mention her name he had said, "Your house and my house, eh, Elder Brother? What is a business contract compared to children and grandchildren growing from double roots?"

Kung Chen had smiled and had nodded his head without speaking. Now everything was confused, Ezra told himself. He often wondered why, when he was a man inclined only toward happiness for everyone, including himself, he should be so often in circumstances that could not bring happiness for anyone, least of all for himself. Thus he found it very uncomfortable to have the Rabbi living in his house—a good man, of course, but thinking of nothing except the old ways of the Torah. The Torah was a rabbi's business, but it brought confusion into a house. Nobody could be comfortable if he was always being reminded of the past. Thus even he, here in his own house, was uncomfortable when he met the blind old man feeling his way along the corridors. He wanted to escape him, and if he met the Rabbi alone, he descended to standing still and not speaking, thus taking advantage of the old man's blindness.

Then Ezra thought of Leah for a while. She was more beautiful and more modest than his Naomi had been. He scarcely ever spoke to Leah, but sometimes in the evening she was in the peach-tree garden. He saw her pacing back and forth under the trees, and sometimes she put up her hand and plucked a fruit. The peaches were fine this year. She did not announce herself by her very presence as Naomi had done even as a young girl. Perhaps David could be happy with her. David was stronger than he himself had been as a young man, and more able to cope with headstrong women. Ezra remembered next that he saw very little of David lately. While the Rabbi had been teaching his son, he had allowed days to pass with no more than a greeting at mealtime. He got to his feet in his impetuous fashion and determined now to go to his son's room, late as it was.

Then he thought of Peony. Did David know Peony's heart? In his own youth it had been different. He was the one who had declared his love to the father. Now it was the girl Peony who spoke first. It mattered even less. He went briskly on bare feet through the cool moonlit corridors to David's room.

Peony had gone straight to the peach garden. It was impossible to sleep after what her master had said. Was it decided that David was to marry Leah? Was this why David was sad? If the father had accepted it, then there was no one left to be convinced. Madame Ezra had won.

She felt panic at her heart. Would Leah allow her to stay in the house when she was the young mistress? Madame Ezra might rule for her lifetime but Leah would be the real queen. She would declare to David, and David would command his mother. Yes, Madame Ezra would allow her son everything if he yielded in her one great command upon him, that he marry the one she had chosen for him.

"Oh," Peony moaned softly, "oh, pity me, my mother."

So she cried to the mother she could not remember. Then it came to her that this same mother had sold her, and could she hear, living or dead?

I have no one but myself, Peony thought. I will cry to myself. So she cried softly to herself, half laughing, half in heartbreak, Help me, Peony—help your poor self! Pity yourself, little one—do everything you can for me.

Then she went out into the peach-tree garden, and there she saw Leah sitting on a bench under the trees. She wore a long white gown, girdled at the waist with gold, and her dark unbound hair was held back with a band of gold. The moonlight shone down on her, and Peony saw in all humility that she had no prettiness to equal Leah's beauty.

"Are you here, Lady?" Peony said in her most childish voice.

"I cannot sleep," Leah replied.

"The moon woke me, too," Peony replied. She came near to Leah and looked through the trees at the full moon. Then she pointed her little forefinger. "See Old Chang up there in the moon?"

"Old Chang?" Leah repeated, looking up.

"He lives in the moon and he gives sweet dreams," Peony went on in the same gay voice. "What dreams will you ask of him, Lady?"

Leah stood tall above her, and Peony looked up to her pure and exquisite face with a sad pleasure. She was too generous a little creature to hate Leah for her beauty, but it made her want to cry again.

"Only God can grant me my dream," Leah said. Her voice was deep and soft.

Peony laughed. "Then we will see who is stronger, Old Chang or your god!"

And in mischief she dropped to her knees and bent her forehead to the earth and then lifted her head and she cried to the moon, "Give me my dream, Old Chang!"

When she rose Leah stood watching her gravely.

"Shall we tell each other our dreams?" Peony inquired saucily.

Leah shook her head. "No," she replied. "I cannot tell mine—to anyone. But when it is given me, I will tell you."

Still they looked at one another. Peony longed to cry out, "But I know your dream—it is to be David's wife!"

To have this spoken between them, to tell Leah that she too loved David and in her fashion she would work to win him away, even for his own sake—ah, what an ease for her heart! But she kept silent. To know a thing and not to tell it was to make it a weapon.

"Good night, Lady," she said after a moment.

"Good night," Leah replied.

They parted, and looking back from the door, Peony saw Leah pacing to and fro under the peach trees.

Now when David had left the synagogue that morning without the Rabbi, he had wept for a few minutes. Then he looked about. No one was near and no one had seen him weeping. The brief yielding had done him good. He was still sad, but he felt relieved. He was committed to no new thing—God had not spoken to him. He was as he had been. He was himself and this seemed good to him. He wanted to see neither the Chinese nor the Rabbi, but only to be alone, and he folded his cap and thrust it inside the bosom of his robe, and alone he went into the streets and wandered about, seeing everything and caring for nothing, and yet aware that his soul was being slowly restored. Thus he went to the court of the Confucian temple, where every strange and curious sight was to be found, the magicians and the jugglers and the dancing bears and the talking blackbirds; but all these things, which usually gave him joy, now gave him none. He looked and he did not laugh. He saw delicate food hot in the vendors' stalls and he bought and tasted and was not hungry and gave what he had bought to beggars. He wanted no friends and he was lonely. Yet in this quiet sadness and loneliness he felt healing.

Thus thinking of everyone he knew and not wanting to see anyone, in the middle of the afternoon he suddenly thought of Kao Lien with some longing to see him and talk with him. Kao Lien would be at his father's shop, but his father would in likelihood not be there, for it was Ezra's habit to go early to the shop in the morning and leave early, whereas Kao Lien did not like to rise until noon, and so he stayed late. To him, therefore, David went.

His father's shop was a very large one. It opened full upon the street, and above the doors long silken banners waved in the wind. Upon these were Chinese letters announcing that foreign goods of all sorts were sold within, both retail and wholesale. When Kung Chen and Ezra made the contract for which Ezra hoped, then these banners would announce both their names. But now there was only the name of "Ezra and Son."

When David came in the clerks all knew him and bowed, and he asked for Kao Lien, and immediately one led him into the back of the shop, and there Kao Lien sat in a large cool room of his own, behind a high desk, brushing Chinese characters upon a ledger. He rose when he saw David, and since David had never come here alone before, he could not hide surprise and some fear. "Is your father not well?" he inquired. "I saw him only an hour ago."

"I have not seen him today," David answered. "I must talk with you, if you please, Uncle."

"Sit down," Kao Lien said gravely. So they sat down and Kao Lien looked at David and waited in such kind silence that everything came out of David at once.

"Ever since you told me about our people being killed I have been wretched," David declared. "I feel I ought to do something—to be some sort of man that I am not. I feel I have no right merely to be happy here, to enjoy myself and my life."

"You feel you should be miserable?" Kao Lien inquired with a wry smile.

"I know that would be useless," David said honestly. "But I think it is wrong for me to live as though our people were not dying as you told us they were."

"The Rabbi has been teaching you, too," Kao Lien said quietly, "and your mother has been telling you that you must marry Leah."

"Then you came and told us that evil news," David said, "and it has made me feel that I must obey the Rabbi and my mother."

"And can you atone by such obedience for the death of our people?" Kao Lien inquired.

"No, no," David answered. Then he beat his breast with clenched fists. "But I can ease myself here!"

"Ah," Kao Lien observed, "then it is for yourself that you would obey the Rabbi and marry Leah. Why not, then?"

"Because I am not sure I want to do that, either!" David cried. "I want to be as I was before—when I did not know about our people."

David sat upon a low cushioned stool, lower than the chair where Kao Lien sat, and when Kao Lien looked down upon his young face, his heart was troubled. "Ah, but you do know," he said, "and you must know. Who of us can escape knowing the truth?"

"What is the truth?" David asked.

Now Kao Lien knew very well the house in which this young man had been reared. He knew the warm, hothearted, pleasure-loving father that Ezra was, in whose blood a strain of Chinese blood mingled, as it did in his own veins. He knew the mother, Madame Ezra, proud of her pure blood, preserving in herself all the ancient traditions of a free people once powerful, once having their own nation, but now no longer free and subject to every nation where they were scattered without home or land of their own. Into her son Madame Ezra poured all her pride, and she was jealous of his very soul.

"The truth is this," Kao Lien said. "You yourself must understand what you are and you yourself must decide what you will be. Your mother looks at the whole world from the center of herself."

"But she only wants me to learn the Torah from the Rabbi," David broke in.

Kao Lien went on, "Then you will look at all the world and all humanity through its narrow window."

David moved restlessly. "Kao Lien, you too are a Jew!"

"Mixed," Kao Lien said dryly. There was a look of humor in his long face. Then he was grave again. "It is true that I felt my marrow cold when I saw the bodies of the dead in the streets of those western cities. But it was because they were dead, not only because they were Jews. I said to myself, Why should these or any men die this death? Why are they so hated?"

"Yes—why?" David repeated. "That is what I keep asking. If I knew, I feel I would know everything."

Kao Lien's small eyes grew sharp. "I will tell you what I dare not tell another soul," he declared. "But you are young—you have the right to know. They were hated because they separated themselves from the rest of mankind. They called themselves chosen of God. Do I not know? I come of a large family, and there was one among us, my third brother, who declared himself the favorite of my parents. He boasted of it to the rest of us—'I am the chosen one,' he boasted. And we hated him." Kao Lien's thin lips grew more thin. "I hate him to this day. I would gladly see him dead. No, I would not kill him. I am civilized—I kill nothing. But if he died I would not mourn."

In the big, silent, shadowy room David stared at Kao Lien with horror. "Are we not the chosen of God?" he faltered.

"Who says so, except ourselves?" Kao Lien retorted.

"But the Torah—" David faltered.

"Written by Jews, bitter with defeat," Kao Lien said. He went on, "Here is the truth—I give it to you whole. We were a proud people. We lost our country. Our only hope for return was to keep ourselves a people. The only hope to keep ourselves a people was to keep our common faith in one God, a God of our own. That God has been our country and our nation. In sorrow and wailing and woe for all that we have lost has been our union. And our rabbis have so taught us, generation after generation."

"Nothing—except that?" David asked. His voice was strange and still.

"For that many are willing to die," Kao Lien said firmly.

"Are you?" David demanded.

"No," Kao Lien said.

David did not speak. His childhood was falling about him like a ruin, echoing through his memory in fragments of sacred days, his mother lighting the candles on Sabbath Eve; the sweet festival of lights, Hanukah, the beautiful Menorah, holding its eight candles at the window, reminding them of the great day when, conquered though they were, the Jews had won their fight to keep their own religion under the Syrian conquerors; Purim, the day when Jews remembered how they had fought against Haman, the ancient tyrant. And most of all he remembered his own special day, when he became a Son of the Commandment.

"Are we to forget all that we are?" he asked Kao Lien at last, solemnly.

"No," Kao Lien said. "But we are to forget the past and separate ourselves no more. We are to live now, wherever we are, and we are to pour the strength of our souls into the peoples of the world."

He shaded his eyes with his long, narrow, thin hand, as though he prayed. They sat silent for a while and then he motioned to David to leave him. So David rose and went to the door. There Kao Lien's voice stopped him. "I do not know whether I have done wrong," he said, "yet what truth have I to speak except what is truth to me? Tell your father and mother what I have said, if you wish. I do not ask that it be kept secret."

"I asked you for the truth," David replied, "and I thank you."

With these words he went home.

When Peony left Leah in the garden, she saw David come in through the first court and she followed him to his rooms to find out if he had eaten and if there was anything he lacked. This was her duty and she did not go beyond it.

"I have eaten," he told her. Then he took his cap from his bosom. "Put that away for me," he said.

When she had obeyed him she came back again into the room where he was, and there he sat by the table, his arms folded upon it, staring at nothing.

"Can I do nothing more for you?" she asked tenderly.

"Nothing—except to leave me until I call," he replied.

He looked so stern, so grave, that she did not dare press him. There he sat, surrounded by books, opened on the table and fallen on the floor. When she stooped to pick them up he said sharply, "Leave them—I threw them there."

So she could only leave him, but now she was in great distress. Never had he refused to tell her what his trouble was. Yet what could she do except continue to love him? She stood a moment, uncertain whether to go or stay. Then, delicately perceiving, she felt the air cold about him. Some struggle went on in him that she did not yet understand.

I must understand, she told herself. Yet nothing could be forced. Events alone could she use.

"Until tomorrow," she said softly, and when he did not answer, she went away to her own room and made ready for the night.

At least one roof covers him and me, she thought when she lay in her little bed. Old Chang, give me my dreams! she prayed the moon. She closed her eyes, and ready to receive her dreams, she drifted into sleep.

As Ezra came near to his son's room he saw that a single candle burned, and without letting David see him, he peered through the lattice. He was appalled by what he saw. David sat in thought and his young face looked so pale, so sad, that Ezra was frightened. This was what came of letting old men and women have their way! What if he lost this darling only child, his one son, his heart's core, the hope of his life and his business?

He burst into David's room like a bear. Peony had not smoothed his hair after she had healed his head, and he had forgotten to put on his little cap. His curly hair stood out in a circle and he had pulled at his beard while he meditated until it was like a broom. He was barefoot and his garments awry because he had a habit of scratching himself here and there while he pondered and ruminated, and David looked at him in astonishment.

But Ezra had already made up his mind what to do. "On such a night, with such a moon, I cannot sleep," he declared. "I shall send Old Wang to see if Kung Chen is awake and if he too is sleepless. Let us invite him and his sons to meet us on the lake. I owe him a feast and tonight I will pay my debt. Old Wang shall hire a boat and we will order wine, supper, and musicians. Come—come—you and I—"

He pulled at David's hand, beaming at him through his beard and flying hair and thick eyebrows. When he saw David hesitate and waver he wrapped his arms about him. "Come, my dear son," he muttered. "You are young—you are young—time enough for grief when you are old."

His father's warm breath, his rich loving voice, his strong hot embrace, moved David's heart. He flung himself into his father's arms and burst into sobs, and now he was not ashamed. This kind father would know how he felt. Ezra held his son tightly against his breast. Tears came into his own eyes but they were tears of anger, and he gnashed his teeth and muttered through them.

"Torture—that's it—they torture themselves and everybody else. But now it's the children. I won't have you tortured—what's it for? To be young is not a sin. Besides, how do we know God? These old rabbis—"

Hearing this angry roar in his father's lungs, David laughed suddenly in the midst of his sobs. Ezra held him off and looked at him. "That's right, my son—you laugh! Why not? Who knows? Perhaps God likes laughter, eh? Now get on your best clothes and let's go. Softly, so nobody wakes! I will wake only Old Wang. We will meet at the gate." He went away, heaving sighs of relief.

David went into his bedroom. He wondered now at the strange release of his heart. The sad quiet of the day had suddenly lightened to joy. No sin was in him, only a vast relief that his father had loosed him somehow from sorrow. He washed himself and brushed back his hair and left his head uncovered. He put on a long robe of bright blue Chinese silk and girdled it with a wide piece of soft red silk. On his feet he put white socks and black velvet Chinese shoes. In a very few minutes he was ready and he went to the gate, where Ezra was.

Ezra looked at his son with overwhelming love. He felt ready to defy anyone to protect his life—yes, even God Himself. His son was his own and he would not yield him up.

"I am not Abraham," he said suddenly. "I will not sacrifice you, O my son!"

He put his arm around David's shoulders and together they went out into the moonlit courts, through the gates, and into the street. On foot they went together toward the lake. The hour was late, but not too late for merrymaking. All sober souls were in bed and asleep, but the young and the old who were lovers of life were making the most of the moon. Summer was nearly gone, the autumn was near, and the lotus flowers floating upon the water would die, the pods be split, and the seed scattered. It was the hour to seize joy with both hands.

Thus Ezra walked with David through the streets, quiet except for a few women still sitting on doorsteps and reluctant to go into their houses. They sat suckling their children and dreaming in the moonlight. So they came to the lake, two men, father and son, and there Kung Chen met them with his own two eldest sons, debonair young men eager for pleasure. The older son looked like his father. He had the same broad face and small kindly eyes and smooth lips. The younger son was slight and pretty, and he reminded David of his sister Kueilan. That little one! Her face rose in his memory, and his blood quickened. The two brothers shouted with lively pleasure to David and clasped his hands and argued with boatmen, while the two elder men stood on the bank waiting.

"We are men of the same mind," Kung Chen told Ezra. "I was about to send a manservant to you to ask you if you would enjoy the moon with us, and he met your man on the threshold."

"My son has been studying too much of late," Ezra said with some reserve. "He needs to forget his books."

Kung Chen was altogether aware of what Ezra meant, but he left further talk until later in the night when they would be mellow with wine. He made no sign even to David that earlier in the day they had met. Each hour unto its own.

By now the young men had the boat they thought best and the boatman held it to the bank with his hooked pole and they all stepped upon its broad flat deck and took their seats. Ezra and Kung Chen sat under the silken canopy but the young men stretched themselves on the deck under the sky. At the stern the boatman's elderly wife fanned the coals in a small earthen brazier and heated water for tea.

"Where will you lords go for your feast?" the boatman inquired.

"Why not have the feast brought on the boat?" Kung Chen suggested. Thus it was decided, and the boatman rowed toward the restaurant called The House of the Golden Bird.

Never had the night seemed so sweet to David, or companionship more pleasant. At first he was quiet. He lay on his back, looking up at the clear and glowing sky. Beneath him he heard the soft sound of the great lotus leaves brushing the sides of the boat. He turned and leaned over the side and plucked a pod and tore it open. Inside the pith was white and dry and embedded in it were the seed pods in orderly rows. He took them out one by one and peeled the green skin from them and ate them, and the cream-white kernels were sweet to his tongue.

The boatman stooped and took the empty pod and thrust it carefully under the lotus leaves. "That son of a turtle Old Liu has bought the lotus this year in advance," he explained. "He commands that the lake police are to fine everyone who picks a pod. But eat what you like, Young Master—the more you eat the less Old Liu will have! Only I beg you to give me a little silver to put into the palms of the police."

Everyone laughed and no one reproved. And David lay on his back and gazed at the moon. He wanted to think no more, to puzzle and doubt and struggle no more with his soul. Let him only live and enjoy his life.

By now the boat was approaching the lower bank where the restaurant stood, and the two young Kungs were arguing over the foods to be chosen.

"Crabs, of course," Kung the First said.

"Fried in oil, not steamed," Kung the Second amended.

"Be sure you young lords order a very potent wine to eat with our crabs," the boatman advised. "They are hearty food, our crabs, for they feed on the refuse that the feasters throw from the boats. Rich fare makes rich meat."

"Let the crabs be steamed," Kung Chen said from under the canopy. "The flavor of the meat is then clear."

So after more argument and talk, crabs were ordered and then roasted duck and vegetables to suit, and hot millet with dates and red sugar for a sweet. This order Kung the First gave to the keeper of the restaurant, who ran down the steps to the water's edge when the boatman shouted, and he stood there, his fat face shining in the moonlight, all smiles and good humor and shouting, "Yes, yes" to every dish. Then he said, "Sirs, will you not have music, too? To eat crabs, as I cook them, with my wine, under such a moon, and all without music, is to marry a wife without a dowry."

They laughed and Kung the Second said boldly, "Send us three singing girls with the food." He turned his head to look at his father slyly. "Will three be enough, Father?"

"Plenty—plenty," Kung Chen said with his slow smile. "We will look at your girls and listen to them sing and that is enough for us old ones, eh, Elder Brother?"

"Plenty," Ezra agreed. He leaned back and sighed with pleasure. "Life is good," he said suddenly.

"For people such as we are," Kung Chen amended. "We who are rich, we who have plenty, why should we be unhappy? There is no suffering necessary for us."

Outside on the wide flat deck the young men lolled on the silk cushions that the boatman had put down for them. The moonlight, flowing about them and over them, gilded them until they were like gods at ease. On the shore the restaurant was bright with lanterns and the mellow light glowed at every window. Voices mingled with singing and the sound of flutes and the beat of drums.

Ezra had looked at the scene scores of times, but tonight its meaning penetrated him. Happiness was waiting to be chosen. In this city there was such happiness, and yet here too was the eternal sorrow of the Rabbi, reminding his people of woe. It was within a man's power to choose happiness and to reject woe. True, it was not within the Rabbi's power. He had chosen sorrow, the endless sorrow of a man haunted by God. He had even transmuted such sorrow into strange dark joy. He was most happy when he suffered most deeply, like the moth that flutters near the flame of the candle. Yes, the likeness was true. Man scorched his very soul in that ecstasy of God. But must all men find happiness in the same way? Let the Rabbi find his own pleasure where he would, but he should not compel the young men—and above all not the one who was his son.

"You are meditating deeply," Kung Chen said suddenly. "I feel a fever in you."

"I am meditating upon happiness," Ezra said frankly. "Can it be for all?"

Kung Chen pursed his full smooth lips. "For the poor, happiness is difficult," he replied. "For the one, too, who fastens his happiness wholly upon another being. Poverty is the external hazard and love the internal. But if one can surmount poverty and can love in moderation, there is no obstacle to happiness for anyone."

"When you say 'being,'" Ezra said, "do you mean human or God?"

"Any being," Kung Chen replied. "Some love a human being too well and are made subject by that love; others love their gods too well and are subject to that love. Man should be subject to none. Then we are free."

This talk was interrupted by a flutter at the door of the restaurant. Three pretty girls came down the stone steps, carrying lute and cymbals and a small hand drum. They were like flowers in the wind, their pink and blue and green robes flowing, and they held their little dark heads high. Behind them waiters brought baskets of food and the boatwoman set up tables. There was a bustle everywhere but in a little while all was ready and the boatman pushed the boat away into the middle of the lake again. The brightly lit shore lay in the distance and soon the voices were only echoes.

Now Kung Chen invited everyone to eat, and the waiter and the cook did their part. The three girls sat down at the bow, their backs to the moon and facing the feasters, and each with her instrument began to play, and they sang in unison a melody so tangled among them and so bewitching that the young men could not keep from laughing. The girls seemed part of the night and the moon, fey and exquisite. Their high sweet voices wandered in and out of the melody, but always in unison, and the young men listened and looked at them, seeing them together, their white pretty faces alike, their wide dark eyes passionless. The exceeding beauty of the night, the delicacy of the music and of the singers, the fine food, each dish seasoned to its capacity and none heavy with oil or sugar, the pleasure of all these stole into David's heart. Grossness would have offended him after the long days with the Rabbi. His soul had been tuned too high and he could not move too suddenly from Heaven to earth. But tonight earth spoke enchantment and Heaven was still.

挑筋教

VII

THE Rabbi did not return to the house of Ezra. When he knew he was alone in the synagogue and that David had gone, he went into his own house. Rachel was surprised when she heard his step, and she came in from the kitchen.

"Well, Old Teacher!" she called.

"I wish to be alone," he told her. "Send word to Madame Ezra and tell her that I will not return. And bid my son come home."

"What of Leah?" Rachel asked.

The Rabbi considered. "Let her remain where she is," he said.

Rachel stared at the old man. He looked exhausted to the heart. His face was white and his beard was unbrushed. His hand, clutching his staff, was trembling, and she saw a slight palsy of his head, which she had not seen before. All this alarmed her and she took him by the sleeve. "Before I go I will make you a bowl of hot millet soup, and you must drink it and rest yourself."

So saying she led the Rabbi to his room, where she kept all ready for him. The old man yielded to her and he let his staff fall and he wiped his blind eyes on his sleeves. "Ah, it is good here," he sighed. "I was not happy in the halls of the rich."

"You are not happy unless you are miserable, and that is the truth about you," Rachel said cheerfully. "Lie down, old man, and rest."

A look of indignation made his face strong again. The Rabbi came to himself suddenly. "What have you done to my bed?" he cried. He had laid himself down on his narrow bamboo couch but now he sat up.

Rachel stood with her hands akimbo. "I put an extra quilt under the mat," she said firmly. "Those old bones of yours with nothing under you!"

But the Rabbi rose to his feet and turned on her with his sightless eyes. "Take it away, woman!" he commanded.

Rachel shrugged her shoulders, shook her head, and made many signs of refusal that he could not see, but so loud and clear was his voice that she did not dare to say aloud that she would not obey him. At last there was nothing for her except to take the quilt away and spread the mat on the hard bamboo. Then the Rabbi lay down again, sighed, and folded his hands on his breast. "Go away, woman," he commanded her, his deep voice as firm as ever. "Go away and leave me to the Lord."

So Rachel went away, disapproving very much; and muttering to herself against the stubborn old saint, she put the quilt into a box. But she was angry and she did not go at once to give his message to Madame Ezra. Instead she kept everything to herself until the next day. When the Rabbi asked her whether Aaron had come home, she told a comforting lie and said that Leah had begged that he be allowed to stay for another day or two with her. The Rabbi sighed at this but said no more. He rose early the next morning, ate his millet porridge, and sat repeating to himself the pages of the Torah.

When the day wore on nearly to noon and she knew that Madame Ezra would be ready, Rachel went to give the message. She found Madame Ezra superintending the cleaning of a fish pond by the kitchen. The angry fish were swarming in tubs while two men raked the muddy bottom. Madame Ezra was scolding fish and men alike, and she was in no good temper to hear what Rachel had to tell her.

"Now what has happened?" she cried when Rachel stopped to take breath. "All was well yesterday—why has he left my house?"

"I know nothing except that the old man came home yesterday alone from the synagogue," Rachel said.

Then Madame Ezra called Wang Ma and Peony to come in.

Wang Ma knew nothing and Peony knew only that David had come home late last night with his father.

"You should have come and told me," Madame Ezra said.

"Mistress, I thought you knew everything," Peony replied.

There was nothing now to do but to dismiss them all, and this Madame Ezra did, except that she held Peony back to give her a command.

"Go and fetch me Leah, while I go to my room and clean myself."

So Peony went to fetch Leah while Madame Ezra gave her last commands to the two men and went to her own court.

As for Peony, she made herself all servant, and she coughed before she entered Leah's door, and when she heard Leah's gentle voice, saying to come in, she went in and bowed and said only this: "My mistress asks for you to come to her." Then she bowed and went away again, and now she went to her own room and thought for a while. What had happened between the Rabbi and David? Did Leah have a part in it?

Waiting became more than she could bear, and she went to find out what she could, by any means. She ran on noiseless feet and hid behind a great cassia tree in Madame Ezra's court. It leaned against the window that was open, for the morning was hot and still. Hidden there, she heard Madame Ezra's voice speaking firmly and clearly to Leah, in these words:

"How can you say that nothing has happened between you and David? I saw you with my own eyes, once, in the peach garden. Certainly you stood very close together."

Leah's voice came rushing softly, full of agitation. "How can I help it, Aunt, if—if—nothing more happened? That once—well, yes, we were very near."

"All these days you have been sitting together over the Torah," Madame Ezra cried.

"He has scarcely spoken to me." Leah's voice died away in this confession.

Madame Ezra flew into sudden anger. "It is your fault, Leah! You never try—you simply wait."

"What can I do but wait?" Leah asked.

Peony listened, her black eyes sparkling, her red lips curving. Ah, then, it was not decided! David did not love Leah! Ah—but what if he did? She slipped from behind the cassia tree and ran to David's rooms. The sitting room was empty, and she put aside the curtain and peered into his bedroom. He lay on his bed still asleep. The noon sun poured into the room. She had drawn his bed curtains last night herself when she made the room ready for night, but he had put them back behind the heavy silver hooks. He lay there in his white silk sleeping garments, his arms flung wide and his head turned toward her on the pillow.

Her heart beat with joy. It was not too late. The Rabbi was gone, and there was no betrothal. Joy ran in her veins and curved her lips and shone in her eyes and danced in her body. It was never too late for happiness.

She stole across the room and knelt by his bed. "David!" she whispered. "David!"

He woke, smiled, and stretched out his arms to her and caught her shoulders. "How dare you wake me?" he demanded, still no more than half asleep.

"It's noon," she whispered. "I came to tell you something—something wonderful!"

"What is it?" he demanded.

But she delayed out of sheer joy. "The sun is shining into your eyes," she said. "Why, they're not black—there's gold in the bottoms of them!"

"Is that wonderful?" he asked, and he laughed aloud and waked himself with his own laughter.

"The sun shines into your mouth," she went on, "and it is as sweet as a pomegranate."

"For this you waked me?" he demanded. He sat up now, wide awake.

"No," she whispered. "David, listen to me!"

She caught his hand and held it against her breast. "David, at noon—*she*—is going to the Buddhist temple to worship and give thanks. She has been ill."

She felt his hand grow tense. "You did not tell me," he said.

"I did not want to tell you," she said. "She is well again—really. David, you can see her for yourself."

His eyes were fixed on hers, and she went on quickly. "If you get up now I will bring you something to eat, and you can enter the side gate of the temple and meet her as she goes to the Silver Kwanyin in the South Temple."

"But she will know I came to see her," he said shyly.

Peony laughed. "How that will please her!" she said with mischief. She put down his hand, and rose to her feet and touched her finger to her lips. "I'll be back with hot food."

She ran away. Ah, but this would take quickness! She stopped only to find her purse and then she ran out of the Gate of Peaceful Escape and down the alley to the house of Kung, and there she asked for Chu Ma and found her at her noon meal. The fat old woman held a huge bowl of rice to her mouth and she pushed in the mingled rice and meats and listened to Peony.

"You must persuade her to be there, mind you, in the court of the Silver Kwanyin, and he will be there within the hour." Peony poured this all into a breath.

"But if her mother forbids?" Chu Ma asked.

"Tell your young lady to weep, to scream, to threaten anything—tell her to say she has a pain in her breast and that she wants to pray. He sends you this."

She emptied her purse into Chu Ma's hands, and then tore at her own ears and took off her jade earrings. "And I give you these."

Chu Ma put the bowl on a table and nodded and Peony flew homeward again. In a few minutes she came from the kitchen with a covered porcelain vessel full of hot rice gruel, which was always on the stoves, and a manservant followed with the small meats and salt dishes for David's breakfast. She trusted that David had loitered even more than usual in dressing himself, and this was true. When she entered his sitting room, he had still not come in.

"Young Master!" she called.

"Shall I wear red or blue?" he called back.

"The wine red!" she replied. Blue was the color he wore to the synagogue and nothing must remind him of that now. She knew the subtle influence of colors, how gray can subdue a man's spirit, how blue uplifts it and sends it wandering, how red, the wine red, holds it to the earth.

Soon he came out, looking so beautiful that she could have wept. His dark head was bare; above the white lining of his robe his face showed brown and red and full of health.

But she subdued herself. "Come," she said, "there is too little time." She uncovered the bowls as she spoke, and he sat down. He ate in silence and he pondered. Had it not been for all that happened to him yesterday he could not have yielded to Peony now. For it was not with great desire that he longed again to see Kueilan. He remembered the pretty Chinese girl with warm pleasure but not with urgency. No, he wanted to see her today at least for his own defense against himself. He knew that Leah was here, and he thought the Rabbi was still here, and he knew his mother was as strong as ever. He needed time against them, time to make up his mind, to be himself before all else. Last night on the lake had calmed him and taken the soreness from his soul. This morning he felt rested and strong and alone.

So he ate and afterward he made himself fresh again, washing his hands in a basin of perfumed water and brushing his hair, without haste, and all so slowly that Peony was half beside herself. "She will have gone, you will not see her!" she wailed. "Oh, when will there be so good a chance again!"

He teased her a while with his slowness and he pretended that he was still hungry and at last she seized the dishes and would not let him have more and he so relished laughing and playfulness again that he set off in good humor, and left Peony to take away the dishes.

Now Peony had reason enough out of love to do all she had done, but what happened next gave her hate for a reason, too.

After Rachel had spoken with Madame Ezra she went to the room that the Rabbi had used, having inquired of the way from the servants, and there she found Aaron still half asleep and barely stirring out of his bed. She told him that his father bade him come home at once, and as she did so she said to herself that it was a shame this was the Rabbi's only son, this gangling splayfooted boy with his long narrow head and his thin crooked face and mean yellowish eyes.

Aaron heard his father's command and he was too timid to say he would not come. Instead he asked, "Is Leah coming home, too?"

"Not today," Rachel replied.

Then because this made him angry he muttered that his father always treated Leah softly, and he screamed at Rachel. "Get away, you old slut! Why do you stand there and stare at me?"

At this she grew angry and she said plainly, "As for me, I hope you do not come home. It will be hard work to cook food to keep you alive."

With this she went away, and Aaron, left alone, began to pity himself and wept a little. He was loath to leave this rich house where the best of food had been given him for his father's sake, and where no servant refused his bidding. He was angry to think he must go back to his narrow life and his lonely room. He loved neither his father nor Leah, but he feared them because they were good and he was not.

So pitying himself and angry at all, he rose, and in great sulkiness he dressed, and then he went out to the hall where the men ate, to look for his breakfast. As it chanced, his path crossed Peony's at the court where the fish pool was. He saw her before she saw him, and she made a pretty sight in the morning sunshine. Her hair was shining black and her cheeks pink and she wore coat and trousers of pale yellow silk and she had thrust a white gardenia in her hair.

He looked right and left. No one was near. She walked with downcast head and smiled as she went. Then she felt his presence as she might have felt a snake near her foot. She lifted her head, startled, and at that moment he ran toward her, seized her in his arms, and pressed his mouth upon hers.

Never had any mouth been pressed upon Peony's. Now she felt Aaron's loathsome trembling hot mouth and she was faint and sick. Her head swirled and she screamed, but so great was her sickness that the scream was too small to hear. Then she felt his hand at her breast. The sickness passed, her strength returned with anger, and she fell upon Aaron with all the fury of her being. She scratched his face and tore his hair and jerked his ears and kicked him when he tried to run, and she held him by his hair with one hand and pushed his face with her other hand, clenched into a fist, all the time silent except for her hard breaths. She did not want anyone to know that the shame of his touch had fallen upon her.

At last, quite spent, she snarled at him, "Dare to touch me again, you cursed son of a hare, and I will kill you with the sword and you will die as your turtle ancestors died!"

Now Peony spoke of the sword that David had chosen out of the caravan and had hung on the wall in his own room. This sword had an exceedingly fine sharp edge, and at this moment Aaron believed that Peony could do what she said. She could not have chosen a keener threat. All the old fear and the weakness handed down to him from his fathers, and bound indeed into the Torah itself, now fell upon him. The old Rabbi was a strong man and he could enjoy the thunderings of Jehovah, but Aaron was a weak worm, and from his pitiful weak childhood he had feared and hated Jehovah, and he longed to be anything except what he was, the son of the Rabbi. When Peony called upon his ancestors he gathered his garments about him and slunk away.

Peony threw him a long look of scorn. Then she walked with firm swift footsteps to her room, and there she washed and scrubbed herself from head to foot and changed her garments and brushed her hair and perfumed herself and put on her best jewels and thrust a fresh flower in her hair. But her anger still burned in her. Now indeed she would rid the house of all who belonged to Aaron. When she was clean again she went to David's rooms and waited, making the pretext of cleaning and dusting and mending a sandalwood fan he had broken.

Her cheeks were still pink with anger when in an hour or two David came back. She sat at the table, mending the delicate fan with a feather dipped in glue. She knew when she looked at him that he had seen Kueilan. He came in, debonair and satisfied with himself. When she saw him, she thought to herself, how smug a man looks who thinks himself beloved! But this she knew was the bitterness of her own hidden love, and she put it aside. She laid the fan carefully down and clothing herself in docility she rose to her feet. His eyes met hers in the old gaiety that she had so missed.

"Tell me," she coaxed, knowing that he wanted to tell her everything.

"What?" he teased.

"Did you see her?"

"Did you not tell me she would be there?" he replied.

"But she was there?"

"Suppose she wasn't?"

To his surprise Peony suddenly began to sob.

"Now what is wrong with you?" he asked.

She shook her head and could not speak.

He came closer. "Tell me," he urged. "Has someone hurt you?"

She nodded, still sobbing and wiping her eyes on her sleeves.

"My mother?" he asked angrily.

"It was—it was—oh, I cannot say his name!" She shook her head. She cried in a small heartbroken voice.

"A man!" David exclaimed.

She nodded. "The Rabbi's son," she whispered.

David stared at her for a second. Then he turned abruptly and strode toward the door of the court. But Peony ran after him. "No, no," she cried. "Never let him know you know. It is too much shame for me."

"What did he do?" David demanded.

"I—cannot tell you," she faltered.

"He did not—" David began, and now the red was flaming in his cheeks.

"Oh, no, oh, no!" she cried. Then lest he think matters worse than they were, she laughed through her tears. "I beat him," she confessed. "I took him by the hair and—and I smacked his face."

David laughed with fierce pleasure. "I wish I had seen you! Did you bruise him, Peony? Let me go and see!"

"No, wait," she coaxed. "Please, what I say is true. He did—he did put his mouth on mine—"

"Curse his mother!" David said suddenly.

Peony laid the little forefinger of her right hand across his lips, and tears brimmed her beautiful eyes. "I am defiled," she whispered.

How could David refuse her comfort? He put his hands upon her shoulders and looked at her soft red lips, and she let her fingers slide away and she said in the softest voice, "Touch my lips—and make them clean!"

She swayed a little toward him, and he bent his head, trying to laugh and make a play of it, and he bent his head still lower until indeed his lips were upon hers. Never had his lips touched a woman's mouth. This was only Peony, only his little same Peony whom he knew so well, but suddenly her lips were sweet and strange.

She drew back and her voice was quick and clear. "Thank you," she said daintily. "Now I can forget. Tell me, Young Master, did you truly see the pretty third daughter of Kung?"

So swift was her change that he scarcely knew how to speak. All was confusion in him. The sweet new warmth that Peony had called up in him she now turned swiftly toward another. Without knowing that he was being stirred, beguiled, led to do what Peony wanted, he let his mind go back to the temple, and to the moment when he had been hidden behind the great Guardian God of the West. He saw Kueilan come in, the embroidered edge of her long skirt of soft apple-green silk sweeping the tiled floor. An old serving woman held her hand, and beside the stout strong figure the young girl had looked like a little willow tree in spring. Then he remembered her face.

"Yes," he said slowly, "I saw her. I had forgotten how beautiful she is."

"She is too small?" Peony prodded.

"A little thing," David said, "not taller than you. But I like small women."

"Her eyes—they are as big as mine?"

Now Peony's chief beauty was her eyes. They were apricot-shaped, the lashes were straight and soft and long, and the color of the iris was a deep warm brown, not quite black. Looking into these eyes, David was constrained to remember Kueilan's eyes, and since he had passed very near her, he said, "Hers are the most beautiful eyes I have ever seen."

At this Peony dimpled and she put her handkerchief to her face to hide her quickening smile—and her tears. "Did you speak to her?" she asked next.

"Yes," David said. "When she passed to go into the inner temple, she saw me."

"And you said?" Peony hinted.

"Only that I hoped she would forgive me because I had come to see her."

This David said very fervently and he sat down beside the table and put away all mischief. "Peony," he said gravely, "you know I cannot marry as ordinary men do. If I choose her for my bride and not Leah, I must wound my mother and the Rabbi and perhaps even my father."

"Your father thinks only of you," Peony put in.

"Ah, but among our people the women are stronger than the men," David said, "and what my mother will do, I do not know."

"Does Leah know—of this other one?" Peony asked.

"No," David replied. He looked rueful. "And I have given her reason to think—" He shook his head.

Peony, who had been standing all this time, now sat down opposite him at the table.

"You have let Leah think you—love her?" So Peony asked in a small frightened voice. Then she hurried on. "How can that be true? You have not spoken to her while you were learning the book. The old teacher sat between you."

"Once, in the peach garden—" David said, blushing heartily.

"In the peach garden?" Peony echoed. "What did you do?"

"It was the day after the caravan came," David said unwillingly. "We were all somehow excited."

"She came to you in the peach garden?" Peony exclaimed. Her divining mind ran ahead. "And do you think she would be so bold as to come to you of her own will? Surely it was your mother who bade her come."

David stared at her, suddenly perceiving that indeed this might be true. "If Mother—" He struck the table with his fists and Peony cried out and drew away the mended fan.

David leaned back, his eyes full of fury. "I shall tell my mother—"

But Peony looked at him over the carved fan, which she held to her face because she loved the scent of sandalwood. "Why need you say anything?" she coaxed. "Let me go to your father and tell him what you feel. Come, I will be the marriage maker for you!"

But David shook his head again. "Nevertheless, it is not honorable for me to allow Leah to remain confused," he said. "I must think of what to say to her."

"Say nothing," Peony pleaded. "What is not said need never be unsaid. If it is put into words, then all is hard and fast. Oh, and she will be very bitter against you."

"Leah bitter?" David repeated. "Ah, there you are wrong! That is what hurts me. She is so good. For her own sake—not my mother's—I wish with all my heart that I could love her." He broke off again, hesitated, and went on, half talking to himself, "I could have loved her, perhaps—had she simply been a woman. But she is much more."

He thought Peony too childlike to understand what he meant, but Peony did understand and she was shrewd enough to keep silent. Leah was more than a woman—she was a people and a tradition and a past, and did David marry her he espoused the whole, and to that he must return. He could not be himself or free, were he to return, for then must he become part of the ancient whole and bear upon himself the weight of their old sorrows. But Peony did not tell him this. Instead she skipped her feet and clapped her hands and pretended to her usual childishness.

"Let me tell your father!" she begged.

And David, his young face shadowed with vague pain, smiled a little sadly. "What can my father do for me?" he inquired. "He was caught as I am now."

"Ah, but he had no one to save him," Peony said gently. "There was no orchid flower in his youth. Think of that little one who sits thinking of you now. Do you know she thinks of you? Ah, yes, you do! Let me tell your father!"

At last, listening to her soft voice, he nodded, and she went quickly lest he call her back. Be sure she went straight to Ezra, and she found him sleeping in his reed chair, his fan resting on his stomach and his legs outstretched. He was snoring and for a while nothing she could do would waken him. She coughed, she sang, she called in a soft voice, careful not to wake him too suddenly, lest his soul be wandering and not come back to his body. At last she spied a cricket on the stones and she picked it up by its jointed legs and put it in Ezra's beard. There it was so dismayed that it began to squeak dolefully, and Ezra woke and rolled his head and then combed his beard with his fingers and found the cricket and threw it out.

"I saw the naughty mite leap into your beard, Master," Peony said sweetly, "but I was afraid to wake you."

"I never had this happen before," Ezra said in surprise. He sat up, stretched himself, yawned, and shook his head to stir his brain. "Does it have a meaning? I must ask a geomancer."

"It means good luck, Master," Peony said. "Crickets come only to a safe, rich house."

She poured a bowl of tea from the pot on the table, and this she now handed him with both hands, and then, picking up the fan from the floor where it had fallen, she began to fan him. When he seemed himself she began her news.

"Master, I must confess a fault."

"Another one?" he asked. He yawned, rubbed the crown of his head, and smiled.

"My young master—your son, sir—" Here she paused.

Ezra was instantly alarmed. She looked too happy. Could it be possible that David had been so foolish as to return her love? It would throw the house into turmoil. A bondmaid! What would Madame Ezra do?

Peony caught the terror in his eyes and tried to smile. Well she knew what he was thinking and her heart quivered. No one, not even this good master of hers, whom she loved as the only father she knew, thought of her as more than a gentle servant, one fit for usefulness and pleasure but no more.

"Do not fear," she said sweetly. "It is not I whom your son loves."

This she said, knowing very well that it was within her reach to make David love her. His heart had denied Leah, and he had not yet accepted Kueilan, and into that emptiness she might have stepped, and his heart might have enclosed her. But she was too wise. Never would she be given the place of a wife, and even if she were, David's life could have no peace. She loved him too well to see him wretched, and she had been reared in obedience to those above. None could be happy if the proportions were ignored. It was not her fate to be the daughter-in-law in this house. No, she was like the little mouse that came out of its hiding place and danced solitary in the sun. So must she find her joy alone, sheltered under the vast roof.

"Then whom does my son love?" Ezra asked sternly.

Peony lifted her head and looked at him straightly with soft eyes that seemed as honest as a child's when she made them so.

"He still loves that little third lady in the house of Kung," she said.

Ezra looked away from her and he did not answer. He sat pulling his beard and sighing and fingering his lips and thinking this way and that and seeing no light anywhere. He discovered only this longing inside himself, that his son might marry whom he pleased and for his happiness.

Have I not been happy with my Naomi? he inquired of his own heart.

He had been happy. If he had not loved Naomi when they were married, neither had he greatly loved any other woman. No, he had not loved Flower of Jade—not enough to give up his parents' favor for her sake. Had David said he loved Peony, he would have chided and forbade, as his father had done in his own youth. But a daughter of the great Chinese house of Kung could not be despised. She was David's equal in all—except in faith. Yet many Jews had married Chinese wives and they had not ceased altogether to be Jews. He would put it so to Naomi.

Now Ezra was a man who had to do a thing as soon as he thought of it, and forgetting Peony he got impetuously to his feet and went in search of his son's mother, leaving Peony to stand and wonder how much she had done. She followed him at a little distance and took her place behind the cassia tree. As for Ezra, he found his wife in her own rooms and in a very ill humor. This he saw as soon as he came to the door, but he supposed that her mood was because of some household matter. Madame Ezra was a very shrewd good manager in her own house and she could be downcast over the theft of an egg or the breaking of a dish. She looked at Ezra coldly when he came in.

"You did not go to the shop today," she said.

He tried to smile as he came in and sat down on the chair opposite her and across the table. "No, for I came in very late last night," he confessed. "Kung Chen invited me to see the moon. He brought his two sons and David went with me."

"How you look!" she exclaimed. "You are yellow as sulphur!"

"Come, come," he retorted. "I am not so bad."

"Blear-eyed," she went on severely, "your hair a crow's nest! Did David drink too much?"

"I have not seen him this morning," Ezra said.

She pursed her lips. "I have been talking to Leah," she said.

Ezra threw her a shrewd tender look from under his bushy brows. "Ah, Naomi," he sighed, "why not let the boy alone?"

"I do not know what you mean," she said angrily.

"He does not love Leah," Ezra went on. "If he marries her it is only to please you, and what happiness can there be for either of them?"

Madame Ezra's handsome face grew red. "David knows nothing about women," she declared. "He is as silly as you were when I married you."

"I was much more silly," Ezra said gently. "I was clay in your hands, my dear."

She was unwilling to let her anger go down. "Besides, Leah loves him," she said.

"Then I pity her," Ezra replied.

"Why?" she turned her head quickly to look at him again. "Why should you pity her?"

Ezra said, "I did not—love anyone else—exactly."

Their eyes met and each looked away. There had been an hour years ago, in this very room, when she, a proud young woman, exceedingly beautiful and stern of faith, had accused him of stealing into a bondmaid's room. Both would have said they had forgotten it, but neither had forgotten.

"If you mean Peony—" Madame Ezra said thickly.

Ezra shook his head. "No, I do not mean the bondmaid. I mean the daughter of Kung Chen."

Madame Ezra rose as once long ago she had risen, and she looked down upon him. "No," she cried, "never! I will not allow it. Why do you speak of her again?"

But Ezra was not now that young peace-loving amiable man. He had grown stout and strong, and after these years of living with her, and learning to love her at last, he could hold his own with her.

"Ah, Naomi," he said gently and cruelly, "when will you ever learn that life does not wait for your allowance?"

With these words he turned away and left her. Peony, behind the cassia tree, pondered what she had heard. Should she return to David and tell him? But what had she heard except the old quarrel between these two elders? Better, then, would it be for her to wait until the quarrel was resolved, as Heaven might will.

She slipped from behind the tree and returned to her own room.

Madame Ezra had goaded Leah to despair. She had not meant to do so, but in the exasperation of her own fear she had harried and blamed and driven until Leah was terrified. This house, which had promised such shelter, was not secure, after all her hope! Her mother's friend, the one nearest to her mother, was angry with her. What would happen to her if Madame Ezra sent her away? She saw the dreariness of her life stretching ahead in her father's little house. When he died, she would be alone, with nothing except Madame Ezra's angry charity. No, she would be worse than alone. Aaron would be there. In fear and despair she gave over trying to defend herself and she ended by utter silence. Whatever Madame Ezra said she did not answer. She stood, her head bowed while

Madame Ezra talked on and on. Her hands clasped before her were so cold that they seemed frozen together. Her whole body felt bruised and heavy and her mind was numb.

When Madame Ezra shouted at her at last, "Leave me—and do not let me see your face again for a while!" Leah had turned and walked away without knowing where she was going.

She had no anger against Madame Ezra. She understood too well the agony of heart that had made the warm good woman fall into such fury. Madame Ezra was in despair, too. It was only despair that made her so cruel—despair and love. Madame Ezra loved David better than she loved anyone, better even than she loved God, and for this reason she wanted to keep her son, to keep him in the faith of her people. Here in this heathen land David would be lost to her if he were not kept in her faith. In her dreams he was the leader who might one day lead them all home again. All this Leah knew, and she saw into Madame Ezra's heart clearly and nothing she saw made her angry because she understood all.

No, it was not Madame Ezra who had been wrong, but she herself, Leah, who had failed. She had not been able to make David love her and want her for his wife. How could she blame David, either, she asked herself humbly? She had done nothing in her life except tend a house for two men. She lifted her hands and looked at them. Wang Ma had taught her how to rub oil in them and she had tried to do it faithfully, but work and poverty had made them big and it was too late to change that. She had tried to learn the Torah, but she kept thinking and dreaming of David, as he sat there. Not once had he looked at her or showed a single sign of remembering the one day when she had moved his heart, the day the caravan came, when God helped her. But afterward she had done nothing —she had not even sought God's help. Instead she had dreamed away the days, foolishly believing. Now, walking blindly along passageways and verandas and through courtyards, seeing nothing, she began to pray half aloud, "O Jehovah, our God, the One True God, hear me—and help me."

And as she walked along blindly praying it seemed that she heard God's voice bidding her to find David and go to him and open her heart to him. She lifted her head and the tears began to flow down her cheeks. If God helped her again, then everything would end as Madame Ezra wanted it—yes, and as she wanted it. She loved David, and how joyfully she would be his wife!

Her feet began to hurry over ways that she had not trod since she was a child. Long ago, when David was seven years old, he had been taken from his mother's court and put into rooms near his father's. The little girl Leah had gone with him one day to see them, and then Madame Ezra had heard of it and had forbade it. No woman except serving women should go to the men's rooms.

Now Leah's feet found the forgotten path, and since it was the hour when the servants were busy preparing the noon meal, no one saw her. Thus she came unannounced to David's door.

David sat as Peony had left him, beside the table. Once he had risen to get a book, but he had not read it. He could not fix his mind upon the words even though he had thought he wanted to find them, because they had made a cluster of verses this morning when he saw Kueilan. They were not simple love verses. They were stern lines about the choice a man must make between love and duty.

And yet, he pondered, even before he opened the book, he was not making a choice between love and duty. His choice lay with duty alone. He could still put aside the pretty Chinese girl whom now he not so much loved as knew he could love, did he make the choice that would allow him. No, what he must decide in the microcosm of his one being was the same decision that lay before all his people. Would he keep himself separate, dedicated to a faith that made him solitary among whatever people he lived, or would he pour the stream of his life into the rich ocean of all human life about him? Dare he lose himself in that ocean? But would he be lost? Nothing was ever lost. What he was, his ancestors in him, his children to come from him, would deepen the ocean, but they could not be lost.

It was at this moment before decision, in the midst of his profound meditation, that he saw Leah upon his threshold. He rose to his feet, amazed that she had come here.

"Did you—are you looking for me?" he stammered.

The moment she looked at him her mind grew clear. There must be no more confusion between them. Soul must meet soul.

"Yes," she said. "Your mother sent for me this morning and blamed me much concerning you."

"That was wrong of her," he said gently. But he was dazed. What did her coming at this moment mean? Did God Himself send her?

She came in and sat down where a little while before Peony had sat. David took his seat again. He saw that Leah had been crying, but something had dried her tears. Her great eyes were brilliant in their clarity and her cheeks were flushed. She was so beautiful that he wondered why he did not love her with all his heart and soul. His heart was silent. He could not love anyone until his soul had made its choice.

At this moment he saw the words of the tablet in the synagogue, engraved upon his own mind:

"Worship is to honor Heaven, and righteousness is to follow the ancestors. *But the human mind has always existed before worship and righteousness.*"

These bold dogged words of some ancient human being now strengthened David's soul, and made him stubborn against God and man.

"You must not allow my mother to disturb you," he said abruptly. "She used to trouble me very much. When I was a little boy it seemed to me that I could never please her. I was never quite good enough." He smiled a little sadly. "She is so good—so full of zeal."

"Your mother is right," Leah said strongly. "It is I who was wrong—you have been wrong. You too, David!"

"Have I been wrong?" He tried to be playful with these words, for he dreaded what he felt in her now, opposed to his own determination to be free.

"If it were not for women like your mother and men like my father," Leah said earnestly, "our people would long ago have been lost. We would have become as all other people are, without knowledge of the One True God. But they are the faithful, who have kept us a living and separate people."

David's eyes fell to her strong young hands clasped together and resting on the table. He was silent for a moment. Then he spoke very quietly. "Yet I wonder if it is not they who turn others against us—still."

Leah's lips parted. He saw that she did not understand his meaning. "It is hard for people to believe that we are better than they," he went on. "And after all, how are we better, Leah? We are good merchants, we get rich, we are clever, and we make music and paint pictures and weave fine satins, and wherever we are we do well—and then we rouse men's hatred and they kill us. Why? This is what I ask myself night and day, and I think I begin to see why."

Leah could not endure these words. "Men hate us because they envy us," she declared. "They do not want to know God. They are evil and they do not want to be good."

David shook his head. "We say they are evil. We say we are good."

Leah was shocked by these words. "David, how can you so willfully misunderstand the meaning of the Torah?" she cried. All her young energy was in the earnestness of her voice and eyes. "Has my father not told you? It is not that we are good. It is that God has chosen us to make known His will, through our Torah. If we are lost, then who will keep alive goodness? Shall the earth belong to the evil?"

To this David replied with some fire of his own. "I know no evil men—or women," he maintained. He felt angry with Leah because she was stubborn also, and he said suddenly, "If I were to speak the name of an evil man I would say it is your brother, Aaron."

With these words he struck her to the heart.

"You—you dare to say that!" she cried. "You should be ashamed, David!"

"Because he is your brother?" David demanded.

"No—because he is—is—one of us!" Leah cried.

David laughed harshly. "Now here is the proof of what I say! Justice is not in you, Leah, any more than it is in my mother. For me a man is good or evil, whether he is Jew or not."

Leah faltered before his wrath. "What has Aaron done?"

David rose and went to the open door and stood, his back to her. "I cannot tell you what he did," he said haughtily. "It would not be fit for your ears." He stared out into the bamboo-shaded court.

"There is nothing my brother does that I cannot know," Leah retorted.

"Hear it, then," David said. "He behaved foully to a woman."

Leah was silent a moment. Wisdom bade her say no more, but she was filled with anger against David. He had escaped her again and she was angry and frightened beyond any wisdom.

"What woman?" she demanded.

"I will not tell you," David answered. His back was still turned to her and he continued to look into the court.

Now at this moment Small Dog chose to appear at the moon gate opposite where he stood. She paused on the threshold and peered at him with her sad round eyes, and her red tongue hung out of the corner of her mouth. It was her habit to follow Peony, but being lazy and slow, she was always late. She followed by scent and not by sight.

But Leah knew that Small Dog always came after Peony, and quick as the flame to tinder, she understood. "I know what woman!" she said. "It was Peony!"

David cursed Small Dog in his heart, but what was there to say? He strode back into the room and he sat down and clapped the palms of his hands on the table. "It was Peony!" he shouted. "A bondmaid in the house where he was guest!"

Their eyes met in common fury, and neither yielded.

"If it had been any other woman, you would not have cared!" Leah cried wildly. She had only one longing now, and it was to wound David with all her strength, and she searched for the words that would hurt him most. "I know why you do not want me!" she cried. "Peony has corrupted you and spoiled you and made you weak to the bone. She has stolen your very soul." She could not go on. She tried not to weep but she began to sob aloud and she hated herself for breaking.

David's anger left him suddenly. Looking into the beautiful distressed face, he was filled with tenderness and pity. "It is not Peony whom I love," he said. "Someone else—perhaps—someone you have never even seen." So his heart made its own choice, after all, and his soul was silent.

Leah stopped crying. She stared at him, her eyes blank, her lips quivering, while the meaning of these words seeped into her mind. She felt them thunder in her heart and drain through her blood like poison. Then her mind grew dark. She leaped to her feet and tore down the sword that hung upon the wall within the reach of her right hand. She seized it and swung it across the table. The sharp curved blade struck David across the head. He put up his hand, felt the gush of blood, his eyes glazed, and he fell. Leah stared down at him, the sword still gripped in her hand.

At this moment Small Dog, who had watched all this, pattered forward and smelled at her master. She touched the tip of her tongue to his blood, and then, lifting her head, she began to howl.

When she heard the sound of the dog's wail the sword dropped from Leah's hand. All her reason came flooding back to her. She fell to her knees and took the sleeve of her robe and put it to David's head. "Oh, God," she whispered. "How could I?" Her whole being melted. "Oh, what shall I do?" she moaned.

And all the while Small Dog continued to wail.

Now Peony was used to Small Dog's voice, and whenever she heard it if the dog did not come she went to find her. She heard the high keening of the dog through the open doors of the courts and she rose quickly and followed the sound, and so she came to David's court. Through the open door she saw Leah kneeling and weeping and the sword was on the floor.

"Heaven—how did he wound himself?" Peony screamed, running into the room.

Then Leah stood up, and all her blood rushed up into her face. "I did it," she said. Her voice was strangled in her throat.

"You!" Peony whispered. She gave Leah one dreadful look. "Help me get him to his bed! Then go and tell his mother!"

She ordered Leah as though Leah were the maid and she the mistress, and Leah, trembling, obeyed her. Together the two girls lifted

David and carried him into the other room and laid him upon his bed, and his head fell back and blood streamed on the pillow.

"Oh, he is dead!" Leah shrieked.

"No, he is not," Peony said hardily. "Leave him to me. Go and tell his mother."

"I cannot, I cannot," Leah wailed.

Peony turned on her. "Shall I let him die while I go?" she demanded.

To this what answer could there be? Sobbing aloud, Leah ran out of the room, and then she paused, weeping and dazed. There was the sword. It lay on the floor beside Small Dog, who sat as though guarding it for a witness. Leah stood beside that sword. Then she stooped and picked it up and Small Dog growled. But Leah paid no heed to the dog. She lifted the sword and drew it across her own throat and the sharp quick blade did its work. She sank down, the sword clattered on the tile floor, and the little dog began to bark furiously.

In the other room Peony heard Leah's footsteps stop. Under her hand she felt David's heart beating and she stood, her hand on his heart, listening. Then she heard the silence and then she waited. Then she heard the dog growl. She waited again. The next moment she heard the clatter, and she ran on noiseless feet to the curtained door. There Leah lay, her neck half severed and her hair already soaked with blood. The sword was beside her, and the little dog barked on.

"Hush," Peony said, "hush, Small Dog."

She stepped into the room and then ran as though ghosts pursued her. Now Peony had bade Leah fetch Madame Ezra, but at this frightful moment she herself had not courage enough to call her. She ran instead for Wang Ma, and she kept silent, not wanting any other to know first what had befallen.

Before she found Wang Ma she found Old Wang. He had taken advantage of the noonday heat, when all slept, to pull a watermelon out of the north well. This melon he had split and now he was enjoying its golden coolness in a quiet and little-used corridor to the kitchen court. Peony had chosen this corridor and so she came upon him. At first he was frightened lest she see the stolen melon; then he perceived that she did not even see what he was doing.

"Where is Wang Ma?" she asked.

"Sleeping under the bamboos yonder." He pointed with his chin.

Peony hastened on, and soon she saw Wang Ma sitting on a stool and sound asleep, her face on her knees.

"Wang Ma!" she cried in a low and urgent voice.

Wang Ma woke instantly from the light slumber of the watchful servant. She stared at Peony, stupid with sleep, and Peony shook her shoulder.

"Wang Ma—here's death! The Jewess and our young master quarreled. She flung the sword at him, at his head."

"Oh, Heaven," Wang Ma muttered. She jumped up. "Where?" she cried.

"In his courts. Wait! Wang Ma, she turned the sword on herself."

"Both—dead?" Wang Ma's voice was a whisper of terror.

"No—only she."

"Do the old ones know?"

"Shall I tell them, or will you?"

The two women looked at each other. Both were thinking fast.

"I will go and prepare for what the old ones must see," Wang Ma decided. "Do you go to tell them."

So they parted, and Peony went to Madame Ezra. It was better to tell her first, she thought, but when she came to the door, there was Ezra too, and so there was nothing but to tell them both.

They cried out at the sight of her face. "What is wrong with you?" Madame Ezra exclaimed.

"Be silent, Naomi," Ezra commanded her. He rose but Peony beckoned with both her hands. She could not tell them, after all. They must see for themselves. "Come—come—the two of you! Oh—oh!"

She began to weep and to run back again from where she came, and they looked at one another and without another word they hastened after her.

With what fearful hearts did these two parents follow after Peony when they saw her footsteps turn toward David's court! They said not one word but hastened on and Madame Ezra was ahead.

At the moon gate Peony stopped. "I must tell you . . ." she began.

But Madame Ezra pushed her aside and went on.

Ezra hesitated. "Is David—?" he asked, and his lips were dry.

"No," Peony said. "Not he—but oh, Master, be ready—Leah has taken her own life—with that sword!"

Now Ezra cried out and he pushed past her, too, and he followed Madame Ezra and then Peony followed. But the room where Leah had lain was empty. Wang Ma had caught Old Wang by the collar as she passed him and together they had hastened on. Together they had lifted Leah from the floor and they had carried her into the room in the next court where the Rabbi had taught David the Torah, and there upon a couch they laid her and Wang Ma tore a curtain from a door and covered her with it. While she did this Old Wang went back and took off his jacket and sopped up the blood upon the tiles and dipped water from the pool and wiped the place clean.

So now when Madame Ezra looked in she saw only emptiness, and then she hastened into David's room and there he lay upon his bed. Peony had bound her own white silk girdle about his head to stanch the wound, and he lay as though he slept, but breathing hard and fast. Madame Ezra was wild with fear. She screamed his name and when he did not answer she abused Peony.

"Wait, Naomi," Ezra commanded her. "We must send for the physician."

"But why did you not tell me he had wounded himself?" Madame Ezra cried at Peony, and she took the girl by the shoulders and shook her and Ezra had to come between them. Peony did not say a word for she did not blame her mistress. She knew that sorrow distracted Madame Ezra and that it would ease her to let her anger out. Old Wang came in at this moment and Wang Ma too, and Ezra commanded Old Wang to go at once for the physician and Wang Ma to go and brew herbs.

So Peony was left alone to tell what had happened. This she did in a few simple words. Ezra and Madame Ezra listened, their hearts beating, their eyes wide, and Madame Ezra sat down beside David and began chafing his hands, and she said nothing.

"But why did they quarrel?" Ezra asked in sad wonder.

"I do not know," Peony said. "I thought only of him when I saw him lying there, and while I bound his head she—"

Madame Ezra burst into sudden loud weeping. "Oh, that wicked, wicked girl—and I treated her as though she were my own daughter! What if she has killed my son!"

"Leah was not wicked," Ezra said sorrowfully. "Something drove her mad—but now we will never know what it was."

Madame Ezra stopped weeping suddenly. "I shall never forgive her," she said.

"Even if David lives?" Ezra asked.

"She tried to kill him," she replied.

At this moment David stirred and opened his eyes, and looked from one face to the other.

"Leah?" he asked faintly.

"Hush!" Madame Ezra said.

"But she—never meant . . ." His voice trailed away.

"Hush!" Madame Ezra said fiercely.

"Do not speak, my son," Ezra said. He came near and took David's hand, and thus the parents waited. But David closed his eyes again and spoke no more. Now Wang Ma brought the bowl of herb tea and a spoon and Peony fed the tea to David slowly until at last the doctor came. He was a small, stooped, silent man and he wore great horn-rimmed spectacles and he smelled of ginger and dried bones.

They rose and stood when he came in and stood waiting and watchful while he examined the wound and felt the pulse and meditated a while.

"Will my son live?" Ezra asked at last.

"He will live," the physician said, "but for a long time his life will not be secure. The wound is not only of the flesh. His spirit has received a blow."

"What shall we do?" Madame Ezra implored.

"Give him his way in everything," the physician answered.

挑筋教

VIII

DAVID woke. He was in his bed. It was night and dark except for the glimmer of light from the small bean-oil night lamp set on the table outside the bed curtains. Night? But the sun had been shining!

"Leah," he called faintly.

Peony heard him instantly. She was sitting on a hard stool, purposely uncomfortable so that she would not doze and would hear the slightest change even in David's breathing. Now she tiptoed to the bed, parted the curtains, and looked down on him. His waking eyes looked up at her.

"Leah," he whispered again.

"Leah is asleep," Peony said.

She took her soft silk handkerchief and wiped his cheeks and lips.

"I feel—weak," he muttered.

"You need food," she replied. "Lie still." She let the curtains fall, and going to a small charcoal brazier set on the table she took the lid from a pot simmering on the coals, and with a long-handled ladle she dipped the soup of rice and red sugar into a bowl. She moved in quietness, soft in all she did, and she went back to the bed.

"I will feed you," she said tenderly.

She feared lest David ask her how he came to be lying in his bed. But he did not ask. He drank slowly, mouthful by mouthful, the warm sweet mixture. Red sugar was to make blood. Then he had lost much blood. That was why he was weak. His head pained him greatly. He remembered why this was. Leah had struck him with the sword. He saw her wild beautiful face, her hands holding the uplifted sword. As long as he lived he would remember. Nothing she could say or do would make him forget. And she was sleeping!

"My head hurts me," he muttered.

"I will give you a little opium," Peony said, going back to the table. She prepared the opium pipe, heating the pill of opium until it was soft, and then going back to the bed she put the mouthpiece to David's lips.

"Breathe it in, Young Master," she said.

He breathed it in again and again and the fumes curled about the paths of his brain. The pain eased and in the gradual relief he saw Peony's face, surrounded by light.

"How kind—how—how kind—how kind—" he began, and he could not leave off babbling.

She put her hand on his lips and stilled them. "I love you," she said distinctly. "I could never hurt you—I love you. Do you hear me?"

He smiled in delightful drowsiness and could not answer. He sank into velvet softness, smelled fragrance, heard music, saw Peony's face over and over again, tender with love, and his eyes closed.

When Peony was sure he slept, she felt the pulse in his wrist. It was stronger than it had been. She could leave him safely for the few moments she needed to go and tell Madame Ezra that he had waked and had eaten and now was sleeping again. Silently she went into the other room and passed Old Wang, sleeping in a chair beside the table, his head on his folded arms. Ezra had commanded him to stay the night, ready for Peony's bidding. Pitying him in his sleep, Peony went on without waking him.

The house was strange at night, silent in the soft darkness. She walked lonely through one court and the next. At each gate a paper lantern was hung to guide her, and she followed the dim light. When she passed her own court Small Dog heard her and pattered after her, sniffing and yawning.

Thus they came to Madame Ezra's court. A light burned in the bedroom and there Peony went. Madame Ezra was sitting up against pillows, asleep in her bed. She had not meant to sleep, doubtless, but weariness had been too much for her. Her head was thrown back, her mouth was slightly open, and she was breathing deeply.

Peony stood between the parted curtains, and dreaded to wake her. "Mistress—Mistress," she called. She made her voice very soft at first, then louder, winning back the wandering troubled soul.

Madame Ezra choked and started. "Eh!" she cried, and opening her eyes, she started forward and stared at Peony. Her soul was still only halfway home, and Peony took her hands and clapped them.

"Nothing but good news," she murmured. "Our young lord waked, he ate, he sleeps again."

Madame Ezra came fully to herself. "Is he asking for me?"

Now Peony did not want to say that he had not asked for his mother, so she replied, "He was still confused with pain in his head, and after he had eaten I made the pipe ready, and eased him. He is asleep again."

"Did he say nothing?" Madame Ezra demanded. She pulled her hands away from Peony's.

"He called Leah's name," Peony replied.

"What did you tell him?" Madame Ezra demanded.

"I told him she was sleeping," Peony said.

Madame Ezra leaned back and sighed.

"I must return to him," Peony went on.

"When he wakes do not tell him Leah is dead," Madame Ezra commanded her.

"I will not," Peony promised, and she went back again, pausing only to lock Small Dog into her room lest David wake.

David was still sleeping when she came to him, and Peony herself felt very weary. Now that he had eaten she did not fear so much that he might die, and she crept upon the foot of his bed and curled herself small on top of the covers and thought how she would conceal Leah's death for a day or two, at least. So tender was David's conscience that he would blame himself somehow for what had happened. Yet how was anyone to blame except Leah herself, and her own god-driven soul?

"How to make him believe this!" Peony murmured distressfully.

Yet he must believe it, or Leah's power would continue over him as long as he lived. He would cling, as all his people did, to his own suffering.

"We must distract him," Peony told herself resolutely. "We must amuse him and make him happy in spite of himself."

Upon this resolution she fell asleep.

Yet how could Leah's death be hidden from David? When he woke in the morning he asked no one where she was, but his eyes were thoughtful. Peony felt him stir and she was up and tending him and Ezra came in soon after dawn, before he had washed or dressed, and Madame Ezra came, wrapped in a great quilted robe, and Wang Ma came and Old Wang, and servants peered in at the door to see their young master so that they could carry the news outside. Still David asked no question of anyone. The old doctor came again and took off the silk bandages that bound David's wound, and he stared at the black plasters that held the edges together, and declared that all was as well as possible, and he ordered the best of blood puddings.

"Pig's blood is best," he declared.

Ezra looked at his Naomi. "We do not eat pig, Elder Brother," he said gently to the old Chinese physician, "but if it is necessary for my son's life—"

"He is young and strong," the Chinese replied, "and chicken blood will do. Were he very old I would recommend woman's milk instead of blood."

So chicken blood was jelled into a pudding with the liver, and red rice was cooked with spinach roots and raw eggs mingled with it, and all this went to mend David's wasted blood. His mother sat beside him all day and his father came and went restlessly, and still David asked no one of Leah.

But the next day and the next, as he grew stronger, his ear caught certain sounds in the house. Stealthy feet came and went, and once he heard the Rabbi's voice raised in a cry. Toward evening he heard the pounding of a carpenter's hammer. His father and mother were with him, and Peony was heating water on the charcoal brazier.

"Mother," David said.

Madame Ezra rose from the chair in which she was sitting and went to his bed. "Yes, my son?" Her voice was so sad and her whole manner so subdued that she seemed strange.

"Where is Leah?" David asked distinctly.

Madame Ezra turned to look at Ezra. He sat beside the table moving one thumb slowly around the other. "We had better tell him, Naomi," he muttered.

"Have you punished Leah, Mother?" David cried out. "Ah, that was wrong."

"God has punished her, my son," Madame Ezra said. Suddenly she began to weep. This tall, strong, hearty woman, who all her life had taken her own way, fell into an agony of weeping. She could say no more and she hastened from the room and Ezra went after her. There was only Peony left, and it was Peony who had to tell David. She went to him and she told him in soft, gentle, quick words.

"Leah went alone into the other room, while I stood here stanching your blood with my silk girdle. She took up the sword and drew it across her own throat—and her life flowed away."

He closed his eyes. That blade, melting through the coarse cloth of the caravan loads! He saw it sink into Leah's flesh. Suddenly he was sick and Peony cried out and held the quilt under his mouth.

"Even dead she hurts you!" she wailed.

David fell back on his pillow exhausted. "Hush!" he gasped. "You can—never understand."

These words dropped like stones into Peony's soft heart. She did not reply; she could not, indeed. She lifted the quilt and took it away to be cleansed, and before she could return to David she paused behind a door and wiped her eyes with her sleeves for a moment. Then she turned aside and she entered the room where the carpenter had finished his work. The heavy camphorwood coffin was made, and the lid stood ready against the wall. Within it servants had already placed Leah's body. They had finished their task. Peony had done nothing, nor had Wang Ma. The undermaids had worked alone. Now only one young maid remained to smooth the robes and put a candle into the folded hands, to light the dead girl's soul upon its way.

"I covered her neck," the maid whispered. She had thrown a fold of silk across the wound.

Peony went and looked upon Leah. The blood had drained away, and Leah's face looked thin and unreal, as though it were made of some clear white substance. Her eyes were sunken and the long dark lashes were thick shadows on her cheeks. Her fine black hair fell back from her pale forehead and her lips were fixed and hard.

Someone stumbled at the threshold and Peony looked up. It was the Rabbi, leaning on his staff. He stretched out his hands, feeling his way on the unfamiliar ground.

"Will someone lead me to my child?" This he asked in his deep sorrowful voice, and Peony went and took his hand and led him in, and stood by him while he seemed to look at Leah's face.

"I see my child," he said at last. "I see her with her mother. Her mother went down to fetch her out of Hell. She will take her child before Jehovah, and she will cry to Him until He hears."

Muttering to himself, the old Rabbi went on. "The mother will weep—she will beat her breast and Jehovah will hear her voice. Leah, my child, the Lord searcheth all hearts and understandeth all the imagination of the thoughts. If thou seek Him He will be found of thee."

So passionate was this old man in his lonely murmuring to the dead girl that the little maid grew frightened and went away and Peony was left. She was frightened too, but she pitied the father. "Come and rest, Old Teacher," she said sweetly, and she took the edge of his sleeve and pulled it.

At the sound of her voice the Rabbi turned on her. His blind eyes opened wide and his long white beard quivered. "Who are you, woman?" he cried in a loud voice.

Peony stood unable to move. This tall old man, towering above her, drove terror into her soul.

His great voice shouted suddenly above her head. "God hath deprived this woman of wisdom! Neither hath he imparted to her understanding! She seeketh her prey and her eyes are afar off. Where the slain are, there is she."

He stretched out his arms as though to seize her, and Peony, seeing those great thin hands, beautiful and terrible in their strength, turned and fled as though she were indeed pursued.

The Rabbi heard her flying footsteps. He listened and a smile of cunning pleasure passed over his face. "Depart from me, ye workers of iniquity," he muttered. He lifted his eyes and seemed to look about triumphantly. Then he sighed and with difficulty he felt his way about the room. Around and around he went, and then he came unaware to the coffin again and he felt it carefully up and down and he put in his hand and touched Leah, her feet and knees, and her cold hands. When he found the candle he took it away and threw it on the ground. Then very slowly with trembling horror on his face and agony in his finger tips he felt her wounded throat and then her thin blood-drained face. He had been told that Leah had lifted the sword against herself. Ezra had told him but he had not understood. Now the knowledge came into him and it was too much. He fell down upon the stone floor, unconscious, and so he was found, hours later, when the burial women came to fill the coffin with lime and the carpenter to close the lid. They lifted the old man up and placed him on a couch and went to tell Ezra and Madame Ezra.

"Let Aaron be brought," Madame Ezra commanded.

But no one could find Aaron. Rachel declared that he had not come home the whole night before. There was nothing to do but tend the old man back again, and under Madame Ezra's direction this was done. He was carried to his bed in the house and laid upon it.

It was Madame Ezra who first perceived what fresh disaster had befallen. The old Rabbi came back. He sighed, a groan burst from his lips, and he struggled as though he fought some unseen spirit. Wang Ma was watching him and she ran to call Madame Ezra. When she entered the room he opened his eyes. Madame Ezra spoke very gently. "Father, I am here."

But the Rabbi's sightless eyes only stared.

Wang Ma cried out in terror, "Oh, Mistress, his soul is lost!"

So indeed it was. For days the Rabbi did not speak at all. He lay on his couch, he took food, but he was silent. Even to pray he did not speak. When one day, without cause, he opened his mouth, it was to speak without knowledge. His soul was gone forever. He knew no one and remembered nothing except the days when Leah was a child, and her mother had been in the house with him.

Thus the Rabbi entered into Heaven before he died, and Ezra in the great kindness of his heart said to his servants, "Prepare a place for him. I will take care of him as long as he lives."

He spoke without thought of his own goodness, but Madame Ezra's heart was shaken. When the servants were gone she turned to her husband and humbled herself as she had never done before.

"You are so good," she sobbed. They stood side by side and she put out one hand to feel for his and covered her eyes with the other. "I wish I had been better to you, Ezra."

"Why, you have been very good, my dear," he said pleasantly. He took her hand and held it.

"No, I have often been bad-tempered with you," she sobbed.

"I know how often I have tried you, Naomi," Ezra replied.

"I shall be better," Madame Ezra promised.

"Do not be too good, my wife," Ezra said, trying to make a joke for her comfort. "Else how can I be your match? I like to have a little temper sometimes."

"You are good—you are good," she insisted, and knowing her intensity, he let this pass. He drew her hand through his arm and led her out of the room, talking cheerfully as they went.

"Now, my Naomi, we must remember that our son lives, and that we have our duty to mend his life and make him happy. Little children must be born here again, and we must forget the past."

So he talked, pressing her heart toward the future, and she subdued herself and tried to be dutiful.

"Yes, Ezra," she murmured, "yes, yes—you are right."

He was alarmed at such submission and anxious lest she were ill. Then he reasoned with himself that it would not last. She was a hearty woman and time would bring back her temper and her health, and so he let her say what she would. But Madame Ezra's heart was sore with sorrow and bewildered with the downfall of all her plans and the loss of all her hopes. She grew weak, for the moment at least.

"Ezra," she quavered when he had led her to her own rooms and had helped her into her chair, "what shall we do with our son?" This was the question that had been tearing at her thoughts ever since she saw Leah lying dead.

Ezra stood above his weeping wife, and for the first time in their life he knew himself master of this woman whom in his fashion he had loved, and he knew that now he truly loved her. He took her plump hand in his and caressed it. "Let us think only of his happiness, my dear," he coaxed. "Let us have the wedding as quickly as possible."

She raised wet and humble eyes to his. "You mean—" She faltered.

He nodded. "I mean the pretty child he loves, the daughter of Kung Chen. I will go to the father and we will set the day and we will bring joy into the house again."

"But Leah—" Madame Ezra began.

Ezra spoke quickly, as though he had already decided everything. "She will be buried tomorrow, and we will allow a month's mourning. By then David will be well."

Madame Ezra could not answer this. A month! She bowed her head and drew away her hand.

Ezra stood for a moment longer. "Are you willing, my wife?" he asked in a full strong voice.

Madame Ezra nodded. "Yes, I am willing." Her voice was weary and she no longer rebelled, and Ezra bent and kissed her cheek and went away without another word.

Upon the day of Leah's burial it rained and Ezra forbade David to leave his bed. This made grief, for David had sworn himself able to get up. Leah dead had laid hold on his thoughts as Leah alive had not been able to do. He felt guilt in himself that he could not fathom. He said to himself that had he been more patient that last day she would never have lost her reason so wholly and he might have saved her. Now it seemed to him that he must follow her body to the grave.

But Ezra would not hear to it, and David was astonished by the strength in his father's face and voice and by the power of his determination. Moreover, his mother did not speak to differ. David looked to her to take his part, but what she said astonished him still more.

"My son, obey your father," she said.

With the two of them thus united against him, David could not contend further, and so he only rose and went to the room where Leah's closed coffin lay. There he stood leaning on a manservant and Peony was beside him to watch lest he faint, and he stood and waited until he was left behind. The bearers lifted the heavy coffin and the few mourners followed. The Rabbi was there, wondering and smiling, but Aaron was not. Until this day Aaron had not been found, and Ezra said that he must have run away from the city.

"When all our trouble is over, I will find him and bring him back," he told Madame Ezra. "As it is, who misses him? The Rabbi has forgotten everything, and Leah is gone."

David stood watching and sorrowful while the little procession went through the court and out of the gate, and then he turned and went back to his bed again. There he lay with his eyes closed and Peony was too wise to speak to him. She sat beside him, letting him feel her presence in silence. David did not speak and Peony did not rouse him. She knew that sorrow must be spent before joy can take its place, but well she knew that sorrow passes, too.

Outside the city, in the lot of ground upon a hill that was the resting place of the Jews, Leah was put into the earth beside her mother. The Rabbi, her father, stood between Ezra and Madame Ezra, smiling and blind in the cool autumn sunshine. But when Ezra spoke, unexpectedly he obeyed.

"Pray, Father," Ezra commanded in a loud voice at his ear.

The old Rabbi lifted his face to the sky. "How warm is the sun," he murmured. And then after an instant he began thus to pray:

"Look down from heaven, and behold from the habitation of Thy holiness and Thy glory! Doubtless Thou art our Father, though

Abraham be ignorant of us, and Israel acknowledges us not. Thou, O Lord, art our Father. Thy name is from everlasting. We are thine. . . ." And then the Rabbi imagined that he was in the synagogue, and from habit he spread out his hands and cried out. "The Lord God, Jehovah, the One True God!"

Around them passers-by had stopped in curiosity to watch and stare, and the Chinese coffin bearers stood wondering in the strange presence of this old man.

Thus unwittingly did the Rabbi pray over his dead child's grave. Ezra saw Madame Ezra weep, and he stepped between them and supported them both, and when the grave was filled and the sod packed hard upon the earth, he led them away and took them home.

挑筋教

IX

In the ninth moon month, at a time when heat was gone and cold not yet come, the day of David's marriage was set. It was the thirty-third day after Leah's death, and the sod upon her grave was still green.

Thus David saw it when he first went to look upon that grave. He had acquiesced by silence when his father told him that the wedding had been decided upon and he had been silent when he heard that exchange of gifts had been made.

"Does this please you, my son?" Ezra had asked at last.

"Yes, Father, if it pleases you and my mother," David had answered. He had recovered from his wound, but it had left a scar across his forehead that would be there until his skull was dust. Though his flesh was healed, his spirit had not recovered. He was listless for many hours of the day, and at night he slept ill, and his old healthy greediness for good food had not returned. All this Peony saw, but she said nothing. She tended him now as she had tended him in the old days when he was a child, and Madame Ezra did not forbid her any more.

"Tell me what will please you, my son," Ezra said anxiously. He put his big hot hand on David's thin one and David shrank from his father's touch. He felt his father too eager and too pressing, overanxious and excessively hearty. His strength was not equal yet to meet his father's love.

"I must marry, I know," David said.

"You need not—you need not," Ezra said. But his face fell.

"Yes, I must," David said.

"Not if you do not love this daughter of Kung," Ezra said.

"I do not love anyone yet, perhaps," David said with a small smile.

Ezra was perturbed indeed. He sat back and put his hands on his knees. "I thought you were writing her poems!" he exclaimed.

"I was—but—" So David said.

"Did you leave off before—" Ezra asked, and could not go on to mention Leah.

"Before Leah died?" David said for him. "No—yes, I left a poem unfinished. That was because I met Leah—in the peach garden."

"Do you mourn her?" Ezra demanded.

David considered long before he spoke. They were sitting in his father's room, for Ezra had sent for him to tell him that the betrothal was completed.

"No," David said at last. "I do not mourn. I wish she had not died—as she did. If she had lived—" He paused again.

Ezra's hair prickled on his scalp and along his arms and legs. "Would you have wed her?" he demanded when David paused too long.

David shook his head slowly. When he did so he felt the scar upon his head ache. "No," he said, and then with more vigor he said again, "No, Father, of that be sure. But had Leah lived I would have wed this other one with more joy. Can you understand that?"

Ezra's jaw dropped and he stared back at his son and shook his head. It was beyond him.

"Poor Father," David said tenderly. "Why should I trouble you? I will marry, and I will have sons and daughters, and I will do well with my life. After the wedding I will come back to the shop and everything will go as before, but better—much better."

He rose, put a smile on his face, and bowed to his father and went away. Behind him Ezra sat doubtful for a long time, sighed, and then went to his shop, his underlip thrust out for the rest of the day and his temper bad.

As for David, he was restless and he was so irritable with Peony that she gave up trying to please him and she sat quietly and did her sewing. This was usually embroidery of some sort, but today she was not working on silks. She had a piece of fine white linen in her hands, shaped to the sole of a foot.

David watched her little fingers moving in and out of the cloth, drawing the needle up and down and through, and at last he asked her what she did.

"Your feet are tender from lying in bed," she replied calmly. "I know that the socks the sewing maids make are painful for you. These I am sewing with flat seams, so that there is no seam inside to tear your skin."

He did not reply to this but he continued to lounge in his chair and look at her idly. "I am to be married, Peony," he said suddenly.

She lifted her eyes to look at him, and then her eyelids dropped again to the sewing. "I know," she said.

"Are you pleased with me now?" he demanded.

"It is not for me to be pleased or displeased," she said gently.

"You shall stay here, Peony, exactly as you have always," he went on.

"Thank you," she said. Then she added, "Young Master."

He paid no heed to this. "I suppose you will want to marry, too, one day," he said abruptly.

"When I do, I will tell you," she replied. All this time her fingers were flying very fast, the needle piercing in and out. He was not thinking of her and well she knew it. His mind was wandering round itself. But she was not prepared for what came next from him.

"I want to go and see where Leah is buried," he said.

She laid the cloth down upon her knees and looked at him, exasperated with love. "And why on this day do you want to go?" she inquired. "It is ill fortune to link death with life."

"If I go and see her grave, I shall know she is dead," he said strangely.

Peony looked at him with concern. "But you know Leah is dead," she reasoned.

"I keep seeing her," he replied.

They sat in the room where Leah had died, and Peony remembered this, but she did not wish to recall it to his mind. She had thought many times that David's rooms should be moved elsewhere in the house, but first he had been too ill to be moved and then when she spoke of it he refused, saying that these had been his rooms since his childhood and he liked them best. Now in the secret place of her thought Peony made up her mind that she would tell Madame Ezra that indeed he must have his married life in other rooms, in larger courts, and these rooms should be sealed or given to visitors.

She folded the cloth and put it into a box inlaid with ivory where she kept her sewing things. "If you wish to go and see that grave I will go with you," she said.

"Now?" he asked.

"Now," she agreed.

So it happened that on this day, a mild still day in the autumn, David rode in his mule cart outside the city wall to the place where Leah was buried. It was a quiet place not far from the riverbank, and not far too from the synagogue. He knew it well, for here his grandparents and his ancestors were buried among many others of the Jews who had died during the centuries of their sojourn here. The graves were tall, like Chinese graves, and the marking stones were small.

To Leah's grave Peony led him, for she knew where it was. She had not come here to the funeral, since she had stayed behind with David, but Wang Ma had told her that Leah's grave lay to the east, away from the river and beside her mother's grave.

There they went and David sat down upon the coat that Peony folded on the grass. The place was still, the air damp and cool under a gray sky. Around them the tall tombs stood, but David gazed at Leah's grave. The earth was fresh beneath the sod that had been placed over it, and the sod had taken good root. A few wild asters of a pale purple were blooming in the grass.

"I cannot feel she is there," David said at last.

"She is there," Peony said firmly.

"Do you believe in the spirit?" David asked her.

"I do not think about spirits," Peony replied. She stood beside him but now she stooped and pressed her palm against his cheek. "Are you chill?" she asked.

He shook his head. "Leave me alone a while," he commanded.

"I will not," Peony replied. "It is my duty to stay with you, or I shall be blamed for any ill you have."

So she stood there beside him, a small straight figure, her face to the grave. But her eyes went beyond it. Over the low wall she saw fields and villages, and beyond them the flat bright surface of the river, and the sail of a boat hanging against a mast. What was in David's mind she did not know, but she would not yield him up to Leah's spirit. She did believe deeply in spirits, and she knew that the spirit of the dead clings always to the living. With all the strength of her inner being she now opposed Leah's spirit.

Stay in your grave, she said silently, and she opposed her will to Leah's will. You have lost him and you shall not harm him any more.

So she held herself hard against every memory of Leah and all that Leah had meant, and at last David sighed and rose to his feet.

"She is dead," he said sadly.

"Let me put this coat on you," Peony said. "Your flesh is cold."

He shivered. "I am cold—let us go home quickly."

"Yes—yes," she agreed, and she hastened him to the mule cart, and when they were driven over the rough cobblestone road to the gate she hurried him out of the cart and into his rooms and she made him go to bed and she fetched a hot stone for his feet and hot broth for him to drink and she sat beside him until he slept. Then she went to Madame Ezra and told her faithfully what had happened. Madame Ezra listened, her dark and tragic eyes fixed on Peony's face, and Peony braced herself, prepared herself for temper. But Madame Ezra was not angry. She heard, she sighed, and then she said quietly, "Now that he has seen the grave, we will forget the past and prepare for the future."

It was the first time in all her life that Peony had heard such words from Madame Ezra, to whom the past had always been most dear, and she pitied this older woman and felt a new love for her. "My dear mistress," she said gently, "I promise you that the future will be happy for you, too."

Madame Ezra shook her head and two tears fell out of her eyes. "If God wills," she murmured.

Peony bowed and did not answer this, but as she went away to her own bed she thought to herself that gods had little indeed to do with mortal happiness.

The day of David's wedding dawned clear and cold. The day stood alone in the calendar of early winter. It was near no feast day, and there were no memories about it. It was simply a day chosen by the geomancer under Kung Chen's direction, a lucky day when the horoscopes of the man and woman met under a fortunate star.

Since David was young, since his strength and health had returned to him fully, since his heart was restless and eager to live again, he rose with some excitement and even with joy. He had allowed himself to become possessed gradually with the thought of the pretty girl coming now to be his wife. It was inevitable, he told himself. Even had his mother wished to put another daughter of their people in Leah's place, there was no other. Among their people the poor were more than the rich, and there was no family to match the House of Ezra. With all her zeal, he knew his mother was too prudent to bring into the house a daughter-in-law with many poor and greedy kinsfolk. If not a Leah, then why not the pretty girl he had seen and knew he could love?

Thus thinking, David loosed the cords that had bound his heart and he welcomed his marriage day.

Never had Peony found him so fanciful and so willful. He rose early and he washed himself in three baths, the last perfumed, and he was dissatisfied with the way his hair curled, and she must brush it as straight as she could with scented oils. He had wanted every garment new, and these new garments had been made of a clear yellow silk, and now he wished them pale green. The yellow, he said, made him look too dark.

Peony lost her patience at last. "But you yourself ordered the yellow!" she cried.

"You should have advised me against it," he said in great discontent.

"Be still," she urged. "There is no time to make others."

So he put on the yellow, and then he was pleased with it after all, for his Chinese robes were of bright blue, and the yellow underlinings were pleasant enough. Over the brocaded blue satin he wore a black velvet jacket buttoned down the front with jade buttons. That his little bride be not frightened, David had chosen to wear Chinese garments altogether for this day, and upon his head he put a round black satin cap and on its top was a round red button.

When all was finished he stood up before Peony for her inspection, and when she saw him there, tall and smiling, his head high, his feet together, the tears swam up into her eyes.

He stepped forward quickly and put his arm around her. "Peony!" he cried softly. "Why do you weep?"

She leaned her cheek for one moment against him. Then she laughed and slipped out of his arm. "You are too beautiful!" she declared. She made herself very busy. "Let me put your collar straight. Have you rubbed musk on your palms as I bade you? David, you will be very happy—I know it—I feel it in my heart!"

"But are you happy?" he insisted.

She turned grave then and she took his hand and put it to her cheek. "I am happy," she said softly. "Now I know that I shall live in this house—forever and forever, until I die."

With these words she fled as swiftly as a swallow. But he took her words and considered them. Did she indeed so love him? He was most tender, thinking of her. Peony would demand nothing of him. She could live quite happily here, content with what her life gave her and asking for no stretch of heart or spirit, or for anything that was beyond right and proportion to what she was. He would look after her welfare and keep her with him so long as they lived, not quite his sister, but something more than servant. He would be good to her.

And now his father and mother were coming. He saw them enter the gate, side by side, dressed in their wedding garments. Each had bought new robes, and Ezra's was of brown satin and Madame

Ezra's was the deep color of purple grapes edged with gold. Ezra had left off his small cap, and Madame Ezra's gray hair was bare. They came with measured steps, in silence, and he went to meet them and bowed before them. He saw his mother had been weeping, for her eyes were swollen and her lips still quivered, but she did not speak. It was Ezra who said what must be said.

"Are you content, my son?" Ezra asked.

"Well content," David replied steadily.

He bowed and they bowed to him and then he went with them to the great hall, and there they waited.

Now in another room Wang Ma and Peony waited, too, for the bride. Whispering and peeping at every corner and window were the women servants and the undermaids, and all were expectant and excited. Was the new bride pretty and would she be good to them? Rumors were that she was the prettiest girl in the city, but these were usual rumors before a bride was seen.

At noon, exactly, the bride's sedan, covered with red satin curtains, arrived at the great gate and a small sedan for Chu Ma and with them panoplied mule carts bringing the bride's family and their attendants. The sedan was carried into the courts and thence into the place where Peony and Wang Ma waited. Chu Ma came out of her sedan first. But Peony herself, with a begging word, opened the curtains of the bride's sedan and offered her arm to the bride.

From all around the court sighs and exclamations rose into the air.

"Ah, she is very pretty!"

"Ah, it is all true!"

"Look at her great eyes!"

"Her little feet—"

If the bride heard, she made no sign. She stepped daintily into the doorway, one hand on Peony's arm and the other on Chu Ma's.

"Carefully, my mistress!" Chu Ma said in a loud voice. She considered it beneath her to notice any other servants, and she went ahead to smooth the cushion on the chair set for the bride and to feel if it were soft enough and she called imperiously, "Where is the tea? Is it the best? My mistress drinks only what is brewed from the leaves plucked before the rains!"

But Peony had all prepared, and after the little bride had sat a while she grew curious, and since only women were there she put aside her veil. She looked about the room with her big black eyes. "Is this to be my room?" she inquired in her high sweet voice.

"Hush!" Chu Ma said. She pursed her lips. "Brides are not to speak—I told you, you naughty child!"

"I will speak," the little bride said willfully. "Besides, you said only if there was a man in the room."

Everyone laughed at this and she laughed, too. Then she saw Peony standing near. "I am glad you are in this house!" she exclaimed. "You are no older than I, are you?"

"I am eighteen, my lady," Peony said.

"So am I," the bride said, and clapped her hands, and everybody laughed again. Then she leaned forward to Peony. "Tell me—is his mother very strange?"

Peony shook her head and put her hand over her mouth to hide her smiles.

"But she is foreign?" Kueilan insisted.

"Yes—but not as much as she was," Peony said.

Madame Ezra had indeed changed very much. She had grown silent and she did not always put her will first. When Leah died, something died in her, too. This all had perceived, without understanding what it was. But Peony knew.

Now there were footsteps in the court. They looked up and there stood David. At once there was confusion, for this was not the time for him to appear.

Chu Ma cried out in alarm, "Your veil, little one!"

But Kueilan did not put up her hand to her veil. Instead she looked at David and he at her. All in the room were astounded at what they saw was happening and they took it to be a foreign custom.

"I know I do what may be considered wrong," David said to Kueilan very gently. He looked at her without shame, and indeed with the greatest pleasure. She did not reply but she gazed back at him as though she forgot that she should drop her eyes. They looked at each other, and then she said in a small breathless voice, "I think it is not wrong!"

"Then we agree," David answered, and after a long look more, he bowed and went away. When he was gone Kueilan sat smiling like a little goddess and heard not one word of Chu Ma's scolding or the smothered laughter from the walls. She let Chu Ma drop her veil and she sat behind it, her eyes bright and her mouth demure.

But Chu Ma continued to scold and she said in distraction, "It is not well for the man to see the woman too early—it brings ill luck to the marriage."

No one gave her heed, for Peony now hastened the wedding. "Let me lead you to the great hall," she said to the bride, and the little figure in the stiff embroidered robes of scarlet satin rose and leaned on her arm and Chu Ma went on the other side, and all followed. In the great hall Kung Chen waited with his wife and his sons by his side. Across the room Ezra and Madame Ezra and Kao Lien stood alone. There had been some talk of the Rabbi's being present, but this morning when Ezra went to see the old man in the rooms where he lived in this house, he found him so dazed and befuddled that he feared to bring him out before guests, and he had left him there under the care of Old Eli, who had been brought here as his servant. As for that Aaron, none had heard of him yet.

The family of Kung missed neither the Rabbi nor his son. They watched the entrance of their child with feelings various and natural to them. The sons were dubious for their sister, but the younger son especially so. The eldest son shared with his father the prudence of business and unity within the nation. Through this little sister the House of Ezra ceased by so much to be foreign, and since Ezra was known as a kind good man, and very rich besides, it was enough. Madame Kung was serene, never exerting herself to worry or overmuch thought, and she saw that the child looked as she should and thought that the marriage was good enough for a third daughter, although she was secretly pleased that the two elder girls were well married to wealthy Chinese families. She held back a yawn, stared at Madame Ezra, and pitied her for being so tall and having so high a nose.

Only Kung Chen held within himself the feelings of love and doubt and tenderness that made him a father. His Little Three! She had grown up in his house and he had paid her no more heed than he had any of his daughters, but now as she tripped with tiny slow steps into the room, he remembered how rosy and laughing she had been as a baby, and how seldom she had cried, and how when she began to walk she had tremendous little tantrums, stamping her feet and clenching her fists, and how he always laughed at her until she gave up being so angry. He remembered that once she had fallen into the fish pond and he had lifted her out and let her cry against his shoulder, wetting him through from her dripping clothes, and how he had bought her a stick of candied crab apples to cheer her again and she came back with fresh dry clothes.

"How came you to be in my fish pond?" he had asked, laughing.

"The fish pulled me in," she had insisted, and he had laughed again.

A small endearing creature, a butterfly mind and a kitten soul, but the slender round body was beautiful. He hoped that the young man would be kind and patient, and his eyes stole to look at him. David stood, his eyes now properly turned away from the bride, and Kung Chen searched his face. Handsome, high-spirited, intelligent—yes, and for a young man, perhaps, very kind, he told himself. Then he sighed. Let it be hoped that the young man did not weary of butterflies and kittens! His mind wandered backward to his own wedding day and the pleasure and the hope and then the long slow disappointment. But he had had children, and he had learned to understand that life is made up of everything and not of a single love. It was enough, perhaps, if the man was kind and the woman pretty.

Now Kao Lien stepped forward as the common friend who was to conduct the wedding, and he called the directions to the young couple. Under his command they bowed in turn to the two families and then to the script upon the wall that took the place in this house of ancestral tablets, and they drank the mingled wine and broke the single loaf. The rites were mixed, based upon the Chinese, but compromised, and like no others.

They were short and soon done, and then the bride was set in her seat where she could be seen, and where all could remark on her, but she must not look up or speak or seem to heed anyone. Nor could David in decency heed her, but he did look at her secretly and his blood began to rise. She was very beautiful indeed. Behind the strands of her bead veil the lines of her little face were soft and lovely, and her mouth was red. He pitied her that she must sit so long under the heavy headdress, laden with gold and silver ornaments, and he promised himself that tonight when he lifted it off he would soothe her and ask if her head ached. Then others saw his looks and began to tease him for impatience and he was ashamed to look any more and he let himself be led away to games of wine drinking and to the eating of many delicacies.

The great gates were thrown open to the streets and all who wished could come in and be fed at the tables that were set up in every court, and hundreds came in to eat greedily and with loud professions of thanks. Ezra, coming and going, saw big bowls of pork meats among the fish and beef and fowl, but he said nothing. There was mutton, too, for the Mohammedans, and let each, he told himself, eat according to his own religion.

So went that wedding day with feasting and music and laughter. Kung Chen and Ezra pledged themselves and their grandsons in wine again and again, and Madame Ezra invited Madame Kung. These two ladies met today for the first time and each found the other strange and hard to talk with, and yet each was determined to do her best. Madame Kung thought privately that Madame Ezra was too firm for a woman and she hoped that her temper was not high. But she granted that Madame Ezra tried very much to be pleasant to her, and although the day was tedious for these two ladies, somehow it passed.

When night was come and the young pair had been ushered to their door, then all farewells were said and the house grew quiet again. It was very quiet everywhere. The servants were weary and full of feast food and they fell asleep quickly. Wang Ma groaned once or twice on her bed. When Old Wang asked her if she suffered somewhere she said, "Only in my belly. I ate three times too much of that sweet and sour carp."

"As for me, I eat as much as I like and I dare my belly to say anything," Old Wang replied.

"Oh, doubtless you are wonderful," Wang Ma retorted bitterly. But Old Wang was already asleep.

Peony's room was very quiet. She had left the company early and had gone into the marriage chamber. She had already put there all the last small touches, the flowers in the vases, the fresh candles and the silver water pipes, a dish of little cakes, hot tea, a plate of late autumn peaches, rosy yellow. She had perfumed the curtains of the bed with musk and had laid a velvet mat upon the footstool before the high bed. Now when she could think of nothing more, she lit the candles and stood looking about the room. There was no repining in her heart. No, she knew what her fate was and what she was born to be, and she was grateful that her life was here, and that into this room she could come every day, though it was only to serve.

Silence stayed in the room when she was gone. Chu Ma broke it for a few minutes when, puffing and anxious, she brought in the little bride. But it was not proper for her to stay, for the bridegroom was coming.

"Sit down, little one," she whispered gustily to the bride. "When he comes in do not look up. Let him lift the veil, but do not look up. When he bids you look up, or he puts his hand under your chin, or if he stands waiting, then look up slowly—as I taught you. The eyelashes are to be raised last, and very slowly, little one. Oh, Heaven help my child!"

Chu Ma began to sob and wipe her eyes on her sleeves. But the bride would have none of this. She stamped her foot and gave her old nurse a push. "Go away, stupid," she said too clearly, and Chu Ma's tears dried at once, and her pity went with them.

"You naughty little one!" she cried under her breath. "I hope he has the strength to beat you." And rolling her eyes and pursing her lips, she bustled away.

Silent the room was when David came in. He waited until the last peal of laughter had become only an echo behind the closed door. Then he turned to his little bride. She sat upon the bed between the parted curtains, her feet together on the footstool, her hands clasped upon her lap, and the veil still hung over her face. Slowly and in silence he crossed the room and lifted the headdress from her head and set it on the table. He stood beside her hesitating, his heart beating fast.

"Does your head ache?" he asked gently.

She did not lift her face. "Yes—a little." Her voice was small and sweet.

He stood, and she waited, steadfastly looking down at his feet. Now that she was alone she was frightened, after all, and she obeyed Chu Ma carefully. But if he did not touch her or speak to bid her look up, had she courage enough of her own to lift her head? And when, if she did, should she look at him?

Before she could answer herself, he stooped and took her face between his hands.

"Let us not talk tonight," he said. "There will be time for talk tomorrow—and in all the days to come."

"Yes," she murmured. He felt her cheeks glow warm between his palms.

"We will be happy," he whispered.

"We will be happy," she echoed.

The night went on in silence until after midnight. Then Ezra was wakened by the sound of someone sobbing. He had eaten so much and had drunk so well that he had dropped into bottomless sleep the moment he laid himself in his bed. Now it seemed to him that he was being drawn up out of peace by something sorrowful and full of pain. He woke groaning and was not able for a moment to know what he heard. Then he knew the sound. Naomi was sobbing! To comfort her he had slept near her that night. He staggered out of his bed and went into the next room, where her bed was. The darkness was throbbing with the sound of her low sobs.

"Naomi!" he cried, and he fumbled for the bed. "What is the matter with you?"

She did not answer and she went on sobbing. He felt his way to the table and lit the candle. The light fell on her distraught face. It was hard for him to believe that this was the handsome woman who had done her duty so bravely at their son's wedding.

"Naomi, are you ill?" he cried.

"No," she gasped. "No—but I—I am thinking of—of all that is over! Oh, I wish I were dead! You wish I were dead, too, Ezra—I know! You want to forget everything."

He sat down on the bed beside her and he took her hand and began to stroke it patiently. He knew somehow that this was but the first of many nights when he must sit beside her in love and patience, waiting for her sorrow to pass.

"Now, Naomi," he said drowsily, "you know we are going to be so happy. David will have children—think of this house full of our grandchildren."

She turned her face away, refusing his comfort. "I have always promised myself—that when I died—I would be buried in our promised land."

"So that is what you are really weeping for this time!" Ezra exclaimed. Then he remembered patience. "Well, dear wife, shall I make you a promise? If you wish, I will promise that when you die, we will take your body to the promised land. I will manage it somehow."

She lay silent for a while. "But will you stay with me?" she asked.

Ezra sighed. "Ah, Naomi, you want your way, and you will not let me have mine! No, dear soul, I will come home alone and here I will die and be buried—here where my fathers lie, and where my children are."

Madame Ezra wept again. "But Ezra, you are a Jew!"

"For that very reason," he answered steadily. "Here even the soil is kind."

And he continued to stroke her hand in love and patience.

The deepest silence of all was in Peony's room. She knew when she laid herself upon her bed that she could not sleep. Through this wedding night she would lie wakeful, her spirit in that other room, hovering over David. But she made all her usual preparations for sleep, washing herself carefully, perfuming her body, cleansing her teeth, brushing her hair, and putting on fresh garments for the night. All day she had been unable to eat, and had made the pretense of being too busy. Now, her head upon her satin pillow, she let herself remember every detail. She could think of nothing that went wrong and for this she praised herself without shame. Every dish was hot or cold in its proper way, and the wines were heated to the right degree and no more. Silver and pewter were bright and ivory was clear and wood was clean polished and even behind a door there was no dust. At the exact moment when the little bride was weary she had seen it and had secretly brought her a bowl of hot soup with rice in it and had managed that none see her eat it. This she knew: that her happiness depended on winning the heart of David's wife. Her new mistress must learn to love her and lean on her. Yes, and far more, she must stand between husband and wife, and bring them together. By no word or deed must she separate them, for in their happiness lay her own safety—in their happiness, and in their need of her.

For this Peony was too shrewd not to see clearly how the future could lie. She knew the measure of the woman, how high, how wide, how small, and she knew David as she knew her own soul. These two would need her often to mend the fabric of their marriage, but she must never let them know she knew their need.

So she lay thinking as the hours passed, thinking and trying to keep herself from seeing with her mind's eye that other room where consummation was. Not tonight was her care, she told herself—not tonight or the many nights to come, not one act or many acts, but the whole, the lives of all in relation to the one life she held most dear.

This she was able to say to herself for many hours, as she lay and gazed steadfastly into the darkness. Then suddenly she heard the cock crow. The night was over and dawn was near. Her heart let down, and she sighed. Tears crowded under her lids and her throat was full, but she would not let her weeping break.

It is over, she told herself. Now I can sleep.

挑筋教

X

THE house of Ezra woke quietly to its new life. Outwardly the old ways went on. Madame Ezra could weep in the night, but when morning came she rose her usual self, except that she lost her temper less often and she did not speak as quickly as once she had. To her son's wife she was scrupulously kind and courteous, and the young woman made no complaint of her mother-in-law. This was surprise and pleasure, for Kueilan was afraid of Madame Ezra. All young wives must fear the elder women who are the mothers of their husbands, but Kueilan had feared more than most. She was a lazy, ease-loving little creature, accustomed to being served and spoiled, and she had no mind to subject herself to discipline and duty. But Madame Ezra asked nothing of her, and behaved indeed almost as if Kueilan were not in the house. When they met, Madame Ezra asked Kueilan how she did, and if everything were to her liking, and Kueilan smiled and looked down and replied that she liked everything. When she saw that Madame Ezra was not inclined to command her, a weight left her heart, and as time went on she grew as saucy and careless as she had been in her own home.

At first Peony could not believe that anything could be the same in the house after the marriage. Then day by day she saw that she was wrong, and that the elders made it the same, and then that David made it the same. David, too, had resumed his own life. The talk that he had put off on his wedding night he put off forever. It had not taken many days of marriage to show him that this pretty wife of his could not talk of anything beyond her daily needs and wishes. But she was ready with laughter, and she knew many games, and their happiest hours together were spent over these games that she taught him, laughing much while she did so. When she won she was as excited as a child, and she clapped her hands and tripped about the room on her little bound feet. These feet were David's pity. He had never seen a girl's feet before so bound, for in this Jewish house Peony's feet had been left free. Kueilan's little feet in their silken shoes he could hold together in the palm of his hand, and one night he did so, exclaiming in sorrow that it could be.

"Little Thing," he said, for so he now called his wife, "how could you let them maim you?"

To his surprise she began to cry, half in anger and half in answer to his pity, and she drew her feet away and hid them under her skirt. "You don't like them!" she wept.

"They make me sad," he replied gently. "How they must have pained you!"

"They don't pain me now," she declared.

"Why not let them free?" he asked.

"I don't want them big," she said petulantly. "Why should I waste all my trouble?"

"Let me see what can be done," he begged, divining her pride and shyness.

"No—no—no!" she screamed. And then she fell to sobbing again and she cried out for Peony so loudly that Peony came running.

At the sight of her Kueilan put out her hands while the tears ran down her face. "He wants to see my feet!" she sobbed, and nothing must do but for Peony to sit down on the bed beside her and soothe her hands and cover her feet in the silken quilt.

"Hush—hush—he did not mean it." So Peony comforted the sobbing girl.

David stood by the bed and looked at the two. "Tell her I want only to help her," he said to Peony. "And it is true that I do not like feet so crippled." With this he walked out of the room and Kueilan clung to Peony and wept mightily and Peony let her weep. When the sobs began to quiet she spoke gently and firmly.

"I will tell my young master how it is that our people bind the feet of women. You must not blame him that he does not know.

His people leave the feet free. Indeed, even their women wear sandals on their bare feet."

"Like farm women!" Kueilan cried through her tears.

"Sometimes their sandals are of gold and silver and set with jewels," Peony went on. "Now stop your crying, Little Mistress. He is kind and good, and once he understands—"

"But there are too many things he doesn't understand!" the young wife wailed.

Peony was very patient. "Each time he does not understand, then send for me, Little Mistress, and I will explain to him how you feel."

Thus soothing and coaxing she comforted Kueilan, and when quiet was restored she said, "A wife must please her husband, Little Mistress. What other man will see you except him? Let me tend your feet then, Lady. I will loosen the bandages so little every day that you will not know it, and then he will be pleased when he sees you obedient. When he is pleased, how happy you will be!"

Kueilan looked doubtful. She lifted her wet lashes and looked at Peony. "I am quite happy now," she declared.

"You will lose your happiness, Lady, if you do not please your husband." So Peony persisted.

The long lashes fell again, and Kueilan said in a small voice, "But I have fifty pairs of new shoes—and they are so pretty!"

Peony laughed. "Lady, if that is all your care, I will copy each pair you have and make new ones for your new feet."

Kueilan was silent for a while and Peony stood waiting. "Shall I not tell him?" she asked, smiling as though at a child.

After a long time Kueilan nodded slowly, and her tears came fresh. But she did not complain while Peony fetched a basin of hot water and took off the tiny laced shoes and then the tight white stockings and then unwrapped the long bandages. Even Peony was sad when the narrow feet lay bare in her hands. She examined each foot carefully to see how much the damage was. Chu Ma had been zealous and eager for her charge to make a good marriage and she had bound the child's feet early. Bones were bent and cramped but not broken. These feet could never be whole, but they could be free.

Yet the task must be done carefully, a little day by day, or the pain of freedom would be as bitter as the binding had been.

"I am glad Chu Ma isn't here," Kueilan said suddenly. Chu Ma had not been allowed to stay with her charge, lest there be quarreling with the other servants in the house. Kung Chen had commanded her to return and care for Lili, his last child.

"And I also am glad," Peony agreed. "Were she here it would be hard indeed for her to see her work undone. When she comes to visit you, Little Mistress, tell her your lord commanded you."

When Peony had soaked the feet and rebound them again with the least loosening of the bandages, she played a game with her mistress, and then, seeing her yawn, she coaxed her to bed and sleep. Only then did she go and find David. He had yielded to his mother's decree, which Peony had secretly suggested to Madame Ezra, and before the day of his marriage he had moved to these new and larger rooms. Now he sat brooding in his library, a great room, high ceiled, and all the walls shelved with narrow shelves upon which the rolls of his books lay. This was his favorite room already, and here Kueilan did not come. She could read—he had learned that—but she considered it useless. To play, to chatter, to tease Small Dog, to watch the goldfish, to make a great ado when she pretended she was about to embroider, to taste many sweetmeats and bite them half through and leave them, these were her occupations. He knew it now, and yet he yielded to the fascination of her prettiness in all she did.

His mind told him that her mind was childish, and her soul sleeping, but his eyes fed his heart, and the roundness of her smooth flesh, her little bones covered with such tenderness, her tiny waist and narrow wrist, the delight that lay in the nape of her neck and the purity of her throat and breast, the scent of her skin and the fragrance of her breath, the endless grace of every movement that she made—all this was precious to him in its fashion. She held him by the pathos of her little hands and crippled feet as surely as she charmed him by her eyes and laughter and her yielding body. It was not love—how soon he knew it was not love! But it was something, for all that, and it was sweet and full of pleasure.

Thus he brooded upon her when Peony came in. She saw his mood and she pretended she had come to fill the teapot and know its heat. "I must bring you fresh tea—this is cold," she said as she had said on every night of his life. He scarcely heard her and he did not answer.

She looked at him and went on. "My little mistress asks me to tell you how it is her feet are bound," she said.

"I know it is Chinese custom," he replied and did not look up.

"A foolish custom," she conceded. "How it came about I do not know. I read once that an emperor was charmed by the small feet of one he loved and other women hearing of it everywhere began to make their feet small. And I have heard that it began long ago when men wished to keep their wives at home. Who knows? But it is a custom now, and small feet bring a price in marriages. We cannot blame my little mistress that she yielded to her elders."

"I do not blame her," he replied.

Peony went on, "She asks me to tell you that she is sorry she cried, and that she will let me free her feet a little every day until they are as free as can be."

He looked up now. "Peony, this is your doing, not hers."

"She was willing," Peony replied and looked away.

"Ah, Peony!" David said, "Ah, Peony!" He felt strangely lonely and he put out his hand and he took Peony's hand and held it. She let it lie for a moment. Then she turned her head and she caught the full warm look of his eyes. Seeing that look, she drew her hand away gently, and with her other hand she lifted the teapot.

"I will fetch hot tea, Young Master," she said in her sweet cool voice, and went away.

He sat there, expecting her return, and wondering why he was not as happy as he wished he were. Peony could help him somehow, as she had always helped him, and yet he did not know what he wanted of her. How could he put into words for her the sadness that he felt, and yet make her know that his little wife was somehow a treasure, too? While he pondered this Old Wang came in with the teapot.

"Peony bade me bring the tea, Young Master," he said. He set it down on the table. "Shall I pour a bowl?" he asked.

"Leave it," David said. "I will pour it for myself when I am thirsty." He watched the old man go, and sat puzzling for a while. Now why had Peony not come back herself? It was not that he had seized her hand. He had often held her hand. He sat a while longer, and feeling neither his sadness lift nor his vague loneliness dispel itself, he sighed and rose and went into the bedroom where his little treasure was.

The house of Ezra shaped itself to its new life. It would have been said that one small woman in the house could not change the laws of generations, but there was this change: Madame Ezra, determined to find no fault with her son's wife, found no fault with her son. But David knew that his mother kept all the old ways. When the feast days rolled around, the house retreated subtly into the past. The ancient rites were performed, the foods of tradition prepared and eaten. But there was no more going to the synagogue. No rabbi stood now before the Chair of Moses to read the sacred Torah. The great red satin umbrella over the platform where the chair stood was folded and laid away. On the western walls still hung the tablets upon which were carved in letters of pure gold the Ten Commandments, but none came there to hear them read. The gates of the synagogue were locked and no one went to them. Madame Ezra could not bear to go alone, and Ezra was busy. His contracts with Kung Chen were signed, and their names stood together in huge letters of black velvet upon the red silk banners that hung outside the shop doors.

A second caravan had been added to the one that each year Kao Lien led toward the west, and besides these, Ezra bought the produce of ships from India, cottons and ivory, silver and jewels, and brought it overland from the south. In return he sent to India Chinese silk from Kung Chen's shops, and there it was rewoven into the gauzes that Indian ladies loved, and that no Chinese looms could weave.

There was no one even to watch at the synagogue gates. Eli the gatekeeper took care of the smiling mad old rabbi, who would listen to no one else. Eli stayed night and day, for the Rabbi could not be allowed to wander about the house lest he frighten the servants.

In the city the remnant of the Jews, less now than two hundred souls, went about their business and forgot who they were. But Madame Ezra in her own house kept the feast days of her people It was lonely keeping, for only she and Ezra and David ate the un leavened bread at Passover.

On the first Passover after her son's marriage she had commanded a place set for his wife. When David came alone his mother looked at him with some of her old impetuous temper.

"Is my daughter-in-law not coming?" she demanded.

David took his place in great quiet. "She says she is afraid to come," he replied.

"Afraid?" Madame Ezra exclaimed. "What nonsense is this?"

"She fears that our sacred foods will bewitch her soul," David replied. Then he said strangely. "I will not compel her, Mother. Perhaps she is right."

Something in his stern still look chilled Madame Ezra's heart and she said no more. Her proud head drooped, she wiped tears from her eyes, but she did not wail aloud. To what low estate had her people fallen! she told herself. Perhaps in a few other houses families worshiped Jehovah in solitary fashion and would for a few years more, but in most of them, and well she knew it, even the pretense of worship had been forgotten and the sacred days passed like any other in business and in pleasure.

So long as his mother lived, David showed no outward discontent with his life. His first son was born a year after his marriage day, and Kueilan, who was pettish before the child was born, delivered him easily although with much wailing and screaming. When she saw he was a boy she gave over her noise, and demanded all her favorite foods. But she refused to nurse the child, and a wet nurse had to be found. This roused Madame Ezra for a moment.

"Must this grandchild drink Chinese milk?" she asked Ezra.

Ezra smiled ruefully. "His mother's milk would be Chinese, too, my dear," he said.

Madame Ezra was struck by her own folly and fell silent, and Ezra had not the heart to remind her that he himself had drunk his Chinese mother's milk. But thereafter he saw that Madame Ezra did not love even her grandchild, and next year when Kueilan had another son, she merely nodded her head when Wang Ma told her of the second birth.

Indeed, Madame Ezra cared no more to live. They all saw it, and each in his way was sorrowful. This strong good woman was the central pillar in the house, and now the pillar was crumbling. She began to lose her taste for food, and she complained that she did not sleep well. When she was alone with Ezra she asked him often what it was that she had done amiss in her life, that it was not to end as she had hoped.

"It is not that you have done amiss, my dear Naomi," Ezra told her. "Perhaps you have only dreamed amiss."

"I have always obeyed the will of God," she replied to this in some distress.

Ezra had not heart to say how often her will was God's will, and so he only said, "Ah, who can tell what is the will of God?"

In the midst of Madame Ezra's own decline, the Rabbi died suddenly in a childish way. As his mind decayed, he had passed from being man to child and then from child to being less than human, and if Old Eli did not watch him constantly, he took up and ate anything he saw upon the ground. So one day he ate some filth, not in hunger, for Ezra kept him well fed and warm in winter and cool in summer, but from some old memory of past hunger. The filth poisoned him and he was racked with cholera and died within a day, bewildered by his pains and begging for mercy from Madame Ezra, whom he now feared as the most powerful being that he knew.

Madame Ezra mourned to see him thus, and she would have stayed beside him to comfort him, but Ezra dreaded the disease and forbade her. The old rabbi died with only Eli beside him, and he was buried in the graveyard beside his wife, who was Leah's mother.

The remnant of his people in the city mourned his death and they followed his coffin, wailing and weeping, and wearing garments of sackcloth, and they stooped and took dust from the road as they walked and poured it upon their heads. All knew that with the Rabbi's death something of their own death had come upon them, too, and they remembered him as he had been in the days when he was young, how good he had been, how strong, and how he had adjured them to remember their God, who was the One True God. Now that he was gone, who would remind them? There was no one even to read the Torah at his grave. His son, that Aaron, was still lost, and the Rabbi was buried with no kin to mourn him or to do his work for him now. David stood there, aloof and silent. His heart was dark, but he did not weep. Neither had he stooped to take the dust nor did he wear sackcloth.

One day after the funeral Madame Ezra felt lonely and sad and she took the fancy that she would go alone to visit the synagogue. Eli had returned to watch the gates, and she went in her sedan chair, with only Wang Ma with her. When Eli saw Madame Ezra he was confused and he begged her not to go into the synagogue.

"Wait until I have time to sweep the floors, Lady," he begged. "The dust lies thick on the Chair of Moses, and I am ashamed for you to see it."

But Madame Ezra would not yield. She had come so far and she would have her way. Reluctantly then he fitted the key to the great lock, and he held the gate closed for a moment.

"Do not blame me, Lady," he begged. "It was like this when I came back."

He opened the door unwillingly indeed, and Madame Ezra stepped into the court and behind came Eli. At first she saw nothing changed except the dust the winds had blown there, and the leaves fallen and rotting under the trees. But when she had crossed the last court and had mounted the terrace and come to the synagogue, she saw change. The two stone lions that had guarded the great doorway were gone, and the iron urns were gone; the curtains over the doors were gone, and when she went inside the candlesticks were not upon the great table, or the silver laver for washing the hands. The separate tables that had held the twelve rolls of the law were gone and the fine silken curtains that had hung over the roll of the law of Moses were torn away.

Madame Ezra stared at loss after loss. She could not speak. She stood in the middle of the synagogue, looking for one well-known object and then another. Then her eyes fell upon the western wall, and there she saw the most vile robbery of all. The very gold had been dug out of the deeply carved letters of the Ten Commandments, which Jehovah Himself had given to Moses. Upon this she turned to Eli and her voice came in a loud cry.

"Who has done this?"

Eli hung his head. "Lady, I fear to tell you all," he muttered.

"Is there more?" she demanded.

In silence he pointed to the door. He led her outside again, and along the walls, and she saw that not only the inside of the synagogue had been despoiled, but thieves had taken the bricks from the walls. These were bricks of a special sort, made new after the great flood that had covered the city two hundred years before. They were finer than any brick made nowadays, for the ancients had the secret of making bricks even from the days when their ancestors had been slaves in Egypt.

"Soon only the shell of the synagogue will be left," Eli said mournfully, "and one day when a storm blows from the south it will fall into ruins and rubble."

Madame Ezra could not speak one word for a long time. She went from one sight to another, and Wang Ma, waiting outside, grew frightened and came to find her.

"Lady, rest yourself!" she exclaimed. "There are thieves in every temple."

Madame Ezra turned on Eli. "How was it that you did not come and tell me this long ago?"

"Lady, I did not know," the old man pleaded. "I could not leave my master night or day, and none of our people came to tell what was happening."

"I cannot think they would have dared to steal from Jehovah's house, unless one led them on!" she exclaimed.

A strange thought came to her mind, but she would not speak it before these two who were not her equals. "I will go home," she said, "and do you watch, Eli. Let it be known that I will demand of the Chinese magistrate that he flog the thieves and set them in racks before the populace to starve."

So saying she went home again, her heart all grief, and she could not wait until Ezra and David came home. She sent Old Wang to fetch them and Wang Ma added her own message that they must come because she feared her mistress was ill. Hearing this, Ezra called David from his own room, which he now had in the shop, and they went home. There they found Madame Ezra waiting and she broke into sobs when she saw them, and they had much trouble amid her sobbing to hear what was wrong, and had it not been for Wang Ma, who stood there with hot tea in a bowl to hold to her mistress's lips, nothing would have been clear.

When all was told, Madame Ezra suddenly stopped crying. Now was the time for her surmise. "I well know the paltry folk our people have become could not have dared to steal from Jehovah Himself," she declared.

Both men waited to hear what came next.

"I tell you," Madame Ezra went on, "there is only one who would do what has been done, and he is that Aaron. He must be found, Ezra. He hides somewhere in the city, and he directs the thieves. Let the curse of God fall on him!"

"How can I find him?" Ezra groaned.

"The Chinese can find thieves," Madame Ezra urged.

"There is a king of thieves in the city," David said. "His name is known at the magistrate's court, where he pays yearly tribute, and through him Aaron can be found."

"Can you do this, my son?" Ezra asked.

David bowed his head. "A sad task," he said shortly, "but I can do it."

So David called upon the magistrate, and paid the money down to meet the king of thieves in that city. On a certain day the man would come to a distant teahouse on the edge of the city, and he was to be known by a red cord twisted in his buttonhole, and he was to sit far inside the house, out of easy sight. David, he decreed, must come alone. When Madame Ezra heard this she was frightened and she insisted that Eli go and stand near the door, unseen. None among the Chinese in the house knew what went on, for Ezra was ashamed, and so indeed were David and his mother.

On the day David went to the appointed place the man was waiting, a thin long smooth-faced man, dressed in a black silk robe, and he sat with a bowl of tea in his hand. This hand David saw as soon as he sat down and greeting had been given. The hand was like a ferret, so narrow and thin and long it was. Seeing it, David loathed the whole man, and he came at once to his business.

"I act for my father," David said. "We would find the thieves who take the bricks from our temple and the sacred vessels and the silk curtains, and all that is gone. If these can be restored, we will pay well. But we will even pay something only to know what has become of them and who the one is that dares to steal from our people."

The man smiled an evil cold smile. "He is one of your own," he said.

Then David knew his mother was right. "His name is Aaron," he said.

"What his name is I do not know," the man replied. "We call him Li the Foreigner."

"But that one could never lift the heavy bricks or the great vases," David exclaimed.

"No, but he puts courage into the ones who help him," the man replied, sneering. "They fear lest the foreign god take revenge on them, but this fellow promises them that no punishment will fall upon them. He is the son of the priest, he says, and he knows all the prayers."

"Where is this one?" David asked.

The man looked very cunning. "If I deliver him to you, how much money will you put in my hand? It is loss for me, you understand."

With loathing in all his blood David contrived to match this cunning. "We do not care whether we see his evil face or not," he said. "Keep him if you wish. But from now on the synagogue is guarded, and your loss is the same."

So bargaining, David promised thirty pieces of silver, and with these he bought the traitor back.

"He lives hidden in a hut inside the gate of a house that stands six doors from here," the man told him. "If you follow me, I will show you. But first I must see the silver."

"I brought no silver," David said. "You know my father's house and that we are in contract with the merchant Kung Chen. You can trust me."

After some demur the man agreed and he rose and they went down the street, and he pointed to the door. "He is always there by day," he said.

"The silver will reach your hand tonight," David said, and then he crossed the street and without fear he entered the gate and suddenly opened the door of a hut and there inside a mean small room Aaron lay huddled on a bed made of boards.

David went to him and shook him, and when he saw David he woke out of sleep and stirred himself sullenly. "What do you want?" he asked.

David stared down at him, and despised him utterly, and yet he could not strike him or curse him.

"I ought to give you to the magistrate to be flogged," he muttered. "And yet you are one of our people! Aaron, how could you do what you have done?"

"I don't know what you mean," the cur replied.

"Ah, you know," David sighed. He sat down on a stool and leaned his head on his hands. "I am glad your father never knew," he said. "I am glad Leah is dead."

Aaron scratched himself and yawned and said nothing.

David stood up again. "Come, I give you a choice! You shall have a place somewhere in the shops—some work where eyes are always on you. If you do not choose this, then I turn you over to the city prison."

The end of this was that after a few minutes more Aaron chose to come with him. With loathing on all sides against him, from that day he ate Ezra's food and wore his castoff clothing, and carried messages from one shop to another between Ezra and Kung Chen. None trusted him alone with goods or cash, and his life sank to less than any in Ezra's house.

As for Madame Ezra, she gave up hope, knowing that never could the synagogue be rebuilt, and she took no pleasure in anything that Ezra said to comfort her.

"See, my Naomi," he told her often. "You have everything to make a woman rejoice. Our son is among the most respected of the young merchants of the city. It was only a few days ago that Kung Chen said to me, 'Elder Brother, your son has saved me the quarter of a year's income.' 'How?' I asked. 'Why,' he said, 'for the last ten years there has been a leak somewhere in my affairs. Try as I have, and my sons, too, we have not known where. Last year I sent even my eldest son to the northern capital to make a written copy of all goods bought and sold. When it came back we found no fault, and yet there was loss. But I gave the copy to your son—' "

She interrupted him here half pettishly, "Tell me the story outright and not this mixture of his son and my son. What did David do?"

Ezra refused to be ill-humored. "Why, the gist of it is, Naomi, David could tell from the figures alone where the dealer had changed the prices of the goods!"

Madame Ezra smiled only dimly at this, and Ezra grew anxious indeed. "Tell me where you feel ill, my dear," he said.

She shook her head. Then she opened her sad dark eyes at him and put her hands on her breast. "I feel heavy here, night and day."

Ezra sat silent a while and then he offered great sacrifice. "Shall I take you westward, Naomi—where you have always wanted to go?" He could not bring himself to say "the promised land," for he did not want to go.

Well she knew his heart, and she shook her head again. "It is too late now," she said, and this was all she would say, and Ezra left her at last with his own heart very heavy.

He made occasion to see David alone that day and he said, "Help me to cheer your mother's heart, my son."

David looked up from his ledgers. "Father, you know she cannot be cheered," he declared. He took up his pen again and worked on. Then he said slowly, his eyes still on his book, "If you wish, I will take her to Palestine and let her see the land. Then perhaps she will be content—either to stay or to come back with me."

Ezra heard this and his jaw fell. "Leave me here?" he exclaimed.

"You can come if you like, Father," David said with a small smile.

"But the business!" Ezra cried.

David shrugged and did not answer. Ezra looked at him. David had grown since his marriage. He was taller and stronger and somehow more hard. He wore a short, curled beard and he was no longer a youth. He was even passing beyond his early manhood.

"What if you two did not come back?" Ezra said strangely.

David did not look up. He finished his line and wiped his brush of camel's hair and put on the brass cover. Then he sat back in his chair and faced his father full. "With you here and my sons would I not come back?" he replied, smiling into his beard.

He did not speak of his wife. Ezra noticed this and said nothing. "There is that war still dragging itself out in the south," he grumbled. "The Englishmen are not content—they force their opium on us. It may be that you will have trouble if you go through India."

"I will tell them we are not Chinese," David said.

"Well, but they will ask you what you are," Ezra went on. Then he said, "How do I know they will be better pleased to find you are Jews?"

To this David could say nothing and Ezra got up heavily, feeling for the first time that since his son was no longer young, he must himself be growing old. "Speak of it with your mother, my son," he said. "Let it be as the two of you decide. You are alike in your stubbornness."

David did talk with his mother and for a few weeks she seemed to revive into someone like her old self. She would not say she would go, and yet she made plans as though to go, and David held himself in readiness. Only Kao Lien opposed the plan.

"Elder Sister will never be able to take the journey," he told Ezra. "Even though we go by India and the sea, there are typhoons upon the ocean, and long days between when the ship will be becalmed. On land it will be worse. The Muslims are wary and fierce and I cannot answer for her life."

"Let her go, if she wishes," Ezra said.

"If she dies there?" Kao Lien asked.

"My son can bury his mother," Ezra replied. But his heart was very sore.

Yet the journey was never taken. Sometime, in some night, Madame Ezra, lying much awake and alone, gave up her plan. David could take her there but he must come back. That she knew. Peony had come that very day to tell her that her young mistress was expecting her third child, and that she wept very much because her husband was leaving her to go on so long a journey.

"My little mistress has had her children too quickly," Peony told Madame Ezra. "She needs rest after this one, and for that reason I said to her that our young lord would be away no more than a year, and when he came back she would be strong and well again. Just now she is sick, Mistress, and she is fretful. But she refused to be consoled. I do not want to trouble you, Mistress, but I tell you this for the sake of your grandchildren."

Madame Ezra waved Peony away with one gesture of her right hand and she did not answer. But in the night she knew that she must not take David away from his children, and she knew that she did not want to die outside this house. That she was soon to die she had begun to perceive. Within her right breast there grew a hard knot, and she felt tentacles from it pulling at her ribs and lungs and under her shoulder. It had been long since she first found it. Now the thing grew and consumed her flesh and she was thinner every day. In the darkness she sighed and gave up her dream. What did it matter now? The synagogue was gone, and of what use was an old woman creeping home to die? She could not bring her children with her.

Within the year she yielded to her inner enemy and with much pain and torture of the flesh she died in her own bed.

Ezra felt his heart broken, and he made a mighty funeral such as the city had never seen. In the long procession every one of the remnant of the Jews walked clothed in sackcloth, and Kung Chen persuaded wealthy Chinese to ride in mule carts twisted with white cloth, and Ezra walked, clothed in white from head to foot, and David by him clothed the same, and behind them came David's wife and children, even to the newborn child; a third son, whom Peony carried. Behind them came all the servants, led by Wang Ma. The people of the city stood thick along the streets to see the sight, and all agreed that never had there been so fine a funeral except that there were no paper images of house and sedan and servants to be burned for the spirit world. Then some said, "These people do not believe in images. Not even in their temple is there an image."

All agreed to this. The western wall of the temple had fallen down in a great wind that came up from the south, and curious people went to stare inside the foreign temple, which had been until now forbidden. It was true there were no images.

The procession walked slowly to the city gate and passed through it and came to the graveyard of the Jews. Then it stopped and David and Ezra stood alone beside the grave. Behind David stood his wife and by her Peony, holding his third son, who wailed without stopping until the funeral was over.

So Madame Ezra was buried, but there was no one to read a prayer beside her grave.

挑筋教

XI

PEONY did not know how to live in this house of Ezra without her elder mistress in it. She came home from the funeral and warmed the crying child and gave him to his wet nurse, and her first thought was for David and his father. Kueilan was weary, and complained that her feet hurt her sorely and that she was hungry and felt weak, and the two little boys wept with hunger. But Peony bade the undermaids serve these, and she and Wang Ma gave their heed to the two men.

Each had gone to his room, and finding this so, Peony motioned Wang Ma to Ezra's room, and she herself went to David. She did not know how she would find him, whether weeping or not, but she was not prepared for his calmness when, having coughed at his door, she heard him bid her enter. He stood there taking off the sackcloth outer garment that he had worn for the funeral, and underneath he had his usual silk robes. They were of a dark blue today, to signify the solemnity of what had taken place. When he turned his head she saw his face grave but not weeping.

"Come in, Peony," he said quietly. "I was about to send for you."

He sat down himself and looked at her most kindly. "Do not wait for me to bid you seat yourself," he said. "You know how much you have become in this house."

She sat down and waited.

"Did I know how I could manage without you, I would not let my conscience trouble me," he went on. "I ought to find a husband for you, Peony. We are all selfish toward you, and I am the most selfish. But the truth is that without you we would be like a boat without a rudder. Now that my mother is gone—" He paused and pressed his lips together.

"I have no wish to wed, Young Master," Peony said.

"You always say that," David replied, "but it does not absolve me from my duty."

Peony put the matter aside. "What did you wish to tell me?" she asked.

David got up suddenly and walked to the door and stood looking out. The winter of the year was over and spring nearly come. The air was mild on that afternoon, and the door was open to the court. "I want to make a journey," he said.

"A journey?" Peony repeated. "Where?"

"You know my mother and I planned to take the journey westward to the land of our ancestors. I have a wish to make that journey now, alone." He paused and then he said abruptly, "There is something restless in me."

"There is something restless in you," Peony repeated. She felt stupid with surprise and yet she knew she needed all her wits about her.

"I feel some hidden guilt in me," David went on. "I have had the guilt ever since Leah died. Now my mother is dead. This journey would somehow be for them."

"Would you leave your father?" Peony asked. She felt breathless, but she made herself calm.

"He does not need me," David said. "He has his friends—and his grandsons. I think sometimes he is nearer to them than to me. And you would be here, Peony—and Wang Ma."

"But your children—and their mother!" Peony urged. "How can I take this responsibility?"

"You do take it, Peony, whether I am here or not," he told her.

Now she could not hold back her fears. "What if you died upon the way?" she cried. "What if you were—were killed?" She remembered the sword with the thin blade that had done such evil to his people in other countries, and had done evil here in this house, too, but she could not speak of it. Old Wang had taken that sword and had carried it to the river and had thrown it as far as his strength could reach, into the yellow whirlpools.

"Many have been killed," David said quietly. "There is no reason why I should not face the same danger."

Now what could Peony say? She longed to cry out to him to stay for her own sake, for he was all her life, and if he did not come back, she too could no longer live. But she was afraid to seize this comfort. His mind was very far away at this moment. She felt a strange jealousy that she had not known since Leah died. She had forgotten Leah for months upon months, even years, but now Leah came back in all her beauty. Did he remember that beauty? She weighed the common sense of speaking Leah's name to him and decided that she would not. If he thought of Leah, to talk of her would be to bring her into this room where they were alone. Let Leah lie dead! Yet what hold was this that clung beyond the grave? What was the conscience in him? She could not answer her own question and she rose gracefully, quiet above her inner turmoil. "Let all be as you will, Young Master," she said.

To her surprise David turned on her with anger. "Do not call me that, Peony!" he said with much impatience. "At least when we are alone call me by my name. Have we not been brother and sister all our lives?"

What words could wound her more than these? But she refused to allow her hurt to show and she answered smoothly, "I will try to remember. Do not take the journey unless you must. Yet if you must I will try to be all I should be while you are gone."

With this she went away, having contrived it so that she did not speak his name. Someday perhaps she would speak it, but not while he remembered Leah.

She went to her own room and sat a long while, pondering what she would do. She heard her name called and she went into her bedroom and hid herself behind the bed curtains, and crouching there she thought a while longer and until her mind was clear. She would go to Kung Chen, and he would help her. Certainly he would not allow his daughter's husband to wander away into the westward country to come back not sooner than a year and perhaps even never to come back. To think of this was to do it, and once again she slipped out of the Gate of Peaceful Escape, which she had not needed to use in these years since David's marriage day.

Kung Chen was at home, for he had been wearied by the long funeral, and he sat inside his own rooms, sipping hot wine and gazing into a small brazier of coals that he had ordered prepared for his comfort rather than for warmth. She was ushered immediately into his presence, since all knew she served his daughter.

"Honored Sir," Peony said in a small sweet voice.

He looked up kindly at her slender, gray-robed figure and remembered that he had seen her standing beside his daughter and holding the wailing child. "Do not stand in my presence," he now commanded her. "We are old acquaintances. Do you remember the morning by the fish pool?" He did not tell her what he thought, that she had grown very beautiful since that morning. Then she had been a rosy girl but now she was a woman, graceful and self-possessed. If the old gay glance of her eyes was gone, a lovely quietness had taken its place. No one would imagine that she was a bondmaid. She had grown far beyond that place.

"What have you to tell me?" he asked.

Peony sat down delicately and folded her hands. She did not tell him what she thought, that he had aged very much since the morning by the fish pool. She had seen him only at a distance since that day. Now she saw him much thinner than he had been. His full face was slack and he had grown a scanty beard that was turning white. But his height remained and his shoulders were still broad. She knew that all his children were married, although for Lili, the child of his concubine, he had been able to find only the son of an ironmonger. Wealthy families did not wish to marry their sons to the daughter of a concubine who had run away with a head servant. This had been grief to Kung Chen, for he loved his little Lili above all the other children.

"Sir, it is for the sake of my young mistress that I come," Peony said. "After we returned from the funeral today, I went to serve hot food to my young master, which is my duty, and I found him distraught, and when I inquired he told me that it was in his heart now to make the journey alone to the land of his ancestors, which he once planned to make with his mother. I said nothing, but I came to tell you. Sir, the journey would take a full year, but this is not the worst of it. The Muslims are very fierce along the way, and Kao Lien told my old mistress so even before she died. My young master will stand in danger of his life if he goes. I think of our lady, your daughter, and the children."

Kung Chen heard this in great astonishment. "How is it that the son would make a pilgrimage when his father does not?" he inquired. "Does this not smack of filial impiety? Would his father not feel reproached before Heaven?"

Peony took her courage in her hands. She had a very delicate web to weave. "Sir, our young lord is the son of our old mistress. Our old lord is the son of one of our own people. The soul of the mother is in the son."

Kung Chen began to understand. He nodded his head slowly and stroked his beard. "Go on," he said.

Peony inclined her own head modestly. The web was well begun but it was not finished. "Sir, there is more than this. I wish to offend no one—but it may be you remember the young lady to whom our young lord was once betrothed—or very nearly."

"The one who—" Kung Chen drew his long forefinger across his throat.

"That one," Peony agreed.

"Did—he—ah—love her?" Kung Chen next inquired. There was some jealousy in him for his daughter, but he did not speak it out.

Peony perceived the jealousy well enough. "I will not say he loved her," she said hesitatingly. "I would even say he did not, for it was at that very time that he loved our young mistress—your daughter, sir. But in some strange way these two young ladies struggled in his heart against one another. Thus the foreign one kept him back from loving entirely our lady, now the mother of his sons, and our lady made him unable to love the foreign one whom his mother wished for her daughter-in-law. The two spoiled one another for him."

Kung Chen pondered this a while. "Was the other more beautiful than my daughter?" he now asked.

Peony considered. "No," she said, then she added, "but she had some hidden power over him. It was the same power his mother had, and he loved and hated it together. While his mother lived, he rebelled against it and he maintained himself. But now that she is dead, he remembers the other one, too, and he feels that somewhere he has a duty undone, and he is restless."

"What has the journey to do with all this?" Kung Chen next inquired.

"They both wanted to leave our land and go to that one where their ancestors were," Peony replied.

Kung Chen mused a while longer. He remembered all that he had learned of the Jews and of the lodestone of faith that drew them back to the arid strip of earth that had once been theirs. Certainly his Little Three must not suffer and she must not be left a widow with many children, and in the height of her young womanhood. He moved to protect his own.

"The young man is restless," he said, stroking his beard. "It is natural enough. He has never traveled. Men often grow restless after the first years of marriage. They know all they have, and they think of new sights. Very well, he shall travel, and my daughter and the children and you must all go with him. I will lend my own mule carts and my muleteers to meet you when you leave the river, and my cooks will go with you, and they will all take the journey to the northern capital. I shall ask the governor of our province, moreover, to send some of his own guards with you, as warning to robbers and river pirates. Spring is just beyond tomorrow and the journey will be pleasant. I shall ask his father to decide that the journey is necessary for our business, and indeed it may well be."

Kung Chen was very well pleased with himself, and he wagged his big head to and fro. His mind ran ahead of his plans. "Yes, and I will see that I have a fine gift that must be presented for me to the two new empresses, and I will send word to my friends to give feasts for my son-in-law, and I will give orders at the Pear Garden Theater to show plays for him and for his friends, whom he must feast in return. Who does not enjoy the northern capital? It is the most beautiful city in the world." Kung Chen's imagination grew warm. He rubbed his hands together over the coals. "All is as it should be," he said. "The Imperial Court is home from exile now—it has returned from Jehol to Peking—and the capital is filled with joy. Truce has been declared with the white men over the opium from India, and the rebel Christians are defeated in the eastern provinces. It is time again for pleasure and for trade."

He clapped his hands on his knees and beamed so brightly that Peony was delighted indeed. She rose, her own face bright too. "It is a plan from Heaven," she declared. "I will wait then, sir, until commands come down." Then bowing she went home again.

Behind her Kung Chen sat alone, stroking his beard and frowning into the fire. His Little Three—was she happy? He had taken it for granted that she was, since each year she had given birth to a son. Once or twice he had asked her mother what she thought, but Madame Kung seldom thought at all about a daughter who had left the house to belong to another family.

His mind went gratefully to Peony. Where she was, doubtless all would be well.

Thus it came about that on a fine day in later spring David, persuaded by Peony, set out for the north. He, his wife, and their children and Peony went aboard a great river junk and sailed for the northern capital. With them were undermaids and menservants and two cooks whom Kung Chen chose because they came from the north and begged to have the chance to see their old home again. On a smaller boat the guards went ahead of them.

Ezra saw them go with a chill heart, and he dreaded his loneliness until they came back. Yet he dared not leave his business, for Kao Lien was about to lead his camels westward again, and the loads must be chosen from the best Chinese goods. Moreover, since peace had come with the white men from India, Ezra had in mind to send down two trustworthy men with Chinese goods to be sold there. He was further persuaded by Kung Chen, who said that his own loss would be heavy if Ezra did not send out these loads early enough to bring back western goods by the next early winter at latest. So Ezra made the best of his lot, and Wang Ma and Old Wang stayed at home, and Kao Lien moved into Ezra's house for the last weeks before he set out, and David made promises to come home soon, and Kung Chen promised that he would dine with Ezra every day, and so the parting was made.

On the junk all was confusion at first. The children cried with the strangeness and they were frightened when with many shouts and curses the boatmen eased the huge junk from the shore and edged their way into the middle of the river, pushing with long bamboo poles and rowing until in midstream the wind caught their sails. Each nurse comforted the child that was her responsibility, and the baby clung to the breast of the wetnurse, and so quiet came. Peony tended her young mistress and saw that she was seated on a couch and that she had tea and sweetmeats, and she unpacked cushions and fans and bedding and charcoal braziers and everything that could be used for greater comfort. This done, she inquired of the cooks what was to be prepared for the day's meals, since they had come aboard at early morning, and only when she was satisfied with their plans did she let her heart rest, and she looked around to see where they were to live.

The junk was a mighty one, for the river, and the bow and the stern rose high out of the water. Upon the bow were painted two great eyes, and upon the stern was painted the tail of a fish. The boatmen lived in two small cabins at the stern, and with them were their wives and children. But gates shut them off from the others and they kept themselves apart. Each child had a rope tied about his middle, so that if he fell into the water, the mother could haul him up again, and Peony exclaimed that such ropes should be put about her charges, too. She took two coils of soft hempen rope that the boatman gave her, but when she tied these ropes about the waists of David's sons, they cried with rage and would not be tied, and Peony had no choice except to bid the maids to hold them by their sashes, and never let them be free for one moment. Thus two maids were continually busy all day and Peony thanked Heaven that the youngest child could not walk.

The kitchens came next after the boatmen's cabins, and the cooks slept in them at night. They were small but there was everything needful for preparing fine food, and soon the cooks were at their duty. In front of the kitchens were the bedrooms for the family and the great central saloon, where they sat by day. Here Peony must sleep by night, for the children and their nurses must have one bedroom, and David and his wife the other, and Peony had no place for her own. This was hardship indeed, but she told herself that when she needed solitude very much she could sit outside the windows of the saloon, where the deck was so narrow that the children could not come and where her mistress would not dare to walk. This place then became her own. In front of the saloon there was a wide deck, and the floors were of fine varnished wood, which neither sun nor rain could spoil. This varnish came from Ningpo, whose people are famous for their junks and seagoing ships.

Thus began the journey that was to last for days. For herself Peony looked forward to every day with pleasure. She had work enough to superintend the life of all, and yet she had hours in which to sit dreaming in her own little place, disturbed only by a boatman when he passed from stern to bow and back again, or when the wind failed and the oars must be used until the tow ropes were out. But she feared very much lest David grow restless. He was used to space and many courts, and would he be patient closed into this vessel with crying children and his wife sometimes impatient? At first she was afraid; then she found she need not fear.

For David found himself absorbed in the sights that passed before their eyes. Sometimes their way was slow enough so that he could walk on the shore, and many miles he walked over new country and through provinces that he had never seen before. Everywhere he was treated with courtesy, and when the towmen stopped to rest and eat and drink tea, he took his meal ashore, too, and the townspeople spoke to him courteously, inquiring only what country he came from. When he spoke the name of his own city they wondered.

"We did not know that foreigners lived there," they told him.

"I am not a foreigner," he replied. "I was born in that city and my father before me."

"But what country did your ancestors come from?" they then inquired.

"From over the mountains," he replied, and they nodded, their curiosity satisfied.

He did not talk often with Peony, for there was little chance for this, and they both, without words, knew that Kueilan would not be pleased if she saw her husband talking with a bondmaid beyond what was necessary. Yet sometimes when Peony had put her mistress to bed, and she went to the foredeck to tell David that all was ready for the night, David lingered a few minutes, especially if the moon shone.

On one such night he said to Peony, "My father has always said that your people are kind to ours, but the depth of this kindness I only now see for myself. These people in the river hamlets and along the shores, they do not know me, and yet they greet me and they make me welcome in the inns. I wonder at this gentleness."

"Are not all men brothers under Heaven?" So Peony replied in the words of the sages.

David shook his head. "These good words are everywhere," he replied, "but not always such good deeds."

He went inside then to his own rest, and Peony stood alone in the moonlight.

It was indeed fair country. The land along the river shores was green with new rice and about every little village the peach trees were in full blossom, pink by day and pearly by night. Distant hills rose against the sky and the water flowed golden under the moon. A good land, and the people were good. There were robbers, it is true, and there were pirates on the river, but these robbed all alike, whatever their color and their shape. With the guards this family was safe, and the governor had given the boatman a flag that announced that they were taking gifts to the Imperial Court and none would dare to rob them.

When all was quiet Peony went into the now empty saloon and she unrolled the quilts that by day she hid under the couches, and she made herself ready for sleep. She slept well, the fresh winds blowing upon her.

Out of one province they came into another and so at last near to the port where the river met the Grand Canal. They did not wish to reach the sea, neither did they wish to change to the small canal-boats. At a given place, therefore, they left the boat that had become a home to them, and they met the mule carts that were to take them north.

Often did Peony wish for the junk again, for now they must travel all day over the rough cobbled roads, stopping to eat quick meals, except at night when they slept at inns. Peony was impatient indeed, for to find a clean, good inn was nearly impossible. Each evening the master innkeeper wherever they were would come out fawning and praising when he saw how long a retinue they had, and he bawled and shouted to his men to prepare food and tea and he promised that he had clean rooms and the best of everything. But when Peony inspected the rooms, they were often filthy. When she saw there were fleas and bedbugs she refused to have the bed rolls opened until water had been boiled and poured over the bed boards. All was done under her supervision, for her mistress was helpless and David was eager to see every new sight, and when they reached a town or city he left his family and went out to look at it.

But Peking was reached at last, and every child was silenced while they looked in wonder as the great walls loomed gray and high out of the surrounding plains. All had heard of the wonders of this capital, but even David was not prepared for the vastness of what they saw. They went through the city gate, and the walls were so thick that it was twilight there between sunlight at the two ends. Kung Chen had written to his shops to prepare a house for Ezra's son and his family, and there they went along streets so wide and all paved with stone that even Peony had no word to say and could only look her wonder.

So they came to a gate set in a wall, and they went in and found Kung Chen's men there waiting to welcome them. David stayed with them in the guest hall, and Peony led the family into their courts, and the servants worked well, and soon all was settled.

The little boys were pleased with what was new, and Kueilan walked about the gardens and exclaimed over the rockery and the dwarfed plum trees. Thus the holiday was begun. But Peony watched above all for David. Would it be holiday for him, too? She was comforted when having sent his guests away he came in to visit his family and her and she saw his face gay and his eyes bright with excitement.

"Let us stay here a long time, eh, mother of my sons?" he said to his wife, and she smiled back at him, excited by his joy. He grew tender to her suddenly. "You little one!" he exclaimed. "You look as you did the first time I saw you!"

Hearing these words Peony slipped away, lest her presence check the renewal of their love. The old deep sadness of life lay in the bottom of her heart and she knew it was there, but she would not allow herself to sink into it. Out of the dark and sullen bottom of a lake the lotus flowers bloomed upon its surface, and she would pluck the flowers.

Peking was at its best that spring. The people, released from the fears and trials of war, rejoiced in the return of the Imperial Court to the city. The two empresses, the eastern and elder and the western and younger, were regents for the young emperor, who was still a child. Both empresses were beautiful, but the Western Empress was rich with love of life and power, and it could easily be seen that under her reign the nation would prosper and every sort of art and commerce would grow strong.

It was the air that David loved best. Old sadness fell from him and the very look in his eyes changed. The tinge of melancholy that had become natural to him left him, and the vitality that only rebellion had lit so far now became his daily energy.

"I love this city," he told Peony one day. "Look at the people—the men tall—the women handsome. Peony, you are like a child here."

Peony was not sure that she was pleased with this comparison. It was true that most of the women were taller than she, their cheekbones high and their frames big. She pouted a little at David and he laughed. "Let us talk of something else, then! The wide streets—I like the space."

To this Peony could agree. There was space everywhere, the

streets wide enough for ten carts to run abreast between shops on either side stocked with fine goods. The people were more than handsome—they were kind and their spirits were noble. There was no smallness anywhere. The largeness of the north was in this city, where the people ate wheat bread with their meat instead of rice. Many peoples met here, and David took pleasure in feasting in the fine inns with the friends whom Kung Chen had provided. To eat roast mutton in a Mohammedan inn, to spend half the night over roast duck in another, to declare both the finest food, was easy enough. The mutton, tender and wisely flavored, was torn in pieces and roasted upon spits over charcoal and brought to the table hot to be eaten with steamed rolls of bread.

And yet Peking duck could still be the finer food. Night after night David sat in one inn or another with men so carefree and so full of humor that he would have said they never worked at anything but pleasure had he not seen them shrewd tradesmen by day. They sat about a great round table, eating small dishes first, until the host of the inn brought in the ducks for their approval, killed and plucked but not yet roasted. When they had chosen a pair of ducks, appraising size and fat and texture of the skin, these were spitted and turned over coals, until the skin was crisped and browned and glistening with fat. Soon the first dish was served, and it was the curls of rich dark skin, and with it came thin pancakes of wheat flour and red jelly made of haws and sweetened. These cakes were wrapped about the roasted duck skin and into each was put a spoonful of jelly and so they were eaten, hot and sweet and bread and meat together, with warmed wine in small bowls. Then in succession came the other dishes, the meat of the roasted duck flavored and mixed with tender cabbage and then with mushrooms and then with bamboo shoots and then with chestnuts, each dish different from all others and each as good as the next, until the final dainty of the duck, now devoured. This was the head split open so that the brains could be picked out with chopsticks and tasted for the fine delicate flavor.

Who could tire of such fare? And yet there were the vegetarian inns where devout Buddhists could feast, those who gave up eating meat for the sake of their souls. At those inns vegetables were shaped and flavored until the feasters could have sworn them meat, except they had no flesh of any animal in them. The eyes of the devout were satisfied and their palates tasted the semblance of the meats they had denied themselves, while their souls were saved.

"How clever are these people!" David exclaimed each day when he discovered such new things. Indeed, the pleasures he had enjoyed in his youth seemed small in comparison to the variety that he now found in Peking. The finest theaters were here, the best shows of juggling and magic, and the most famous singers and musicians and scholars.

While he waited for audience with the two empresses, David released his soul and he enjoyed every pleasure that the city had. Nor was he selfish and solitary. Each morning he spent on business for his father and Kung Chen, and he visited every rich merchant in the city and he made many new contracts for the delivery of goods and he took orders for fabulous articles from Europe and from India. For the merchants here knew of machines and cloths and lamps and toys made abroad and they craved these things for themselves and for sale. Especially did they want clocks. The great gilt clock that years ago Kao Lien had brought as a gift for the Emperor was now matched by many others in the palace. In one room, so David heard, there were more than a hundred clocks. What had been a royal gift for one now became a thing coveted by common men, and David wrote to his father:

"Clocks can be sold here by the many thousand, I think, especially those not too high in price, yet ornate with gilt and figures. But all foreign goods are valued. These people have the best of everything, the finest silks and satins and embroideries, the richest jewelry and furniture, and yet their love of novelty is such that they will buy any trickery of foreign stuff."

When the morning's business was over David spent his afternoon with his family, unless the day was raining or, worse than rainy, clouded with dust, which the high winds blew over the city from distant deserts. Holding his sons' hands, David walked in temple forests and sat in theaters and visited every bazaar and fakirs' show place, and with him often was his wife, shy at being seen abroad and yet made bold by curiosity. Whether Kueilan went or not, and sometimes she complained that her feet hurt her and she could not walk, Peony went always with the children, and now she too knew the happiest times of her whole life. With David and his sons she laughed and watched and was amazed at many sights. She was never tired, and she was always amiable, and as the weeks passed easily, more and more it was she who went and not her mistress.

For Kueilan had made friends with some of the ladies of the merchants, and she grew fond of gambling with them. From one house to another these ladies went, one day here and one day there, traveling in their curtained sedans, and they spent the whole afternoon and evening at mah-jongg, until it became their passion. In this the serving maids encouraged them, since before each lady said good night to the others she must for courtesy's sake put silver in a bowl upon the table, and this the maids divided between them. Peony took no share, for she considered herself above such money, but careful always to wound no feelings, she excused herself to the others saying, "Since I must stay with the little lords and their father and I cannot help you who serve our mistress, it would not be just for me to share the serving money."

There was no talk of quick return to their old home. For one thing, the presentation of the gifts David had brought to the empresses was delayed until they were ready to receive him, and the delay stretched into months because they were busy with the repairs needed for the palace. While the court had been in exile there had been much ruin, and this must all be mended. But far beyond this were the vast plans the Western Empress had for a new palace and for added courts and pools and bridges and rockeries and gardens. The Imperial Treasury was impoverished by wars with the white men and by the rebellion of the southern Christians. The Western Empress demanded therefore new taxes and tributes, especially for the building of the Summer Palace and for the beautifying of the lake there. She dreamed of a marble boat set in the lake that would be large enough for all her ladies to dine in and then to see a play whose actors might number into hundreds. Her ministers groaned to think of such expense, and rumors went out over the city of her ambitions and her willfulness. The ministers besought her to remember that the wars with the white men had been lost for lack of a good army, and that swords were not enough these days when outer nations had gunpowder. But the Western Empress answered arrogantly thus: "When the Imperial Court is glorious, the nation shares its glory," and the rumor of this went over the city, too.

Yet the people laughed when they heard of the pride and strength of the young empress and they took it as a good sign. Weakness and languor in the ruler were feared, and there was neither in the Western Empress. Even rumors of her quarrels with the Eastern Empress were made the stuff for jokes and songs, and hardihood and willfulness entered into the spirit of the people because it was in the young empress.

Early in the summer David received at last the summons to the court and he made ready to appear. The hour was soon after dawn, when the audience with the ministers was over, and the empresses were ready to receive proposals of new revenue and gifts.

Peony rose early indeed and she helped David to dress himself and saw to it that he had food and that all was in readiness. She went with him to the gate and behind her stood the servants, awed to know their master was to be received at court. They all gazed at David, very fine in new garments of blue silk and black velvet, his tasseled hat upon his head and jade rings on his thumbs, as he stepped into his great sedan chair.

Peony watched until the chair disappeared and then she went back to bed. She could not sleep—that was beyond her—and in an hour or two she must rise and see that the children were fed, cared for, and happy, and later than that the feast was prepared for her mistress that night, for the ladies were to play mah-jongg here. When David would return she did not know, but the house must be ready for that, too, and her mistress up and dressed and waiting to hear the story he would have to tell. For Peony was always careful to prepare her mistress to be all that she should be as a wife. She did not allow Kueilan to appear before her husband with her hair uncombed or her dress wrinkled. Kueilan grumbled often, saying, "I am an old married woman now, Peony, and shall I have no peace? First it is my feet I unbound to please you and now it is my hair to be a trouble to me and then it is my eyebrows to be plucked and my fingernails painted and you have me perfumed like a flower girl. When am I to have some peace?"

To this Peony only smiled and said, "It gives your lord pleasure, does it not, my lady?"

One day when Peony had so answered Kueilan threw her a shrewd look and she said, "It is only to please him, then? You do not care for me."

Peony felt her heart stop. Then she said smoothly, "I take it that what gives him pleasure gives you the most pleasure, too, but if I am wrong, Lady, please instruct me."

This put Kueilan in a difficulty, for how could she say she did not wish to give her husband pleasure? She was silent, but after that Peony took care never to mention David to her again. She learned more wisdom, and her soul grew deep as life itself.

When David came back at midmorning, looking weary but triumphant, the whole house was waiting to receive him, his wife dressed and pretty, the children clean and eager, and the servants respectful and yet curious.

Peony met him at the gate. "Is it too much to ask that you tell us what has happened? We wait to know, and with one telling it will be told to all."

"First let me eat and drink, for I am faint," David replied. "We were not allowed to sit down and I had to bow myself on my knees until they are sore."

She followed him into the house and to his own rooms and took the heavy hat from his head, and the stiff brocaded robe he next laid aside, and the high velvet boots. Then she fetched his easy robe of summer silk and his low satin shoes and he ate and drank food that she ordered brought to him and he slept an hour and then he was ready.

In the great hall of the house Peony assembled all, and David sat down in the highest seat and looked about at his family and servants. The day was fine and the summer sunshine fell into the court and shone through the wide-open doors and he thought to himself that what he had was well enough to make a man proud. His wife sat across the table from him, and she wore a soft green satin robe, and jade was in her ears and in the knot of her hair and gold and jade were upon her hands and wrists. She was as pretty as the girl he had first seen in Kung Chen's hall. Near her stood his two handsome sons, dressed like little men in long silk robes, their hair braided in queues and corded with red silk. The third son was now beginning to walk, and his nurse held him by a broad silk girdle and followed him as he staggered everywhere. Peony sat near the door, and he knew her quiet beautiful face. The servants stood together clean and waiting. He took up his tea bowl, sipped and set it down, and then began:

"You must understand that it is no easy matter to appear before the empresses. I waited for more than two hours in an anteroom with others who had been granted audience today, and we were given no seats or tea. A eunuch led us there and bade us wait, and it was the Chief Steward himself who was to call us. But when he came he had first to teach us what to expect and how to behave. The Eastern Empress, he told us, was ill today and only the Western Empress would receive us. We were not to look at the Imperial Screen behind which we sat—"

At this point David's elder son cried out, "Dieh-dieh, did you not see her?"

David shook his head. "No one is allowed to see her, my first son. She is empress but she is also a woman—a beautiful one, and a widow. Her behavior is correct.

"Well, we all went in, and I was given the third place—"

"Why the third place, Dieh-dieh?" his son asked again.

At this David looked impatient and Peony rose softly and led the little boy to her side and held him in her arm. Then David went on: "That I am third is because I have no official rank and there were two before me who had. I was the first of those without rank, and this is because Kung Chen has special favor in our province and has been mentioned at the court by our provincial governor."

So David went on, and he told how he came in and how he bowed his head to the floor and how he must stay in that position until his name was called, and how then he stood with bowed head and presented his gifts, which had been taken from him at the door when he entered. He explained that the gifts were from Europe, not as good as anything already here, but still he hoped that Her Majesty would find a moment's idle pleasure in their curiosity. Then he spoke of the House of Ezra and its contracts with the House of Kung, and he thanked the Empress because although his ancestors came from foreign lands, yet they had lived here in peace.

At this point David stopped and looked at them with some pride. "When I said this, the Western Empress spoke to me."

"What did she say?" Kueilan asked.

"She asked me if you were foreign too, but I said no. Then she asked me if I had children and I said yes, three sons. Now hear me—she commanded me to bring my sons and let her see them, because she has never seen children of foreign blood!"

What consternation, pride, and excitement now fell on David's family!

"Did she set a day?" his wife exclaimed.

"Tomorrow, at four in the afternoon, we are all to go. I am to wait in the anteroom, but you and the children and their nurses must go to the garden where the ladies of the court will be gathering flowers. The Chief Steward will take you there and you are to stay only as long as he says and then come back."

"Peony must come with me," Kueilan said immediately.

"Oh, no!" Peony exclaimed.

"Yes, you must go," David said with authority. "It is only you who can stop a child from crying."

So it was decided, and for once Kueilan was too distraught to play her mah-jongg well and that night she was peevish when Peony came to put her to bed because she had lost so much money.

"Your lord is rich and generous," Peony reminded her. "He will not reproach you, Lady."

But Kueilan did not want to be comforted and she continued peevish until Peony left her in bed and went to tell David that she was ready to go to sleep.

She found him very meditative in his garden, sitting under a twisted pine tree in a bamboo chair. He heard her message and inclined his head but he did not rise for a moment. Peony waited, perceiving that he had been thinking and might want to tell her what he thought. When he did not speak she asked a question to excuse her lingering.

"How did the voice of the Western Empress sound in your ears?"

"Strong and fresh, but without sweetness," he answered.

Then he said what was in his mind. "Peony, I never felt so clearly before the imperial clemency that has been shown to my people. She knew me foreign, she heard me give her thanks—and all she wished was to see my children."

"Woman's curiosity in an empress," Peony said smiling.

"But no dislike!" he exclaimed.

"Why should there be dislike when your people have never made a war here or taken what was not yours of land or goods?" Peony asked warmly. "You have been good people—and you and your father are good men."

David looked at her strangely. "Our goodness has not saved us elsewhere in the world," he said.

"Those other foreign peoples are unreasonable," Peony retorted. "We have been taught reason with our mothers' milk."

Upon this she went away, and the more she pondered what David had said, the more she was not certain whether it had been well to have him grateful to the Empress or whether it were a good sign that she had made him feel foreign again. Peony sighed and for the first time wished that a day had been set for their return to their own city.

There was no time for thinking or wishing on the morrow, be sure of that. All day Kueilan spent in bathing and powdering and dressing, and the hairline of her forehead must be straightened and every little hair pulled out that did not lie flat, and only Peony could do this without hurting her. The long fingernail on the third finger of her right hand broke off and this made her shed tears of anger.

"How shall I hide this?" she demanded of Peony, and she held out her little hand, which was still like a lotus bud.

"We will put the silver shield on just the same," Peony replied. "Who will know the nail is gone beneath? Sit still, Lady, please, and let others serve you, lest you break another nail."

By now it was her feet that distressed Kueilan. She looked with much distaste upon her shoes, which needed to be so much larger than they had been. "I am ashamed to show these huge country-woman's feet," she declared to Peony. "I wish I had never listened to what you said."

"Your lord was very pleased, Lady," Peony reminded her, forgetting that she was not to speak of him.

"Only for a day or two," Kueilan said pouting. "He never sees my feet now. He has forgotten all my suffering. But I have to see my feet every day and now they will disgrace me before the empresses. I dare say their feet are very tiny!"

Peony remembered her books at this moment. "No, Mistress, there you are wrong. The empresses are Manchu and not Chinese and their feet have never been bound, and therefore how much bigger are they than yours!"

Kueilan exclaimed at this but she was consoled, and at last she was dressed and beautiful and she sat motionless in her chair so as not to spoil her looks while Peony superintended the dressing of the children before her eyes. This, too, was a task needing much patience, for Kueilan did not like the robe for her eldest son, and when at last all were ready, the third son was overcome with excitement and too much noise and he cast up his food and spoiled his garments and had to be made ready afresh.

"I wish it were all over and that I were in bed!" Kueilan exclaimed when she rose at last and went to the gate, where the sedan chairs waited.

"Lady, you will tell your grandchildren of this hour," Peony said, smiling, to comfort her.

So they set forth, David ahead and all his family behind, and they approached the great foursquare walls of the palace. At the gate they were delayed for bribes to the gatekeepers and then the chairmen were allowed to enter. Then the gates closed again after them and the chairs were set down and David came out first and then waited while they all came out. He surveyed them and felt his pride rise at the sight of his pretty wife and healthy children. Then he turned to Peony anxiously.

"Stay close by each one, Peony! Do not let the little boys run here and there—help their mother to answer well when she is spoken to."

"Rest your heart," Peony replied, but her own heart was far from at rest.

So they left him there, and a eunuch led them to an inner gate, and then the Chief Steward met them. He was a tall strong man, a eunuch as all men were in these walls, except the Emperor himself, and Peony instantly disliked his looks. He was handsome, his face full and smooth, his voice high and soft, but cold. But his eyes were not the eyes of a eunuch. He stared at her with instant and insolent admiration, and she looked away. In spite of her wish, she felt herself blush and then she grew cold. What if he took that blush to be a sign that she felt his look? She stayed close to her mistress and she took a hand of each little boy, and together they walked behind the Chief Steward to the gardens. At the gate he paused, and again his insolent eyes were on Peony while he gave them commands in his high cruel voice.

"Their Imperial Majesties are now examining the water lilies," he told them. "You are to stand by the great pine tree inside the gate. When they pass you must all bow, even to the children. Do not speak unless Their Majesties address you. If they do not speak and pass on, I will lead you away again. If a question is asked, I will repeat it, and you are to answer me, and I will repeat your answer to Their Majesties."

He led them in, and they waited by a great pine tree and he waited with them. In the distance, among the flowers in the sunshine, they could see the empresses, followed by a score and more of ladies all in beautiful robes of many colors. It was a pretty sight and Peony wished to enjoy it, but she could not because of the Chief Steward. What did he do now but take his place directly behind her? He stood so close to her that she could feel his hot breath on her nape, and she knew this meant that he was staring at her hair and at her neck and shoulders. She stepped forward and he stepped forward and suddenly she felt faint. The sunny picture before her swam into a mist, and all the brilliant colors mingled in a rainbow haze. If she stepped farther, it would be unfitting to her mistress, and yet she could not endure the terror of this man behind her. While she wavered she felt him press yet closer, and he made pretense to speak in a low voice: "The tall one is the Western Empress. She will speak if either speaks, for the Eastern Empress never speaks before her."

While he said this he peered over Peony's head and she felt his huge body press loathsomely against her. Now she could not bear it, and she slipped to one side and put the third son's nurse in her place. Peony did not look up while she did this, but he reproved her. "Make no commotion, woman. Their Majesties are near!"

"Be still, Peony!" Kueilan whispered loudly.

What could Peony do but stand? She felt her face flush again and all the joy was spoiled. She scarcely heard what came next and she could scarcely keep from weeping.

For the Western Empress had paused and then the Eastern Empress also and all the ladies.

"Who are these?" the Western Empress now asked of the Chief Steward.

He answered her, and they stood while the Western Empress looked at them. Peony did not lift her eyes, knowing it was forbidden, but she saw the royal hands, one holding a jade fan, the other hanging down empty. They were strong hands for a woman, not small, but beautifully shaped. Upon each finger was a nail shield of gold, embossed and set with jewels. The feet beneath the long robe were in embroidered shoes, and under the shoes were satin soles padded six inches thick to the give the Empress height.

The Eastern Empress did not speak, but the Western Empress looked her fill at the children. "They do look foreign," she declared to her ladies. "Black hair, but not smooth. The eyes are round, their noses high. Yet they are handsome and they look healthy. I wish our royal son looked so healthy."

She sighed and ordered sweetmeats given them all and Peony thanked Heaven that the baby did not cry. Then she heard the Western Empress ask yet another question. "Who is this pretty girl?" She knew the question was of her, and she hung her head yet lower.

"She is our bondmaid," Kueilan told the Chief Steward, and he shouted, "A bondmaid, Majesty!"

"Too pretty for a bondmaid," the Western Empress said coolly.

That was all. The Western Empress swept on and with her the Eastern Empress and the ladies, and the Chief Steward led them out again. Now he was very affable and he heaped sweetmeats on the children, and he put his hand into his bosom and took out some money.

"Here is something for yourself," he said to Peony. "Her Majesty never sees another woman, and it was most unusual that she spoke of you. A word from me will bring you into these courts and you will have all you need for life."

While he spoke he held the money on his big open palm, but Peony did not take it. She hastened on with the children and shook her head and was not able to speak. Never had she been so glad to see David as she was now. He came forward to meet them and she answered his questions quickly while she busied herself.

"Yes, the children were good. Our lady was beautiful. Her Majesty spoke of the children's health."

And all the time she made haste to be hidden behind the curtains of her sedan chair, for the Chief Steward stood staring at her. When the curtains were drawn about her and she felt the chair hoisted to the men's shoulders, she took out her handkerchief and wept heartily and well. She had been thoroughly frightened and now she was safe. Never would she leave the walls of the house again until they went home. A man so powerful as the Chief Steward in the Imperial Palace could reach out his hands and clutch her anywhere in the streets. She would persuade David to go home as soon as they could. Yet how could she tell him?

All the way home she wept, wiping her eyes dry only when they turned into their own street. When she was in the house she was busy again and she kept her face turned away, and in the weariness of all, the fret of her mistress and the crying of the children, she was not noticed, for David withdrew to his own rooms as he always did when the children were troublesome. So this day ended, and when all were at rest Peony went to bed too, without having seen David. She wept again and asked herself whether she must tell David, but being weary with fear and excitement, she too fell asleep before she could answer her own question.

David discovered her plight himself the next morning before Peony had so much as seen him. He had finished his breakfast and was about to set forth on a visit to a new shop in the south end of the city where rugs were being woven in new patterns, when a messenger came to the gate in the yellow garments that meant that he was from the Imperial Palace. He was very haughty and he frightened the gateman and the servants by his loud voice and his high manners, saying that he brought out a letter addressed to "The Foreigner Surnamed Chao, from the City of K'aifeng, Now Resident in the Hutung of the Silver Horse."

Chao was the Chinese surname of Ezra's family and the letter was for David. The gateman received it, and begging the imperial messenger to be seated, he ran with the letter to the head servant, who took it to David as he was about to come out from his own door.

"Master—from the palace!" the servant gasped.

David took the letter with wonder, and opened it. His face changed as he read the words it contained. He looked astonished and then stern.

"Does the messenger still wait?" he asked.

"At the gate, Master," the servant replied.

"Pay him well and tell him that I shall send an answer when I have considered the proposal."

The man went away and paid the messenger and then spread throughout the household the rumor that the master had been offered a high post in the Imperial Court. This rumor came to Peony and immediately she grew afraid. If David were tempted indeed to stay near the court, then how could she remain with him? She could never be safe from that evil eunuch. Her life fell into pieces before her eyes, and she felt so faint that she could scarcely continue with her task of arranging lilies in a bowl. Now indeed she must speak to David and tell him what had befallen her.

But David sent for her before she could speak. It was not usual that he sent for her, since when he had anything to say to her he strolled about the house until he found her. Peony knew, therefore, that he wished to speak privately to her, and she inclined her head when the servant came to call her and she put the flowers into the water and went at once.

David stood in the middle of his sitting room when she came in. In his hand was a large yellow envelope. When he saw Peony he held it out to her. "What is the meaning of this?" he asked.

She took the letter and read it. It was an offer from the Chief Steward to purchase her as a maid for one of the ladies of the court. Arrogantly phrased, it was all but a command. She folded the letter and thrust it into its envelope and looked speechlessly at David. Tears welled into her eyes again.

David sat down. "Sit down, Peony," he said.

She sat down, bending her head and wiping her eyes with the edge of her sleeve.

"Do you know any reason for this?" he asked kindly.

To her dismay she saw that he imagined she knew that this offer was to be made. She shook her head and could not speak for weeping.

"Come, Peony," he said at last, growing angry with her. "Have the courage to tell me if you want to leave my house!"

His anger dried her tears immediately. "Dare to say that I have no courage!" she retorted.

"This is more like you," he said. "Now tell me everything."

So Peony told him what had happened the day before, and the further David heard the more angry and dismayed he was.

"What a quandary!" he exclaimed. "We cannot stay here any more, or the Chief Steward will make our life wretched for us. A word from him and the very merchants will fear to deal with us!"

"It is all because of me," Peony said in much distress. "Let me go."

"Sell you?" David exclaimed. His voice was so hot that Peony took heart.

"I could run away," she said.

"You could run away!" he repeated. "And what would become of me, Peony? Could I forgive myself?"

"If I ran away I might be able to find my way to you again," Peony faltered.

They looked at one another and it was a strange long look. Peony was humble and trembling and frightened and David was fearful not only at what he saw in her face but at what he now perceived in his own heart. He could not let her leave him. He was jealous that the Chief Steward had so much as seen her and he blamed himself.

"How dare I let you out of my gate?" he muttered.

Peony looked down and did not answer. He saw her long straight lashes lying upon her cheeks and he rose abruptly.

"Prepare everything," he commanded. "We leave for home tonight."

She rose slowly, and lifted her eyes to his face.

"David," she whispered, and did not know she spoke his name. "Do not think of me!"

"I do think of you," he said shortly. "Obey me, Peony! I give it as my command."

"I obey you, David." Her voice was as soft as her breath.

That night soon after midnight David and his family left the city in hired mule carts. To his friend who was the head of Kung Chen's shops in the city he explained truthfully why he must go. "The young woman has been like a sister to my wife rather than a bondmaid, and it cannot be allowed," he said.

"That Chief Steward is a very devil," the merchant agreed. "How many families in this city have suffered the loss of their daughters through him! You do well to escape."

To his wife David also told the truth in a few simple words, and

Kueilan was half frightened and yet unwilling to yield to fear. "It might be very well for Peony to be in the palace," she reasoned. "We would have a friend there and she is so clever—who knows, she might even be a servingwoman to the Empress!"

To this David would not listen. "Peony has been in our house always, and it does not become me to sell her like a slave." If Kueilan looked at him with suspicion he refused to see it. "Come," he said. "Hasten yourself, Little Thing! We go tonight whether you are ready or not."

It was a silent going. The city gate was closed and David had to bribe the gatemen well before they would open the great locks. But once they were open the carts passed through swiftly, and by morning they were well on their way to the canal.

挑筋教

XII

UPON that homeward journey David said little indeed to anyone. The pleasure he had taken in the new countryside when they were going northward he scarcely felt now. The country was as beautiful as ever, and perhaps more beautiful, for every tree and field was at its ripest growth. Wheat had been harvested, and, in the north, sorghum corn stood high. This was the season for banditry, for the corn was so tall that robbers easily hid in it, and he was uneasy until they reached the canal. But good fortune was with them, for though they heard of highwaymen before them, none came near on the days when they passed.

The reason for this was that through some stupidity the robbers had not known that the governor of the province was traveling to the capital and they had taken him to be a common rich man. When his soldiers sprang at them they were so confounded that after a short battle they withdrew in dismay and hid in their caves and hills for a few days. It was held a crime to attack a governor or some high official, and the king of the bandits sent tribute quickly to the governor and cursed himself heartily for molesting so august a personage, and he promised that he would cut off the heads of those who had led the attack, and deliver them to the governor on any day he was ready to receive them. To this the governor replied that the men were to be spared. He set a punishment, nevertheless, that for a month there was to be no robbery whatever along the roads from the capital to the river. Within this month by luck David and his family went southward to the river and took a junk homeward. River pirates there were, but David bade the boatmen use the same flags that he had used before, which had on them the name of the Imperial Court, and under these they were safe.

The journey was slow, for in midsummer the winds are soft and mild, and as they went westward the current of the river was against the travelers. There was time for David to be alone with his thoughts, and he was much alone on the decks, gazing at the slowly moving countryside on either side of the junk. The sun was hot and the boatmen put up a wide awning to shade him from the sun, and beneath it he sat on cushions, in comfort as to body but much disturbed in his mind. This disturbance made him very gentle toward his children and his wife, and to them he gave more heed than usual, listening to their chatter, and courteous to any whim that Kucilan made known. He had through the years allowed the habit of impatience with her to grow upon him somewhat, but now he curbed it, and he answered her gently, even when what she said was foolish. To his sons he made endless explanations in answer to their many questions, and sometimes he even held the end of the sash around his youngest son's waist, so that the child would not fall into the water. Altogether David was unlike his usual self.

Peony perceived all this, and then with pain she discovered that this new kindness was not given to her. David avoided her, and this she saw plainly as the days went by in the enforced closeness of the junk. He took care not to be alone with her, and if she came out on the deck in the evening, after her charges were ready for the night, David was never there, although the moonlight was splendid upon the river. Day after day went by but David never spoke to her alone, and seldom spoke to her at all except to give her a command concerning his sons or their mother. Peony was wounded to the heart at first, and she thought this change in him must be because it was for her sake he had left the capital when he would have liked to stay longer. She sighed to believe that he was like other men in this, that he loved least that one for whom he must sacrifice. She began to blame herself that she had allowed him to give up anything for her and pride crept into her with despair, and she planned that if this change stayed in him, she would keep to herself, and even perhaps leave his house. But where would she go?

She had no answer to this question. I must still stay hidden in his house like the mice and the crickets, she told herself.

If David noticed her silence and her pride, he made no sign. The days went one after the other through the midsummer and they drew near to their home. He sent runners ahead to tell his father that if there were winds they would reach home within seven days, and if winds delayed or if a summer storm fell, it would be at most as many as seven days longer. He was anxious to get home before the late summer season of storms, when all river craft must be ready to seek harbor.

The winds were with them for a few days and they were towed the rest of the journey, and at the end of the tenth day they saw the city walls upon the plains. All were glad to see the shores they knew so well, and Ezra was at the riverbank to meet them, and so were Kung Chen and his sons, and there were mule carts and sedans and carriers.

"Well, my son!" Ezra cried with gladness. He took David into his arms and pressed his cheek against his tall son's shoulder. "I did not expect you for another half year, but how heartily I welcome you!"

Kung Chen shook his hands clasped together and nodded his head and greeted his daughter and her children and acknowledged Peony, and so they got into carts and chairs and went homeward. The city officials had ordered firecrackers to be lighted at the city gate and at the gate of Ezra's house. Old Wang and Wang Ma stood holding many feet of firecrackers in strings and they lit them, and thus in the midst of din and rejoicing the family was reunited.

How glad was Peony to be safe inside these gates again! "Everything is the same," she murmured to Wang Ma when she had stepped into the courtyard.

"There has been one small death," Wang Ma said. "Otherwise all is well."

Now Peony had already missed the voice of Small Dog, but she had taken it that the little beast was sleeping somewhere, for she was old and lazy.

"Not Small Dog!" she exclaimed.

Wang Ma nodded. "The creature pined when you went away and would not eat. I tempted her with meat scraped fine to spare her teeth and I bought fresh pig's liver for her, but she could eat nothing."

"I wish I had taken her with me," Peony cried in sorrow.

"She would have longed for home," Wang Ma replied. "Either way she was doomed to die."

Peony said no more but she missed Small Dog exceedingly. When she had settled her mistress and the children in their rooms she went to her own small court and the quiet was too heavy for her to bear. She felt cut off from everyone, and she sat down and wept a while softly, sighing now and then. Small Dog's cushion was still under the table and she looked at it mournfully and asked herself if she should get another small dog. Dogs were many and could be replaced easily and no one cared whether they lived or died. Yet somehow she did not want any dog except the one she knew and had lost, and she cursed herself that she was so singlehearted.

"I am a fool," she murmured aloud. "I love too narrowly." She thought of Small Dog, but now her mind went on and she cursed herself that this same narrowness of heart made her cling to David when another woman would have given him up and chosen a good husband for herself and welcomed her children and been merry even though she could not have the man she loved. But all her cursing could not change her stubborn heart. I must put up with myself as I am, she thought mournfully, and when she had wept for a while she washed her face and brushed her hair and changed her garments and went out to do her duty to her mistress and the children.

David sat late that night with his father. They had dined alone together this first night and had promised to dine tomorrow with Kung Chen. Each had news to give the other. Ezra said he was well, but he looked thin, and David, seeing him freshly now, perceived that his father was growing to be an old man. Ezra's cheeks were lined under his beard and his left eyelid drooped somewhat. He complained of stiffness in his left side and that his left foot dragged when he walked. Yet his eyes were still bold and bright, and his voice was as loud as ever.

"Did the stiffness come slowly or quickly?" David asked.

"I woke up so one morning two months ago," Ezra answered. "For a few days my tongue was thick and I could not say my words clear. Wang Ma fetched the physician and he gave me an herb drink and I was better."

"Father, you must let me help you more," David said.

To this Ezra replied, "I have already done so, my son. While you were away I made you the head of the business, and from now on you are the one to say yes and no and to plan everything. Kung Chen has done the same with his eldest son. You are the partners and we two old grandfathers will stay at home unless we please to give you advice."

David was moved and proud, and yet a vague sorrow fell on him. This was the beginning of the end of his father's life. As he himself came into his prime his father must decline. It was the inevitable march of the generations and none could stop its course, but he told himself that from now until the day his father died he would be always gentle to him and he would defer to his wish in everything.

"I miss your mother, my son," Ezra said suddenly.

He looked at David and his eyes watered and he brushed his tears away with his fist. The hour was late, the house was still, and the great candles flickered in the summer wind blowing through doors open to the soft darkness in the court.

"We all miss her," David said quietly. "The house has never been the same house since she went away—for any of us."

Ezra seemed scarcely to hear him. He leaned back and his thick hands clutched the arms of his chair. "I think about our life together, hers and mine," he went on. "It was not an easy marriage, my son. She was unyielding—until I learned to know her. I could never deal with her twice the same way. She was a woman of many changes. Sometimes I met anger with anger, and sometimes I met anger with love and again with laughter—I had to choose my weapon. I had to be new to meet her newness. Yet underneath all her change there was a purity unexcelled. The heart of her was goodness. I could trust her. God she never betrayed, and me she could not betray. She was a true wife."

David did not speak. To him his parents had been merely parents, but now dimly he began to see them as man and woman. He was abashed to think of them thus, to contemplate these two from whom he had sprung as separate from him and leading between them the vigorous and private life of a man and a woman.

"She was never stupid," Ezra began again. "Well, sometimes that was almost too much, for I saw in how many ways she was more clever than I! When I was young this roused my spleen sometimes, but as I grew older I saw how fortunate I was. Look at Kung Chen! A lonely man, eh, my son? He never speaks to me of his children's mother, but the few times I have seen her—a bit stupid, eh, David? And he is a fastidious man—he cannot go out and pluck wild flowers along the road. No more could I. When a man has known a woman like your mother—body and soul—" Ezra broke off, sighed, and went on again. "While you were gone, my son, and when Kao Lien left me to go westward with the caravans, I had time to myself, and I remembered all my life with your mother. Much comfort she took away with her when she left me, but here is something strange: I have never been devout, as you well know, David, but while she was in the house I felt all was well with my house before God. She was my conscience—which pricked me sometimes and against which I kicked, but which I valued. Now I feel lost. God is far from me—if there is a God?"

He put this as a question and David did not know how to answer it. He kept his silence.

When he did not speak, Ezra began to speak again. "You and I cannot answer that question. By that much we are no longer Jews, my son. I made my choice, you made yours. Would I go back? Ah, but I am what I am, and did I go back I would make the same choice, and so would you."

"I am not so sure as you are," David said now. "I could have been one man—or another. Had Leah lived—" He broke off.

"Had Leah lived," Ezra repeated. He turned this over in his

mind. Then he said, "Had Leah lived, perhaps your mother would be living too. Everything would have been different. But first we would have had to be different."

"We would not have been here," David said.

Ezra looked across the table at him surprised. "You mean—"

"We cannot live here among these people and remain separate, Father," David argued. "In the countries of Europe, yes, for there the peoples force us to be separate from them by persecution. We cling to our own people there because none other will accept us, and we are martyred and glorified by our martyrdom. We have no other country than sorrow. But here, where all are friends to us and receive us eagerly into their blood, what is the reward for remaining apart?"

"Indeed—indeed, it is so," Ezra said. "All that has happened to us is inevitable."

"Inevitable," David agreed.

"And your sons, my grandsons, will proceed still further into this mingling," Ezra went on.

"It will be so," David said.

Ezra pondered. "Shall we then disappear?"

David did not reply. It was inevitable, as he himself had said, when people were kind and just to one another, that the walls between them fell and they became one humanity. Yet he could not contemplate the far future when his descendants knew him no more, when perhaps they would have forgotten the very name of Ezra, and when indeed they would be as lost as a handful of sand thrown into the desert or a cupful of water cast into the sea. He gazed down the long line of those who would come from his loins and the loins of his sons and his sons' sons. He saw the faces turning toward him, and they were the faces of Chinese.

"We grow too mournful," Ezra said suddenly. "What has been has been, and cannot be avoided. Tell me about your journey, my son."

So David roused himself and he told his father everything, the beauty of the great northern capital, and how the people looked and how noble their nature was, and what he had eaten and drunk and what all the gaieties were that he had enjoyed and how he had been given an audience before the Western Empress, and he told of the rumors about her, and so telling all he came at last to the reason why they had left the city so suddenly by night, for Peony's sake.

Ezra listened closely, laughing sometimes and his eyes shining sometimes, and shrewd and careful when David spoke of business. When he heard of Peony, he grew very grave indeed. "What misfortune!" he exclaimed. "The long arm of the Chief Steward can reach anywhere, and we must tell Kung Chen this tomorrow."

"I could not have done otherwise, Father," David said.

"No—no." Ezra hesitated, then he said firmly, "No, my son, no! To be sure, had she been like other women and had she welcomed the chance to go into the palace—well—hm—then, ah, it would have been fortunate for our house. We would have had a friend in the highest quarters. But being what she is—no, certainly not. Yet we must take every opportunity to ward off evil results. It would be a great sacrifice to make only for a woman, if our business were spoiled because of spite at the court. Your mother always said we made too much of Peony."

At this David felt some sort of heat rise in him, mingled with anger, and to defend himself he spoke coolly. "Well, my father, if I have done unwisely, I must make amends in some other way, for Peony has been like my sister, and I could not put her into that evil steward's palm at any price. That much I know."

"As long as she is no more to you than a sister I will not complain," Ezra said.

This speech was so plain that David was confounded by it. It probed him too deeply, beyond what he himself was willing to know, and he did not answer it. He looked at the candles and saw them guttering and he made excuse to rise and use the snuffers on them.

"It is late!" he exclaimed. "Tomorrow I must be early at the shops, Father, and so I will say good night."

Wang Ma had been waiting outside the door, and when she heard this she came in with the fresh tea and the rice gruel that Ezra drank before he slept, and so the day was over.

But for David there was no sleep. He did not go to his wife. Instead he stayed in his room, finding there every sign of Peony's thought for him, the bedquilt folded, the curtains drawn, the teapot hot, his pipe prepared, the candles trimmed. But she herself had gone.

He made himself ready for bed and he put out the candles and parted the curtains and laid himself down. Still he could not sleep. His father's talk had stirred afresh all that had been in his mind these many weeks on the journey. His mother, Leah, Peony, Kueilan, these four women who had somehow between them shaped his life were shaping him still. He longed to be free of them all, and yet he knew that no man is ever free of the women who have made him what he is. He sighed and tossed and wished for the day when he could return to the shops and the men there who had nothing to do with his heart and his soul.

Peony, too, was restless that night. David had been long with his father, she knew, for Wang Ma told her that the two were talking gravely hour after hour and she dared not go in, even though it was long past midnight. She had waited with Wang Ma, outwardly to keep her company but secretly because she hoped to see David's face at least as he passed. Yet he had not seen her, and she had not dared to call him. She sat in the dark court outside the range of the mild candlelight flowing through the open door and beyond, hearing their voices, and he passed her so closely that she could have touched him, but she did not put out her hand. Doubtless he had told his father why they had left Peking, and perhaps Ezra had reproached him. Well she knew that danger of trouble from the Chief Steward was not past, even here, and she shrank from being the cause of it.

When David had gone she went to bed herself, and lying alone in the moonless summer night, she considered her plight. Rich folk could be kind, as the Ezra family had always been kind to her, but if one of the lesser ones to whom they were kind should also become a trouble, their hearts could cool quickly. She remembered how she had thought that David loved her, perhaps, and she thought of the look in his eyes sometimes. Then she remembered how cold he had been all these weeks. Doubtless he regrets already what I have compelled him to do, she told herself.

Pride came to her help again, and she decided that at the very first moment he allowed her, she would go to David and tell him that she wished to enter the Buddhist nunnery that stood inside the city gate. There she would be safe from any man, and he could send word somehow to the Chief Steward that she had long been dedicated and only waiting for the journey north to be finished before she became a nun. Inside that quiet haven, where only women lived, she would be safe, and it seemed sweet to her.

The more she thought of this plan, the better she considered it to be, and she held it in her mind for a few days until the first rush of David's business was over. Yet she dared not be silent long, lest that strong soft hand from the Imperial Palace should bring trouble in its grasp.

On the fifth day she saw David linger after his noon meal as though he were not in haste to return to the shops. Ezra went to sleep on the long couch that in this summer weather was set under the bamboos, and Wang Ma sat by him to keep the flies away. The children slept, the servants slept, and her mistress too was sleeping. Peony had made it her business today to superintend the noon meal, and while the underservants took the dishes away, she handed the bamboo toothpicks to David and she said, "Will you not sleep a while, too? The air is heavy and there are thunderclouds in the south."

"I will sleep an hour in my own court," he replied.

Thither she went to set a bamboo couch under an old pine tree there, and while she was spreading a soft mat over it, David came in. He had taken off his robes when he came in and he wore his inner garments of pale green silk.

"All is ready," Peony said, and she prepared to leave him. The day was so hot that clear little rills of sweat ran down her cheeks and she wiped them away and laughed. "I am melting!" she exclaimed.

Her eyes met David's unconsciously, and instantly her laughter died. She had never seen him look at her thus. His eyes were on her passionately, grave and warm. The red flew into her cheeks and her knees trembled. Her tongue began to speak at random, without her mind, and yet repeating what her mind had been thinking.

"I have—have been—looking for the moment—to—to say something." So she began.

"This moment," David said.

She clasped her hands in front of her. "I—I have wept so much—"

"Why?" he asked.

"Because of what happened in the capital." Her words rushed out now, hurrying to be said. "I want to ask you—I beg you—I would die if I had brought harm to you, or even a little trouble. I can—I will—go into the Buddhist nunnery. It is safe there, and you could tell the—the Chief Steward—I am to be a nun."

"You a nun!" David cried in a low voice. He laughed silently, as though he wanted no one to hear him.

Yet who was there to hear? The house was sleeping and around them the hot afternoon sun shone down. There was not a sound even from outside the walls. The city slept and the very cicadas were still. And Peony stood before David as though she were caught fast in a web. She did not try to speak again. She could not, indeed.

What had brought him to this moment she could not imagine. She was amazed and fearful and love heated her veins and throbbed in her heart. He whom she had thought so cold all these weeks was suddenly all molten fire.

"Peony, follow me," he commanded her.

He turned and she followed him into his sitting room. He leaned against the table and faced her. "I tell you this now and it must last our lives through. If I tell you, will you remember?"

"Yes," she whispered, and her eyes did not waver from his.

"I have cheated myself all these years by saying you were like my sister," he said. "I have been a fool. You have never been like my sister. Never could I have loved a sister as I loved you when we were children—and as I love you now."

He looked at her steadily and she returned his look. This was the gift life gave her, this moment when he spoke these words. It would have been easy to put out both hands and take the gift, forgetting all else. But this was not possible for Peony. Too many years had she taken care of him and shielded him and strengthened him, planned for him and loved him. She could not think of herself now.

She tried to laugh. "All the more reason for me to be a nun, I think!"

He put aside her pretense at mirth. "Do not escape me by laughter," he said sternly. "I know as well as you do what it means for me to—to say what I have said. Yet I had to say it so that you know now why I could not leave you in the palace. As long as I live you must stay in my house, Peony, for I cannot live without you. I know it at last."

"Is this why you have been so cold to me all these weeks on the journey?" she asked.

"I was not cold to you. I was thinking of you, by day and by night," he replied.

She could not pretend to laugh now. He was sorrowful and resolute and she could not bear to know that his love for her should bring with it trouble to him. "I thank you for telling me what you have in your heart." Her voice was clear and grave. "I will keep your words in my heart forever. They are my comfort and they make my home."

She clasped her hands together and she bowed and turned away to leave him.

At the door his voice held her again. "Further than this I have not thought. Yet what is to become of us?"

She paused, one foot on the threshold, her hand on the lintel of the door. "Time will show us," she said gently, and then fearing lest he step forward to catch her hand or touch her shoulder, and dreading the weakness of love in her heart, she went quickly away.

That night it was impossible to sleep. She was glad that the bright moon that had attended them on their journey was gone. She crept through the darkness into the peach garden, and sat there alone under the trees. The stars were hidden by clouds, and the air was damp with coming rain. Yet she could not sit too long, for soon the mosquitoes began to whine about her. She lifted her wide sleeves and waved them like wings about her, and then she rose and walked to and fro. This walking—it was what Leah used to do, hour after hour, and when she thought of this suddenly Leah was here again and she could not shake off the sense of her presence. Yet why should she be afraid of Leah any more? She had the weapon now to still that ghost forever. If she would, she could go to David at this very hour and seal her love with her body, and what could Leah do to her—Leah, whose flesh was dust? She lifted her face to the dark sky, and ecstasy brimmed her heart. What if she went on silent feet while the house slept and took her advantage of David's love? The victory would be hers.

She stopped alone in the darkness, her finger to her lip, smiling to herself. Into her secret life in this house he would come, and she would be alone no more. She shook her head and her hand fell and her smile was gone. Her heart beat hard. Why should it be secret? There was no law against a man taking to himself the woman he loved. All through the city men did so, even as Kung Chen had taken his pretty singing girl, who afterward betrayed him. None would raise a cry against David. Indeed, it would be the better for him, for it would bring him closer to his friends. There need be no ceremony. She would yield to her heart and go to him now, and in the morning she would tell Wang Ma and soon all would know, and her mistress could accept it and allow her the second place, or she could refuse to know and all would go on as before.

Thus Peony's soft heart reasoned. Then her mind, solitary so long, grew hard and clear. Is David like other men? So mind inquired of heart.

At this moment, before she answered, she was suddenly startled by a strange thick cry. She lifted her head to listen, and her thoughts paused. There was no second sound, but feeling herself always responsible for this family, she went at once through the dark garden into the dimly lit great hall, and listened. Ezra's rooms opened eastward from the hall and his windows into the garden, and she pressed her ear against his closed door. She heard his breathing coming from him in groans, very heavy and slow, and she opened the door softly.

"It is I, Peony!" she called softly. "Are you ill, Old Master?"

He did not answer but his loud breaths came and went as though he dragged them out of his bosom. She ran in then to his bedroom and blew alive the brown paper spill always smoldering in its urn of ashes, and she lit the oil lamp and held it high in her right hand while with the other she pulled aside the curtains. Ezra lay there, his pillow pushed aside, his head thrown back until his beard stood upright into the air. His eyes were open and glazed and his whole face was purple and his back arched and stiff. He did not see or hear her, for his whole attention was fixed upon drawing his breath in and pushing it out again.

"Oh, Heaven!" Peony cried. She dropped the curtain and ran to David's room and beat upon his door. Then she tried to open it. It was locked! Even in the midst of her terror she paused. Why had he locked the door—except against her? Or perhaps against himself! He heard her now and he answered, "What is it?"

"It is I, Peony!" she cried. "Your father has been smitten down!"

He came out almost at once, tall in his pale night garments, and fastening his silk girdle as he came out he passed her.

"I heard your father cry out—and I went in—being in the peach garden—" She stammered this as she followed him, and they entered Ezra's room.

There was no sound of breathing now. When David parted the curtains and Peony looked in by his shoulder, she saw the old man lying with his arms and legs flung wide, as though embattled against death. But he had lost. He was dead. His beard lay on his bosom, and his eyes stared up severe and cold. She pushed David aside when she saw those eyes, and with her fingers she drew down the lids, lest they stiffen in that stare until they fell into decay, and she drew his arms to his sides and laid one foot beside the other and covered him. "So that he looks only asleep," she murmured.

All this time David had stood there. Now he fell upon his knees, and he took one of Ezra's hands and held it. There was no doubt of death. He knew the moment that he saw his father that there could be no use in doubt. He must rouse the household, call Kung Chen, make the death known through the city. Everything had to be done, but he delayed in disbelief.

"We were talking only a few hours ago," he muttered.

"It is a good way to die," Peony said gently. But suddenly she was frightened. Without Ezra in this house, would the heart of kindness be gone from it? Why—why had David locked his door against her? She knelt and put her head down upon the bed and began to weep. "He was so good!" she sobbed. "He was so good —to me!"

She waited, wondering, half heartbroken, if David would put his arm about her shoulder to comfort her. But he did not. Instead he began to stroke his father's hand gently, as though Ezra still lived.

挑筋教

XIII

So Ezra ben Israel died, and he was buried next to his father, and a little above the place where Madame Ezra's dust mingled with the Chinese earth.

This was the thought that struck itself into David's mind as he stood beside his father's open grave. He thought of his mother, and of how strong she had been, and still was, in his being. The struggle that she had maintained all her life to keep herself and her family separate was over now. Death had vanquished her. The early evening air was sweet upon the hillside, and David was not unmindful of the great crowd that stood here with him to see his father buried. He was almost glad that his mother was not living to see how the kindness of Ezra's many friends had made the funeral so nearly like that of a Chinese official that it would have been hard indeed to discover in it anything of his people. Only in David's heart was there the knowledge of his own origin. He understood now, for the first time in his life, why his mother had longed so deeply to return to her own land and there be buried. She knew, doubtless, as she knew much beyond what she ever told, that if she died here, her very dust would be lost in the dust of the alien earth. Five layers deep did the cities lie dead under the ground upon which he stood, and generation had built upon generation in this old countryside and no grave could be dug deep enough to escape the ancient dead. His father and his mother were inexorably committed to the common human soil, and nevermore could they belong to a separate people.

The chant of Buddhist priests startled him for a moment. David had earnestly wished to refuse when the abbot of The Temple of the Golden Buddha came to pay his respects to the dead, and he tried to find the courage to say that Buddhism was not the religion of his father. With what courtesy he could muster he had tried to tell the old priest that it would not be fitting to allow Buddhist music at the grave. The abbot had replied with great dignity:

"Your father, although a foreigner, had a large heart, and he never separated himself from any man. We wish to honor him with what we have, and we have nothing except our religion."

The low soft wailing of the chants rolled over the hillside and rose toward the sky, and David pondered while he listened, his head bowed and his hands clasped before him. On either side of him stood his sons, dressed as he was in coarse white sackcloth. Even the youngest child was so dressed. Behind him his wife wept dutifully aloud and he knew she leaned on Peony.

Peony! Of all that was dear in his childhood, only she remained. He thought of the hour, three days ago, when he had told her that he loved her. What he had not dared to tell her was how he longed to possess her wholly. He was uncomfortable even now when he remembered his longing, remembering his mother's wrath whenever his father had reminded her that his own mother had been a concubine. Yet here, among his friends, these people who supported him so warmly today, not a voice would be raised against him were he to make Peony his concubine. They would congratulate him on her beauty and welcome him as one of themselves. Even his wife might not complain—would not, indeed, for Peony was too delicate and courteous to wound her, and her manner would never change to her mistress.

Yet, that night, when all his heart and flesh longed to call Peony to him, he had suddenly locked the door of his bedroom. He had forced himself to take up a book—what chance had made his hand fall upon the Torah itself? He had been awestruck at such coincidence, and he had sat hour after hour reading, until Peony's cry had startled him.

His mind flew back to the days when Leah was alive, and his heart had trembled between love and fear. Had he and Leah met later in his life, after the youthful tide of rebellion against his mother had passed, perhaps he might have loved Leah. He thought of her even now with a strange regret, remembering her beauty, her simplicity, her high proud spirit. Her desperate death, for his sake, had given her a power over his memory that he did not deny. Something of Leah lived in him still, though no more than a dream of what had never been.

Yet it was hard to imagine his life without Kueilan, and only with Leah—and Peony. Ah, but Leah would never have allowed him Peony! Kueilan had been more generous, and he liked this generosity. He knew that had his mother been living at this moment, he would not have acknowledged to her his disappointment in his wife. He had married Kueilan for her pretty face and her rounded creamy flesh, for her dark eyes and her little hands, for her heart as free as a child's from fear of God. If she had been lacking in other ways— He lifted his head suddenly and straightened his shoulders. Let him acknowledge the truth! With Peony always in his house, he had known no lack. She met his mind fully. With her he discussed his sons and his business and all his problems, and she had arranged his pleasures and his household affairs, and she had shielded him from petty cares. His life had been good.

The chanting ended, and he heard the first clods fall upon his father's coffin. The magistrate had presented that coffin, and it was made from a huge log of cypress wood, carved and gilded. Kung Chen, standing across the grave in somber purple robes of secondary mourning, wiped his eyes. He had not wept aloud as the lesser mourners had done, and even now he was silent while the tears kept running down his cheeks. He had loved Ezra well, and that he had never trusted him wholly did not make his love less. No man was perfect, and he had been amused to discover that not even the union between their families could ensure him against Ezra's love of money. Yet in other ways Ezra had been warmhearted. He could be tempted to cheat me himself, but at least he would never allow another to cheat me, Kung Chen thought sorrowfully, and he grieved sincerely that he would see no more the ruddy bearded face of his friend. He felt eyes upon him and he looked up and found David's gaze fastened upon him across the grave.

David looked down again, and he thought, Kung Chen is nearest now to me as a father. He loved the good Chinese merchant, and yet the knowledge of his new nearness startled him. The last root was cut with his mother's people. Here he was now, forever, irrevocably. The memory of old conscience stirred in him unhappily.

When at last the long funeral was over, David went home again, bearing this prick of conscience in him. It remained upon him alone to keep alive the vestiges of old faith—or let them die.

Peony had managed to reach home early, and it was her face that David first saw when he entered the gate. She perceived his relief.

"Ah, Peony, see to the household," he murmured. "I must be alone for a while."

"Leave all to me," she replied steadily.

He thanked her, with a smile warm in his eyes and touching his lips, and passed her and went to his own rooms. There was enough for Peony to do with the children, and the youngest was crying loudly now for comfort. She took the child from the weary nurse and hushed him in her arms.

"Go and change your garments," she bade the woman. "When you are in your usual ones he will not be so frightened."

She held and coaxed him with soft words. So had she held and comforted all of David's sons, for they were the only children she had. Each one of them recognized her for someone not quite his mother, and yet somehow stronger than his mother, a decisive voice in his life and a comfort when his mother was cross or sleeping. Peony never changed. Kueilan could love her children extravagantly and heap them with sweets and pattings and pressings of hands and smellings of their cheeks, but she could slap them, too, and scold them loudly. Peony was always gentle, never too warm and never cold. She was the rock in the foundation of their lives. The child stopped crying and she took off his outer garments and she made him dry and warm and fed him a little fresh tea from a bowl, and when the nurse returned her charge was cheerful again.

So Peony went from one to the other, and saw that each child was made happy by some small attention and at play. She kept a little store of hidden toys, trifles that she bought here and there, always new to the children, and she brought out something now for each child, to cast out the thought of death.

"Shall we never see Grandfather again?" the eldest child asked.

"His spirit is always here," Peony replied.

"Can I see his spirit?" the child asked again.

"Not with your eyes," Peony replied. "But in the night sometimes think of him and how he looks and then you will feel him with you. Now here is a little book I have kept for you—see if you can read it."

Peony had been the tutor for the little boys. Now she sat down and the two eldest leaned their elbows on her knees and she opened the book and they tried to read. She took pride in their quickness and she praised them heartily and they forgot the sadness in the house. The book was one she had found on Madame Ezra's own shelf. Long ago Peony had sorted these books and she had put some in the library and some in the box of Madame Ezra's private possessions with the shawls and trinkets and sacred emblems that suited no one else now. But Peony had kept for herself a little book written in simple Chinese words that told the story of Madame Ezra's people, how they had once been held slaves in Egypt, and had been set free by a favorite of the queen, who had in his veins some of the strange blood. This story David's sons now read with wonder.

"Where is this Egypt?" one son asked.

"Why were those people slaves?" the eldest asked, and again he asked, "Who was the Moses who set them free?"

He looked very solemn when the story was finished. "But it was not kind of their god to kill all the eldest born, like me. I am glad that god is not here."

None of the questions could Peony answer, and so she said, "It is all only a story, long ago finished."

After she had put the book away and had seen to it that the children had their supper and were playing, she pondered these questions in her heart. Surely someone in the house should answer them, lest later, when the children were grown, they would know nothing of their ancestors, and this would be an evil. Ancestors are the roots in any house, and children are the flowers, and the two must not be cut asunder. She made up her mind that when she had time she would delve into Madame Ezra's old books and discover for herself enough to answer the children's questions.

Now she must go to her mistress and see that she was comfortable and in fair spirits. The twilight was falling and the air was still and mild as she crossed the courts. The house was very quiet, and she missed with some sort of heartache the two who were gone. Yet the generations passed, and now David was the head and the oldest living generation. She thought suddenly of the locked door. Indeed, she had not for one moment forgotten it. He had locked his own door against her, for the first time in their lives. What if it had been against himself? Still, it was against her. She would never go to him now. The door was locked forever—unless he himself unlocked it.

Yet she was unchanged. She must do much for him, more than ever before. Comfort and amusement were no longer enough. She must study what would add to his dignity and his growth. His life must be of fullest worth, so that he could find strength and peace in himself. She lifted her face to the sky for a moment. She had never made a prayer in her life, and she knew no god, but her heart searched Heaven and fastened upon the god of his people, whose name, she remembered, was Jehovah.

Deign to hear the voice of one unknown to You, she prayed within herself. Inform my spirit so that I may serve with wisdom the man whom I love.

She stood a moment, waiting, but no sign came. The bamboos rustled slightly in the almost silent air, and somewhere in the city a woman's sorrowful voice called in the distance to summon home again the wandering spirit of her dying child.

Inside the house Kueilan sat in state. She was now the mistress, the eldest lady of the ruling generation. She had recovered from the discomfort of the journey to the grave on the hillside, and she was eating sweetmeats and drinking hot tea with relish. Even her eyes were no longer red from weeping.

When she saw Peony come in she made a plaintive mouth, nevertheless, and put down the cake she was about to eat. "I shall miss our dear old lord," she said.

"So shall we all, Lady," Peony replied quietly. She saw that her mistress was ready to talk, and she sat down on a side seat and folded her hands.

"He was so kind to me," Kueilan mourned. "I never felt in him anything hard or cross."

"There was nothing," Peony agreed.

Tears came to Kueilan's eyes. "He was kinder than my own lord," she declared.

"Your lord is very kind, Lady," Peony said gently.

Kueilan's tears dried suddenly. "There is something hard in the bottom of his heart," she replied with energy. "I feel it there, and so would you, Peony, if you did not think him so perfect. But you are not married to him, and I am. I tell you there is something very hard in his heart—I can see it in his eyes sometimes when he looks at me."

Peony sighed. "I have told you, Lady, that he likes to see you always fresh and pretty, and sometimes you will not let me dress you for his coming or even brush your hair. And there are nights when you are weary and will not let me bathe you before you go to sleep. Those sweetmeats, Lady—you know he has never liked the smell of pig's fat, and these are larded. Why do you eat them?"

Through the years Peony had learned to speak very honestly to the beautiful little creature who now sat frowning at her. Yes, Kueilan was still beautiful, although it was true that a layer of soft fat was creeping over her dainty skeleton, and she complained that her feet had hurt her ever since Peony took away the bandages. She seldom moved unless it was necessary, and she loved sweets and delicate foods. Now Peony laughed at her frown. "Do not hate me, Lady, for I love you too well."

Kueilan clung to her scowl as long as she could until her own laughter compelled her to give it up. "You scold me too much," she declared. "I tell you, Peony, you must give it up. I am the elder lady now and you must obey me. It is not right any more for you to tell me what to do."

This little creature drew herself up straight and looked at Peony with something more than laughter sparkling in her big black eyes.

Peony saw this with astonishment and wonder. Willful her mistress always was, but she could always be coaxed and teased and made to laugh. If now she grew proud and high, then indeed David might lose his patience with her. The bond between them was only of flesh, and it could be easily broken. David was not a man of lust. Passion he had, but it was entangled with spirit and mind, and he could not separate into parts that which was his whole being. So long as his wife was pretty and warm and sweet-tempered enough in his presence not to offend him, quiet enough not to rouse his contempt, she could hold him by the strands that touched his heart. But let her offend him somewhere, and her hold was too light to keep. She did not possess him.

These things Peony knew. There was so much time in her life for musing, and since all her life was in this house, she had mused about each soul under its roof, and most of all she had pondered upon David. She told herself that now she had passed beyond jealousy or hope, and her concern was only that he might receive from each source all that was there for his happiness and health.

She curbed her astonishment at the new pride she found in her mistress. "You know very well that you do all for your lord's sake and willingly, Lady," she said quietly. She moved into the bedroom then to see that it was prepared for the night. It was a lady's room, made for her mistress, but she knew when David had come to it. There were always signs of his presence in the morning, his pipe, his slippers, his white silk handkerchief, a book he had chosen to bring with him. Such books she often examined. At first they had been books of poetry, but now they were always books of history or philosophy, abstruse pages that assuredly he could not read aloud to his wife. Since they had come home, the books had been from his mother's library, which for the first time he was beginning to read; why, Peony did not know, and she pondered very much what change had come into David, that in the last few days he should recall his ancestors.

When she had seen to the lamp, had dusted the table and folded the quilt ready, had loosened the heavy satin bed curtains from their silver hooks, had closed the latticed window against moths and mosquitoes, and had lit a stick of incense to pour fragrance into the air, she stepped softly from the room. Her mistress still sat idle by the table.

"Shall I help you to undress, Lady?" Peony asked.

Kueilan shook her head. "It is too early to sleep," she declared imperiously. "Leave me alone a while."

Peony obeyed the command and went away. It would indeed be a different house if her mistress were to shape its daily life. She stopped in the third court and considered. Should she go to David? If she did not, he would think it strange. And might he not need her? She could not go. The memory of the locked door was there. Instead she went to a side court in search of Wang Ma, and found her sitting on her bed, and Old Wang near her on a bamboo stool. Both were weeping.

She had forgotten them in all her duties, for as the years had passed it had come to be that more and more they had served Ezra while she had served the next generation. Now they were bereft. She did not presume to comfort them, but she took her sleeves and wiped her own eyes and waited until Wang Ma spoke.

"Sister, I ask you a favor," Wang Ma said sobbing.

"Ask it, Elder Sister," Peony replied.

"I have no heart to stay here in this house any more, I and my old man. We will go to the village and live with our eldest son and our own grandsons. Speak for us to the new master."

They were so broken by sorrow that Peony had no courage to say what she had been about to ask, that they go and serve David in her place.

"I will speak to him as soon as he is able to forget his own sorrow for an hour," she promised, "and be comforted, the two of you, for he will refuse you nothing. Yet how shall I manage alone, Elder Sister? I have always leaned on you."

"I have no heart any more in this house," Wang Ma replied, and she began to weep again.

So Peony left them sadly and found a manservant and bade him go and see if the master wished food or anything, and so she went alone to her own rooms. It was night and she felt weary indeed and the future was not plain before her eyes.

Now Ezra had had no time to tell Kung Chen of the reason why David and his family had left the northern capital so suddenly, and David in his grief had forgotten it. As if the grief were not enough, the ships loaded with goods from India sent word that they had reached port, and that the goods was being brought overland by carriers. Yet since the wars were so recently over and the people everywhere were poor there were many robbers, and David must arrange for guards and soldiers in each province through which the loads would pass. He had no time for mourning even for his father. Immediately he must return to his business. In the midst of all this trouble, he still forgot to tell Kung Chen of what had happened in regard to Peony. He was troubled within and without, for in the house he soon saw that Peony had separated herself from him, and this fretted him, even though he knew it was her wisdom so to do. He told himself that when his troubles were settled and the goods safely in the shops and the continual pain of seeing his father no more were all over, then he would face his own heart again and know what he must do with Peony.

He was in no wise prepared for Kung Chen, therefore, who came to him one morning with looks of consternation. David was in his own part of the shop, computing the quantity of the goods that were beginning to arrive each day, and appraising the quality of the fine cotton stuffs that had been woven in India. With him sat his partner, Kung Chen's eldest son, and the two were deep in their affairs. Both were surprised when Kung Chen came in.

"David, come aside with me for a moment, and you, too, my son," Kung Chen said gravely.

Both men followed him into a small room, where Kung Chen

shut the door. His full face was gray with alarm, and his lips were pale.

"A messenger has come to us from our shops in the northern capital," he said in a voice scarcely above a whisper. "He tells me that there is anger in the palace against us, David. The Chief Steward has sent out the rumor that one of your bondmaids was rude to the Western Empress. What is the meaning of this?"

David's heart fell. All was clear to him in an instant, and with difficulty he told the story to the two, who listened in silence.

"The Chief Steward will certainly demand that Peony be sent for on the pretense of punishment," Kung Chen said when David had finished. "If we refuse to give her up, then we must never hope to do good business again. The arm of the imperial favorite is long."

"I will return to the capital alone," David said. "I will seek audience with the empresses and tell them the truth."

Both Chinese cried out at this. "Folly—folly!" Kung Chen declared. "Can you hope to prevail against the Chief Steward? He is in the imperial confidence and you would only be casting away your own life. No, there is no hope except to make her go."

"That I cannot do," David said.

Both men looked at him strangely and he had much difficulty in not allowing his eyes to falter before theirs. Then father and son looked at one another. They remembered how beautiful Peony was. Indeed, Kung Chen had remarked once or twice to his son that it might be difficult for any man to remain unmoved by so beautiful a bondmaid, who was clever and learned besides.

For David the moment was intolerable. "You wonder at me," he said stiffly, "but I assure you, what you think is not possible. In my religion—the religion, that is, of my people—a man is allowed only one wife. I feel—gratitude to the bondmaid—who has been like a daughter in our house. I cannot deliver her to—to the eunuch."

Kung Chen grasped at a hope. "If she is willing to go of her own will?"

David could not tell the truth, nor did he know why he could not. These men would not blame him did he say openly that he loved Peony and wanted her for himself. They would have laughed and pondered how to save her for him. He could not say it. He bowed his head. "If she wishes to go—for her own sake," he stammered, "let it be so."

They went back to their business then, and David tried to apply himself. Yet how could he think of figures and goods or even of profits? Kung Chen would summon Peony and force her, he would press her to realize how great a damage she would do to David and to all their two houses, and in her soft unselfishness Peony might yield. His mind misted and he could not go on.

"I feel ill," he told Kung the First. "I shall go home and sleep a while and come back tomorrow."

His partner stared at him and said nothing, but David saw the shrewdness in his small kind eyes and he hurried away. He could not delay one instant. As soon as he reached home he sent for Peony and waited restlessly until she came running to his rooms, still wiping her hands dry.

"I was in the kitchens," she confessed. "They told me the jar of soy sauce was not thickening properly and I went to see."

He paid no heed to this, but he saw her beautiful and strong, the pillar of his household. He could not live without her. "Peony, sit down," he commanded abruptly.

She sat down on the edge of her chair, alarmed at his looks and at the sound of his voice. "What has happened now?" she asked.

He told her roughly and quickly, eager to get the burden off his own heart and knowing her able to bear anything. But he was frightened when he saw the pink drain from her cheeks and the strength from her frame. "I told you I must be a nun," she whispered. "I shall not be able to save you otherwise." She rose and began to untie the blue apron she had forgotten.

"Wait," he commanded her. "There is another way for you to stay with me."

Peony knew well what he meant, but her heart had hardened at last and she would not spare him.

"What way?" she demanded.

"You know," David said in a low voice, and he would not look at her.

She was angry that he turned away, and she spoke for him firmly. "You mean—take me as your concubine?"

"Yes," he said, and still he did not look at her.

She saw his face was fixed and strained. There was no joy in his eyes. The apron dropped from her hands. "You locked your door against me," she said. "Why?"

"How do I know?" he asked.

"You do know," she retorted. "You were afraid of the very thing that now you ask. You were afraid of yourself—of that which is in you still and will be in you so long as you live!"

"I deny it!" he said in a loud voice.

"It will not be denied," she said. "It is born in you."

He bent his head on his hand and did not answer. As clearly as though she lived, he saw Leah and heard her voice, and her voice was the voice of his mother and the voice of all those men and women who had lived before him. It was the voice of Jehovah Himself.

"If I yielded to you," Peony said in her gentle swift way, "your own conscience would grow more dear as you loved me less. No, David, I dare not. Let me go. Yes, I will go of my own free will —but not to the palace!"

She ran out of the room and David could not pursue her. What she had said was true. That which his mother had pressed into his unwilling soul had taken root there. He had defied it and crucified it, but it was not dead. It lived in him still, the spirit of the faith of his own people. It had risen from the dead and claimed him. He could not free himself. He fell on his knees, his arms folded upon the table, and leaned his head upon his arms. "O Jehovah, the One True God, hear me—and forgive me!"

Across the city Peony sped on foot, her head down, her hands empty. The gate of the nunnery was open and she entered it. The courts were still, but she cried out, "Oh, Mother Abbess, I am here!"

A gentle old woman dressed in gray robes came out and her hands were outspread to receive. "Come in, poor soul," she said.

"I am in danger," Peony gasped.

"Here the gods protect us from all men," the Mother Abbess replied.

"Ah, lock the gate!" Peony begged. Now that she was here she was terrified at what she had done to herself. She seized the old woman's hand. "If I ask to go out—do not allow me!" she implored.

"I will not," the Mother Abbess promised, and she drew the iron bar across the gate.

How could David believe that Peony would not come back to his house? He waited for several hours, his mind thick with confusion. Then, too restless for longer waiting, he sent for Wang Ma and bade her go to the nunnery and see if Peony were there. So dark was his look that Wang Ma did not dare ask a question, and she went off in silent consternation.

In his secret heart David was afraid lest Peony had thrown herself into the river, and his spirits lifted when Wang Ma came back in an hour to say that Peony was indeed in the nunnery. He heard this news in silence, and then, knowing that it would soon spread in the house, he saw that he must tell Kueilan immediately what had happened. That is, he would tell her that Peony had feared lest the chief eunuch reach out his arm and seize her in spite of all that could be done. He would not tell Kueilan of the confusion that had been in his own heart or of the strange stillness that he now felt when a gate had been locked between him and Peony. Yet had not she left him? He was somehow wounded that she could leave him, running out of his house like a beaten slave, although he had loved her from their childhood so well that he did not know when childish love had changed into something more. He feared to face this love, whatever it had become, and fearing it now, he turned away from it and reproached Peony in his heart. She had no right to leave me so suddenly, he told himself, and feeling ill used, he let himself be angry with her, and upon this anger he went to find his wife.

As it chanced, Kueilan was this day in her sweetest mood. She enjoyed being the mistress of the house and knowing that her husband was master, and that there were no elders above them. All that was foreign here was now gone, and she smiled easily and was patient with servants and children. When David came to the moon gate of her court, he saw a picture that might content the heart of any man. This pretty woman who was his wife sat surrounded by her children playing about her. His sons had taken a holiday since Peony had not come to teach them, and the eldest was playing shuttlecock and the second was playing with a cricket on a string and Kueilan held the third in her lap. Chrysanthemums were blooming in the terraces against the walls and the afternoon sun shone down upon flowers and children. Now David saw again what sometimes he forgot—how great was Kueilan's beauty. Her creamy skin was as smooth in the clear light as the baby's, her lips were red, her hair, under Peony's long care, was shining black and oiled. This very morning Peony had put jade pins into the knot of rich hair to match jade earrings and a coat of apple green.

Why should I not be happy? David inquired of his own heart.

He paused at the gate and now they all saw him. Kueilan rose and the boys ran to their father. The maids were busy elsewhere and Kueilan followed him. The sun had been as kind to David as to her, and for the same moment he had seen again how beautiful she was, Kueilan had seen her husband as he stood at the gate, tall and at the best of his manhood. He had never allowed his beard to grow too long, as some foreigners did, and his smooth face, large dark eyes, firm lips, and above all his strong frame stirred her heart. She loved her husband, but in the round of days she had forgotten how well. She sat down near him, and their eyes kindled to each other. David took his youngest son from her arms. "Let me see how big he is," he said.

Kueilan made haste to put under the child a padded cloth. "Not so big, naughty fellow, that he cannot wet you!" she exclaimed.

David laughed, and the two elder boys, hearing this, came and leaned their elbows on his knees. Above the three fine children, the eyes of the parents met again and smiled.

"How is it you are home at this hour?" Kueilan inquired.

"A very strange thing has happened," David said. "You remember the chief eunuch, who wanted Peony?" How easily he said this to his wife! He was amazed at his own calm.

"Do not tell me he still wants her!" Kueilan exclaimed with lively interest.

David nodded. "Since Peony will not go, there is only one way to escape without bringing danger to our house."

Kueilan was watching his face very closely. He felt—ah, but he knew—that he could never tell her the depths of his heart. Did he himself know those depths? What man knows what is dearest to him when all he has is weighed and measured, one love against another?

"She has gone to the nunnery," he said quietly.

"To stay?" Kueilan asked, her eyes very wide.

"How else can she be safe?" he replied.

Now the children began to ask questions. "Will Peony never live here any more?" the eldest asked.

"If she is a nun she must live in the temple," Kueilan said.

The younger son began to cry. "I want to see Peony again," he sobbed.

"Be quiet!" his mother said. "She can come to see us—as soon as she is a real nun."

David sat silent, toying with his little son's hand. Upon his open palm he spread the baby hand, and the child's palm was warm upon his own.

Kueilan was gathering her wits together. She, too, was weighing and measuring good against evil. She would miss Peony sorely—but Peony could come here as often as she liked after her novitiate was over. True, she must always return to the temple at night, but then it might be pleasant not to have Peony here always. She did not need her as she had before the old people died. It did not matter now whether everything was done according to the rules and traditions. Yes, perhaps it would be better not to have Peony here. Sometimes it was almost as if Peony had been the mistress. A secret jealousy that had slept in her because Peony was useful to her now sprang alive. Peony was much too beautiful. Peony could read books and David liked to talk with her.

"It is a good thing for Peony to be a nun," Kueilan suddenly declared. "She would not marry, and what can a woman do then except be a nun? Many times I told Peony that we should choose a husband for her, but no, she would not hear me. A woman gets no younger. She would have had to be a nun one of these days—that is, if she would not enter the Imperial Palace. If she had gone there, then of course—"

"She could not," David said abruptly, not looking up.

Kueilan felt her jealousy. "She could have gone if she had loved us as much as she always pretended," she cried. "What could have been better for the family than to have her in the Imperial Court? She might have spoken for you there, and when our sons grew older, she could have had them to visit, and I could have visited her, too, and all sorts of favors could have come from it."

David did not reply. The baby's fingers curled into his palm and he closed his hand over the little fist. Suddenly he stood up, and stooping he put the child into the mother's lap. "It will be strange here without Peony," he said quietly. "But she has decided wisely. I must go back to the shop for an hour."

He touched his wife's round cheek with his hand and went away. A stillness was in his heart. Some part of his life was ended. He had made a choice without declaring even to himself what that choice was, but he knew the struggle was over. He was master of his heart as well as of his house.

When Wang Ma had gone to find Peony, the nun at the gate had refused to let her come in until she asked permission of the Mother Abbess. The cloisters were whispering with the excitement of the nuns and novices over the coming of the beautiful young woman from the house of Ezra. All knew that the old master there had died only a short time before, for who in the city had not heard of his splendid funeral? The Mother Abbess heard the whisperings but she had not yet questioned Peony. There must be time for sorrow to spend itself. She had commanded that Peony be given a large quiet room facing a small bamboo grove. Hot water was taken to her by the novices that she might bathe, and fresh soft robes of smooth gray grass cloth were laid upon a chair. When the novices reported that Peony had bathed and had dressed herself in the gray robes, the Mother Abbess commanded that Peony's other garments be taken away and locked in a chest, and then that vegetarian foods be put before her and a pot of the most delicate tea. All this was done.

When the Mother Abbess heard that an old woman was at the gate she herself went to Peony. There Peony sat by the window, her hands folded. In the gray robes she looked so beautiful that the Mother Abbess felt her heart ache. Long ago when her own young husband had died, less than a month after their marriage, she had come to this place. She had first waited to make sure that her womb held no fruit, and then she had sworn herself away to Heaven. She understood the look of a woman who knows that she must live alone.

"There is at the gate an old servant, surnamed Wang, who wishes to see you, my child," she said gently. "Shall I bid her come in?"

Peony rose and turned her great sorrowful eyes upon the kind face of the Abbess. She was about to shake her head, and then she could not. What she had done had been so quickly done. Doubtless David had sent Wang Ma to find her.

"It is better that she come in," Peony said.

So Wang Ma came in, and when she saw Peony in the gray robes she was speechless and the tears began to run down her wrinkled cheeks. She held out her arms and Peony could not hold back. She ran to Wang Ma and the two women wept aloud together and the Abbess bowed her head, waiting.

It was Wang Ma who wiped her eyes first. She sat down. "My legs are trembling," she muttered.

Peony stood, the tears on her cheeks.

"What did he do to you?" Wang Ma asked.

Peony shook her head and wiped her eyes on her sleeves. "Nothing," she answered in a small voice.

"So he did nothing," Wang Ma repeated. She continued to gaze at Peony.

Peony looked at the floor. "That eunuch sent to find me again," she said in the same small voice.

"And you being neither wife nor concubine—" Wang Ma went on.

"I have no one to protect me," Peony agreed.

Wang Ma sighed loudly. "Is it too late for you to come back?" she asked.

"What is there for me except sorrow?" Peony replied.

"If you had only done as I did," Wang Ma complained. "I took the man they gave me and I lived on with the family, and I served my master until he went to the Yellow Springs. Now even my old man is a comfort to me."

How could Peony tell her that David was different from his father, and she different from Wang Ma? She smiled with her lips while her eyes were filled with tears. "Do you remember you told me once that life is sad?"

This she said in so gentle and distant a voice that Wang Ma did not reply. She groaned two or three times, her hands planted on her knees while she stared at Peony, and then she stared at the Mother Abbess.

"Will you shave her head?" she asked the Abbess.

"I will be obedient to law," Peony said, before the Abbess could answer.

Wang Ma sighed and got up. "If your heart is set on Heaven, there is no use for me to stay," she said sharply. "Have you no message for our master?"

Now the Mother Abbess, watching Peony, saw the story plain. A rich and lovely rose color spread over Peony's neck and face. Her red lips quivered and the tears hung heavy on her lashes. "I may never see him again," she murmured.

At this the Mother Abbess took pity on Peony. Long ago she had wept the nights through, thinking that she could never be free from the love and longing in her heart. Yet somehow the heart had healed, and agony was lost in the past. What she remembered now, when she remembered at all, was the sweetness of the days when her husband had been living, and the pain of her loss had faded.

"It is not necessary to say that now," she told Peony. "We will see how the heart heals."

Wang Ma nodded shrewdly at this and went away.

After she had gone, the Mother Abbess sat down while Peony continued to stand. These words of the Mother Abbess had been spoken very quietly but they rang in Peony's heart like bells. She looked up. "Do you mean, Mother, that I shall cease to love him?"

The Mother Abbess smiled. "Love changes," she replied. "When the flame dies, the glow remains, but it no longer centers upon one human creature and it warms the whole soul. Then the soul looks at all human creatures with love diffused."

Peony listened to this and was silent. She stood there, her robes flowing away from her, and the Mother Abbess felt her pity rise and surround this younger woman.

"Shall I tell you why I came here?" Peony asked after a while.

"Only if it comforts you to do so," the Abbess replied.

"There is no law that I must tell why I escaped?" Peony asked.

"None," the Abbess answered. "We are all here for some sorrow or other. What was our life became monstrous, and we found refuge. The only thing that I must have known was whether you had a husband's power over you, so that I might have bargained for your freedom from him."

"I have said truly that I have no husband," Peony replied.

"Then live here in peace," the Abbess said. "Heaven is above and earth is beneath us all."

So saying she rose and went away. Peony stood for a long time more, feeling neither weariness nor pain. A deep stillness stole into her being.

For three years Peony lived behind the gate of the cloisters. So long did it take for the flame in her heart to change to that glow of which the Mother Abbess had spoken. In all that time she did not see David. No man was allowed to step within the gate and she did not step outside. The very day after Wang Ma had left her she took up the life of the cloisters. When she had studied the sacred books, had learned the ritual of prayers, had taken her share of labor in caring for the gods, in tending the garden, and in serving in the kitchen, when the older nuns cut off her long black hair and shaved her head, she ended her life as a novice. She took the vows and she became a nun. The secret life of her heart was over. The Mother Abbess gave her a new name, Ching An, or Clear Peace.

But during these three years Kueilan had come often to see Peony. In the first year she had come only twice. Peony had sat almost silent while Kueilan, her usual self, had chattered, lively and curious about all she saw and telling Peony the gossip in her own house. Thus Peony heard that Wang Ma and Old Wang had returned to their village and lived now with their sons. Thus she knew, too, that Aaron after Ezra's death had gone back to his old idle ways until David in anger had bade Kao Lien's sons take him away when they traveled with the caravan, now that Kao Lien was too old. This they had done, and they had left him in some country west of the mountains, where there were Jewish people living who could teach him to mend his heart, and he was never heard of any more.

But after the first year Kueilan came often. She had borne another child, a fourth son, and when he was a month old she brought him for Peony to see. Kueilan was proud that she had so many sons, but when the nuns went away and left her alone with Peony, she poured out her dislike of this new child.

"Look at him!" she exclaimed as the nurse stood and swayed with him in her arms. "Is he my child, Peony?"

Never could Kueilan remember to call her anything except this old name.

"You bore him," Peony said, smiling. Heaven had made her Kueilan's equal now, and she needed no more to call her Mistress.

Kueilan pouted. "He looks like his foreign grandmother."

Peony could not but laugh. Indeed the tiny boy did look strangely like Madame Ezra. His big strong features did not fit his small face. She motioned to the nurse to let her hold the child. When he was on her lap she looked at his feet and hands. They were big, too. "He will be a big man," she declared. "Look at his ears, how long the lobes are—that means boldness and wisdom. This son is a lucky one."

So she consoled Kueilan, and Kueilan, feeling warm toward Peony, coaxed her thus: "Come and visit us again—why not? The maids do not listen to me as well as they did to you, Peony. My eldest son is lazy at his books and his father beat him for it yesterday and I cried and then he was angry with me. If you come, they will all listen to you, Peony, as they always did."

But Peony, still smiling, shook her head and gave the baby back to his nurse.

"You are the same Peony, even if your head is shaven," Kueilan coaxed.

Peony was startled. Did these words uncover her heart? Was it because she was shaven and a nun that she did not want David to see her? She grew grave, and by her silence Kueilan thought she had won her way. When she went home that day she told David that she had persuaded Peony to come and visit them for a day, and then he turned grave, too, and silent.

In her cell again, Peony cruelly examined her heart. It is true, she thought. I dread his eyes upon me.

There was no mirror in any nun's room, but she filled her basin with clear water and she bent over it in the faint sunlight at the end of that day and she saw herself dimly. For the first time she saw her hair gone, and she thought herself ugly. Nothing else could she see, not her dark quiet eyes or her red lips or the smooth outlines of her young face. Her whole beauty, it seemed to her now, had been in her hair, in the braid she used to knot over one ear, in the flowers she had loved to wear in it. For one long moment she looked at herself. Then she lifted the basin and poured the water out of the open window upon a bed of lilies that grew beside the wall.

It is my punishment to let him see me, she told herself.

Yet she did not go for two full years more to the house of David. Kueilan bore her fifth child, this time a daughter, and had conceived her sixth, when one day a servant came in haste to the nunnery to beg Peony to come, because the eldest son of the house lay dying. She gave Peony a folded paper, and Peony opened it, and there David had written a few words.

"For my son's sake, come."

"I will come," she told the maidservant, and she hastened to the Mother Abbess for permission. The Abbess had grown old and frail in the last few years and she never left her cell. To all she was kind, but Peony she loved exceedingly, as the daughter she had never had. Now she clasped Peony's hand and held it a moment.

"The fire in you is quenched?" she asked.

"Yes, Mother," Peony said.

"Then go, my child," the Abbess replied, "and while you are away, I will pray for the boy's life."

So Peony went out that day from the refuge that was now her home, and as she walked along the street she quieted her beating heart with steady prayers, her rosary of brown satinwood twisted in her fingers. When she entered the familiar gate David was there waiting for her, and her heart quickened until her will commanded stillness. She looked at him fearlessly, determined that their eyes should not speak anything but cool friendship.

"Peony!" David cried, and she felt his eyes searching out the change in her.

"My name is Clear Peace," she told him, smiling. No, she would not be afraid to smile.

"I think of you always as Peony," David replied.

She did not answer this. "Where is your son?" she asked.

They were walking side by side now, she quieting her heart, her fingers busy with her rosary. She had forgotten how tall he was, how strong. The air of youth was gone, and he was a man powerful and grave. She took pride in him without feeling sin, and she looked up at him and met his eyes again. "You have not changed so much," he said abruptly. "Well—except for your hair."

"I have changed very much," she said cheerfully. "Now take me to the child."

"Ah, my son," he sighed.

So they quickened their steps and went into the rooms where David and his two elder sons now lived. Each boy when he had reached the age of seven had left his mother's courts and come to live with his father, and David led Peony into his room and there in his own bed lay the sick boy. He was no longer a child—that Peony saw at once. His tall slender frame lay outstretched on the bed. He was breathing but choking at every breath, and his face was flushed and his eyes were closed.

Peony took his wrist between her fingers and felt the pulse too swift to count. "We have no time to waste!" she exclaimed. "There is poisoned mucus in his throat."

Now Peony, as all the nuns must, had been much with the sick, and she knew a disease had fallen upon the city this year, borne hither upon evil winds from the north. So she ordered a servant to bring a lamp with a strong wick, and another to cut a length of soft new bamboo and bring it to her. While she waited she dipped cloths in hot water and bound them about the boy's throat to warm his muscles. As soon as she had the thin bamboo tube in her fingers, she bade David hold the boy hard, and set a manservant to hold his feet. Then delicately pressing the thumb and finger of her left hand to his jaw, she forced open his mouth and she put down the tube and sucked on it slowly. The boy choked and struggled but she persevered until a clot came up into the tube and he fell back with a great gasp.

"Burn this tube in fire," she told the servant. "It is full of poison. And bring me wine to give him."

She stood watching and motionless until the wine was brought and she poured some of it into the boy's throat, and then she washed her own mouth with the wine, too, and spat it out into a silver cuspidor that stood by the bed.

"He is better!" David exclaimed with joy.

"He will live," Peony said.

Nevertheless she did not leave the bedside until near dark, when the laws of the nunnery said she must return. The next day she came back, and every day indeed until the lad was well again.

By that time she knew that she must come often. David needed her sorely, for he was perplexed by growing children and impetuous sons and too many servants who were lazy and disobedient, and harassed because his own prosperous business took him much away. Peony saw clearly the years ahead when sons and daughters must be betrothed and weddings planned and all the life of a great and busy house be carried on to other generations. And she could come safely, for David loved his wife. This Peony saw with lingering pain. Indeed, she asked herself, why should there be any pain? Had she not brought Kueilan into this house? It was not Kueilan who had sent her out of it. The marriage she had fostered had flowered and borne seed. Between David and Kueilan now there was the close fleshly bond of house and home and children and prosperity, and all their life was entwined together. Was this not what she had hoped would be?

The restlessness in David was gone. He had forgotten, or so it seemed to her, that there had ever been a life in this house different from his own. Even the vestiges of his mother had been taken away. The scroll above the table in the great hall was gone and instead a painting hung there of crags and clouds and pines. By whose command this was done Peony did not ask, but there it was, and it signified the change in the house—yes, and in David, too. He was content.

So Peony came and went through many years, and she met David and Kueilan as equals, and as time went on as something more than equal. They came to lean on her and to wait for her advice, and she spoke with authority in their house.

When Peony had been for ten years the nun named Clear Peace, the Mother Abbess died. During those years Peony had grown to such a place of reverence that when the old abbess had been buried, she was chosen by the nuns to take her place as mother abbess. She had less time then to visit David's house, for she had her own house of women to govern, and she did it wisely, without casting down the spirit or wounding the heart of any creature, even to the lowliest kitchen nun.

Now followed the years when Peony and David came to perfect understanding. She, being Mother Abbess, was free to go out as she liked, and none could breathe against her name. Neither was she any longer young. David's two elder sons were married and their wives and children lived in his house, and the next one was betrothed. His eldest daughter married young into a Chinese house, and his sons' wives were all Chinese.

It might have been forgotten that this house was anything but Chinese except that David's fourth son grew up so different from the others that he reminded his father now and then of what his ancestors had been. Hothearted, impetuous, excitable, strong, this fourth son kept the household in turmoil. Peony laughed at him and loved him best of all, and in some strange fashion he became the son of her childless heart.

"Leave him to me," she told David one day when the father and son had quarreled again, as they did so often. "I understand him better than you do—because he is more like you than you know."

"I was never like this young fool!" David protested.

To this Peony only smiled.

So the years passed, and as the three, Peony, David, and Kueilan, grew old, each year was better than the last. Between the two wiser ones Kueilan was treated as a dear and older child, and they made much of her and laughed a little over her head. She allowed herself to be spoiled and she used her tongue to berate them sometimes and she pouted when they laughed at her, but she leaned upon their love.

It was a prosperous house, and David was one of the city's honored elders and Peony was its wise woman. Their age fell gently upon them all.

In the city, the synagogue was now a heap of dust. Brick by brick the poor of the city had taken the last ruin of the synagogue away. The carvings were gone, too, and there remained at last only three great stone tablets, and of these three, then only two. These two stood stark under the sky for a long time, and then a Christian, a foreigner, bought them.

This made an uproar in the city. The son of David's fourth son, surnamed Chao, had sold the stones. Upon his head the wrath of the city's governor fell. "How is it you, unfilial son, have sold the stones of your ancestors to a Christian foreigner?" the governor demanded. "He must return them, lest he take them away from our country to his own and the dead of your house rise up to reproach us." And he ordered his guards to throw this Chao into jail.

But Chao had the blood of Madame Ezra still strong in him and he shouted through the bars, "Though you heap a fortune on me, I will not ask this Christian to give back the stones! They belonged to our religion, which has come to an end in this land, but his religion sprang from ours and let him keep the stones."

Now this Chao was supported by all that family of Chao which had sprung from the loins of David ben Ezra, and they pointed out to the governor of the city that for scores of years the stones had stood under snow and rain and sun until they were cracked, and none had protected them. Why then should there be complaint if they were sold?

There was no one to make compromise until it was remembered in the city that the Mother Abbess had known the family well, and so the governor sent his messengers to her and she received them at the gate of the nunnery, since it was the law that no man could step beyond the threshold.

Peony was very old now, but her mind was clear and cool and she heard the messengers. Then still standing she gave out wisdom, and these were her words:

"This one surnamed Chao was a lively child and he grew into the man you know. It is his nature to spend his life in the jail unless a way is found for him to come out without leaving his pride behind him. I knew his father before him and his father before that. I will tell you the way: The foreigner shall keep these sacred stones he has bought but he shall not take them from our city. Let him set them before his own temple, and let him build a pavilion over them to preserve them for the generations to come."

The men looked at one another and scratched their jaws and acknowledged that the Mother Abbess was wise indeed, and they thanked her and went away.

Even as Peony had said it was done. There in the new temple the stones stand to this day, under the shelter of the pavilion. Upon them are carved the ancient words "The Temple of Purity and Truth," and beneath the words are carved the history of the Jews and their Way, and it is there said, "The Way has no form or figure, but is made in the image of the Way of Heaven, which is above."

When Peony had returned to her cell she pondered long. Her memory brought back to life all the story of the House of Ezra, in which her own life had been entwined by some chance, for some purpose she did not understand, except that she knew that whatever happened was Heaven's will. That strong and powerful family, the seed of Israel and Ezra and David, were they one day to be no more, even as the synagogue was gone, which their ancestors had made for a temple of their God? Had she done evil when she had enticed David away from Leah to marry Kueilan?

Long she pondered, and as often happened to her in her great age, the answer came to her. She had not done wrong, for nothing was lost. "Nothing is lost," she repeated. "He lives again and again, among our people," she mused. "Where there is a bolder brow, a brighter eye, there is one like him; where a voice sings most clearly, there is one; where a line is drawn most cleverly to make a picture clear, a carving strong, there is one; where a statesman stands most honorable, a judge most just, there is one; where a scholar is most learned, there is one; where a woman is both beautiful and wise, there is one. Their blood is lively in whatever frame it flows, and when the frame is gone, its very dust enriches the still kindly soil. Their spirit is born anew in every generation. They are no more and yet they live forever."

AFTERWORD

Afterword
by
Wendy R. Abraham, Ed.D.

The Chinese Jews of Kaifeng represent one of the most obscure, and one of the most fascinating chapters in the annals of the Jewish diaspora. Throughout *Peony*, interwoven within the fictional events surrounding the House of Ezra, Pearl S. Buck has managed to convey with historical accuracy the Jews at the twilight of their existence in Kaifeng–a people at once assimilated and yet set apart from their neighbors.

That the daughter of Protestant missionaries could so effectively impart the depth of feeling and concern behind a Jewish family aware of its imminent spiritual demise, yet deeply cognizant of its obligation to carry on the traditions of its forefathers in a foreign land–all the while exhibiting authentic Chinese sensibilities–is a testimony to the greatness of the writer herself.

Origins of the Chinese Jews

The actual history of the Jews in China dates back at least to the 8th century C.E., when Jewish merchants and traders from Persia and India travelled overland along the Silk Road to trade in the Middle Kingdom during the Tang dynasty (618-906 C.E.). Testimony of this early history exists in bits of archaeological evidence which came to light at the turn of this century. A Judeo-Persian business letter, dating to 718 C.E., was discovered in 1901 by the archeologist and Orientalist Sir Marc Aurel Stein, along the the Northern caravan route of the Silk Road. Nine years after this discovery, a Selichah, or Hebrew penitential prayer sheet, was unearthed in the Dunhuang Caves of Gansu Province, along what was the Southern Caravan route of the Silk Road. Dating to 708 C.E., it represents the earliest known Hebrew manuscript still extant. What makes these two pieces remarkable is the fact that they were made on paper, which at the time was only made in China, proving a Jewish existence in Chinese territory at least as early as the 8th century.

Some scholars theorize that the Jews came to China by sea, noting the various coastal Jewish communities which sprung up in Canton, Hangzhou, Yangzhou and other cities. Of these, Kaifeng was the grandest, with its opulent synagogue dating to 1163 in what was then the capital of China.

Early information about the Jews in China is scanty. Between the 9th and the 14th centuries, well-known Arab travellers and historians such as Abu-Zaid and Ibn-Battutah reported the presence of Jews in China. Although these constitute the first available observations noted by Westerners, they said little about the daily life of the Jews themselves. Pointing to Moslem countries for the origins of the Chinese Jews–in particular Persia, they confirm that they lived in the same major cities as did the Moslems, having arrived approximately the same time and in the same manner. Indeed, the Chinese often confused the Jews for Moslems, calling the former "blue capped Moslems", since the real Moslems always wore white skull caps, while the Jews wore blue. (In *Peony,* David is depicted at one point, as donning a blue silk cap. This was not a chance color chosen by Pearl S. Buck.)

Early European travellers in China during the Yuan dynasty (1280-1367) also reported sighting Jews. Remarkably, Marco Polo made it a point to mention in his memoirs that the Mongol ruler Kublai Khan (for the Yuan was a "foreign" dynasty), celebrated the festivals of the Moslems, Christians and Jews. During the same period European missionaries such as Andrew of Perugia reported Jewish resistance at attempts to convert them, or to be otherwise swayed from their convictions. It is clear that through the 14th century, at least, the Jews in China had contact with other foreigners, and that their religious life and identity as Jews remained intact, undisturbed and unchallenged by the exceptionally tolerant Chinese people and government.

For their part, the native Chinese left negligible information about the foreigners in their midst. Only six references to Jews have ever been found in official government documents, all dating to the Yuan dynasty. Extensive contact with foreign peoples and cultures was one of the unique features of the Yuan dynasty, during which time commerce flourished. It is therefore not surprising that the only bits of information on the Jews found in official Chinese government sources should appear during this dynasty. Mentioning Jews in the same breath as the Moslems, the Statutes of the Yuan Dynasty decreed a prohibition on ritual slaughter on January 27, 1280. Forty years later the same Statutes mention Jews, Moslems and Nestorians with regard to the payment of taxes. The Official History of the Yuan Dynasty contains the remaining instances in which Jews are mentioned, for the years 1329, 1340 and 1354. Jews were prohibited from tax exemption and the ancient practice of having a widow marry her deceased husband's brother — a practice common to both Moslems and Jews.

Local gazetteers dating to the 17th century indicate that a great number of Chinese Jews attained high rank in the civil service system. While the gazetteers attest to the great success the Jews had in Chinese society by virtue of their disproportionate numbers having passed this difficult exam, they also serve as the first indication in Chinese sources of the tremendous degree of assimilation which must have taken place in advance of the Jews' ability to master the Confucian Classics by then, for the Classics were essential for any hope of passing the exams and attaining high rank in society.

History Etched in Stone

The bulk of our knowledge of early Jewish life in Kaifeng comes not from the Arabs and not from the Europeans or the native Chinese, but rather from the Jews themselves, in the form of inscriptions found on steles (stone monuments) which they erected in the synagogue's courtyard as early as 1489.

The steles offer a fascinating glimpse into the way the Jews portrayed their history and customs, both to themselves and to their Chinese neighbors. Dated 1489, 1512, 1663 and 1669, two of these stone monuments are all that is left of this exotic community today in Kaifeng.

The 1489 stele was erected in commemoration of the rebuilding of the synagogue, which had been destroyed in a flood during 1461. It speaks of the Emperor granting express permission to the Jews to build their first synagogue on that very spot in the year 1163. Chronicling the history of the Jewish religion, it mentions at the outset that the patriarch Abraham was the nineteenth generation descendant of "Pangu-Adam." That the stele was erected at all shows the point at which the Jews can be said to have truly assimilated into their environment, since it was a Chinese, rather than a Jewish, custom to do so in houses of worship. And that the first man in Biblical creation could be combined in one breath with the first person in the Chinese story of creation is further testimony to the degree of assimilation the Jews felt with their Chinese neighbors by the 15th century.

From the 1489 stele we learn that the Jews made no images, fasted four times per month, and observed Jewish laws and rituals–in a language filled with Biblical wisdom, yet interspersed with sayings from the Analects of Confucius! Moses and Ezra are mentioned early on in the stele as well, and seem to take on the qualities of Confucian gentlemen rather than those of wandering Israelites. The Jewish religion, so it goes, came from India. Originally, seventy or more clans came to Kaifeng, where the Emperor of the Song dynasty said to them: "You have come to Our China; reverence and preserve the customs of your ancestors, and hand them down at Bianliang (Kaifeng)."

It is generally believed that 17, rather than 70, was the number of clans meant to have come, since the pronunciation for "70" and "17" in Chinese is so similar that mistakes could have been easily made. Of those clans, only seven particular surnames have remained and are to this day indicative of Jewish origin: Ai, Gao (Kao), Jin (Chin), Li, Shi, Zhang (Chang) and Zhao (Chao).

It is also clear that the Jewish community of Ningbo donated a Torah scroll to the Kaifeng community after the devastating flood of

1461. The contributions of individual members to the reconstruction of the synagogue, and the high civil service ranks attained by others, was duly noted, as was the fact that Judaism was in no way in conflict with the other great religions prevalent in China–Buddhism, Daoism and Confucianism. In fact, it went out of its way to explain that the Jews were not only loyal to their G-d, who must have seemed so foreign to the Chinese, but also quite loyal to the Emperor. In contrast to this, however, is the fact that above the Imperial Tablet, which was placed in all authorized temples symbolizing the protection and authority of the State (and proclaiming "Long live the great Emperor!"), the Jews placed a Hebrew inscription in beautiful gold letters, which only they could read. It was the Shema, the Hebrew article of faith, proving that although they were respectful of the government, G-d alone was higher than the Emperor.

The second inscription, dating to 1512, was actually carved on the reverse side of the 1489 stele and further details the Jewish religion, taking great pains to note the many similarities between Judaism and Confucianism. In particular, the notion of zedakah, or charity, is explored in detail. "A Record of the Synagogue Which Respects the Scriptures of the Way," this stele claims the Jews entered China as early as the Han dynasty (206 B.C.E.-220 C.E.), but offers little new information about Judaism that was not already described on the first stele. Once again, Jews from other communities (this time a Mr. Jin of Yangzhou, who donated a Torah and set up the second archway to the synagogue) are noted for their donations and efforts on behalf of Kaifeng's Jewish community.

Although the 1663 stele is now lost, rubbings of it still remain. Commemorating the second rebuilding of the synagogue, which had again been destroyed in a flood by the Yellow River in 1642, this stele was most likely not written by Jews at all. In it, Adam is described as the nineteenth generation descendant of Pangu, and the Jews were said to have entered China during the Zhou dynasty (1100-221 B.C.E.), an even more fantastic claim than that on the 1512 stele. The 1663 stele is replete with quotations from the Chinese Classics — all of which signifies an even greater desire to appear Sinified.

Lastly, there was a stele erected in 1679 by the Zhao clan, commemorating the setting up of the Zhao Family Memorial Archway and enumerating the many contributions this family made to the Jewish community throughout the years. It was discovered built into the wall of a house occupied by a Zhao family, on the southern perimeter of the synagogue enclosure. In fact, this area is where many members of the Zhao clan can still be found today.

That Pearl S. Buck made a point of mentioning the Ezra family was of the Zhao clan is worth noting here, since the Zhao's have represented the most prominent members of the Kaifeng Jewish community over the centuries. Local gazetteers give us the most information about the Zhao clan, due to their extraordinary success in the civil service exam, and hence, in Chinese society. One Zhao family is the direct descendant of the man who built Kaifeng's first synagogue in 1163. And in 1421, it was Zhao Cheng who was responsible for the reconstruction of the synagogue. Two Zhao brothers and other leaders of the community are credited with having saved several Torah scrolls after the 1642 flood. In 1653 they actively helped rebuild the synagogue and restore the manuscripts. In the 19th century, two of their members were invited to go to Shanghai to relearn Hebrew and Judaism, as shall be seen shortly. The Zhao's remain the spokesmen for the history of the Jews in Kaifeng into the 20th century.

Discovery by the Jesuits

Aside from these silent testimonies in stone and early Arab and European sightings of Jews in China, nothing else remains to tell us the story of the Chinese Jews through the 17th century. Then a funny thing happened in 1605...

When the Jesuit missionary Matteo Ricci entered China in 1583, he could scarcely have imagined that barely a quarter of a century later he would be the first Westerner to come face to face with a Chinese Jew, and bring the continued existence of this community to the attention of the West. One summer day in 1605, a Chinese Jew by the name of Ai Tain was on his way to Peking to take the civil service exam. Along the way he had read a book called "Things I Have Heard Tell" that there were Europeans living in the Middle Kingdom who proclaimed their faith in the one true G-d, yet steadfastly maintained they were not Moslems. What else could they be, he reasoned, but Jews, having never heard of such a thing as Christianity.

Ai Tian determined to locate these men, and when he reached the capital he inquired and was directed to the Jesuit rectory. After knocking on the door and being greeted by none other than Ricci himself, Ai proudly proclaimed himself to be his co-religionist, never once using the term "Jew." Ricci must have been equally delighted, thinking he had come face to face with a Chinese Christian, even before serious proselytizing efforts were underway in China.

Writing in his diary a few years later, Ricci, referring to himself in the third person, recalls the comedy of errors which then ensued:

"On entering our home he seemed to be quite excited over the fact, as he expressed it, that he professed the same faith that we did. His whole external appearance, nose, eyes, and all his facial lineaments, were anything but Chinese. Father Ricci took him into the church and showed him a picture above the high altar, a painting of the Blessed Virgin and the child Jesus, with John the Precursor, praying on his knees before them. Being a Jew and believing that we were of the same religious belief, he thought the picture represented Rebecca and her two children, Jacob and Esau, and so made a humble curtsy before it. He could not refrain, as he remarked, from doing honor to the parents of his race, though it was not his custom to venerate images. This happened on the Feast of St. John the Baptist.

The pictures flanking the altar were those of the four Evangelists and the Jew asked if they were four of the twelve children of the one represented on the altar. Father Ricci, thinking that he had made reference to the Apostles, nodded in agreement. Actually, however, each one was mistaken as to what the other had in mind. When he brought the visitor back to the house and began to question him as to his identity, it gradually dawned upon him that he was talking with a believer in the ancient Jewish law. The man admitted that he was an Israelite, but he knew of no such word as Jew. It would seem from this that the dispersion of the ten tribes penetrated to the extreme confines of the East. Later on [Ai] saw a royal edition of the Bible... and though he recognized the Hebrew characters he could not read the book. We heard from him also that there were ten or twelve families of Israelites in his home town and a magnificent synagogue, which only recently they had renovated at a cost of ten thousand gold pieces. In this same temple, as he related, the five books of Moses, namely the Pentateuch, had been preserved in the form of scrolls, and with great veneration, through a period of five or six hundred years. In Hamcheu... he claimed there were a far greater number of families, with their own synagogue, and others scattered about, who had no place of worship because their numbers were almost extinct."

Ricci was also asked to return with Ai to Kaifeng and become their Rabbi, since he knew so much about Judaism–the only stipulation being that he had to promise to abstain from eating pork! Through this chance encounter it was learned that the Jews had a full religious life with a synagogue and a rabbi, and observed all the usual customs and holidays as did their counterparts in the West. Other Jesuits whom Ricci sent to Kaifeng to confirm what the Jew Ai Tian said, did just that. Unfortunately, the great flood of 1642 destroyed the synagogue and scattered Kaifeng's Jewish inhabitants for close to a decade. The Jesuits who had begun to live in their midst and record what they saw were killed by the waters.

During the early part of the 18th century, several other Jesuits were sent to Kaifeng with the specific intention of procuring a copy of the Torah belonging to the Chinese Jews. At this time in Europe it was believed that the rabbis of the Talmudic era had purposely excised out of the Torah, references to Jesus as the Messiah in specific terms. If they could only locate the Kaifeng Torah, untouched by the corrupt European versions, the specific portions could be found. Thus, the Jews in Europe would see the error of their ways and how their own rabbis had deceived them, and would come to embrace

Christianity.

The Jesuits who did get to see the Kaifeng Torah, however, had to concede that, indeed, it was exactly like that of the European Jews, with not one letter altered. The same Jesuits also left a precious legacy in the form of sketches of the synagogue itself, both its interior and its exterior. They noted that the synagogue faced West, towards Jerusalem, and that the Jews turned in this direction when they prayed. From the outside, the synagogue looked as though it were any other Chinese temple, replete with archways and courtyards. Of the many memorial halls, the very innermost one held the Ark of the Covenant. Two marble lions flanked the pathway to the Front Hall, in between which was a large iron incense tripod–a Buddhist, rather than Jewish, convention. There was a hall for the kosher preparation of meals, a Hall of the Founder of the Religion, a Hall of the Holy Patriarchs, ancestral halls of the Zhao and Li clans, and memorial archways of the Zhao and Ai clans.

Inside was a main ceremonial table on which were placed censers, flower vases and candlesticks. Behind this was the Chair of Moses, upon which the Torah was placed for ceremonial reading. Also evident were the Imperial Tablets mentioned earlier, and many wall inscriptions in Chinese.

These early Jesuits were able to preserve for posterity many of the stele inscriptions and writings of the Chinese Jews. Their reports remain the only sources of first-hand information on the daily life of the Chinese Jews which captured their existence in both the heyday and twilight of their lives as a religious community. While their knowledge of Hebrew was said to be somewhat tenuous at this stage, the Jews nevertheless held fast to their religion and to each other, taking great pride in their beautiful synagogue, which was captured for eternity in the sketches made by Father Jean Domenge in 1722. The synagogue had stood by now for 600 years. Although obvious signs of assimilation into their Confucian surroundings abounded, their ties to their Jewish ancestry proved too strong, and attempts to purchase copies of the Kaifeng Torah at this time were futile.

In 1723 the missionaries were forced to leave China, and a general ban on proselytizing was enforced as anti-foreign sentiment began to set in. It would not be until 1850 that foreigners were able to have direct contact with the Chinese Jews again.

Historical Setting of Peony

It is towards the end of this time of suspended communication with the outside world that Pearl S. Buck set the novel *Peony.* The primary intimation we have for its initial setting as being in the last decade of the 18th century or possibly the first decade of the 19th century, is the fact that the last rabbi was still alive, albeit in his last years. Scholarly research has ascertained that the last rabbi died between 1800 and 1810, thus verifying the time frame in which the story of *Peony* begins.

At the outset, Madame Ezra is said to be almost fifty years old, which would mean that her own parents were members of the congregation during its heyday, described by the Jesuit missionaries in letters to the Vatican. Madame Ezra's great love of Judaism is all the more plausible, seen in this light.

Ezra ben Israel's family was said to be one of seventy families which came scores of years ago through Persia and India, by land and by sea, as merchants and traders, and later surnamed Zhao. This, too, would be historically accurate according to the steles. That Madame Ezra should later on declare to the Rabbi that theirs is the leading Jewish family, is all the more true, since the Zhao's held a remarkable place in the annals of Sino-Judaic history.

The synagogue, described as falling slowly into ruin, was said to be on the Street of the Plucked Sinew. While that street today is known as South Teaching Scripture Lane, before the early 1900's it was called just that—the Street of the Plucked Sinew. The rabbi was described as standing beside the Chair of Moses, "upon which the sacred Torah was placed. He wore long black robes and about his black-capped head was wrapped a fine white cloth that streamed down his back." This description coincides perfectly with a photograph found in *Chinese Jews*, written by Bishop William Charles White, an Anglican bishop who spent almost twenty-five years in Kaifeng, from 1910-1933. Elsewhere, Pearl S. Buck's description of the synagogue coincides exactly with that portrayed in sketches by Father Jean Domenge in 1722, which was also reproduced in Bishop White's book. A partial translation of the 1489 stele is given as well. Thirteen Torah scrolls were said to be in the synagogue, held in long cylinder boxes. References to inscriptions by Jews from other cities in the form of vertical tablets was also made.

Where Pearl S. Buck appears to take literary license is in the time sequence of the story. Although the real last rabbi of Kaifeng was supposed to have died by 1810, she alluded to the period of the Opium War (1839-1842) for the time of his death.

Later, when David ben Ezra journeys with his whole family to Peking, it is said to be at the time of the Empress Dowager, who then asked to see his "foreign" children. Since the Empress Dowager's influence was most prominent from 1898 to 1908, it is inconsistent with the story that a period of over fifty years could have elapsed between the time of the rabbi's death (assuming he died during the Opium War), and David's visit to Peking with small children.

By the end of the novel, the synagogue was finally only a heap of dust. The carvings were gone, and only three steles remained for a time, then later only two. They stood "stark under the sky" until a Christian foreigner bought them. In fact, Bishop White *did* buy the steles, moving them for safekeeping into the cathedral compound. But this was in the year 1912, and if, as we surmised at the outset, the story was set at the turn of the century with the real rabbi's death, then the novel would have spanned one hundred years ...

Although we are encouraged to picture Madame Ezra, the Rabbi and his children as having distinctly Western features, by the 19th century the Chinese Jews were for the most part Sinified racially. Sketches of two Kaifeng Jewish brothers of the Zhao clan around the year 1850 do show high foreheads and decidedly Semitic profiles, yet exhibit Oriental eyes and hair. Although impossible to verify, by the latter half of the 19th century most likely no Kaifeng Jews retained a strictly Western appearance.

Chronological inconsistencies notwithstanding (and perhaps even *because* she took such literary license), Pearl S. Buck managed to reveal the sweeping panorama of Chinese Jewish history all at once in this way through the rise and decline of Jewish observance in the Ezra family.

19th Century Contact with the Chinese Jews

The end of *Peony* is by no means the end of the story of the Chinese Jews, however. Contact with Kaifeng's Jewish inhabitants resumed after a 130-year hiatus in the year 1850, when the London Society for the Promotion of Christianity Among the Jews sent two Chinese Protestant delegates (converts from Shanghai) to Kaifeng. They reported that the synagogue was in a woeful state of disrepair and that the last rabbi had died about fifty years earlier. The community had some years before petitioned the Emperor to allow them to repair and rebuild their temple, but they had received no reply. Their condition was so desperate that the delegates were able to purchase close to seventy Hebrew manuscripts and six Torah scrolls from the synagogue over the course of two visits to Kaifeng. In addition, they bought the Chinese-Hebrew Memorial Book of the Dead, which was first assumed to be a genealogy. (All of these can now be found in the Klau Library of Hebrew Union College in Cincinnati.)

The delegates invited two members of the Kaifeng community (the Zhao brothers described above) to return with them to Shanghai in order to relearn Hebrew and Judaism, with the hope of resuscitating the community upon their return. Zhao Wenkui and Zhao Jincheng were circumcised Jews, a custom still practiced in Kaifeng at that time. The latter stayed only briefly, but the former remained until his death, and was buried in the communal cemetery which 19th century Jewish emigrants had established in Shanghai.

Only a year before, a sergeant in the Chinese imperial army, Tie Dingan, wrote to the British Consul in Amoy, T.H. Layton, that eight families still existed in Kaifeng. He reported they were Chinese in appearance, but exhibited "straight features like people in the center of China." There were no rabbis, and none could read Hebrew.

Once Jews and others outside of Kaifeng learned of their existence, attempts were made to send letters to the Jewish community, but only one was ever acknowledged–possibly the only one ever received. On August 20, 1850, Zhao Nianzi of Kaifeng wrote to T.H. Layton (in response to an 1847 letter by James Finn, a career diplomat and missionary, who was fluent in Hebrew and knowledgeable about Judaism). He described the dismal state of affairs in Kaifeng at that time, mentioning that since 1800-1810 the religion had been "imperfectly transmitted," though religious writings were still extant. The synagogue, he mentioned, had long been without "ministers." The structure of the synagogue itself was in ruins, and he mentioned those who were willing to mortgage or sell the synagogue and materials from the Gao, Shi and Zhao clans.

Zhao's letter was a cry for help from the Jews of the West, as their poverty and by now general ignorance of Hebrew and most of Judaism's religious tenets had turned them into a desperately isolated community on the threshold of total assimilation into their Chinese surroundings.

In 1860 another catastrophic flood from the Yellow River hit Kaifeng. Perhaps this marks the last time the synagogue was swept away–this time for good. For in 1866 the Reverend W.A.P. Martin visited Kaifeng, at which time he declared that the synagogue itself no longer even stood on the site at which it had been for the past seven centuries, and which, although in a dilapidated state, had been visible to the 1850 delegates.

The plight of the Jews of Kaifeng by this time is poignantly conveyed by Martin when he related learning that after the last rabbi had died, the Jews still cared enough to leave a copy of their Torah in the marketplace in the hopes that a Jew from afar who might perchance be in Kaifeng would notice it and teach them once again its contents. All he reported standing at the time was a solitary stone.

Western Jewish Contacts with Kaifeng

The first Western Jew to visit Kaifeng did so for ten days in July of 1867. Jacob L. Liebermann, an Austrian Jewish merchant, went not on behalf of a religious organization, but of his own accord, and wrote a series of ten letters to his father. He described that while the Jews lamented their degree of assimilation, they also recounted stories of a brighter past.

It was not until the turn of the century, however, that Jews, then living in Shanghai, made a concerted effort to establish close contact with the Chinese Jews in Kaifeng, attempting to help resuscitate the community. This was in response to their discovery that a year earlier, in 1899, the Jews sold the last remaining Torah scroll to the Apostolic vicar of the Henan Mission, a Monsignor Volonteri.

Until the turn of the 20th century, relatively few Jews had heard of the Kaifeng community, and even fewer made the journey there, since they had not the financial backing afforded representatives of missionary groups.

The successful Sephardic and Ashkenazic Jews who had taken up residence in Shanghai during the 19th century, represented best by the Sassoons and the Kadoories, however, became alarmed when they learned of the sale of Torah scrolls and the generally decayed state of the Kaifeng Jewish community.

Banding together, they formed the Shanghai Committee for the Rescue of the Chinese Jews in 1900, hoping to save the Kaifeng Jews from spiritual oblivion. Communication with Kaifeng thus took place, prompting several Kaifeng Jews to travel to Shanghai where they reported that they still observed some of the Jewish dietary laws, and that some were even circumcised, but that the community no longer consisted of practicing Jews. They expressed the fervent hope that their synagogue could be rebuilt with the help of Shanghai's Jews, which might revive even a semblance of the sense of community that once united them.

When pogroms and immigration of the Russian Jews began to occur soon after, however, attention and funds were diverted from the original intention of rebuilding a synagogue for the Kaifeng Jews. Almost all those who had come to Shanghai hoping to find some Western Jews who could help rebuild their community, returned to Kaifeng with their hopes dashed and their hearts heavy, realizing that the former grandeur of their synagogue and pride as a Jewish community were never again to be.

Bishop White

From 1910-1933 the Chinese Jews had in their midst the Canadian Church of England's first Anglican Bishop of Henan Province. No other Westerner lived among the Chinese Jews as long as did Bishop William Charles White, whose magnum opus *Chinese Jews* was published in 1942. White succeeded in getting the heads of the seven clans agree to have his church take over protection of the two extant stone inscriptions in 1912. Two years prior to this, the Jews would not agree to give up legal title to the synagogue site. A year later, however, after a conflict over the possession of the steles with the local authorities, White was able to purchase the stones on the condition that they not leave the province. And in 1914 the site of the synagogue itself was sold by the Jews to the Mission, representing the first time in over seven centuries that someone other than the Chinese Jews owned the site.

By now no more scrolls of the Law were left, and parts of the synagogue were already being used by others in Kaifeng. A Confucian temple had obtained one of the marble balustrades of the former synagogue for over fifty years; two stone lions were said to be outside one of the Buddhist temples, and even the green roof tiles were now part of the local mosque.

In May of 1919, Bishop White held a series of meetings with the Chinese Jews to try to educate them and revive some kind of communal ties between them. Heads of all seven clans were present, and forty families out of the estimated 200 participated. They did not know one another, and only the Shi clan was reported to have kept family records.

The many Chinese-Jewish artifacts which Bishop White purchased while in Kaifeng have since passed into the hands of the Royal Ontario Museum in Toronto, where they now remain. Among those bits of Chinese-Judaica in the Museum's possession are a black marble chime used to call the Jews to prayer, two stone lotus-carved bowls and a large, cylindrical case for the Torah scroll.

One of White's main contributions while in Kaifeng was to attempt to revive the community by bringing together the seven major clans, documenting the occasion with photos and articles. However, nothing came of these meetings, as the Jews had by now lost all sense of community and all hopes of rebuilding their synagogue or re-learning Judaism, much less practicing it.

As a community the Jews had by now come to an end, although a strong individual sense of ethnic identity has remained with them, even through the 20th century.

Between the downfall of the Qing dynasty in 1911 and the establishment of the People's Republic of China in 1949, Kaifeng saw an array of visitors during the turbulent first years of the Republic of China. Some claimed to still notice physical characteristics among the Chinese Jews which stemmed from their Semitic origin, but all noted the tremendous amount of assimilation into their Chinese environment which had by then taken place. Nevertheless, it can be seen from conversations with the Chinese Jews that they still longed for some contact with Jews from the West which would enable them to revive at least their knowledge of Judaism. In particular they asked for schools for the young. Their numbers fairly decimated, the Chinese Jews of Kaifeng proved nevertheless to be resilient and driven to retaining whatever sense of ethnic identity they still possessed.

Chinese Jewish Descendants into the 20th Century

After the creation of the People's Republic of China, little contact was had with the Jewish descendants in Kaifeng. In 1952, a census of all minority peoples in China was carried out, "minority" being defined as a group whose members spoke a common language of their own, and retained common traditions and cultural traits different from the Han ethnic majority. As Michael Pollak explained in his *Mandarins, Jews and Missionaries*, "several hundred inhabitants of Kaifeng, apparently unaware that Jews did not fit into any of the minority classifications set up by Peking, trooped to the various census centers, where, to the utter bewilderment of the clerical staffs, they attempted to register as members of a minority that, officially at least, did not even exist. Their efforts were of course to no avail."

The decade of turbulence and violence which began with the Cultural Revolution in China in 1966 prevented most Westerners from making their way to Kaifeng until the late 1970s. A UPI journalist in 1980 was the first Westerner to visit the Jews of Kaifeng since the 1960s, meeting several members of the Ai and Shi clans who told of the existence of dozens of other Jewish descendants in the city. Although claiming to be Jews on the basis of their ancestry alone, none were said to observe any of the Jewish customs or rituals. The existence of the steles in a safe place in the warehouse of the Kaifeng Municipal Museum was confirmed.

A flurry of activities ensued in 1981 in attempts to contact or research the subject of the Chinese Jews. A survey was conducted by the former curator of the Kaifeng Municipal Museum, Wang Yisha (who is arguably the one person in Kaifeng today who personally knows more Chinese Jews than anyone else), which concluded that there were still 140 families of Jewish descent with six surnames. Of these, 79 families live in Kaifeng and 61 have moved to other parts of China. The 79 families in Kaifeng numbered altogether 166 persons.

The year 1981 saw the publication of an article by Jin Xiaojing, entitled "I am a Chinese Jew." Jin, a sociologist at the National Minorities Research Institute of the Chinese Academy of Social Sciences in Beijing, only discovered her Jewish roots in 1980 while attending a professional conference. At that time she learned that two of the men whose names were mentioned by others as being Jews, were actually paternal uncles of hers. Although her ancestral home was Kaifeng, it never dawned on her that she might be of

Jewish descent, since she was raised as a Moslem!

My own visits to Kaifeng began in 1983 with special interest tours I led for the American Jewish Congress. Each of my groups was allowed to meet with three particular individuals, representing the Zhao and Shi clans. We went to South Teaching Scripture Lane, where the synagogue once stood but where now only a hospital exists to mark the spot. We also saw the 1489/1512 and 1679 steles, stored in a warehouse of the Kaifeng Municipal Museum.

Although discussions with the Jewish descendants were fairly formal, and no mention of Israel was allowed, we were able to glimpse for the first time those people whose ancestors and ours once spoke the same language in prayer, and equally longed for a return to their ancestral homeland.

In 1985 I returned to Kaifeng alone, and managed to speak with six heads of Jewish-descended families and some of their family members, representing the Ai, Li, Shi and Zhao clans. Each day in Kaifeng was an adventure in discovery of this remnant community. I gathered informal oral histories, testaments to how much has lingered on for some, and how much has been forgotten by others.

One member of the Ai clan could not recognize a Star of David as relating to Judaism, and knew nothing of the religion or history of the Jews in Kaifeng. He knew only that he was of Jewish descent because his father had told him so, and for some reason he, too, believed it important to pass down this knowledge to his sons. This, I surmised, was more representative of the Chinese Jewish descendants in Kaifeng, than those few brought before groups of tourists to recount their family's and people's history in China and religious customs.

Another member of a different Ai family, the oldest, being in his late seventies, had one of the most interesting stories of all. He was chosen in 1952 by his neighborhood committee to go to Beijing to represent the Chinese Jews as one of the national minorities, for a ceremony held by the three-year-old government of the newly created People's Republic. Ai met and shook hands with Mao Zedong, Zhou Enlai and Deng Xiaoping. This leads one to believe that the Jews were at one point, soon after the establishment of the PRC, close to being declared a national minority.

An elder statesman for the Zhao clan — the clan which figured so prominently throughout Chinese Jewish history and in Pearl S. Buck's novel — has begun to build his own mini-museum to commemorate the many contributions of his family's ancestors to the Kaifeng Jewish community. To this end, he has built a model of the old synagogue as his father and grandfather told him it looked, including the two stone lions which are missing on the model of the synagogue found in Israel's Museum of the Diaspora.

One of the most enterprising of the Chinese Jews, he and one of this daughters had begun to make Chinese-style yarmulkas which they hoped to be able to sell to visiting tourists within the next few years. Zhao, in fact, found himself in a peculiar position with five daughters, since Judaism had been passed down patrilineally in Kaifeng for centuries. As one of the few Chinese Jewish descendants with an extensive knowledge of his people's history, he has decreed that any children which his daughters have should be registered as "Youtai," (meaning Jewish, rather than "Han," for ethnic Chinese) even if their fathers are not of Jewish descent, on all Certificates of Registry next to the space allotted for nationality. The Zhaos still live on South Teaching Scripture Lane, near the hospital where the synagogue once stood.

A senior member of the Shi clan I met exhibited a deep desire to recover his heritage. His childhood memories were still vivid, recalling yarmulkas made in six sections (in honor of the six days it took G-d to create the universe, so his mother had told him), brass Stars of David kept locked in a medicine chest but lost over the years, and Passover rituals... red paint mixed with water, a substitution for the traditional chicken's blood, was spread over the doorpost of his home with a Chinese writing brush. This festival was combined with the Chinese New Year, while a second, separate custom taking place a month later called for the baking of cakes without yeast.

Shi has been working closely with Wang Yisha to reconstruct the genealogies of the Kaifeng Jews, in particular those of the Shi clan.

To this end, Hebrew Union College in Cincinnati agreed to donate two microfiches of the Chinese-Hebrew Memorial Book of the Dead to Kaifeng–one to the Kaifeng Municipal Museum and another directly to Wang Yisha.

I returned to Kaifeng for the last time in 1988, and came away feeling that a renewed sense of purpose had taken root, both in those Chinese Jewish descendants actively pursuing knowledge of their past, and in the Westerners who have been lucky enough to re-establish contact at this crucial time, when the last generation who can even purport to have such memories, still lives.

In June of 1985, two months before my own solo journey to Kaifeng, the Sino-Judaic Institute was created in Palo Alto, California to promote scholarly research and exchange of information on the subject of the Chinese Jews around the world. In support of the creation of a Judaica Wing of the Kaifeng Municipal Museum, it publishes a newsletter to disseminate information, old and new, on the Chinese Jews, as well as accounts of recent visits to Kaifeng.

Reminiscent of the Shanghai Committee for the Rescue of the Chinese Jews established at the turn of the century, it attempts to focus attention on this miniscule remnant of the Jewish diaspora so that their story may be made known, and efforts on behalf of the promotion of friendship and understanding between the Chinese and the Jews may succeed.

As for Chinese interest in the subject, since 1988 the Shanghai Judaic Studies Association and the China Jewish Studies Association in Nanjing have been established. The latter organization is planning an exhibit of Chinese scholarship on Judaic studies, and the former is amassing a Judaica library to be shared with scholars and others interested throughout China, among other projects.

Other indications that the Chinese are officially interested in fostering closer ties with Jews around the world is the fact that for the past four years a pilot Hebrew program has been conducted at Peking University for six undergraduate Chinese students. Other older scholars from various Chinese universities have also been to Israel from time to time. A tour of the exhibit on the Chinese Jews is being planned in China for the near future as well.

Although the Chinese government has long sought to avoid mention of Israel between Jewish visitors and the descendants in Kaifeng, 1990 has seen the establishment of Academic Exchange offices between China and Israel in Beijing and Tel Aviv. Just how long it will be before formal diplomatic relations are established between the two countries is impossible to predict, but the likelihood appears to be greater each year.

Pearl S. Buck's knowledge of the Chinese Jews can only be explained by a possible association with missionaries who were in Kaifeng while she was growing up in Nanjing at the turn of the century, or in her discovery of Bishop White's *Chinese Jews*, published just six years before *Peony* was written. The details of daily life and customs prevalent among the Chinese Jews which were incorporated in the story of the Ezra family can only be described as uncanny. In writing *Peony*, Pearl S. Buck did much to foster greater cultural understanding between the Chinese and the Jews. And in republishing *Peony* at this particular point in Chinese-Jewish relations, one cannot help but imagine what the future holds in store for continued contact between the two oldest civilizations on earth.

WENDY R. ABRAHAM, Ed.D., author of the Afterword for this edition, is a scholar of the history of the Jewish descendants of Kaifeng. Her dissertation at Teachers College, Columbia University was on the Chinese Jews of Kaifeng, 1605-1985.

A frequent lecturer on the topic, she serves on the Board of the Sino-Judaic Institute, Palo Alto, CA., and is currently teaching Asian studies at NYU and the New School for Social Research in New York City. She has visited China six times since 1981, and in 1985 recorded oral histories of the oldest descendants of Chinese Jews in Kaifeng which she hopes to publish.

BIBLIOGRAPHY

Abraham, Wendy R. "Kaifeng's Legacy, A Chinese Jewish Identity," *Hadassah Magazine,* vol. 69 no. 1, August/September 1987, p.20-25. (Illus. with photos by the author).

Kublin, Hyman, ed. *Jews in Old China: Some Western Views.* New York: Paragon Book Reprint, 1971.

Leslie, Donald Daniel. *The Survival of the Chinese Jews.* Leiden: E.J. Brill, 1972.

__________. "The Kaifeng Jewish Community: A Summary." Jewish Journal of Sociology 9, no. 2 (December 1969): 175-85. Reprinted in Kublin, Studies, pp. 187-97.

Martin, W.A.P. "Account of a Visit to the Jews in Honan." *The Chinese: Their Education, Philosophy, and Letters*, New York, 1881.

Perlmann, S.M. *The History of the Jews in China.* London, 1912.

Pollak, Michael. *Mandarins, Jews, and Missionaries: The Jewish Experience in the Chinese Empire.* Philadelphia: The Jewish Publication Society of America, 1980.

__________. ed. *The Sino-Judaic Bibliographies of Rudolf Loewenthal.* Hebrew Union College Press, Cincinnati, in association with The Sino-Judaic Institute, Palo Alto, CA., 1988.

White, William Charles. *Chinese Jews.* 3 vols. Toronto: University of Toronto Press, 1942. (Reprinted (3 vols. in 1), Cecil Roth, ed., New York, Paragon Book Reprint, 1966.

Model of synagogue of Kai-Feng-Fu, China, built originally 12th cent.; reconstruction based on Jesuit missionary drawings of the 18th cent.

Photo by Edgar Asher. From Beth Hatefutsoth, The Nahum Goldmann Museum of the Jewish Diaspora, Tel Aviv

Chao Wen-k'uei, a teacher from the Kaifeng community, who learned Hebrew in Shanghai from an emissary of the London Society for Promoting Christianity Among the Jews.

Chao Ching-ch'eng, of the Jewish community of Kaifeng, around 1850.

ABOUT THE AUTHOR

Pearl S. Buck *

1892-1973

Pearl Sydenstricker Buck was born in Hillsboro, West Virginia, to Presbyterian missionary parents who brought her to Chinkiang, China, where she learned Chinese before she knew English. She was educated in both China and the USA, at Randolph Macon College in Virginia and at Cornell University, where she received an M.A. in English. Intermittently, the family was forced to leave Nanking because of political changes, but she managed to teach literature at several Chinese universities before 1932, when her literary career blossomed with the 1931 publication of *The Good Earth*, which later became a popular Hollywood film, and for which she received the Pulitzer Prize.

During her lifetime she wrote more than 80 works which included fiction, non-fiction, juveniles, books of opinion on social issues of the orient and the biographies of her parents, cited when she received the Nobel prize for literature in 1938. Her books have been translated widely and are known the world over.

Mrs. Buck had one child of her own when she was the wife of John Lossing Buck, whom she divorced. She then married Richard J. Walsh, president of the John Day Company, her publisher. With him she adopted five children, and established at their home in Green Hills Farm, Perkasie, PA., the Pearl S. Buck Foundation, where her humanitarian work for Amerasian children continues today.

* The photo shows her in 1940; the same period as the publication of PEONY.